# H THE ERETIC OF THE NORTH
## THE CHRONICLES OF THE STAR CALENDAR

VOLUME I

# TIMOTHY BROMMER

Runestone Hill, Ltd. Co. • Louisville

THE HERETIC OF THE NORTH

Copyright © 2004 by Timothy Brommer.
Cover art copyright © 2003 by Larry Elmore.
Cover design by Ken Whitman.

Maps designed by Timothy Brommer.
Maps drawn for this edition by Gretchen DeChurch.

ISBN  0-9726344-0-1

http://runestonehill.com

PRINTED IN THE UNITED STATES OF AMERICA

0 9 8 7 6 5 4 3 2 1

*To the Marines, who taught me to persevere through adversity.*

*Semper Fi* –

Nick & Shannon

Find the good
in every situation

Jim Brown

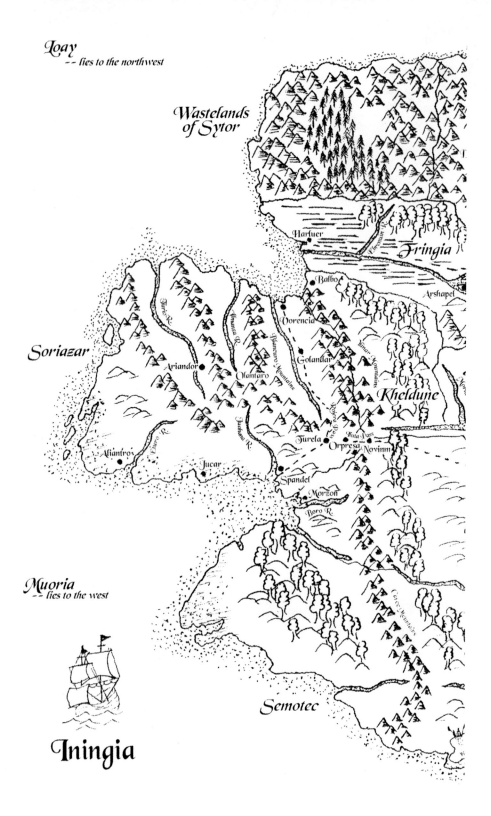

Loay
-- lies to the northwest

Wastelands
of Sytor

Soriazar

Fringia

Harluer

Balbo

Arshapel

Vorencia

Golandar

Kheldune

Olantaro

Turel R.

Amatra R.

Blancaro Mountains

 Limar Mountains

Ariandor

Turela

Hutz Pass

Orpresa  Novinn

Afiantros

Ituro R.

Duchara R.

Jucar

Spandel

Morzon

Boro R.

Muoria
-- lies to the west

Croc Mountains

Semotec

Iningia

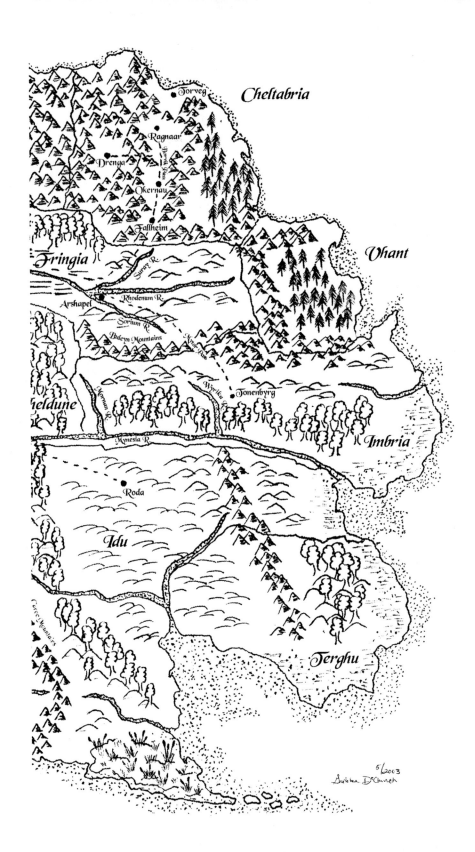

# Prologue

Rain lashed the basalt cliffs of Loay. Foaming waves broke against them in great geysers. The wind moaned as it swirled through the jagged clefts and defiles of the rugged island. Six figures stood upon the edge of a precipice, facing the raging sea. Their ash-gray robes flapped about like wet banner flags.

One of the figures raised a spyglass to his hooded face. Lightning flashes confirmed what he suspected – a ship was foundering in the storm near the shore.

He lowered the spyglass. "One can see the lanterns on the aft castle."

The robed figure beside him, with a silver embroidered moon on his robe, raised his pale hand. A ball of fire streaked from the palm, briefly bathing his companions in a reddish-orange glow. The fireball hissed and steamed as it cut through the slashing rain. He kept his hand directed at the ship. The fireball arced through the air, following its caster's will. It burst upon the vessel, spreading across the deck like a flaming liquid. The screams of dying sailors reached the figures on the cliff, in between the roar of the breaking waves and the wind's howling.

Another fireball lit the night and struck the ship. Fire crawled up the riggings and masts. Flickering yellow balls leaped over the gunwales into the foaming black waves. A third fireball lit the ship from stem to stern. More writhing yellow flickers dropped into the sea.

Morning came hours later. Blackened flotsam rolled back and forth in the waters at the base of the cliffs. Five bedraggled sailors had managed to swim ashore onto a narrow beach. The robed figures found them, pulled them out of the surf, and brought them to a nearby grotto. Two of the sailors were badly burned and drifted in and out of consciousness. The robed figure with the moon emblem slid his sword from its scabbard and thrust the point of it into one of the injured sailors' chests.

"In the name of Ghyo," begged the other burned man, "spare my stricken soul."

"Ghyo has abandoned you upon our shore," a voice hissed back from within the gray hood. "I offer your dying soul to Eo."

The sailor feebly threw up his hands and screeched as the sword crunched through his breastbone. The pale hands of the other robed figures appeared from their sleeves and seized the remaining sailors, who did not have the strength to resist. The one with the sword, the leader, turned toward them.

He approached and placed his pale, bony hand upon the first sailor's forehead. "This one suits me not," he said. He then laid his hand on the second one. "This one suits me not." He came to the third and wrapped his fingers over the top of that sailor's head. He paused for a few moments before saying, "This one shall I spare."

Blood, from the sailors passed over, stained the sand nearly before the leader removed his hand from the third. The survivor shook violently as he knelt, pleading for his life.

The leader said to him, "Take what I offer. And through serving me, you will serve Eo. And you shall be given power."

## The Year 220 After the Great Schism

A human forger, with an eel tattoo circling his arm, stoked the white-hot coals. Molten metal bubbled in the small crucible. Two terrified, bound hostages knelt on the dirt floor, one Human and one Syt. Eo's stillborn child, the moon, was visible through the opening in the hut's roof. The leader stood beside a table with a mold on top of it. The silver-threaded moon on his robe reflected the reddish light of the furnace.

"It is ready," the forger said, as he lifted the crucible with a pair of metal tongs. He poured the gold alloy into the mold. Four reddish circles took shape. A silver light radiated from the leader's hands.

Two Syts pushed the human hostage near the table. An irresistible urge to speak at the rings came into the hostage's mind. The frightened, dark-skinned man spoke in Semotec, and the molten rings rapidly cooled and hardened as he did so.

"Pour the next set," the leader said. He tipped the mold and spilled the finished rings onto the table.

The forger filled the mold again and the Sytish hostage was dragged forward. He spoke in Sytish to the fast-cooling rings, as the light from the leader's hands bathed them in a milky hue.

"Come forward and receive your charges," the leader said to his companions.

Six figures, robed in gray, stepped out of the shadows around the edges of the hut and held out their pale hands. Six of the rings were divided up among them. They each slipped one upon a finger and instantly clutched their throats. The robed figures screamed out in pain as the power of the rings twisted and constricted their vocal cords. Their tongues rolled about their mouths as they tried to speak in their native language, but they were changing. The pain moved to their heads and scrambled their thoughts, as a lifetime of knowledge rushed into their minds. They grasped the sides of their heads and cried out more. But slowly, their thoughts became ordered and their tongues began to form words. Semotec and Sytish soon flowed from their lips.

A thin, ominous laugh issued from the leader's hood. "Go forth and do your duty. Eo's might is waxing."

# Chapter 1

## The Light Emerges
### 5 Janoban, 229 A.G.S.

In the valley of Northern Cheltabria, in the center of the steep-roofed village of Ragnaar, two men circled each other, slogging about in thick mud. A large crowd of fur and flax-clad Chelts surrounded them. They cheered for their chief, Worgoth, a huge Chelt with massive arms. Worgoth, stripped to his waist, wore buckskin breeches and boots. He bore a scowl on his ruddy face, curling back his lips, baring his teeth. His blonde hair hung in a thick braid beside each ear. He held a double-headed battle-axe before his body. He breathed deep and steady.

His opponent stood nearly a foot smaller. Clumps of mud plastered his black hair to his head. He too wore buckskin breeches and was stripped to his waist. Mud clung to his knees, elbows, and backside. Unlike Worgoth, his face showed exhaustion; his chest heaved with each breath. His tired arms trembled slightly as he held his axe before his body. Orius Candell feared he might not live to see sunset.

*I could conjure fire and end this now*, Orius thought. *But I must prove to these people that I'm worthy enough to lead them.*

Worgoth bellowed and rushed forward, swinging his axe above his head. Orius threw his up and countered the strike. The axe handles clashed with a crack, but Orius lost his balance and landed on his back. Worgoth's blue eyes widened.

Orius watched the Chelt lumber toward him, the mud sucking at his feet. Worgoth's wicked half-moon blade sliced through the air.

*Move!* Orius's mind screamed, as he rolled to his left.

The axe whistled past his ear and sank into the soft ground. Mud splattered several of the Chelts nearby. Orius hopped to his feet and growled like an angry wolf. He caught Worgoth bent over, freeing his axe from the ground. For an instant, Orius could not see Worgoth's eyes, which gave him a sudden burst of courage. *Ghyo, forgive me.* He brought his axe down across the back of Worgoth's neck. Astonished cries came from the villagers as Worgoth's head landed in the mud, with his eyes looking skyward. The chief's body fell forward and a stream of blood stained the ground.

Orius fell to his knees beside Worgoth's corpse. He turned his exhausted face toward six Chelts sitting on a log. They stared back with grim but approving faces. Worgoth's wife wailed and two other weeping women took her away. Orius rose to his feet and turned toward the villagers. The shock of the violent scene showed on their faces. He fought to control the sickening feeling growing inside him. He had killed and killing was a sin.

He spoke to them. "By Right of Combat, I, Orius Candell, declare myself the Chief of Ragnaar and Chief of the Northern Valley." He gestured at Worgoth's body, lying at his feet. His stomach quivered as Worgoth's lifeless eyes stared back at him. Revulsion rose to the back of his throat, but he forced the acidic taste back down. "Worgoth was a brave warrior. We will prepare a funeral for him, fitting of a chief." The Ragnaardars nodded with hesitative approval. *I didn't wish this combat to happen. Please, believe me.* "I tried to convince Worgoth to join us, like the other chiefs did, but his pride would have none of it. So his pride cost him his life."

Orius walked around the circle as he spoke, looking into as many faces as he could. *These people only respect strength, but I'll show them another way. I'll teach them Ghyo's way.* "I bring peace to you and to *all* of the tribes." The people stared at him in silence. He knew they did not understand the peace he spoke of; they only knew he was their new chief, and Worgoth soaked the ground with crimson blood. The change of power was abrupt, like it always was in Cheltabria.

Orius pulled Worgoth's axe from the mud. He propped it over his shoulder and strode over to the Chelts sitting on the log.

Culley Magolin, an old and weathered Chelt, rose to his feet. The sound of old joints popping accompanied his movements. He offered Orius his hand and whispered, "Boy, I thought you'd gone the way of the Departed. Ghyo blessed you with that opportunity."

A nervous grin formed on Orius's lips. He nodded and patted his old friend on the shoulder. "I did not want it to be like this. Worgoth was a fine warrior. He would have been useful to us, but he challenged me, so I had to fight him." He looked Culley straight in the eye. "We will move past this. We have much work to do."

A wide grin etched its way across Culley's face. "That we do, my boy," he growled. "That we do."

Kathair Vorhenin rose from the log and slapped Orius on the back with his muscular arm. "Do you always fight sitting on your ass?" he joked. "I was sure you were going to change your mind and burn him."

"Maybe you would like to do the honors for me next time," Orius said, wiping mud from his face. Suddenly, he realized - there could be a next time.

"I'm not the ambitious one," replied Kathair, shaking his blonde head. "I'm just here to watch your back." His tone then became serious. "But I'm glad you're alive to drink with me tonight."

Orius pointed a finger at Kathair's thick chest. "You know I had to defeat Worgoth through force of arms and not by force of nature. The tribes will soon learn of that, anyhow."

"Right now, all I can smell is that meat roasting," Argus Dolke, a massive Chelt, bigger than Kathair, interrupted them. He patted his round belly and sniffed at the scent of roasting meat. "The Ragnaardars have prepared a feast to celebrate Worgoth's victory, but tonight it's not to be. The feast will honor Orius."

"Worgoth's warriors must pay homage to you," said Culley. "That'll be a bitter herb for some to take."

"They have heard through the gossip of what I am," said Orius. "I must now prove the rumors true and show them who I am." He looked at each of his companions. "They *will* follow me. I have brought the Faith back to the North. That is why the other village chiefs elected me as the leader."

Orius retired to a small log hut. He leaned Worgoth's engraved axe against the doorframe. A bucket sat on the ground beside a barrel of water. He picked up the bucket, filled it from the barrel, and poured the water over his head, rinsing the mud from his face and hair. He dropped the bucket and entered the hut. He stripped off his soiled garments and dropped them on the dirt floor beside a wooden chest, held together with metal bands. Black breeches and a black woolen tunic hung from pegs on the wall. A pair of knee-high black boots sat on the floor. Orius dressed himself in the tunic, breeches, and boots.

A black cuirass of boiled leather and a studded black leather gorget lay on top of the crude wooden bed. Orius strapped the cuirass to his torso. He then knelt and opened the chest. Inside, a pair of leather gauntlets lay on top of a white, short-sleeved surcoat. The gauntlets were dyed white, except for the palms, which were dyed black and made from rougher cuts of hide.

Orius bowed his head and pressed his hands together in front of his chest, fingers joined and pointing up. He raised his arms skyward, gazed toward the ceiling, and mouthed a silent prayer. He spread his arms parallel to the floor; his palms faced upward, each glowing with the Light of Ghyo. Orius reached into the chest, removed the surcoat, and slid it over his head. Wavy gold embroidery circled the ends of the surcoat's sleeves and a large gold sun, with wavy rays of light extending from it, was embroidered on the chest. He cinched a black leather belt about his waist and put on his gauntlets. Lastly, he placed the gorget over his shoulders.

He emerged from the hut and stood before the doorway. Nearby, the warriors and villagers of Ragnaar waited for him. Orius closed his eyes, breathed deeply, and collected his thoughts. He sniffed the wetness from the rainfall of that morning, and he sensed a perceivable hint of tension in the air. He paused for only a moment and then strode toward his companions. The six of them stood in a line.

As Orius approached, Culley knelt, took his right hand, and touched it to his forehead. "May the Light of Ghyo deliver us from the darkness," he whispered.

Orius stepped past him and was greeted in kind by Kathair, Moreena Odel, Alana and Fayne Carlainen, and big Argus. After Argus rose from his knee, Orius faced the Ragnaardars who had gathered to pay homage to him. Fifty warriors knelt before him and most of them grudgingly pressed Orius's hand to their foreheads and acknowledged him as chief. Even the ones that did not take his hand did mumble their homage.

When the last warrior rose, Orius raised his right hand. Amber light radiated from it like a torch, illuminating the faces of the Ragnaardars gathered before him. Several women fell to their knees and wept at the blessed sight, a sight heard of only in the tales of their ancestors.

"I have brought back the Light of the Creator to this land," Orius said. *Until now, I was but a rumor to these people. Now, seeing is affirmation.* "Long ago, the Church left you and let darkness fall upon these mountains and valleys." He watched their faces; their eyes were transfixed upon him. "Ghyo has never forgotten His followers, but the worldly dealings of His Church did. As you know from tales of long ago, a great schism cast the Church asunder. Your priests were called away to the south to fight the battles that ensued the schism's chaos." Orius glanced at Culley, who gave him a slow, solemn nod.

As Orius spoke, the Light of Ghyo reflected in the wide eyes of the Chelts of Ragnaar. Not only were they naturally uncomfortable with strangers, but Orius was a foreigner with dark hair and dark eyes, although he had lived in Cheltabria for all but four of his twenty-seven years. But he knew the people, their language, and their customs. And he knew they needed leadership, and he needed a united Cheltabria.

He closed his palm and the light faded. "We will work the land and make it prosper. There will be no more starvation and sickness. Let us eat the food you have prepared and begin the preparations for Worgoth's Passing."

The feast commenced, but the mood was somber. Upon Worgoth's commands, the Ragnaardars had scraped together what food they could spare. There would be lean times ahead because of the feast, and on top of that, Orius wanted their warriors to march south with him to fight the Oruks.

Orius's companions sat close together, picking at the meat roasting above the fire and popping the sizzling pieces into their mouths. His small group had grown close to him since joining him eight months prior. Orius's future had given them purpose and an opportunity for adventure - two things they had found lacking in their ordinary lives at home. They came from the village of Torveg, a day's walk from the northern coast of Cheltabria. They had known each other all of their lives. They had played together as children and had hunted together as they matured. In times of need, they had fought together. But their lives had changed that spring, when the dark-haired stranger, the old Cheltan warrior, and the mother came down from the ancient keep, which crowned a nearby mountaintop.

"Drink no wine tonight," Fayne said. "Those warriors might come up with some trickery. And I want to see the sun rise."

"There's no need for such caution," Alana scoffed at her brother and drank wine from a skin, whipping back her long golden hair as she did so.

"I hope you are right," said Orius. "But another warrior may have designs on becoming chief."

Alana blushed then, and put the skin aside.

"Now that Worgoth's out of the way, we can march south and west," said Kathair.

"In three days, the other warriors will be here," said the slender, muscular young woman named Moreena. "And we shall then take our vengeance on the Oruks."

"Orius, do the warriors here march with us?" Fayne asked.

Orius cocked his head. "I believe I can explain the situation to them. The thought of their homes being torched and their families being carried off into the wastelands should be all the reason they need."

Culley chimed in as gracefully as a bull. "All of them know this problem arises every third generation or so. I only hope the numbers we confront aren't too overwhelming."

Alana's sapphire eyes showed lines of worry at the corners. "But the danger is an opportunity. Isn't that so, Orius? That's what you said."

"Yes, but we must we plan our moves carefully. Our army will attract attention in the lands to the south," Orius said.

Argus butted in, his speech slurred by a mouthful of meat. "Just show me where to plant my axe and the problem's solved."

Kathair laughed and slapped Argus on the shoulder. "Save some for me, you brute." The two of them roared heartily.

Culley was not amused. "You two keep your wits about you. We need thinking men as well as fighters on this trip. Only Ghyo knows how many Oruks wait for us down that road." He pointed southward, toward the Borvik Pass.

Orius motioned to Fayne and Alana to sit beside him. He spoke to them quietly, "I want the two of you to ride south before dawn. Scout the valley and hills around Drenga. You should be able to make it there in two days. Spend a day there, then ride back and meet us somewhere along the road."

Fayne looked like he was already going over the preparations he needed to make before leaving. But Alana's eyes widened and she worked her lips about.

"Alana," said Orius, "you seemed troubled."

"Are you sure you're sending the right people?" Alana swallowed and looked at her brother. "I mean, me."

"You and your brother have spent your lives hunting and tracking," said Orius. "This job needs those abilities. If you do this right, you should be able to avoid unwanted contact."

"And if we can't avoid contact?"

Orius leaned closer to her. "Then you will have to use that bow of yours. Fayne will be counting on it."

"I know of no one else who can loose arrows with your precision," Fayne told his sister. "And should you have to use your bow, you'll only be killing animals." He placed his hand on hers and looked into her eyes. "I need you."

Alana smiled plaintively. "I came along with Orius to find adventure. I just didn't expect to find it so soon."

Orius stood up. "It is time I speak to these warriors." He looked at Culley. "Will you accompany me? The presence of an old warrior lends weight to my argument."

Culley smirked, scratched his graying beard, and followed Orius over to the Ragnaardars, who were huddled around their fires. When Orius and Culley approached, the Ragnaardars' talking changed to whispers, and then died into silence. Some of them began to rise and Orius raised his hands, motioning them to sit. He and Culley made their way into the center of their gathering. All eyes were fixed upon them.

"Warriors of Ragnaar," Orius said. "I ask you to join me by my fire." He paused. What he had to say next was a gamble. Including people of questionable loyalty in on his plans was risky - even if they had sworn allegiance - but he needed their swords and axes. "As warriors, you must join your chief's war council." He beckoned and then walked with Culley back toward their companions. "Are they coming?" he asked.

Culley looked over his shoulder. "Aye, they are coming."

Purple hues colored the clouds hanging over the mountains in the east. The cool morning air was thick with the woody scent of dying campfires. Birds were awake and chirping. Fayne's black horse whinnied, and he patted its neck and whispered into its ear. Alana steered her chestnut mare closer to Fayne's. Orius stood before the horses, gently stroking their noses. He looked around, trying to spot any curious faces in the windows of Ragnaar's huts. It was still dark in the valley, and it was difficult to tell if anyone watched them. Orius raised his right hand, and the palm began to glow.

"May the Light of Ghyo guide you through the darkness," he said quickly, extinguishing the amber light almost before he was done.

Fayne shook Orius's hand. "Thank you for the blessing. We'll meet you in a few days."

Alana reached down and took Orius's hand from her brother's grasp. She touched it to her forehead, and then kissed it. "I truly believe the Creator sent you to make Cheltabria a great nation. Your blessing lightens my heart. I've found the strength to carry out this work."

"Ride forth and complete this task," Orius told them. "Ragnaar's warriors march with us. Keep peace in your hearts, but war on your minds. Our enemy will not leave without a fight."

Alana and Fayne steered their horses down the road that ran south to the Borvik Pass, which connected the north of Cheltabria with the south.

# Chapter 2

## The Oncoming Tide
### 5 Janoban, 229 A.G.S.

Furiously urging his horse onward, Tarik Torenyo traveled north along the road running parallel to the Gudor River. He weaved his way through columns of farm carts, merchant wagons, and people carrying wares on foot. The traffic had grown heavier the closer he got to the city of Golandar. He cursed loudly and yelled for people to make way. As a Royal Messenger, he carried urgent correspondences for the king.

He had been on the road nearly three days, running from horse to horse at relay stations, stopping only to relieve himself, to eat, or to bed down for the night. Summer neared its end, but the heat was intolerable. The valleys and plains of Soriazar remained sun-baked and blistering, even at this time of year.

The formidable fortress of the Alcazar loomed on the horizon, situated on a rock outcrop rising from the white buildings of Golandar. Villages, olive groves, and fields of grapevines and wheat radiated from the city to the Yunar Mountains rising to the east. Barges unloaded cargo at Golandar's riverside docks.

The city rested on a huge, gently sloping hill on the river's east bank. The city walls boasted forty round towers, thirty feet high and constructed from precisely cut blocks of stone. Four gates controlled access to and from the city.

Tarik galloped his horse up to the southern gate. A sweating guard came forward. He shifted the halberd in his hands and raised an arm, signaling Tarik to stop. Tarik presented his signet ring to the guardsman, which denoted him as a Royal Messenger. With a loud sniff, the guard motioned him through the gate. Tarik buried his spurs into the flanks of his brown pacer and charged into the city.

Shoppers, hawkers, wagons, and kiosks crowded the streets of Golandar. Loud voices haggled over prices. The smells of spicy food from a nearby tavern lessened the stench of the pack animals and unwashed people. Azaris sat around tables in front of the tavern beneath the shade of an awning: eating, conversing, conducting business, and drinking beer and wine.

Tarik licked his parched lips with envy as he guided his horse down a winding street leading to the city's main thoroughfare. He had

to move slowly to avoid trampling anyone, but he shouted for the
people to make way. He soon turned onto the main thoroughfare,
which ran from the city's west gate to the road leading up to the Alcazar.

The vertical cliffs supporting the fortress rose abruptly from the
houses nestled at its feet. A narrow road rose from the western end of
the rock, running nearly the length of it before turning back on itself
and running to another switchback at the western end, until ending
in front of the Alcazar's solitary gate.

Tarik's horse was exhausted when it reached the gate. White foam
dripped from its neck and flanks. Tarik displayed his signet ring to
the guards at the entrance, who instantly waved him through. He
dismounted, led his horse through the gate, and headed toward the
stables a short distance to the right. His legs and back ached from
the hard ride. The pungent odors of manure and hay hung in the air.

A young groom jumped up from the stool on which he sat in the
shade of the fortress wall and took Tarik's reins. The servant gave a
concerned look to the exhausted horse and an accusing look to Tarik.

Tarik gave him a hard stare in return. "Water," he rasped.

The servant went over to a wooden bucket that sat on the ground
beside his stool. He scooped out some water with the ladle resting on
the lid. Tarik swallowed the water in two gulps and tossed the ladle to
the servant. He then pulled a chain with a key from under his green
tunic. He unlocked a saddlebag and removed a worn leather folder
containing the message for the king.

Tarik marched past the stables as quickly as his stiff legs could
carry him. He passed beneath the arch cut through the high hedge
on the border of the stable's courtyard. He walked down the brick
path, which ran between waist-high hedges. The branches of birch
trees mingled above the path, creating a shaded passageway.

He passed the Muori-style fountain, with eight stone lions supporting its bowl. The fountain sprayed cool moisture into the air
around it. After pausing briefly to let the cool moisture cover his face,
Tarik followed the path to the main doors of the palace. His journey
neared its end.

Two soldiers of the Eagle Guard stood by the palace doors.
Sunlight glittered off their polished breastplates and morions. As
Tarik approached, they crossed their halberds and blocked the entrance. He showed them his ring and they snapped their halberds
back to attention. Tarik crossed the palace threshold and immediately the coolness of the shaded interior washed over his face and
neck. His boots made echoing clicks as he crossed the polished marble tiles, passing by immense woven tapestries depicting battles of
long ago.

Tarik stopped at the entrance to the audience chamber. He held up a hand to the servant who was stationed at the double-doors, motioning him to wait. Tarik looked into the large mirror to the right of the doors. His dirty reflection surprised him. He wiped the dirt from his eyes, primped his black goatee and mustache, and straightened his clothing. He handed his baldric and morion to the servant, who stepped forward and patted dust from Tarik's tight-fitting green tunic. Tarik rubbed his boots on the back of his hose, completing his hasty preparations, but it was useless – he was filthy. He then nodded to the servant, who opened the door for him.

The green marble floor of the audience chamber reflected the sunlight shining through the partitioned glass ceiling, filling the room with an amber glow. A forest green carpet, with gold embroidered laurel leaves, branches, and acorns skirting its edges, led from the door to a three-tiered marble dais. Two handsomely carved mahogany chairs, upholstered in gold damask, sat atop the dais. A forest green tapestry hung behind the chairs, with embroidery at its borders identical to that of the carpet. A golden eagle rested in its center - the Royal Eagle of Soriazar.

Gray-haired Beltram Zepio, the sagely Royal Steward, greeted Tarik and bade him wait by the door. With a soft ruffling sound from his black jerkin, Beltram turned away and approached the dais. The creaking of old joints accompanied his movements. A dull metallic thud, from his silver Staff of Office, accompanied his steps. He halted behind the man who occupied the king's attention.

Rodrigo Mendio sat upon the right hand chair atop the dais. He wore a red, thigh-length tunic with shining gold buttons running from his waist to a tight, high collar. He patiently listened to his son-in-law Borto Camidor, a wealthy merchant and the Duke of Golandar, recount the success of his latest enterprise. Borto was loyal, but Rodrigo never cared for his in-law's personality and boasting. But Borto brought much revenue to Rodrigo's coffers, so he tolerated him.

Rodrigo noticed Beltram approach; he also saw the messenger waiting at the opposite end of the carpet. He raised his hand to Borto, who stopped talking. "Beltram, bring that man forward."

Tarik wiped his palms on his hose and approached the dais, passing by the twenty finely dressed and perfumed Azaris attending court. He stopped when he reached Beltram and handed him the leather folder.

Rodrigo recognized Tarik. "What news do your bear from Spandel? We were not expecting any correspondence from my cousin the marquis. How is your father?"

"The marquis is in good health, Your Majesty," said Tarik. "And he wishes the same to you." He kneaded his hands before continuing. "But Your Majesty, I have the misfortune to report that Semotec warriors have crossed our frontier and raided three villages."

*And so it begins.* Rodrigo pursed his lips. His stomach twitched and his neck turned hot. At times like these, he paid close attention to maintaining his composure. He took a deep breath and exhaled. He gestured and Beltram handed over the message.

Rodrigo broke the red wax seal on the yellowish parchment bearing the emblem of the marquis. He slowly unfolded the letter and read it. He took another deep breath after finishing the first paragraph. His instincts told him to make a statement to the curious members of the court.

"It appears the Semotec problem is no longer an Iduin problem," Rodrigo announced to the people gathered. "They have taken many Azari men, women, and children prisoner. No doubt, they are to be sacrificed by the heathens. Beltram, summon General Mazrio and the princes. We shall meet in the council chamber. Borto, we shall continue our conversation later."

Borto bowed deeply as Rodrigo rose from his seat and strode toward the doors. A scribe packed up his portable desk and writing utensils and followed Rodrigo.

Beltram slowly turned around. "Court is adjourned. Unfinished business shall be resolved tomorrow." The audience bowed as Rodrigo walked past them.

The darkened council chamber resembled the inner deck of a ship. Square wooden beams ran from the floor to the ceiling, across to the other side, and back to the floor. A pair of windows on the right side let in the sunlight, but not enough to illuminate every recess. Heavy curtains hung from each window.

Rodrigo seated himself in the high-backed chair at the end of the table in the room's center. A map of Soriazar covered the table's surface. Small painted wooden blocks were situated on the map along the frontier of Soriazar and Idu. Each block represented the last known positions of Semotec troops. The scribe took a seat in a corner and prepared to dictate dispatches.

Rodrigo knew he had time before the others arrived, so he finished reading the letter:

*...have mobilized the militia units of the march from the towns and villages furthest from the frontier, to march toward Spandel with all*

*possible speed. I have ordered the militias between Spandel and the border to fortify their homes and resist the Semotecs until relief can arrive. I also request that Your Majesty dispatch a general to take command of the defense of Spandel March.*

*Your faithful servant,*
*Gregor Torenyo, Marquis of Spandel*

The heavy door opened and Rodrigo glanced over the top of the letter. Beltram entered, followed by General Todu Mazrio, dressed in a green tunic with wide sleeves beneath a burnished breastplate with the Royal Eagle emblazoned on it. Todu's black hair was streaked with gray, like his thin beard and goatee. He cradled an ornately engraved morion in the crook of his arm. His stern green eyes were locked on Rodrigo.

*His very presence commands authority.* Rodrigo smiled at his old friend. "Todu, although you stay in Golandar, I do not see you often enough."

"My apology, sire." Todu snapped his right arm to his heart. "The new army requires much attention."

"Right you are. Soriazar remains ever in your debt, senyor. I should not be so selfish." *You've served Soriazar well for thirty years, old friend.* "These troops you are training will soon be asked to demonstrate their abilities. Are they up to the task?"

A smile stretched Todu's peppered goatee further than what seemed natural. "These Semotec raids are just what I need to initiate the army."

Rodrigo nodded with approval. "It has been years since the nation has been threatened like this. Your enthusiasm reminds me of the time we spent fighting Kheldune. Hopefully, this will not prove as difficult."

"I have hardened these boys into men as best I could. The only thing we have been lacking is a war," Todu told him. "Other nations will fear us when I finish with these savages."

*And nations will scramble to match us.* Rodrigo glanced toward Beltram. "We need wine."

Beltram bowed, exited, and closed the door. But moments later, it burst open and a large swaggering man, with reddish-brown hair, strode into the chamber. Sandovar Mendio wore a light-blue silk tunic tailored to accentuate his muscled chest. The silver quatrefoil of the Order of Olantaro hung from a chain around his neck.

"Father, what is this news of invasion?" Sandovar's voice boomed. He stopped beside the table, hands on his hips. He pored over the map, appearing to take mental notes. "What moves have you decided upon? Who is mustering the troops?" He then stared at Rodrigo. "Who is to *lead* them?"

Rodrigo moved his eyes from Sandovar to Todu and back to Sandovar. *I must handle this lightly.* "We have not begun the council. You and Todu are the first to arrive."

Sandovar glanced at Todu, wrinkled his nose, and walked around the table. He knelt beside Rodrigo and placed a hand on his arm. "Father, if I am to rule this land, I must be given a chance to command in battle. You know this. I am twenty-seven and have never led troops in battle."

Rodrigo fought to keep a calm face. Arrogance and pomposity often affected Sandovar's judgment. Thirty years of peace and prosperity had pampered the prince and the nobility. Rodrigo motioned to the chair on his right. "Sandovar, take your seat. There is much to be discussed besides who is to command."

Sandovar's face turned to scorn. He plopped his large frame into the chair, and the wood groaned beneath his weight. "I must be involved," he said. "I must bring honor to this family."

*And I must keep control of this family.* "I am sure you will bring this house great honors," said Rodrigo. "However, we must all do our duty in the coming days, or we could be faced with disaster."

Sandovar leaned back in his chair, cupping his chin in his hand.

"The king is correct," Todu said. "You do not have to worry about being left out. There will be plenty of fighting - for all of us."

"Only if you use the knights," Sandovar snapped. "I have seen your new army. There is no personal honor in the way you fight. People of land, title, and position are to be entrusted with the defense of Soriazar. Not the common foot soldier."

"As Your Highness already should be aware," Todu responded. "The ground dictates the tactics used by the commander. More so than the type of troops."

Sandovar jumped from his chair. "You dare insult me? I am your future king! Father, this upstart should be whipped for his words. He forgets his place."

"If you spent more time on the drill field and less time on *other* pursuits," said Todu. "You would understand how your future military operates."

"Father, I claim my right as a knight to challenge General Mazrio to a test of arms." Sandovar pointed at Todu. "You, senyor, shall witness how I handle my weapons firsthand."

"Enough!" Rodrigo slammed his fist on an armrest. *This never ends. Whom do I side with – my son or my best friend?* "There will be no more of this. There is no time." He glared at Sandovar. "My cousin has massed Spandel's militias. General Mazrio will command the operations along the border. Sandovar, you will be second-in-command."

Sandovar's brown eyes bulged. His mouth fell open. "Second-in-command places me in the *rear* of the fighting!"

Rodrigo held up his hand and continued in a softer tone. "My son, Todu and I have commanded in many battles. It is true you need to lead men in war, but you must first learn how. You have no real experience. Todu is our greatest general, and he has much to teach you. You will be king, but you must learn how."

Todu smiled slightly. Sandovar gave him a menacing stare in return. "I will serve as your second," he said. "Only because it is the wish of the king."

A high-pitched squeal came from the hallway, followed by a young man's laughter.

"I shall catch up with you later," said the male voice.

"You're so sure about that," replied a female voice. "Don't count on it."

Prince Javior, Beltram, and a serving girl, bringing bread and cheese, appeared in the doorway. The girl used her hip to nudge her way past Javior. She placed the heavy tray on a long, narrow table against the wall. Her black, ankle-length skirt fluttered as she spun around and curtsied to Rodrigo. She then walked toward the door, pausing only long enough to flash a flirtatious glance at Javior.

Javior grinned and sighed. Of all the noblewomen flocking at the chance to be introduced to the youngest and most beautiful of Rodrigo's sons, he paid more attention to the female commoners working in the palace - a habit his father found intolerable.

Javior, too, wore the medallion of Olantaro. Rodrigo had knighted him only a few months earlier. Javior was intelligent and as skilled with the sword as he was in horsemanship. He took his seat, three chairs to the right of his father. The second chair was reserved for Prince Masuf. "Will Masuf be joining us?"

"No," said Rodrigo. "Masuf is at his post in the Yunars."

Todu took the seat on Rodrigo's left. Beltram took his seat beside the doorway. They waited for one more to arrive.

A male servant entered with a silver decanter and goblets on a tray. He went to the table along the wall and set it down. He placed a goblet in front of each man and one in front of the empty seat to Todu's left. Each man held up his goblet as the servant poured red wine from the decanter. When the servant finished, he bowed and left. Another then entered and placed a silver tray, heaping with fruit, on the table. He too bowed and departed.

"The Mistress of Trackers should be arriving soon, Your Majesty," Beltram said.

Rodrigo nodded. He raised his goblet and sniffed the wine's fruity scent. He loved the sweet muscatel from the vineyards of Vorencia. He took a sip and set the cup on the table. He looked at the men seated around him. *I'll be relying on these people in the coming days and weeks.* Of the many uncertainties that war brings, he worried much about the ego and temperament of his son Sandovar, who was a grown man and fast becoming unyielding to changing his nature. Rodrigo's heart felt heavy in his chest. He had gotten that sensation from time to time during the last year, mainly when he thought about how Sandovar would handle being king. Rodrigo felt the years creeping up on him. He was fifty-nine, and he knew he had time left, but the ache in his chest made his heart feel as though it were sinking.

Rufina Manda opened the door and entered the council room. She was tall, confident, and athletic. She raised her hands to her head and flipped back the hood of her mottled green and tan cape, which nearly reached the floor. Her thick red hair was tied in a braid. She directed her tanned face and emerald eyes towards Rodrigo. "Your Majesty."

*Such a beauty,* Rodrigo thought. *But her looks pale beside her swordplay.* "Mistress Manda, take your seat and we shall begin."

Rodrigo commenced the meeting by going over the contents of the marquis' letter. He then said, "We shall react to these events by sending Todu and the Royal Army to Spandel. They shall be on the road within three days. We have been expecting an incursion and have planned for it. Princes Javior and Sandovar shall accompany Todu. The general is to command all the Azari soldiers within Spandel March. His objective is to expel the Semotecs from Azari soil." He looked at Todu for emphasis. "But you are not to send troops across the border into Idu." Rodrigo sipped his wine. "Mistress Manda is to dispatch Prince Masuf and a company of Trackers to join the Royal Army. They will be under Todu's command and serve as his scouts. Admiral Amadora's ships will depart from Spandel's harbor and raid the Semotec's coastal villages."

As Rodrigo spoke, the others circled the table, noting to where he pointed on the map. The council lasted two hours. Comments and suggestions were voiced. Plans for supplies, weapons, and wagons were finalized. The scribe furiously dictated letters. With the completion of each message, Beltram took it into the hall and handed it to one of the Royal Messengers, standing by.

Rodrigo adjourned the meeting, and the council members paid their respects and left, except for Beltram and the scribe.

Rodrigo said to the scribe, "Edero, I have one more message to send. Do you have strength for another?"

"Yes, Your Majesty," the weary scribe replied.

"Thank you. You have done a great service today. Are you ready for the most important one?"

"It would be my pleasure, sire."

Rodrigo knew the scribe lied, but he cleared his throat and placed his hands behind his back. He hated the sound of the words he had to say, but he knew he must take advantage of a great opportunity. "To the Senate of the," Rodrigo hesitated and said the word, "*Republic* of Idu."

It took half an hour to complete the letter. "Beltram, is Tarik waiting outside?" Rodrigo asked.

"Yes, sire."

"Bring him in. This job requires family."

# Chapter 3

## The Scent of Heresy
### 5 Janoban, 229 A.G.S.

Pendros swaggered jauntily down the cobblestone street, which led to Ghyo's temple in Fallheim. With each step, his rapier bounced off his leg. It was mid-morning, and the street was filled with women returning home with baskets containing bread and fruits for the noon and evening meals. Pendros flashed his practiced smile at them and doffed his wide-brimmed black hat, decked with a slender white feather, to the ones he found enticing - especially to the younger ones, whom he presumed to be unmarried, but that was not so important. The women blushed or giggled in return.

Pendros had received a sealed letter from the High Priestess of Fallheim. The letter requested that he present himself to her, to pass along some information he had that was of interest to the Church. So, Pendros had concluded his normal business early and headed off to meet the high priestess. As he arrived at the temple's steps, he glanced up at the twin stone spires, rising a hundred feet above him. They stood out starkly against the clear sky. A gentle breeze blew down from the mountains to the north. Pendros hoped the meeting would not consume the entire day.

A knight of the Holy Order of Ilyas stood guard at the temple's entrance. The knight wore a shirt of mail covered by a sleeveless, white surcoat with a gold embroidered sun stitched into the cloth at his chest. A longsword hung from his stout black girdle, and a shining barbuta, studded with rivets, covered his head. White gauntlets with black palms covered his hands and forearms. The knight's eyes stared at Pendros from the shadowed recess of the barbuta's T-shaped opening.

Pendros found it disgusting that the Church never disbanded the knights after the Great Schism. Ghyo's priests preached peace, eased the suffering of the sick and injured, but the Church still kept the ruthless knights in their employ. *They're masters at shaping a good reputation,* he silently admitted.

Pendros set his foot on the first step and placed his hands on his hips. "I am Pendros Lillelin, the Iron Merchant. High Priestess Jurdana has sent for me." He grinned as widely as he could. "And here I am!"

"Wait here."

*He's as rigid as an oak. They all are.* The knight entered the temple's darkened foyer, Pendros heard his muffled voice, and the knight then reappeared with an acolyte.

"Master Pendros, you may follow me," a thin, male voice said from within the acolyte's white cowl. "Her Holiness awaits." He motioned Pendros to follow him and walked inside.

Pendros marched up the steps and entered the temple. The dankness of the interior touched his face. It took a moment for his eyes to adjust to the foyer's dimness. Two bronze sconces, hanging from the walls, cast flickering shadows. A faint scent of incense lingered on the air.

A quiet voice addressed Pendros from behind. "Master, leave your sword with me." It was a second acolyte, who had appeared from a niche to the right of the entrance.

Pendros bowed slightly, drew his rapier like a flash of lightning, and handed it to the robed figure. Small feminine hands emerged from the wide sleeves of the acolyte's robe and took the sword.

"This way, please," said the male acolyte.

The entrance to the temple's sanctuary lay at the foyer's end. Across it, Pendros saw the marble dais and altar where the priests conducted their rituals and ceremonies. Daylight shined through the large stained-glass window above the altar. Pendros's boots knocked against the rough-hewn stones of the temple's floor. The stones' unevenness resembled ripples on a lake. He followed the acolyte to the left along the sanctuary wall, behind a row of stout columns. They passed several doors and stopped when they reached one with a lighted bronze sconce to either side of it. The acolyte turned the handle and opened the door to the audience chamber.

A blue carpet ran the length of the room to a single-stepped dais. A slender, regal-looking blonde woman sat on the chair atop the dais. She wore a low-cut, white silk dress that ran to her ankles. Above her blue eyes, she wore an engraved band of gold around her head. A golden sun with eight wavy rays of light was fastened to the band and sat in the middle of her forehead.

The acolyte entered the audience chamber and knelt a few paces from the woman. Sunlight streamed through the stained glass windows behind dais, casting patches of red, green, blue, and yellow across the acolyte's robe. "Your Holiness, I have brought the merchant with whom you wished to speak."

Pendros removed his hat and bowed deeply. His brown leather doublet made a creaking sound as he did. As he straightened himself, he ran his eyes along the priestess's body from her feet to her face, pausing a little too long at her breasts. He breathed in her perfume before he spoke. "Your Most Lovely Holiness, I have come as requested. I must say it is always a pleasure to meet you. What service may I be to you?"

Jurdana looked down her delicate nose at him. "Spare me your flattery," she said. "I govern the churches of the Southern Valley. I am not a mere tavern girl you can woo with silky words."

Pendros looked down at the hat in his hands and slowly ran his fingers along the brim. He felt abashed by her rebuke – slightly. *No harm in a little flattery.*

Jurdana continued. "You recently returned from trading for iron in the North."

Pendros cleared his throat. "That is true, Your Holiness. I traded for iron in the village of Ragnaar."

"Your caravan guards have spread rumors of a priest gathering the tribes in the Northern Valley. If it is true, that is heresy. The Holy Tower is sensitive to matters of heresy. It stains the dignity of Ghyo's Church." She glanced at the acolyte after she spoke.

Jurdana's bluntness surprised him. "Yes...you are quite right. Word of this will reach Arshapel. That is inevitable." *She is rather agitated by all this.* Pendros had returned the day before, and it always amazed him how quickly stories brought in by the caravans spread through Fallheim.

"I want to hear what you have to say about this." Jurdana raised her hand, signaling the acolyte. "Bring him a chair."

The acolyte brought a leather folding chair. Pendros sat, placed his hat on a knee, and leaned back, testing the strength of the chair's rivets. "I heard stories of a priest of Ghyo, named Orius Candell, who preaches for a crusade against the Oruks. Rumor says a sizeable host of them have crossed the border near Drenga. The fighting there is said to be fierce." His eyes strayed from her face to her breasts again.

"A crusade?" asked Jurdana. "Mind your eyes!" She glared at Pendros. "Why do you use that word?"

Pendros's eyes darted back up to hers. "Because it was explained to me that this priest is using the name of the Creator to rally warriors to his banner. That seems like a crusade to me."

"Who spoke to you of this? I trust it was not some farmer or woodsman."

"No, Holiness, it was Worgoth, chief of Ragnaar. The priest had communicated with him about joining forces to fight the Oruks. But Worgoth told me he would have none of that. He said his warriors fight only in defense of his land. Drenga and Candell must fend for themselves." *Arrogant bastard. Worgoth is useless to us, Jurdana.*

"The northern tribes and their petty differences." Jurdana shook her head. The corners of her lips sagged. "This nation could be strong and respected, but outside influences and the squabbles of the North keep it down and divided."

"Cheltabria would be great if Fringia was not its neighbor," said Pendros. The massive Fringian population sucked the life out of the Southern Valley. More food and money flowed south than north.

"Is there anything else you can tell me?" Jurdana's voice echoed finality to the meeting.

Pendros struggled to keep his eyes from wandering again. "Yes. This priest uses the Gift to prove his legitimacy to the people of the North. He conducts the Celebration of the Light, and he heals the injured and sick."

"Master Pendros, you have again done the Church a service," said Jurdana. "I shall arrange a payment to you in gold for this information. You are dismissed."

Pendros rose from his seat. Being rewarded for passing along gossip surprised and pleased him. He bowed deeply and made a sweeping gesture with the arm holding his hat. The acolyte came to his side.

Pendros turned to leave, but then he spun around and said, "I forgot one thing, Holiness." He smiled his practiced smile. "This Orius refers to himself as Chief of the Northern Valley." His smile turned mischievous. "I apologize for the omission. I was entranced by your beauty." He did not wait to see the cold stare that cut through his back.

The door clicked shut behind Pendros. Jurdana stood and crossed the carpet. Her silk dress floated about her. *So it's true, the tribes are uniting.* She left the audience chamber and crossed the sanctuary. Her pulse quickened with each step. To the left of the altar was a stout door in a niche beside a column. Jurdana removed a key from the pouch on her gold-threaded rope belt and unlocked the door. Once inside, she locked the door behind her and stood in pitch darkness. She raised her hand and the palm radiated an amber light. Her hand trembled with trepidation. The glow intensified and illuminated the passageway. Stairs led into the temple's foundation. They were shaped from the same rough-cut blocks of stone that made up the sanctuary floor. Only one person at a time could descend the passageway.

The stair's bottom opened into a small chamber. Shelves covered the walls, filled with leather-bound books and tomes. Jurdana felt the chamber's dampness on her chest. The scent of old leather and moldering paper permeated the air. A hand-carved wooden table sat in the small room's center. A small wooden box with a lock dangling from its latch rested on a corner of the table. A two-foot diameter translucent crystal sphere, suspended a few inches above the table by a golden hoop mounted on three golden legs, took up the table's remaining space.

Jurdana reached into her belt pouch and produced a second, smaller key, which fit the lock on the box. Inside the box, a thin silver tiara rested on top of dark blue velvet. Jurdana removed the gold band from her head and replaced it with the silver one. She knelt and mouthed a silent prayer.

Jurdana rose and stretched out her arms, so the sphere was between them. She then made her other palm glow and a bluish-white light appeared in the sphere's center. It began as a small, dim ball that grew as the light intensified and filled the sphere. A milky mist swirled around the light. A man's face appeared within the mist and gradually became clearer; a room came into view behind his image. After a few moments, the mist dissipated. The man wore a golden sunburst on a band above his somber eyes.

"Sister Jurdana," the man said in Tradcspcak. "What trouble compels you to call upon the Holy Tower?"

Jurdana grimaced at his tone. *He knows I wouldn't use the sphere unless there's good reason.* "Brother Gaetan, I have received word of strange occurrences in the North. The Tower should hear of this from me, instead of through other channels." She was conscious of the slight tremor in her voice.

Gaetan looked over his shoulder and dismissed someone from the room. He returned his attention to Jurdana. "What could possibly be happening in the North?" His face showed no emotion. His hazel eyes lacked any luster of life. "I trust this is not about the Sytish raids."

Jurdana chafed at his remark. As the Holy Legate, he was her superior in the Holy Tower's hierarchy, and he did what he could to make her seem incompetent in the eyes of the Holy Council. "Brother Gaetan, there is a man, a priest of Ghyo, roaming about Northern Cheltabria. He gathers warriors for a crusade against the Syts." Jurdana felt a release of tension after she spoke. Gaetan would have found it impossible to believe that she had not heard of Orius Candell, if he found out about it from another source. Ignoring heresy was a serious matter. Besides that, and more importantly, it was Jurdana's responsibility to report these matters to the Holy Tower. A failure to do so would bring her competence as a High Priestess into question, which could bring about her replacement, which would dash her hope of creating a united Cheltabria.

Gaetan's eyebrows rose. "Continue."

"I assure you I have no involvement in this heresy and have sent no missionaries to the North," Jurdana told him. *I despise having to always make divulges to clear my name. There's too much intrigue inside His Church.* "Have any been sent by the Holy Tower?"

Gaetan shook his head. "I do not know, but I can look into that for you." He cocked his head to one side. "Why does this man refer to himself as a priest of the Faith? Have you spoken with anyone who has seen him?"

"No one I have spoken with has seen him. However, the information I have speaks of this man using the Gift and presenting the Celebration of the Light to the tribes."

Gaetan rolled his eyes. "There have been dozens of stories of farcical prophets who claimed to wield the Gift. You have told me nothing that has justified the use of the sphere. Though, I will see if there was a mission dispatched to Cheltabria. And any heresy will be dealt with." He paused for a moment. His eyes darted from side to side as though he pondered something. His furled eyebrows had the look of someone recollecting something mentioned long ago. "Let me know what else you learn of this," he added. "Good day."

"As you wish, Brother Gaetan," Jurdana answered, feigning respect for him.

She lowered her hands. The image inside the sphere faded into a milky mist, and the blue light fell in upon itself. Though Gaetan had been irritated by her summons, he had failed to mask his interest in her story. Jurdana would remember that and filter the information about Orius Candell she passed along to him. Any pursuit of heresy in the North would place a lot of attention on Cheltabria - attention she and others did not need.

# Chapter 4

## Shoring Up the Weak
## 7 Janoban, 229 A.G.S.

Tales of the Semotecs and their savage rituals of human sacrifices terrified the Azaris. Merchant caravans had brought to Golandar the stories of the brutality being committed upon the Azari people in Spandel. The Semotecs were heretical worshippers of Ghyo who sacrificed humans to give back the power of life given to them by the Creator. But their priests wielded the Gift. A fact the Church quietly ignored, leaving the people of Iningia to wonder how the Creator would allow the architects of such savagery to wield His power. Would the Semotecs invade deeper into Soriazar? People anxiously discussed it in the taverns and markets, but that was only part of their anxieties.

There was uncertainty about what the future would bring, and the merchant class had taken steps to protect their livelihoods. They sharply raised the prices of their goods, and the Golandarii complained of this to Rodrigo Mendio. They felt the merchants had taken unfair advantage of the situation caused by the Semotec invasion. The March of Spandel produced citrus, olives, wine, and grapes, but the price of bread had risen threefold since news of the invasion reached Golandar. Cloth, pottery, and other goods suddenly doubled in value, as well. Rodrigo responded to his people's complaints.

Late in the afternoon, thirty angry merchants stormed the Alcazar's gate, demanding an audience with Rodrigo. To their surprise, he granted them entrance. It took the Eagle Guard an hour to ensure the merchants were disarmed, and the merchants then packed into Rodrigo's audience chamber. The air soon became stuffy from the heat of their voices and their failing perfumes.

The sound of boots striking the marble caused the merchants to fall silent. Ten Eagle Guardsmen marched through the audience chamber's double-doors and shoved the crowd aside with the poles of their halberds. They made a space for Rodrigo to walk to the dais. Beltram Zepio followed close behind and took a place on Rodrigo's right side. The guards formed a cordon around the dais.

Beltram banged his silver staff on the floor three times. "His Majesty, King Rodrigo Mendio, extends his gracious invitation to all who attend this special session of the Royal Court. The king wishes to address your concerns during the time he has set aside for you this afternoon. Have you decided upon a spokesman?"

All the merchants shouted out in a chaotic outburst of demands, questions, and complaints. Rodrigo held up a hand, motioning for silence. He was satisfied. *I can wield more influence over an unorganized mob than over a cohesive coalition.* Slowly, the merchants ceased talking. Rodrigo said, "The decree I issued on 5 Janoban was made in the interest of the well-being of my subjects. Prices shall remain where they were prior to the fifth. The action I took affects all corners of Soriazar. Golandar has not been singled out."

A dubious merchant named Uroyo Senen suddenly spoke out. The nervous man struggled to keep his hands at his side. "King Mendio, not all of your subjects benefit from what you have proclaimed. This fighting could be lengthy. My fields are where the war is being fought. I'll lose all of my olive groves." A handful of other merchants roared in agreement.

"Senyor," Beltram said, pointing his staff at Uroyo. "There is protocol to follow. There will be order at Court."

"I agree, Senyor Senen," said Rodrigo. "The devastation could be massive." He studied their faces, trying to penetrate their stares and see into their minds. He rarely meddled in the merchants' affairs. He had known the decree would alienate them, but the merchants were not the nobility, and the nobility held the real power in Soriazar. Rodrigo kept a stern face. "It is a fact that our villages have been sacked. I promise you, the Semotecs will be punished for this. They sent a huge army into Idu, and they are rapidly exhausting the food there. Their invasion of Soriazar is a raid to gather supplies." Rodrigo pulled a kerchief from the white sleeve of his tunic and dabbed sweat from his forehead. "I have allowed you access to my chambers, so I may make one point clear. I will enforce the decree at sword's point, if need be. There is no reason for the cost of goods not originating from the regions around Spandel to be increased. I find your reasoning for the higher prices to be dubious."

The merchants gave each other astonished looks. Many cupped hands to their mouths and spoke to their neighbors.

Beltram banged his staff on the dais. "Silence! There will be silence as His Majesty speaks."

The noise abated. An arrogant cloth merchant stepped out of the crowd and looked at Beltram. "I, Prosporo Rabago, wish to be heard in the presence of His Majesty."

"You may speak, senyor," Beltram replied.

"Your Majesty, with this decree, you interfere in circles you said you would avoid," said Prosporo. "Why, now, do you choose this course?"

Rodrigo pointed a finger at Prosporo. "Senyor, you are plagued with the affliction of a short memory. Soriazar has not been threatened this way in thirty years. Peace has pampered you." The merchants whispered again in harsh voices. Rodrigo spoke louder. "Those of you who are old enough to remember will recall that I made a similar decree during our war with Kheldune. That decree eased the fears of my people. I will *not* allow bread riots in the streets while the stocks of grain are plentiful. You will not unnecessarily bring the suffering of the people of Spandel to Golandar and elsewhere."

The merchants stood in silence. Rodrigo signaled the room to be emptied, and Beltram ordered the guards to escort the merchants from the Alcazar. Conversation sprang up among them. The sounds of their voices echoed off the marble floor and faded as they left the palace.

Rodrigo and Beltram were alone in the audience chamber. Rodrigo fixed his gaze upon the green carpet running the length of the room. *I now have a list of troublemakers who may interfere with my governing of the country and the running of the war.* "Their greed runs deep," he said. "I doubt softer words would have swayed them. They are a pack of hounds when it comes to matters of gold. Especially that slimy, boastful Prosporo Rabago. He holds much sway over many of the nobles of this city. He heartily satisfies their desire for fine clothing, and he revels in the fact he spends much time attending their feasts."

"Making profits certainly comes before the good of the nation with that lot," Beltram agreed. "Uroyo Senen surprised me though. He is a soft spoken and nervous man. If he feels compelled to speak out, who else can we expect to do the same?"

Rodrigo shrugged and smiled. "I do not know. But I have them to thank for giving me the pretext to issue a price decree. We must find the good in everything."

Beltram leaned his aging body against his staff. "You have turned their greed to our benefit."

Rodrigo rapped his knuckles on an armrest. "It is imperative that I keep the support of the common people, should things with the Semotecs and Idu go awry. I will call up more soldiers after the harvest, and the price decree will lessen the burden of supplying my army." Rodrigo had to pay like everyone else. Gone were the days of tyrant kings who took what they pleased from their subjects.

He shook his head. *They'd sell out their families for profit, and many of them have.* "When this war is over, we will have to appease some of the merchants. Our coffers will need to be refilled with their taxes."

Beltram sniffed. "That is an unfortunate fact, Your Majesty."

The merchants had their arms returned to them, and they passed through the Alcazar's gate, making their way on foot or horseback down the winding path to the city. Uroyo and Prosporo walked together, and two others joined them. They were Aurelo Irigo, a famous, popular wine merchant, and Faquezia Letio, a shrewd grain merchant. The quartet reached the bottom of the path and walked down the wide thoroughfare leading to the western gate. At an intersection, the group bid each other good evening.

"We will meet at sunset tomorrow," Prosporo said. And they dispersed.

A man clad in a mottled brown and green cape rode a white gelding through the departing merchants. He guided the horse through the crowds of Azaris going about their business. Some of them greeted him, and he touched his right hand to his brow and greeted them in return. The horse seemed to know where its master wished to go. Without coaxing, it trotted up the winding path to the Alcazar.

As they ascended, the rider looked out over the landscape. Beyond the city's massive walls, the river Gudor stretched its way back toward its source in the mountains at the valley's southern end. The valley floor was green and lush. The growing season was almost over, and the fields were bountiful. At the gate, the guards snapped to attention. The rider returned the gesture with a salute and spurred his horse ahead. He dismounted and left the exhausted horse in the hands of a livery servant. He then marched with the confidence of a soldier through the gardens to the palace. His worn leather boots, folded over at the tops, made dull thuds upon the marble of the grand hallway. He stopped at the doors leading to the audience chamber. The room was empty except for the servant standing next to the entrance.

"Where's my father?" he asked.

"Your Highness, the king has retired to his council chamber," replied the servant.

His mottled cape made a rustling sound as the man headed further down the grand hall. He quickened his pace and entered the door to the council chamber.

The lanterns hanging from the rafters were lit and the heavy curtains were drawn. Rodrigo sat in his chair behind the large table, scribbling his name on the documents in front of him. When the door opened, he looked up and frowned, but his face instantly brightened. He pushed himself up from his chair. As he walked around the table he held out his arms. Masuf Mendio met his father's embrace.

"I had no idea you had returned," said Rodrigo.

"I left my company at Todu's camp and came right here," Masuf said. He stood an inch shorter than Rodrigo and lacked his father's and his brother Sandovar's heavy build. Campaigning against the bandits in the mountains bordering Kheldune had trimmed him of excess weight. Masuf wore his dark hair long, unlike his father and his brothers. His face was gaunt and sunburned, but his brown eyes were clear and alert. "We rode all night and through today. I only received your summons after midday yesterday."

Rodrigo beamed with pride. Masuf and his men had indeed completed a hard ride out of the Yunar Mountains. He released Masuf from his grip and placed his hands upon his son's shoulders. "You are strong. I can feel it. You are prepared for the campaign ahead. Your skills will be of the utmost service to the Royal Army."

"What'll you have me do?" Masuf asked.

"Todu requires scouts for his army. I have ordered Mistress Manda to release your company from your duties along the Khelduni border." Rodrigo turned away from Masuf and stood next to the table. He leaned over the map and extended his hand towards the blocks of wood around the city of Spandel. "I want you in Spandel with Todu. You have been chasing bandits for how long now?"

"Six years, Father."

"A long time. You are a veteran Tracker." Rodrigo thought about Sandovar one day sitting upon the throne. The corners of his mouth sagged with worry as he looked at the map. He ignored the ache beneath his breast.

"Father, what's the matter?" Masuf asked.

"To satisfy Sandovar's ambition, he has been made Todu's second on this expedition."

Masuf's eyes widened. "Father, Sandovar's never been involved in a fight off of the tournament field."

*Why couldn't you have been born first?* "I know, Masuf. But if he is to be king, he must learn of war, and Todu is the finest teacher we have. He taught me much, thirty years ago, and he will do the same for Sandovar. But they are at odds with each other. Your brother's pride will be a serious obstacle." He looked up at Masuf and his mood lightened. "You can ease the tension between the two of them."

"Father," said Masuf, "I'll serve you and Soriazar as faithfully as I can, but Sandovar is stubborn. We don't get along."

Rodrigo glanced at Beltram sitting beside the door, then back at his son. "I also chose you to go with the army, because of your prowess and cool-headedness in a fight. Rufina keeps me informed of your deeds."

Beltram said, "Your Highness, you are of equal status to the prince. Todu and his officers are not noble born."

"When I am in camp, I will *try* to play peacemaker," Masuf said.

"We ask nothing more from you," said Rodrigo. "But let us move on. Our problems with the Semotecs could be greater than we think. Idu's army has retreated into the mountain passes and abandoned their coastal plain. They hardly fought them, and that is very strange. They let them walk right into Soriazar. And we now stand alone."

The scent of roasting pork and herbs wafted in from the kitchens.

"All of your siblings shall dine with us tonight," said Rodrigo.

Masuf smiled. "I haven't dined with everyone in over two months."

Rodrigo gestured toward a chair at the table. "Please sit and rest a while. You look tired."

"If I may, I'd retire to my room and nap a while. I promise to not keep you waiting. Have my goblet full."

Rodrigo chuckled. "Get going," he said, as if Masuf were a child again.

Masuf trotted down the grand hall and passed through the double doors leading to the Mendios' private apartments. The red-marbled hallway was empty, but he abruptly slowed his pace. He stopped, listened, and sniffed the air. He placed his hand on the hilt of his dagger and slowly approached his room. It had a recessed door for an entrance, flanked by two columns. As he approached the darkened alcove, a strong, green-sleeved arm flashed out of the shadows, grabbed the top of his leather cuirass, and pulled him through the doorway. In an instant, he was on his back inside his room.

The door slammed shut and his attacker jumped on top of him, straddling his body. She tossed her mottled green cape aside and stared down at Masuf with emerald eyes. She gripped his face between her hands, bent down, and kissed him deeply. She sat up and slid her hands from his head to his chest. A grin appeared upon Rufina Manda's lips.

"You didn't remove enough of your perfume," Masuf said. "I could smell it in the air."

"I wanted my ambush to be sporting," she said. "I could not take undo advantage of you."

She bent low again and kissed Masuf. He kissed her back.

"I'm to attend dinner with my family tonight," he told her. "There isn't much time."

"Then we shall have to make do," Rufina said as she unbuckled his leather armor.

They made frantic love beside the door. They had been separated nearly four months. Rufina's position as the Mistress of Trackers kept her in the Alcazar far more than in the countryside. Afterwards, they rested upon the carpet, wrapped in each other's arms, panting from their coupling. Rufina stroked the side of Masuf's head.

"I must get dressed soon," he said. "My family has probably started without me. I promised Father I wouldn't keep him waiting."

Rufina closed her eyes and nodded. She sat up, folded her arms around her knees, and rested her chin there. "Todu and his troops march south tomorrow. Fate lends us no time."

Masuf looked up at Rufina. "Fate robbed you of your father and now it takes you away from me."

Rufina's lips quivered. "Making love in the mountain air has a seduction to it I cannot describe. It hurts too much to remember those nights."

Masuf stroked her bare shoulder. "Do you wish they never occurred?"

Rufina's head darted up. "No, how can you ask me that?"

Masuf smiled wanly. "I'm sorry. We should ask my father's permission to marry."

Rufina shook her head. "Our personal wants cannot come before the wants of Soriazar. It would be selfish to discuss this with His Majesty while a war rages. I inherited command of the Trackers from my father, with the blessing of King Rodrigo. We must wait."

A knock at the door startled them. A muffled voice said, "Your Highness, the king has sent me to inform you that everyone has gathered in the dining hall. What shall I say is your reply?"

"I'm almost ready." Masuf smiled at Rufina who chuckled quietly. He kissed her softly on the lips and laid her down again.

# Chapter 5

## For Love, or Love of Duty?
### 7 Janoban, 229 A.G.S.

Knocking interrupted Tarik's sleep. He grunted loudly, letting the innkeeper's son know he was awake. He lay on the bed a while longer, allowing sleep to drain from his body. He rose and stumbled over to the small table in a corner with a ceramic pitcher and basin on top. He poured some water and washed the grime from the previous day's ride off his face, neck, and hands. The water turned cloudy after he took a couple of handfuls from the basin. When he felt refreshed, Tarik opened the door and found his clothing hanging on the door handle. The innkeeper's son had done well at brushing away the dust. He threw his clothes on the bed and began to dress. His body ached from two days of hard riding, and he had many more ahead of him, but the grueling part of relaying from horse to horse was over. He hung his baldric over his right shoulder. He yawned and stretched, clearing away any lingering traces of sleep. The air in the room was warm and close, so he turned the latch on the window and opened it, letting in the morning air.

He poked his head through the window, and the scent of baking bread greeted him, quickly followed by the stench of manure. Below him, on the right side of the high-walled courtyard behind the inn, two grooms with pitchforks cast soiled straw from the stables. They chattered loudly as they went about their chores. The sound of banging pots from below then caught his attention, and his nose picked up the scent of the bread again. He looked at the window beneath his. Muffled female voices drifted up from behind the iron grating mounted into the whitewashed walls of the inn, covering the window. Breakfast was being prepared, and his stomach growled. Tarik shut the window and gathered his saddlebags, containing Rodrigo's correspondence and his personal belongings. His stomach urged him to hurry. He walked down the hall to the stairs, leading to the tavern on the first floor.

Tarik was staying in the village of Turela, nestled against the feet of the Blancuro Mountains, which rose steeply to the north. The road connecting Golandar and Spandel descended from the Rojera Pass and ran through the village center. Turela was a stopover for merchants and travelers, boasting more inns and taverns than other villages its size. The village was a day's hard ride from Spandel, or three days at an ordinary pace.

Tarik stayed at the Wandering Troubadour when he passed through the town. The inn was a modest two-story structure, tucked away down a narrow street. Two swordsmen stood watch always at its entrance. Carlos, the innkeeper, ran a prosperous enterprise, and his guards kept out rowdies. The merchants who stayed there appreciated the security and rewarded Carlos with generous gratuities. The Wandering Troubadour was a quiet place to conduct business, and it was a safe place for a man like Tarik, who carried State messages, to stay.

He reached the stair's bottom and found a table next to the wall. He draped the heavy saddlebags across one chair and sat in another. Three other customers occupied the tavern; other than them, the place was empty of patrons. Tarik glanced toward the long bar on the opposite side of the room. Carlos stood behind it, cleaning glasses. He noticed Tarik and nodded. Carlos called for the serving girl, his daughter, Aida, who appeared in the opening leading to the kitchens at the end of the bar. Aida was a petite girl with a round face and long, dark hair. When she saw Tarik, her brown eyes widened and a giddy expression appeared on her face. She placed a hand on the bar, rounded the end of it, and sauntered across the room.

Aida had not been working the night before. Tarik had heard from Carlos that she was at a festival. He had hoped to catch a glimpse of her before he retired for the evening. As usual, the loneliness brought on by traveling had weighed heavily on him. He always looked forward to flirting with her and trying to arrange a rendezvous. He played that game each time he stayed at the Wandering Troubadour. However, Aida was shrewd and eluded Tarik. Maybe it was the challenge that kept Tarik from feeling rejected – maybe, it was more.

Tarik was twenty-four and quite unlike the older merchants who ogled Aida's voluptuous figure. Tarik never groped her, like others did. Her father's guards watched over her and had tossed many a lecher onto the cobblestones in front of the inn. Although Tarik was flirtatious, he kept his honor and never imposed himself upon her.

"Good morning again," Aida said as she stood over him. She bit her lower lip and swayed her hips. "What can I get for you?"

Tarik slowly stroked his goatee. "If seeing you were breakfast, then I would have no need of ordering." He smiled, hoping he did not sound ridiculous.

Aida blushed. "The sun has barely risen above the mountains, Senyor Tarik, and already you try to woo me with your words. I believe the summer heat has affected your senses." She spun around;

her whirling skirt brushed his leg. She gave him a seductive glance over her shoulder. "I think I know what you need."

His stomach fluttered when her skirt touched his leg. The sensation lingered longer than he wished. A tight feeling formed in his throat. He waited for her to look away, and then shifted with discomfort. There had been women in his past. Frequent traveling provided him opportunities to satiate his needs, though no attachments were ever formed; but with Aida, it was different. The thought of being with her made Tarik question his livelihood. Royal Messengers gave up much in their service to the Crown. There was no time for marriage and child rearing. Though Tarik was proud of his work, he sometimes felt there must be other courses to pursue, but being the marquis was not open to him. His two older brothers stood in line before him.

Aida returned with a tray, containing a plate of toasted bread, a ceramic jar of greasy red pork butter with small pieces of meat mixed in, and a steaming cup of herbal tea - his usual breakfast when he stayed at the inn. She set the tray on the table and smiled at him. "Is there anything else you would like?"

*Her voice is smooth as silk.* "This will be fine, thank you," Tarik said.

"So, you'll be leaving after you eat?" she asked, sounding pouty.

"Yes, Aida." His throat became dry when he said her name. He took a sip from his cup. "I have quite a journey before me. I cannot remain here long."

"I see," she said sadly. "You're always rushing off. Important errands for His Majesty, I assume." She looked at him with an inquisitive face. "Does it bother you to not have a home?"

Tarik looked down at his plate. The question caused a sickening ache in his chest. He did have a home, sort of. He maintained a comfortable apartment in the castle at Spandel, but he did not have a true home, which bothered him. "I have learned to live without having an ordinary home. However, I do enjoy my service to the king. Being a messenger is a great responsibility, which comes with an equal amount of trust. It is good to be needed by His Majesty." He looked into her brown eyes, which sparkled with interest. The sudden thought of being needed by king and country made him remember why he did not have his own family. *I'm a creature of duty.* Tarik smeared some of the red butter onto his toast and bit off a mouthful. He chewed the hardened bread, and then sipped his tea.

"The people around here are scared," said Aida. "The militia was called up and they were sent to Spandel. Turela isn't well-guarded." She pursed her lips. "Do you bear any news for us from Golandar? I mean, what's the king planning to do?"

The three other men in the tavern overheard Aida's question. Their faces piqued with interest, and they fixed their gazes on her. By their style of dress, Tarik figured them to be merchants. He paused before answering her question. *I must phrase this carefully.* Information about troop movements was something not to be shared with everyone. The Royal Army at Golandar had been packing when he left the city.

The wealthiest looking merchant, a man with numerous baubles on his fingers, spoke up. "Yes, Messenger, the girl is not the only one interested in learning how His Majesty plans to deal with the Semotecs."

Another merchant, wearing a floppy hat with a yellow feather, added, "My business suffers because of those heathens."

Tarik frowned, looked at Aida, and then turned toward the men. "Senyors, I can assure you King Mendio is taking the situation seriously. He will not allow his subjects to suffer more of these injuries."

The merchant with the baubles complained and shook his head. "Typical ambiguous answer. We want specifics, senyor. Our livelihoods are threatened."

"King Rodrigo must react with speed. Hopefully, he will not drag his balls on the ground," the one with the floppy hat griped with a common-born Azari's sarcasm.

"Senyors, I understand your concern," responded Tarik. "My home and family are in Spandel. But the king is an honorable man. He has ruled during times of trouble before, and he prevailed. Have faith in him."

"Hah!" the baubled merchant shouted. "I will believe it when I see it. Do not lie to us. Your faith is based on your wages. You are like other men. *Gold* is loyalty." He rubbed a thumb and forefinger together.

Tarik's eyes bulged. In an instant, his hand was on the hilt of his sword and he was on his feet. "You dare question my loyalty! I love King Rodrigo and Soriazar. I assure you, senyor, that there are many more people like me."

The three men were startled by Tarik's aggression. Their hands fumbled for concealed daggers. Aida jumped back; her hand flew to her neck. From behind the bar, Carlos called for the guards, who appeared like ghosts.

"Senyors, senyors," Carlos said calmly. "Let us have no bloodshed in my inn. I run a respectable business."

Tarik removed his hand from his sword, and the merchants slipped their daggers back into their hiding places.

One of the guards at the door said, "Carlos, should we clear out these troublemakers?"

"They can stay," he said. "If there are no more problems."

Tarik returned to his seat and continued eating, but he kept an eye on the merchants. Aida remained next to Tarik's table. Her face was flushed. "Would you have fought all of them – single-handed?"

"Aida!" her father broke in before Tarik could answer. "Return to the kitchen and finish your chores."

Aida gave Tarik a sheepish look. "Good luck to you, Tarik. I hope to soon see you again." She walked away and disappeared into the kitchen.

Tarik smiled a little as she left. He enjoyed the notion of having a woman care about him. He hoped his travels would soon return him to the Wandering Troubadour. *Maybe I'll retire when I am done with this trip.* "Thank you," he called out to her. "I hope so, too."

The merchants finished their breakfast before Tarik and left the inn. Tarik finished his soon after, but he waited for a few minutes. He gave them time to retrieve their horses, if they had any, and to put some distance between themselves and the inn. For all he knew, they could be waiting in ambush in the stables, or in one of the many narrow streets and alleys. Tarik was upset with himself for losing his temper. Being killed in a dispute over honor was foolish, and dangerous to the nation. The message he carried was of utmost importance to Soriazar. Thousands of lives relied on him to reach Idu and deliver it.

When he supposed sufficient time had passed, he rose from his seat and picked up the heavy saddlebags. He weaved his way through the tables and chairs scattered across the red brick floor and stepped outside. He glanced left and right. The street was empty. The arched entrance to the stables was to the left; he entered and called for the grooms. One of them appeared and motioned Tarik to follow.

The Wandering Troubadour's stables were large. Ten of the stables were reserved for horses owned by the Crown. The inn served as a relay station for the Royal Messengers. A fresh horse, a black gelding, waited for Tarik. He hefted the saddlebags onto the animal's back and fastened them to the saddle. He then retrieved a key from his pocket and moved over to a large locked chest, with the Royal Eagle emblazoned on the side. He opened the lock and raised the lid. The chest contained a crossbow and other equipment - blankets, a one-man tent, a lantern, rope, and other items used by people who had to spend nights in the outdoors.

He took the crossbow and a quiver containing thirty bolts from the chest, and strapped them to the horse's saddle. He returned to the chest and selected a rope, a blanket, a small cooking pot, a bundle of wooden rods held together by two leather belts, metal rods shaped to form a cooking spit, and a box containing flint and steel.

These, too, were packed onto the horse. Lastly, Tarik checked the two fat skins hanging from the saddle; one of them contained water and the other wine. When he was satisfied with the arrangement of his gear, he handed a few coins to the groom and mounted the horse.

Tarik emerged from the stable's dim light onto the cobblestone street. The street, like most in Soriazar, was a narrow, winding whitewashed canyon of connected houses and shops. Balconies with flowers and plants protruded from the second stories. Tarik guided the horse toward Turela's main square. As he rode, he caught the scent of meals being prepared and the sound of families chattering.

Tarik arrived in the central square. Merchants were already there, setting up their goods for market. The sight of Tarik attracted stares. He ignored most of them, but he greeted the few people he recognized. Tarik took the street leading east. His horse was frisky, so he allowed it to trot a little faster. He soon reached the edge of Turela. Despite the early hour, there was activity on the road. Groups of farmers walked to the fields surrounding the village, carrying their lunches wrapped in cloth, hanging from the farm tools on their shoulders. They talked and laughed amongst themselves and seemed oblivious to Tarik, as he wove his way past them.

The barren, rolling foothills of the mountains to the north dominated the land. The hills had once been dotted with oaks and clumps of large stones, but they had been cleared to make room for vegetable fields, cotton fields, and olive groves. The nobles of Soriazar, who dwelt in the country in their large whitewashed estates, owned the fields. The people of the surrounding countryside worked their land.

A few merchant wagons traveled east. Like Tarik, their destination was the Iluta Pass, on the frontier bordering Idu. As the morning went by, the eastern mountains loomed larger, rising high above the rolling hills. The sky was devoid of clouds. The road wound its way back and forth and up and down the slopes of the foothills, and it ran through half a dozen tiny, whitewashed villages. The sun beat relentlessly upon the road and the land. Tarik paced his horse in the oppressive heat. He figured he would reach the mountains around mid-afternoon.

The Iluta Pass looked as if a giant had cloven the mountains with an axe. It loomed high above the walled town of Orpresa, which sat atop a conical hill aside the road, at the point where it began a winding ascent into the pass. Several merchant caravans were camped around the walls, awaiting the customs inspectors to appraise the value of their goods and collect taxes. The citadel of Orpresa, crowning the hill, served as a Royal Customs House.

A column of smoke rose into the sky along the southern horizon. Orpresa lay a half-day's ride from a village being plundered by the

Semotecs. Tarik guided the horse through Orpresa's main gate, which was heavily guarded by the town's militia. Crossbowmen manned the crenellations. Tarik sensed the nervousness in the faces of the townsfolk, soldiers, and merchants and in the sounds of their voices. The raids had driven hundreds of people from their homes, and the streets were crowded with displaced Azaris, who begged Tarik for money or food. As he passed them, they told him of the Semotec's crimes and begged him to relay the information to King Mendio. They spoke of murdered brothers, sisters, parents, and children. They told him of burned houses, looted possessions, and of family members carried away by the heathens. Trembling, hollow-eyed children stood beside their parents, faces taut with grief and shock.

Sadness took hold of Tarik. *I'll finish this task,* he silently resolved. *These people suffer, and the message I bear can help them.* He had planned to spend the evening in Orpresa, but he changed his mind and would camp in the Iluta Pass instead.

Tarik found a tavern with a stable and spent an hour there, resting and eating. He sat alone and eavesdropped on the other patrons' conversations. Revenge was the underlying mood of the talk. People discussed the future and expressed their anger about the food shortages of the coming winter months. If the Semotecs raided any deeper into Soriazar, other regions of the nation would have to feed them. Lean times lay ahead. The people had coped with poor harvests before, but nature had induced those. It was to be different this year, and that brought rage to their hearts. The people wanted revenge and the local militia was prepared to march – alone if necessary.

While Tarik finished his meal, he kept his head down, trying to remain inconspicuous, but someone recognized his green uniform, the emblem on his breast, and the ring on his finger. A drunken peasant, dressed in a loose, dirty shirt that had once been white, shuffled over to Tarik's table. He looked down at him through bloodshot eyes, holding a wooden mug against his round stomach. The man bent forward as he spoke, and his sour breath clung to Tarik's face. "A Royal Messenger! Do you come from Golandar, or some other place?" He slurred the last few words.

"I come from Golandar," Tarik answered.

A woman with her black hair tied in a bun, her drunken husband who appeared to be a shopkeeper of sorts, and a plainly dressed merchant moved closer to the table.

"Are you carrying instructions for our militia?" the woman asked.

"No," said Tarik. He closed his eyes and sipped his wine. It had been a mistake to answer the first man's question. Now he faced interrogation.

The woman's husband clenched his jaws. "Then, if you are not here for our militia, what message do you carry?"

Tarik frowned and rubbed his temples with a thumb and middle finger. "I cannot tell you the specifics of what I carry." *You know too much already.*

"An important message," the merchant said, pointing at Tarik. "You bear a message of importance. If your destination is not Orpresa, then you can only be traveling farther east. Orpresa is the only town of importance in this area." The merchant took a drink of wine and mulled over the issue. "The Semotecs crossed our border over a week ago, and now a Royal Messenger, not just *any* messenger, has come to Orpresa, and he is not stopping here." A crooked smile came to his face, and he pointed at Tarik again. "You are going to Idu. And I wager that King Rodrigo is planning something, hopefully a military campaign, and he needs to consult with the senators of Idu." The merchant swayed drunkenly as he stood beside the table.

Tarik sat up in his chair and chuckled. "Senyor, when you see the direction I take when I leave, you will then know if your speculations hold any weight." He hoped the hint would satisfy the man and end any further questioning. He added, "Other than that, I am bound by oath not to discuss my assignments." *I should've ridden past and camped by the roadside.* But the services of the tavern's stable had saved some the provisions he carried.

The woman's husband grew agitated. "Burn your oath. The enemy is but a day from here. Tell us what you know."

The woman with the bun tapped the shoulder of the man behind her and said, "This man is a Royal Messenger, and he is carrying a message from King Rodrigo to the land of Idu."

That man repeated what he heard to the group he spoke to, and those then told others. Suddenly, the tavern was silent and all eyes were upon Tarik. Their stares hungered for information. A man who possibly knew the mind of their king sat before them. The attention made Tarik uncomfortable. Typically, the presence of a messenger did not attract such notice, but the troubles had changed that. The silence did not last long; people clambered to get to a better view of Tarik. He was then confronted with a dozen, simultaneous questions and a couple of threats. He raised his hands and motioned for silence. It took several moments for the crowd to become quiet. Tarik stood and placed the saddlebags containing the message over his shoulder. *I must be tactful, or they could tear me apart.* He conspicuously placed his hand on his sword.

He tried to sound official. "Good people of Orpresa. Be assured that your Sovereign knows of your plight and is coming to your aid." He took a couple of steps toward the door, but the woman's husband blocked him. Sweat rolled down Tarik's back. "I know not what his plans entail, but you must have patience, and you must protect your town and buy time for His Majesty." A handful of people blocked the door. "Now, I must be on my way. Time is crucial - for *all* of us."

The woman's husband grabbed the arm that Tarik held onto the saddlebags with. But Tarik punched him in the nose. The man dropped to the floor.

"That's my husband!" shrieked the woman with the bun in her hair, as she clawed at Tarik's face.

Tarik rammed the heel of his hand between her plump breasts and knocked her on her rump. The merchant with the mug of wine raised his drink above his head and dexterously spun away from the melee.

Tarik put his shoulder down and forced his way to the tavern's door. A wall of noise broke the silence. People grabbed at him as he fled, but he shrugged them off. The chaos spread across the tavern and turned into a flurry of flailing fists and grappling bodies. Two men jumped over the bar and waylaid the bartenders. They then opened the spigots on the wine casks and lapped up streams of red and tawny liquid.

Once in the street, Tarik bolted to the stable, where he screamed at the grooms to shut the doors. A few people followed him into the street and blocked the road. Tarik hurriedly secured the saddlebags and checked the bit, bridle, and harness. His heart thumped heavily and his limbs shook with excitement.

When he was satisfied his equipment was in order, he paid the grooms and asked, "Has he been fed and watered?"

"I took good care of him, senyor," one of the young men said anxiously.

Tarik mounted the gelding and a groom opened the large wooden doors. Dusty beams of sunlight rushed in and illuminated the stable's interior. Tarik drove his spurs into the gelding's flanks and charged out of the stables. Once outside, he whipped his head around and saw a gathering crowd outside the tavern's door. Tarik steered his horse in the opposite direction, and he wound his way through the maze of streets to the town's gate.

He rode for a quarter of an hour, until the road climbed into the pass. It wound its way up the slope to a place where the pass opened into a narrow plain, and then the road ran straighter from there. The bottom of the pass was covered with boulders and scrubby pine bushes, and an occasional cork oak. Tarik stopped, turned his horse, and looked westward. Orpresa was a small, white oval sitting beside the reddish strip of the road, which slithered its way back to Turela. Fields of tans, browns, and greens flanked the road, dotted here and there by the white houses of the landlords. Just visible on the horizon, Tarik could see the white specks of three of the villages he had passed through.

A sensation of relief released the tension in his arms. It was his first mission outside Soriazar, and he barely made it out of the country unharmed. He wondered about the temperament of the populace on the other side of the mountains. A twinge of homesickness tugged at his stomach as peeled his eyes from his homeland and turned his horse eastward.

# Chapter 6

## Pressing Wills
## 7 Janoban, 229 A.G.S.

Half-columns graced the walls of the Alcazar's dining room, with either a sculpture or painting displayed between each pair. The vaulted ceiling rose fifteen feet at its apex, with decorative ribs traversing and intersecting in three places. Gilded chandeliers hung from the ribs' intersections. A long, lacquered table stood beneath the chandeliers on a prismatic hand-woven Muori carpet.

Two tall, partitioned windows occupied the wall opposite the double doors. A life-size portrait of Rodrigo Mendio hung between the windows, which he had commissioned after Soriazar's victorious war with Kheldune. The portrait depicted a young Rodrigo in a full suit of armor. His right arm rested on the pommel of a drawn sword. His left arm cradled a flagpole with a banner of a golden eagle on a forest green background. A small bronze plaque with the inscription, "Rodrigo I, Guardian of the Realm," was fixed to the bottom of the frame.

White porcelain plates with gold trim and sparkling crystal goblets sat before the diners. Half a dozen chickens sautéed with wine, fried tomatoes, green peppers, onions, garlic, and bits of cured ham lined the table's center. There were also platters with mushrooms in garlic and wine sauce, three types of bread, and four types of cheeses.

Rodrigo sat at the head of the table beneath the painting. He wore an emerald silk tunic with gold embroidered epaulettes. Queen Khalia sat at the opposite end. Her dress was tailored to match Rodrigo's attire.

"Oh, thank you, General," Caermela Mendio-Camidor said from where she sat between her brothers, Sandovar and Masuf, near Rodrigo's end of the table. She glanced at her tight blue velvet dress. "I purchased it this afternoon. I found it at Angelo's - just off the western thoroughfare." Her ruby earrings waggled each time she moved her head.

With his napkin, Todu whisked crumbs from his crimson tunic. "May I say you have excellent taste, Your Highness."

Caermela giggled and speared a piece of chicken with her knife. "Oh, you may, senyor."

"Masuf, I see you have again managed to look your best for dinner," Khalia said. Her nostrils flared a bit as she looked down her delicate nose at his murrey-colored tunic.

"Yes, Mother. Your perception never surprises me," Masuf answered. "It seems the mountains have taken the luster from my refined upbringing." He sipped wine from a crystal goblet and smiled and nodded toward Todu, who quickly raised his napkin to conceal his smile.

Javior turned toward his mother. The gold embroidery of his black tunic caught the light of the chandeliers. "Mother, please. We have not had Masuf in the palace for months. Let us be content with seeing him again."

"Perhaps what you say has merit." Khalia's expression softened as she responded to her youngest son. Then her eyes narrowed. The candlelight winked off her tiara's emeralds and diamonds. "But I did not raise my children to be ordinary."

"Your Highness, I think Masuf looks striking in his attire," Faquezia Letio said from her seat to the right of Khalia. "I think he is handsome, in a rugged sort of way." She raised her wine glass to her lips and looked over the top of it, fixing her eyes on Masuf. The ruby, pearl, and diamond rings on her hand sparkled. Masuf raised his glass to her.

High Priestess Serophia and Princess Drucilla Mendio sat quietly, eating their meals. They did not take interest in the others' jests and comments. Khalia sipped her wine and watched Serophia take a bite of chicken.

"Holiness, I hope you find the meal to your liking," she said. "The white wine is from Spandel March. His Majesty ordered it served in honor of those fighting the heathens."

Serophia, who sat beside Faquezia, dabbed the sides of her mouth with a napkin. Her sunburst tiara was the antithesis of Khalia's royal tiara. "It is most delicious, Your Highness. Your cooks should be commended. Over the years, I have become accustomed to Azari cuisine, almost over that of my native Fringia."

"Indeed," Faquezia interrupted. "Azari chefs inject a piece of their soul into their creations." Her black, silver-brocaded dress displayed her womanly curves.

Khalia focused on Drucilla. "Have you received your first assignment?"

"No, Mother," Drucilla said quietly. "I am presently charged with conducting Vespers." Half of Ghyo's sunburst on her white dress was visible above the tabletop.

Khalia's eyebrows rose. "Holiness, is there no diplomatic task that the princess can work on? I understand the Church has daily functions to complete. But Drucilla was trained for a specific purpose. Have I not donated enough to the temple?"

"Your Majesty, I understand your concern. There will soon be work for Drucilla," she glanced toward Rodrigo at the table's opposite end, "considering the present political state."

Rodrigo noticed Serophia looking at him. There was a lull in the talk at his end of the table, so he had heard what she had said. "And what is the Church's opinion on the matter?" he asked.

"We are interested in knowing the extent to which you wish to prosecute this war, King Rodrigo," Serophia answered.

Rodrigo hesitated before responding. He wondered exactly to whom Serophia referred to when she said "we." *As far as the outside world is concerned, this fighting is a border problem.* "I intend to pursue the matter until a favorable conclusion is in our hands. If it would please Your Holiness, I would prefer any further discussions about this to be held later this evening."

"Agreed."

"I also want to speak with my fine son-in-law and with the lovely Mistress Letio this evening," Rodrigo added. "Will the two of you indulge me?"

"Certainly, Your Majesty." said Borto.

"And I too, sire. I was waiting for your cue," replied Faquezia. "Your gracious invitation to dinner rang of business." She bit into a garlic mushroom.

Rodrigo nodded to them both and returned to speaking with the people at his end of the table. Livia Mendio rested an elbow on the table and pressed her forehead into the palm of her hand. Tears glistened in her eyes. Her wrinkled mouth showed her distress.

"Livia, my dear," Rodrigo said. "It is a normal thing for your son Tyrel to accompany his father on this campaign. He will learn much, and it will be good for him to become accustomed to life in a military camp."

"My little dove, my father is correct," Sandovar told his wife, the daughter of the Duke of Aliantro, who followed Azari custom by sitting opposite her husband. "Tyrel will someday succeed me to the throne. He must be exposed to these experiences. Besides, we will not be leaving the country."

Livia turned away from Sandovar. "I know," she replied sullenly, "but he is only six. He is too small. He may get stepped on by a horse...or worse."

"Livia, Devio will watch over him," said Sandovar. "He is our most trusted man-servant."

"And Devio is a skilled rider," Rodrigo said. "He will keep the prince out of danger." A scene from his childhood flashed in his mind - he saw the Iduin cavalry charging at him.

Masuf gave Livia a smile. "Javior and I will be there too. Extra eyes to watch over the young man."

Their attempts to comfort her were futile, and Livia began to cry. The love of a mother for her child is not easily assuaged. Her boy would leave Golandar in the morning with his father and the army, against tens of thousands of foes.

After a dessert of custard and fruit, servants cleared the table and placed clean goblets in front of the diners. They then brought out bottles of Vorencian port and charged the crystal for toasting. A servant stood behind Khalia, holding a full bottle, concentrating on the diners' glasses. Rodrigo slid back his chair and picked up his wine glass. The others rose and raised their glasses as well.

"The first toast is to General Todu Mazrio. May Ghyo's Light guide you and grant you success," Rodrigo said.

Family and guests cheered the toast, touched their goblets, and drank.

"The second toast is to Sandovar, my eldest son and heir to the throne. May he gain wisdom during the upcoming campaign." Sandovar huffed at Rodrigo's toast.

Again, the crystal chimed and they drank. The servant circled the table, recharging the glasses.

"The next toast is to Masuf. May his prowess in combat bring him glory and keep him safe."

Masuf grinned at his father and bowed, and the diners drank to the toast.

"My final toast is to Javior. May his youth be a strength and not a hindrance to him." Javior straightened and thrust his chin forward.

The toasting then passed to Sandovar. "I thank you, Father, for the chance to lead troops in battle."

Then Masuf toasted. "May we return to the Alcazar in safety." He touched his glass to Sandovar's, Javior's, and Todu's.

"To the valor of the Knights of Olantaro," Javior said.

"Hoorah!" Sandovar cheered, drowning out the others.

Lastly, Todu raised his glass. "To the good fortune of the Royal Army." To which Sandovar grunted and shook his head.

After the toasting, Beltram stepped into the room and said, "His Majesty wishes to speak privately with Her Holiness, the High Priestess Serophia." He tapped his silver staff on the floor and servants entered and cleared away the goblets, but they left four glasses of wine on the table. When the servants left, everyone bowed to Rodrigo, and then to Khalia, before filing out of the room. Khalia departed last, and

Beltram shut the doors and took a seat beside Rodrigo. Serophia remained, too. Rodrigo gestured to the seat on his left, and she sat down.

Serophia began the conversation. "I suppose you are in need of the Church's aid for your expedition. Which do you require, money, priests? Or both?"

Her question insulted Rodrigo, though he kept calm on the outside. Rodrigo despised her. Her arrogance had always been an obstacle when he dealt with her. She always acted as though he was some tenant who had fallen behind on the rent. *Oh, how I wish an Azari held your position.* At one time, that had been a possibility, but events had to follow a different course. *Supporting your Ascension was a mistake.* And there was always a question of where her true loyalty lay - to the Church, or to Fringia. "I hope you realize the situation is grave and members of your own clergy are at risk, too," Rodrigo said. "The Semotecs do not respect the priests of other nations, or faiths."

"I am fully aware of the consequences in the event you fail," Serophia told him. "Meetings such as this occur each time a monarch wants to go to war. They wish to spend as little of their own money as possible, so they come to Ghyo's Church, seeking funds."

Rodrigo took a deep breath, calming himself. He glanced at Beltram, whose eyes, too, betrayed his dislike of the High Priestess. "Holiness, you will address me by my proper title. I have called you here because the army needs priests to ease the suffering of the wounded and to perform religious services for the troops. I ask for no money." Serophia blinked several times. *She's surprised. Good.*

"You shall be given two priests who are skilled at healing," she said. "Now, I need to address the Church's wish to fund your expedition, King Rodrigo. The Tower wishes to know how far you are willing to press your campaign."

Rodrigo sat up straighter, his mind suddenly raced along. *What does she know? Has there been a leak? Only Beltram, the scribe, Todu, and I know the contents of the message to Idu. Did one of the others talk? Not likely. Maybe the scribe talked, but not the others. Maybe Tarik had been waylaid along the road? That's possible. I have to find a way of discovering what the Church knows.* He carefully worded his response. "Our plans are to defend our country by preventing further raids. This is a border issue, nothing more. Things like this are rather common. Why is the Holy Tower so interested in this fighting? How far do they wish us to press this?"

"Are you sure you are only planning to defend your borders?" Serophia asked. "You would not be trying to take advantage of the situation in Idu, would you? History speaks loudly."

Rodrigo kept a straight face, but his thoughts were whirling. *Despite centuries of decline, the Church's insight into the affairs of nations is still amazing. How could they have squandered such influence and power?* "Holiness, my land is overrun. The enemy still advances. This is hardly a time to begin expanding our borders."

"We always take interest in those who fight against heretics," Serophia went on, seeming to ignore what he had just said. "The Church *will* back a holy cause. Is Your Majesty's a holy cause?"

Rodrigo now understood the meaning behind Serophia's words. The Church never revealed their true intentions, until they received guarantees from all the parties involved. *The Holy Tower wants my army to pursue the Semotecs through Idu and into their homeland.* Soriazar's war had given the Church a solid pretext to punish the Semotecs for their sins and to take up the sword. And Ghyo's Church never tolerated the existence of the blasphemous Semotec cult, with its offerings of human blood to Ghyo, the Creator. *But the Church hates Idu as much as it hates the heathens...they wish to injure two enemies with one stroke.* If he campaigned through Idu as far south as the jungles of Semotec, Rodrigo knew the Church would throw a lot of money at him. *But never mind the fact that the Iduin won't enjoy Azari boots trampling their soil, nor sit idly by as we do so. In the eyes of the Church, a strong Soriazar's a counter-balance against a powerful Idu. Even after two centuries, the wounds of the Great Schism remain raw. The Holy Tower wants revenge.*

Rodrigo sat back in his chair and stroked his goatee. "The Semotecs cannot ravage our land with impunity. We *will* strike them back. However, a campaign across land into Semotec is not practicable. The distance to the Semotec border is considerable, and an invasion would require our troops to march through Iduin territory. Idu will not allow that without resisting. Also, there are tens of thousands of undefeated Semotec warriors inside Spandel March." Rodrigo sipped from his wine glass, wetting his throat. Then an idea flashed in his mind. *Always find the good in every situation.* The Church's warlike attitude was an unexpected surprise. "Naval action would be an effective course for the Church to support. Our ships will raid the coasts of Semotec. Great damage can be done to their homelands that way. In time, we could invade Semotec from the sea and cause great damage to their lands. Would the Holy Tower be interested in supporting that course of action?"

Serophia cocked her head and smiled a bit. "I shall inform the Holy Tower of Your Majesty's suggestion. I cannot speak on their support for naval action. At this time, it would be speculation."

Rodrigo rose from his chair, as did Serophia, silently acknowledging that the meeting had concluded. Serophia bowed slightly, gathered her dress, and turned to leave. Beltram bowed to her and opened the door.

After she passed, Beltram straightened and asked Rodrigo, "Sire, shall I summon them?"

"Please do."

Faquezia and Borto entered. Rodrigo gestured for them to sit. Borto adjusted his parti-colored tunic and took the seat to Rodrigo's right. Faquezia sat on Rodrigo's left.

Borto did not wait for Rodrigo to speak. "Your Majesty, what service may I perform for you? I am yours to command."

Faquezia rolled her eyes. Duke Borto's mannerisms in the presence of Rodrigo Mendio were infamous. She reached for a glass of wine, and then she stopped. "If His Majesty permits me to drink from my cup?"

"You may," Rodrigo responded. *Always impetuous aren't you?*

Faquezia took a sip and gazed at the closed doors as she said, "King Rodrigo, it surprises me that I was summoned to this audience."

"I am pleased you were available to answer my invitation," said Rodrigo, knowing it was a grave insult to turn down a Royal Invite. "I realize I did not give you much notice beforehand." He paused. "You were present during my audience with the merchants this afternoon. Will your dissatisfaction with my decree about the prices preclude you from conducting business with the Crown?"

"That depends on the *business* arrangement Your Majesty desires," Faquezia answered. Her tone was icy. "Borto, I was not surprised you were not there this afternoon. I am sure your business does not suffer from the decree."

A smug grin came to Borto's lips. Being the Duke of Golandar and being wedded to Caermela Mendio were his life's two greatest achievements. His position brought him power and great wealth.

"Mistress Faquezia," said Rodrigo. "We need to purchase grain for the army. Your family's granaries in the Juahana Valley are perfectly situated to suit our needs. The Royal Army will need to purchase large amounts of grain."

Faquezia's face reddened. Above the table, she clenched her hands. Rodrigo noticed the change in her mood. Borto said nothing and quietly awaited Faquezia's famous temper.

Her words burst out rapidly. "Your Majesty insults me and my family with your request," she said, gesturing wildly. "You issued your decree, and now you come to take advantage of the low prices. How far will the tentacles of your influence extend?" She bit her lip and then buried her face in her hands. "Already, I am calculating the lost profits."

Rodrigo glanced at Borto and returned his attention to Faquezia. "I figured you would react as such. Sometimes, I believe your reactions are staged. Remember, I am King in this land, and I will take steps to ensure the Monarchy will not be eroded." He sipped his wine and continued in a softer tone. "My sources tell me your granaries are fat from last season's harvest, and this year's harvest will be equally fruitful." Faquezia's eyes widened upon hearing what Rodrigo knew. *Here's my opportunity.* "I am giving you a chance to sell a lot of grain before a greater surplus arises. You are very gifted at operating your business. Maybe too gifted, considering the bumper crops you grow and the trouble you have in selling it all."

Faquezia nodded at the compliment to her skills, and then she sighed heavily. "I admit you speak the truth. Once again, you have displayed your greatness, King Rodrigo. However, I must consider the risks of dealing with Your Majesty. Your decree is not popular with the merchants. As news of it reaches the far corners of Soriazar, other families will be resentful, too. Some of them will not approve of me dealing with you. It could damage my business relations. What can you offer to make the deal more palatable?"

*The woman still negotiates for terms that are more favorable. That's remarkable, considering her financial situation.* Rodrigo respected and feared that trait. He thought that if he offered no other condition other than relieving her of excess grain, he could still form a contract with her. But with the merchant class angry with him, Rodrigo offered Faquezia a generous concession. *I may need the Letios later on.* "Your family will be exempt from the next levy of the Military Tax. That should help you recover some lost revenues."

Faquezia's jaw dropped. The Military Tax was the method used to pay for the Royal Army. The Letios, like most merchant families, avoided providing people for the militias by paying the tax. Azaris who did not pay the tax had to serve in the militias and maintain their own weapons and armor. But the nobility chose to serve in the militias, reflecting their sense of duty to the country and to the king. And that put them at odds with the merchant class, who opted out of military service.

Faquezia said, "Your Majesty, I find your offer to be acceptable. I will sell you all the grain you require. Shall we discuss the arrangements for transporting the grain? There will be additional charges to cover that expense."

"That will not be necessary," Borto interrupted. "I will be shipping the grain." Faquezia glared at Borto, and he smiled politely in return.

"Yes," said Rodrigo. "Borto has two barges in Spandel. They will travel up the Juahana, collect the grain, and deliver it to General Mazrio. Beltram will arrange to have a contract drawn up - tonight.

You are doing a great service to Soriazar, Senyora Letio. Please accompany Beltram." Faquezia rose and curtsied. Beltram opened the doors and stretched out his arm for her to follow. They departed, and he shut the door behind them.

Rodrigo turned to Borto. "I must know if the merchants will cause problems. If you hear anything - rumors, whatever - keep me informed. I need a secure country behind me while I prosecute this war."

Borto placed his right hand beside the ducal medallion on his chest and bowed to Rodrigo. "Of course, sire."

*There's sincerity in your voice.* Rodrigo heard it. However, like the hundreds of people he had dealt with during his long reign, Borto's loyalty came at a price. But the money, gifts, titles, and favors he had heaped onto Borto Camidor were the greatest bargain Rodrigo had ever struck. And the arranged marriage to Caermela bound it all together.

# Chapter 7

## A Bright, Dark Omen
### 7 Janoban, 229 A.G.S.

ayne and Alana descended from the narrows of the Borvik Pass into a heavily wooded glen. They came to the spot where the road continued south, but branched off to the west. The western road turned into a trail, scarcely wide enough for a single cart. Towering conifers pressed against its sides, blocking out much of the sunlight and bathing the forest in an eerie, greenish glow. The woods were silent, aside from the occasional chirping of birds and the chattering of small mammals. It was a serene place where one could find solitude - if that was what one wished for.

They rode a way down the western path and found a suitable place to camp in a small open area off the road, obscured by a large fir tree. They had ridden since daybreak, and they needed rest. Fayne and Alana first unsaddled the horses and fed them. Then Fayne lit a small fire to cook their supper, while Alana spread out two blankets on the ground.

"We'll arrive in the area of Drenga sometime late tomorrow," Fayne said quietly, as he stoked the fire. "That'll give us time to find a hideout and then maybe an hour or so to do some scouting. I'll cook enough meat for tonight and tomorrow. We'll make no fire tomorrow night."

Alana threw aside a fallen branch and smoothed out a blanket. Her eyes darted about the forest. "No fire tomorrow," she repeated. "Fayne, I don't think it was wise of Orius to have sent me. One of the others would've been a better choice."

"Keep your voice down," Fayne said. "This is like hunting deer. From now until we reach Drenga, we need to speak quietly." He reached out and touched her on the shoulder. "Don't let your fears get the best of you. You and I were raised in the woods, and we're the best trackers Orius has. Trust your senses and instincts. Besides, the Oruks don't know we're coming. That's an advantage for us."

Fayne unpacked some of the meat he had wrapped that morning and spitted it on a stick. Alana retrieved the water skins from the saddles. Fayne cut a loaf of bread; all the while, he eyed their surroundings. They finished their meal as dusk gave way to pitch-blackness. Fayne covered the fire's embers with dirt. They slept in shifts and relieved each other every two turns of the small hourglass Fayne had brought with him. Only the sounds of owls, crickets, and small animals broke the night's silence. Tension made the night pass by slowly.

Gradually, daylight filtered through the forest canopy. Alana awoke her brother, and they packed their equipment and breakfasted on dry bread and water. Fayne checked the crossbow strapped to the back of his saddle. Alana plucked the string of her bow, testing its tension, and slung it over the leather quiver of arrows hanging on her back.

Fayne wore a loose fitting green tunic, with buckskin breeches and boots. A brown leather girdle supported his short sword and long dagger. A green bandana, with holes cut into it for his eyes, covered the top of his head and his cropped blond hair. He had smeared a greasy green pigment over his exposed cheeks, ears, and neck. Alana wore the same outfit, but her other weapon was a short sword. She had covered her exposed skin with the pigment as well.

The morning air was cool and scented by the pines, moldering leaves, and damp mosses. Fayne and Alana walked their horses to the road and mounted them. A thin ray of sunlight suddenly shone through a gap in the forest canopy and illuminated Alana. She felt its warmth upon her face and closed her eyes.

"It's going to be a lovely day," she said.

Fayne saw how the sunlight touched his sister. "Yes, I think it will be a lovely day. The sunlight upon you must be an omen. A good one, I'm sure." He was in front of her, and he reined his horse around, until their mounts faced in opposite directions. "Keep a sharp watch today. Oruks are good at fighting in cover. If we run into trouble, we need to stick together."

Alana frowned and nodded. "One more thing to remember," she murmured.

"It's all right to be afraid," said Fayne. "I am. Fear sharpens your wits. Just keep it under control." He cocked his head over his shoulder and turned his horse westward. Alana followed about a horse's length behind.

After a couple hours, they reached the edge of the woods, where the land opened up. Fayne reined his horse and spent several minutes observing the valley, which was not more than half a mile across. Boulders and short evergreens dotted the valley floor. The ground gradually rose to the left to the base of a rocky mountain. To the right, it sloped away to meet the base of the opposite mountain, covered with a forest of pines. Seven miles to the west, at end of the valley, the trail wrapped around the northern base of another mountain, covered with more rocks than trees.

"What is it?" Alana asked.

Fayne pointed to the right. "We need to ride along the trees. We should assume unwanted eyes watch the road. That far mountain is a good spot to observe the entire valley."

"We can keep to the shadows over there," she added.

"It will take us longer a little longer to arrive in Drenga, but it'll do us no good if the Oruks are waiting to welcome us."

"I wish we knew the land around here," Alana fretted.

Fayne clicked his tongue and got his black horse moving. They soon reached the tree line and there discovered a gully with a shallow brook meandering through it. The gully's bottom provided concealment. They would follow its course upstream for as long as possible.

A half hour passed. Fayne and Alana were a third of the way across the valley. They came to a place where the gully bent to the right. Fayne rounded the bend, and a log hut came into view, squatting upon the left bank. Tightly woven evergreen branches made up the hut's roof, and the walls were in good repair. A small stone animal pen sat to the hut's left. Fayne halted his black mare and waited for his sister. Alana reined her chestnut next to him.

"It's awfully quiet," she whispered.

"Draw your bow and cover me," Fayne said.

He spurred his horse and slowly approached the dwelling. There were no windows built into the hut's walls, and Fayne could not see the door from the gully. He turned the horse and climbed the bank; Alana followed. As he reached the top, he got a better view of the ground around the animal pen. The animal pen's wooden gate had been torn apart, and dozens of wide, stubby footprints marred the pen's damp soil, mixed in with cattle prints. The footprints formed into a trail leading west, until they disappeared into the gully. The hut's door was on the south side, and it hung awkwardly from its bottom hinge. Fayne dismounted and wrapped the reins around a part of the fence that had not been torn down. His slid his sword and dagger from their scabbards.

He looked back at Alana and spoke softly, "I'm going to look around inside."

Alana maneuvered her mare so she could loose an arrow in the doorway's direction. Her heart pounded and her breathing grew heavy. She mumbled a prayer for the strength to loose – to put down a target.

Fayne approached the door, hunching his shoulders. He stood with his back against the wall and peeked around the frame. He could not see far into the heavily shadowed interior, but a sickly sweet odor reached his nostrils. Butchered animals gave off that type of smell. Fayne looked at the broken door and saw congealed blood splattered on it. He paused a while longer, listening, then he gestured to Alana with his dagger hand.

In an instant, he slipped inside the hut. The slaughterhouse smell was twice as strong inside. Murky shadows filled the corners and rafters. Crude wooden furniture was strewn about, broken and up-ended. Dust motes floated in the light shining through the doorway. There was no sound or movement.

Across the room, where the light ended and the darkness began, was a small table tipped over at an angle with two legs broken off. A sandal, wrapped around a foot, stuck out from behind it. Fayne slowly approached the table, placed his sword on the table's edge, and pushed it aside. He gasped so loud he scared himself. An arrow stuck out of the corpse's chest, and there were several gaping wounds from axe blows on the head and torso.

Fayne stumbled out of the hut. His face was pale, and his eyes wide. He paused for a moment, shook his head, breathed deeply, and exhaled. He wiped his brow with his sleeve.

"What did you see?" Alana exclaimed.

Fayne sheathed his weapons and walked to his horse. "It was...the owner of the farm. I guess." He untied the reins from the fence and mounted the black mare. "He's dead. The house has been torn apart. It's a pity we don't have time to burn him."

"Where is his family? Was he alone?"

"He was the only one inside. There's not much left in there. No clothes or food. Just broken things."

"Cattle thieves don't murder the owners of the herds they steal. It must've been the Oruks who did this," said Alana. "If they've come this far, what's become of the people of Drenga?"

"We may not have to ride that far to find out. Let's follow the tracks." Fayne pointed to the gully.

The trail was a day old, and the tracks followed the streambed. Fayne and Alana followed the trail for an hour and a half. The tracks continued westward.

Ahead of them was another bend in the gully, which was actually the tip of a large spur, rising from the stream and running northward to the mountain's peak. Like the rest of the mountain slope, pine trees and brush covered the spur. The stream flowed around it to the right. A light breeze blew in from the west, carrying the sounds of laughter and shouting.

Fayne and Alana halted the horses. Alana glanced up the slope. "That looks like a good place to observe the land on the other side."

Slowly, they picked their way through the undergrowth. They left their horses a short distance below the spur's crest, and crept the remaining few yards to the top, where they sought cover amidst the bushes. An encampment was visible through the trees, not more than fifty yards from where they knelt. A hundred Oruks had gathered in a circle, sitting in packs of fives and tens, trading jokes, insults, and wineskins. There was great merriment in their voices and on their faces. In the gathering's center, two Oruks butchered a cow. Five other cattle stood nearby, quietly observing the fate of their companion.

The Oruks were the cousins of humans. The average one was a head shorter than a human, but wider in the shoulders and longer in the arms, which hung to a little below their knees. They possessed bonier brow lines and larger jawbones, with large, square teeth. Interbreeding with humans was impossible.

The Oruks inhabited the area of northwestern Iningia known as Sytor. Their race's proper name was Sytan, and they referred to themselves as Syts. But in the parts of Iningia populated by humans, they gave the Sytish people the unflattering name Oruk, which mocked the Syts' rough sounding language.

Alana's eyes widened upon seeing the large host. The Oruks' guttural language made her queasy. She had not expected to see so many. She felt faint.

Fayne quietly counted them. "There are many Cheltan weapons down there."

"No! Not again!" A woman's scream broke through the din of laughter and shouting. Alana and Fayne flinched at the sound.

A human female jumped up from behind one of the large rocks sticking out of the ground. Her eyes were wild, her face contorted. Her torn dress exposed her breasts. She stumbled and fell to her knees. An Oruk called Grundish appeared from behind the rock, wiping blood from the scratches on his cheek. He glared at the woman, baring his thick, square teeth. Other Oruks gathered around, pointing fingers and laughing. Grundish approached the woman, his arms clutched for her.

"No!" she screamed in Cheltish.

A larger Oruk suddenly stepped out from the growing audience. He wore a tarnished metal breastplate, while the others wore skins and flaxen shirts. Grundish stopped and stared in surprise at the larger Oruk.

"Grundish, I am leader," the larger Oruk croaked. "She is mine."

"Shizak, you are leader only because the Outsider says so," rasped Grundish. "You did not earn your place."

Shizak lunged forward and shoved Grundish to the ground. In a flash, he drew his sword and jabbed the point of it into the soft flesh of Grundish's throat.

"I should kill you now," Shizak said, "but I need your mangy carcass." He stared at the others gathered about. "There is a new way. It must be followed, or the Outsider will make our families and us pay for our disobedience – with our *lives*."

Fayne and Alana watched the scene from their hidden perch. Their jaws slackened when the woman appeared.

Fayne shut his eyes and bowed his head. "They're savages," he whispered. "They kidnap, plunder, rape, and murder Chelts. I want to ride down there and kill them all. But Ghyo forgive us, there's nothing we can do for that woman."

Alana knelt beside him in silence. Her eyes were fixed upon the surreal scene unfolding a short distance away. Tears glistened in her eyes.

Shizak looked back down at Grundish and pushed the sword into his neck until blood began to trickle. Grundish let out a sharp cry. "This is the only time I will be merciful with you," Shizak said, sneering. "Next time, I will kill you." He withdrew the sword and slid it into its scabbard.

Grundish gasped with relief and rubbed the cut on his neck. He crawled away and hid behind a rock. Shizak turned toward the woman, who cowered on the ground. She clutched her stomach and gagged. She could not understand a word of what was spoken, but her eyes met Shizak's.

"My men cannot wait their turns," Shizak said in Sytish. "I have not finished with you. I will have you again." He grabbed a handful of the woman's hair and dragged her to a large rock with a flat surface.

"Don't let my children see this," she pleaded in Cheltish.

Shizak smiled. He plopped her down hard onto her back and ripped off her dress. The woman kicked and clawed at him. A couple of Oruks moved in and grabbed her arms, sneering and laughing as they did so. Shizak undid the straps of his breastplate, removed it, and leaned it against the rock. He then untied his flaxen brown breeches and ungraciously let them fall to his ankles. He took hold of the woman's legs, roughly forced them open, and entered her.

An unearthly howl burst from the woman. Alana covered her mouth and nearly retched. She tried to force herself to look away, but she could not. Her tears suddenly dried up. Her right arm bent up behind her ear. Her fingers wrapped around an arrow's fletching. Without thinking, she notched it and drew the bowstring. Fayne whipped his head around.

"Alana, no!"

The missile streaked through the air and slammed into Shizak's spine. He arched his back and unleashed a hideous scream. He looked down at his chest, at the tip of the arrow that had broken through his skin. Blood dripped onto the woman's stomach. A new wave of screaming overcame her. Shizak slumped heavily on top of her and died. The Oruks holding the woman's arms released her and jumped back. The second arrow was already in the air. It struck the Oruk on the right and burrowed into his heart. His dead body flopped onto the ground. The Oruks began shouting and running about.

"To arms!"

"Find them!"

"Arm yourselves!"

Alana moved like an automaton. She notched another arrow.

Fayne grabbed her arm. "Alana! We have to leave."

She shrugged off her brother's grasp, drew the bowstring to her chin, and loosed the arrow. Another Oruk fell.

"They're coming for us!"

Alana blinked and looked at Fayne. Her face was expressionless, but her eyes burned with hatred. Blandly she said, "I guess we can do no more today."

They ran to their horses and leaped into the saddles. Fayne and Alana's eyes were wild with excitement. In their haste to escape, they violently tugged the reins, causing the horses to bolt recklessly downhill. The horses weaved their way through the trees. They burst out of the foliage and galloped across the stream, kicking up spouts of water. The Oruks had already rounded the bend and caught sight of their prey. Fayne and Alana heard them splashing through the water and screaming in Sytish. Fayne glanced back and saw at least thirty Oruks running after them. Two of them knelt and loosed arrows, but they fell wide of their mark. They charged the horses up and out of the gully. The Oruks stopped their pursuit as they disappeared over the gully's lip.

After they had ridden for a mile, Fayne and Alana halted their horses. Sweat darkened the bandanas wrapped around their heads. They looked behind them for some time, until they were satisfied that the Oruks had given up the chase.

"We need...to meet with Orius as quickly as possible," Fayne panted. "The Oruks have advanced...a long way. Over a day's march east from Drenga...I believe."

Alana's voice shook. "Fayne, did you hear...that woman speak of her children?"

Fayne nodded slowly. "Yes, I did. I guess...we have to get used to dealing with things like that."

"I don't think I'll ever get used to such things. What they did to that woman...was not right."

Fayne moved his horse closer to Alana's and wrapped an arm around her shoulders. "You did well today," he said. "I hurt inside, too. But we need to move on now."

Alana wiped her runny nose and her eyes on her sleeve. "Some warrior I am."

Fayne smiled. "Nonsense. I'll ride with you again."

They spurred their horses into a full gallop and only slowed their pace when they reached the edge of the woods, where they had camped the night before. They rode through the woods and continued on until afternoon. They camped that evening in the Borvik Pass in a copse of trees along the trail. From there, they could watch the valley where the road disappeared into the forest, where it met the road leading west to Drenga. There they waited for the Oruks to come pouring out of the trees.

# Chapter 8

Setbacks and Obstacles
8 Janoban, 229 A.G.S.

arik rose and gazed into the reddish dawn. Dark clouds glided on the wind toward the east, the sun painting their underbellies purple. To the west, he saw lightning flashes moving in his direction. Nearby, a slender waterfall cascaded from a precipitous cliff, forming the headwaters of the Mynesia River, which served as the border between the lands of Imbria and Idu, sealing one off from the other, so much so that their cultures developed differently.

Tarik bundled up his blanket, packed his belongings in his saddlebags, and retrieved an oilcloth cape. He tied it around his shoulders and pulled the cowl over his head. The wind picked up as the first raindrops fell. He had camped at the highest point of the pass. The morning ride would thankfully be downhill, but the rain intensified, and the dirt road turned into a viscous river of mud.

He guided the horse off the road to walk on the grass alongside it and resigned himself to a day of slow plodding. He hoped the weather would soon clear, but the torrent continued. After half an hour, rainwater seeped through his cape and soaked him to his skin. The howling wind chilled Tarik beneath his drenched clothing. It being summer, he was not used to the cold. He shivered.

Suddenly, lightning struck a nearby cork oak, splintering it with a deafening crack. The flash blinded Tarik and his horse reared. He lost his grip on the reins. His body floated in the air...

Tarik's eyes popped open. The world was upside down. His knees were before his face. He rolled onto his right side and a shocking pain bolted through his body. He writhed in the mud. He cried out in horror and pain, when he discovered what had happened. His right arm hung awkwardly from the shoulder socket. Tarik cradled his useless arm and sat up. Rainwater ran down his uncovered head, washing the mud from his forehead into his eyes.

He placed his injured arm in his lap and ran the sleeve of his other arm across his eyes. He blinked until his vision cleared. His horse stood nearby, grazing on wet grass. He turned his head left and squinted through the downpour. There he saw the smoking remains of the mangled tree. The acrid smell of burnt ozone permeated the air. The lightning had ripped the trunk into four jagged pieces, and around it laid hundreds of large pale splinters, contrasting with the green grass.

Slowly, Tarik rose to his knees. He then stood. The world spun. He staggered on wobbly legs to his horse, firmly planting one foot before taking another step. His cowl hung against his back and rapidly filled with water. The weight of it dug into his shoulders. He pulled the cape's drawstring and let it slide off his shoulders. He focused on the horse, which swayed back and forth before him. His head bobbed with each step. *Stay on your feet. Please, stay on your feet.*

"S-steady," Tarik said to his horse, his voice quavering.

The horse snorted and stamped with each thunderclap, but Tarik got a grip on the saddle's pommel. He tucked the fingers of his injured arm down the front of his breeches. With his left hand, he clumsily undid the straps of one of the saddlebags. It took him five tries to get the bag open. He retrieved a bundle of wooden rods bound together by leather straps. *I never thought I'd be using these on myself.* For as long as he could remember, he had had good luck on the road, excepting this journey.

A shock of pain caused him to lose his balance, and he dropped the bundle of rods. He grabbed the pommel again. His shoulder throbbed with each heartbeat, and he felt nauseous. The bundle of rods lay at his feet. He grasped the saddle girth with his good hand and slowly lowered himself to the ground. It took several minutes for him to loosen one of the straps around the rods. He was careful not to let the strap's tip slide out of the buckle as he re-fastened it. He then slid the strap around the back of his neck, pulled his arm from his breeches, and slung it.

Tarik used the girth to help himself to his feet. He then carefully knelt, picked up the bundled rods, and put them back into the saddlebag. He removed the stopper from the skin containing wine and hefted it to his lips. His head spun more as the wine's intoxication made its way there. He clumsily put back the wineskin and slowly climbed into the saddle, as the rain slackened.

"Figures," he grumbled.

Tarik clicked his tongue and the horse moved down the road. He tottered back and forth in the saddle, moving with the horse's rhythm. His shoulder continued to throb, though the pain was slightly duller. He wanted more wine, but he feared falling from the horse in a drunken stupor. He had no idea how long he had lain in the mud, but he had only traveled a short distance from his campsite. He figured he was at least ten hours from the border at the pace the horse was moving.

The storm passed, but the clouds remained. The horse plodded along the muddy road for hours, with Tarik slumped over in the saddle. When the pain became unbearable, he drank wine until it lessened. It felt like a week had passed since the horse threw him. *I want to return home,* he told himself repeatedly, but too much depended on him delivering the message. He had to succeed. *I must press on.*

A vision of Aida came to him through his wine-clouded thoughts. He dreamt he was back at the Wandering Troubadour. He listened to her voice and watched the way she sauntered about the inn...

A wolf appeared from behind a bush and fear stabbed at Tarik's chest. His throat constricted, stifling a scream. To his dismay, his sword arm hung uselessly in the leather sling...

He awoke suddenly and grabbed hold of the pommel as he began to topple out of the saddle. His pounding heart cleared some of the fogginess from his head. *It was only a dream.* He looked at the sky to find the sun, but it was still overcast. He had no idea how long he had been traveling; his shoulder throbbed intensely. His eyes were bloodshot and his face was pale. Tarik lifted his head and noticed that the pass had widened. It sloped down toward rolling, tree-covered hills. *Idu!*

"We're getting closer," he mumbled to the horse as it followed the road. But he did not have the strength to ride harder.

He rode for another hour before catching sight of a town, surrounded by a stout wooden stockade with stone watchtowers built into it. The town straddled the road leading down from the pass. The land around it had been cleared of trees for nearly a mile in each direction. The black gelding followed the road and walked up to the gate. Tarik swayed in the saddle; his head lolled. Two soldiers in mail shirts approached, and one of them placed a hand on Tarik's reins.

"Who are you, and what business have you in Novium?" the guard asked in Iduin.

Tarik slowly opened his eyes, but the guard's face was blurry. Tarik summoned the strength to whisper a reply in Tradespeak. "I do not...speak your tongue."

The guard cocked his head and looked at Tarik's signet ring with the eagle crest of Soriazar upon it. "We should call for the Watch Commander," he said to the other soldier. "I think this may be important." The other soldier jogged through the gate.

The Iduin set his rectangular shield on the ground, gestured to Tarik, and spoke again in Iduin, "Put your arm around my neck, and I'll help you down."

Tarik did not understand, but he acquiesced. The soldier reached up, wrapped his arm around Tarik's waist, and gently pulled him from the saddle. The man grunted as Tarik's weight fell onto his shoulder.

The other soldier returned with the Watch Commander, who wore a shining cuirass of metal segments banded together with rivets and leather straps. The officer spoke to Tarik in Tradespeak. "My soldier tells me your presence here is important. Who are you?"

Tarik leaned against the soldier. "I am...a Royal Messenger in the service of..." He grit his teeth as a wave of pain interrupted him. "...King Mendio of Soriazar."

The Watch Commander placed his hand to his breast in salute. "How did you injure yourself?" he asked with a touch of concern.

The pain made it difficult for Tarik to concentrate. It also did not help that he had not spoken Tradespeak in months. He silently mouthed the words he wanted to use. "Lightning startled my horse. It threw me...from the saddle."

The officer pursed his lips. "Soldier Regius, take him to the guard-house and put him on the bed." He turned to the other one. "Soldier Philatus, tie up this man's horse at the guardhouse and see to it that his belongings are secure."

The soldiers saluted the officer as he spun around and marched through the gate. The soldier called Regius helped Tarik through the gate, and Philatus followed with his horse. They took him to a small wooden shack near the main gate, which contained a wooden bunk bed, a tiny table with two stools, and a small stone hearth. Regius sat Tarik on the straw-stuffed mattress of the lower bunk. Regius frowned and placed a hand to his chin. He gestured for Tarik to wait and then waved his hands about Tarik's injured shoulder.

"Thank you," Tarik mumbled in Azari, as the soldier left. *They're bringing me a priest.*

The Watch Commander appeared in the doorway, casting a shadow across Tarik. "Are you well enough to answer some questions?"

Tarik looked at the man's feet, then he shifted his gaze to the darkened face. "What do you need...to know?"

"What is your assignment?"

Tarik again mouthed what he was going to say before he spoke. "I am delivering a message...from my king to your senate. I request...safe passage to the city of Roda. I am instructed to deliver this message...in person."

The officer's eyes widened. "I see. I will report this to the commander of the garrison." And he disappeared from sight.

A short while later Tarik heard voices. When they stopped talking, a priest entered the room, wearing his white vestments. The gray-haired and balding priest asked in Tradespeak, "Where do come from?"

Tarik frowned and cocked his head. "I am Azari," he answered in Tradespeak.

The priest smacked his forehead, and he began speaking Azari. "Ah! I, too, am Azari. I am Father Grigorio. Just now I noticed the emblem on your breast."

"Are you skilled in the ways of healing?" asked Tarik. "I fell from my horse."

"Do not worry, my son." Grigorio reached for a stool and pulled it over. He sat and gently probed Tarik's shoulder. "I will need to remove your tunic. I must have flesh to flesh contact when I lay hands upon you."

Father Grigorio slowly pulled Tarik's arm from the improvised sling, slightly moving the injured arm. Tarik's face went pale and he gasped.

Grigorio smiled. "Depending on the injury, sometimes the healing is the more painful part of the process."

He unbuttoned Tarik's tunic. He helped him slide his good arm from the sleeve, and he carefully pulled the injured limb out of the other sleeve. Again, Tarik's eyes bulged from the pain of moving his arm.

"I think that will be enough," Grigorio said. "I will not remove your undershirt."

Grigorio bowed his head and pressed his hands together before his chest. Keeping the palms pressed together, he raised his arms skyward and mouthed a silent prayer. He separated his arms and lowered them until they were parallel to the floor, palms facing up. Tarik watched as the priest's palms began to glow. Grigorio leaned forward, slid his left hand under Tarik's armpit, and placed his other hand on the front of Tarik's shoulder.

A warm sensation transferred from Grigorio's palms, through Tarik's skin, and deep into his shoulder's muscles and ligaments, dulling the pain. Tarik watched his shoulder. He saw the bones moving beneath the skin, but Father Grigorio's hands did not move.

Tarik's body reacted involuntarily to the popping sound of his shoulder sliding back into socket. A cold sweat broke out across his body, and his chest and shoulder muscles twitched spastically. He became dizzy and his head lolled. He then fainted from the masked pain.

"The Gift fools the mind, but the body reacts naturally to the injury," Grigorio said as he laid Tarik back on the bed. "Sleep now."

It was dark inside the shack. The sun had disappeared behind the stockade and shadows enveloped Novium. Tarik lay on the bed. In the hearth, embers glowed beneath a blackened pot, suspended on an iron hook. The scent of stew wafted from that direction. Tarik's stomach growled, and he sat up on the bunk. He swung his feet over the side and glanced down at the cloth sling cradling his arm. He probed his shoulder, which was swollen and tender to the touch, but his pain was dulled and his mind was clear.

As Tarik stood, he felt aches in places that had not been there earlier. *I must've fallen hard.* Stiffly, he shuffled to the hearth and grabbed one of the wooden bowls and spoons, which rested on the crude table. He set the bowl on the mantle, removed the lid of the cooking pot, and used his left hand to clumsily scoop some stew into the bowl. He recognized barley in the stew, but not the other root-like ingredient, and he avoided the chicken's foot. After he replaced the lid, he sniffed the contents. Though he was famished, his nose wrinkled at the stew's scent. *I almost forgot why I'm not a soldier.* Tarik sat by the table. He had to eat slowly, because of the awkwardness of eating with his opposite hand. More stew plopped back into the bowl than he put into his mouth.

When he had finished, he left the bowl on the table and walked over to the bunk bed. He retrieved his tunic and managed, after a couple of tries, to wrap it around his shoulders. His sword and baldric hung from the top of the bedpost. He went to the door. Outside, he saw the black gelding tied to a hitching post in front of the shack. His saddlebags appeared to be unmolested. He dug through his shirt and found the key to the saddlebags' locks, hanging from the chain around his neck.

An Iduin soldier stood watch beside the horse and came to attention when Tarik appeared in the doorway. The soldier wore a mail shirt and carried a rectangular shield, which covered him from his chin to his knees. A rounded helmet, with wide cheek guards fastened together beneath his chin, protected his head. The guard looked back over his shoulder and called out to someone Tarik could not see.

Tarik unlocked a saddlebag and retrieved a leather tube, which he tucked inside his shirt. Moments later another soldier appeared, wearing similar panoply, but with a crest of horsehair fastened to the top of his helmet. He said something in Iduin and motioned Tarik to follow.

The soldier led Tarik through the darkened streets of Novium. Only the torch he carried cast any appreciable light. They passed many connected two-story wooden buildings, which housed shops on the ground floor and the private apartments of the owners on the upper floor. Most of the top floor windows were open and Tarik heard people talking, laughing, or arguing. The garlicky scent of their evening meals accompanied the sounds of their voices. Occasionally, children darted in and out of the shadows, playing hide-and-seek.

The soldier led Tarik across Novium's central square to a single-story, windowless brown stucco residence, with a set of stout wooden doors. The soldier rapped twice on the door with the large iron knocker. A servant opened a square peephole.

"I am Proculus, Sergeant of the Watch," the soldier said in Iduin. "I was ordered to deliver this messenger to the Garrison Commander."

The peephole slammed shut and the sound of scraping metal came from beyond the door. The hinges groaned as it slowly swung open. The male servant swept his arm in a wide arc, gesturing toward the interior of the house. Proculus removed his helmet, marched through the door, and crossed a short marble-floored vestibule. Tarik followed.

The vestibule opened into the atrium of the house. Tarik found the interior more pleasing than he would have guessed from the plain-looking exterior. The square atrium had a trio of columns on three sides of it, with two columns standing astride the entrance to the vestibule. A bronze sconce hung from each column, lighting the area with a flickering yellow glow. A breeze blew in through the open roof and rustled through the leaves of ferns growing from fat, terra cotta pots in the atrium's corners. A shallow impluvium rested in the center of the marble floor with a sculpture of a nude woman rising from the water on a plinth, holding a jar next to her hip. Water trickled from the jar. Overhead, a cloud passed by, revealing a crescent moon.

The servant closed the door with a bang and slid the locking bar in place. He joined Tarik and Proculus and led them down the gallery to the right of the impluvium. "Wait here," the servant said to Proculus in Iduin. "I will inform the Master you are here."

After a couple minutes, a tall man appeared from the doorway the servant had entered. He wore a thigh-length white tunic with red embroidery around the neck and the ends of the short sleeves. A belt, with a dagger dangling from it, was cinched about his waist. His legs were bare and he wore sandals with laces that extended to the bottoms of his knees. His black hair was cut short. He scowled as he approached Tarik. Proculus snapped to attention and thumped his arm to his breast.

"I am Cuentis Attalus," the man said to Tarik in Tradespeak. "I am in command of this garrison. I am told you bear a message to be delivered directly to the Senate. I order you to hand the message over to me for delivery to them."

Tarik shuffled his feet. Cuentis's tone surprised him. Thoughts raced through his mind about how to address a man who was not used to being told no. His orders came directly from King Mendio. He was not about to willingly give Cuentis, or anyone, an opportunity to read the message.

He cleared the dryness from his throat. His stomach twitched as he said, "I apologize, Commander. But I cannot hand over the sealed message to anyone, except the Presiding Senator of Idu. The penalty for that is severe in my land. It can even mean death." *Knowledge is power. Do you think I'm stupid?*

Cuentis's faced reddened. His dark eyes switched from Tarik to Proculus and back to Tarik. "Listen to me, Messenger. I will forward the correspondence to the Senate, along with the other messages I send each week. Idu is at war. I cannot allow a foreigner to travel alone through my land. You may be a spy."

Tarik shook his head, his insides fluttered. "The message I bear is of great importance. King Rodrigo stated this fact to me, himself. I am instructed to request an armed escort from Novium to Roda."

Cuentis crossed his arms, leaned back slightly, and cocked his head to one side. "And what type of escort am I to provide you?"

Tarik had not thought about that. He shrugged. "Whatever you can spare, though I need to arrive in Roda as soon as practicable."

Cuentis laughed. He did not hide his sarcasm. "Whatever I can spare, you say." His eyes glanced down at Tarik's sling. Then his voice became menacingly softer. "You will travel by chariot. It is faster than horseback. My son Murius is an officer in this garrison. He will accompany you. You will leave in the morning. And that is all I will spare for you." Cuentis turned and walked away, disappearing through the door from which he had appeared.

# Chapter 9

## Tempered Aggressions
### 9-11 Janoban, 229 A.G.S.

The fog swirled around Orius, obstructing his view of the land. Occasionally, the wind stirred it and created openings through which he could see the mountains towering above him. But then the fog grew thicker, and the wind no longer caused it to swirl about. The cold, dank air enveloped Orius's face. He turned in his saddle. Culley had been close behind, but he was no longer visible.

"Culley!" Orius called out. There was no answer.

"Culley, I *know* you can hear me!" Silence.

Orius tightened his grip on the reins. A sinking feeling grew in his chest. The silence unnerved him. The wind had stopped blowing and he felt alone.

"Mother?" he called out.

A woman's voice answered from beyond the fog. "I am here, son."

"Mother, I have lost my way."

"No," the voice said. "Your way is clear. Apprehension clouds your vision."

Orius shook his head and looked into the swirling fog. "Mother, there are many uncertainties. I do not have all of the answers. There will be many questions asked of me."

"My son, you wield the Light of Ghyo. Use your power to bring change. You must fight for your birthright."

Orius's voice was strained. Tears came to his eyes. "But, Mother. How many will rise against me? How many lives must be sacrificed for the sins of my father? The Faith defies the use of violence."

"Others are willing to spill blood to oppose you," the voice said. "You must be willing to do the same. Someone must lead. It is the destiny of common people to follow such leaders." There was a portentous pause. "There are people searching for us across Iningia – people who wish to kill us. Orius, our exile has lasted a lifetime…"

Orius awoke suddenly; sweat drenched his body. He normally awoke refreshed, but he felt drained. He lay on a cot in a log hut in the village of Ragnaar. The warriors from the northern villages had arrived the day before. It was time to lead them south to Drenga.

Orius whispered, "Mother, I will spill not one drop of blood more than is necessary. If there is to be *real* change, I will give peace an opportunity to..."

A knock at the door interrupted him. "Orius, my boy," Culley growled. "It's near dawn. Are you awake?"

Orius yawned and licked his lips. "I am awake. I will be with you shortly."

"The campfires are being lit for breakfast. Are you hungry?"

"Yes, and make sure everyone is fed. Today's march will be long. They will need their strength."

Culley left the door ajar and the morning light entered the dark hut. Orius heard Culley's feet shuffle against the ground as the old Chelt walked away. He sat up and stretched his arms. He looked toward the door as if he could see through it. Outside was an army of Chelts, waiting for their commander to appear. He got out of bed and lit the candle on the table in the center of the room, dressed himself, and sat back down on the cot.

His dream lingered in his thoughts. *I have special abilities, and I'm trained and educated in the ways of using them.* Orius knew he would not have been elected chief if he was not a priest and the Oruks had not invaded Cheltabria. The Chelts' faith and fear of the Oruks turned out to be stronger than their dislike of foreigners. The Northern Tribes had pledged their support for him, so he would lead their warriors into battle. For the time being, religion and necessity had cast aside the Chelts' petty squabbles, and the Oruks had provided the glue that tenuously bound them together. The Chelts needed a strong leader to unite the country, and Orius needed a strong Cheltabria to claim his legacy.

Orius walked outside. Morning dew dampened the air, which was permeated with the scent of burnt wood from the dozen small fires that glowed in a field on the outskirts of Ragnaar. Orius watched his warriors huddle around their fires, sipping tea, and eating cheese and bread. He listened to their laughter and stories. An argument flared up around one fire and two Chelts wrestled with each other. They rolled through the campfire, sending a shower of embers in every direction. The Chelts nearby howled with laughter.

*Save that aggression for the Oruks,* Orius thought. *A few months ago, these warriors represented opposing villages, competing for land, cattle, and game. Now, they band together to fight a common enemy. How long can I keep the peace between them?* He saw Culley, Kathair, Moreena, and Argus standing around a fire.

"Orius!" Kathair called out, holding a tin cup in his hand, motioning him to come over. "I have your breakfast."

Orius took the cup and sipped the hot tea. "Thank you, I needed this."

"We have a fine army gathered here," Moreena Odel said. "I've never seen so many warriors in one place."

Argus glanced over at the wrestling match. "And they aren't even tearing out each other's throats. Well, most of them, anyhow." He laughed at his own joke.

Orius's eyes widened. Culley glanced around at the other campfires.

Argus shrugged. "What did I say?"

Moreena whacked him on the arm, causing hot tea to splash onto his hand. "Keep your voice down. There are warriors about who bare the scars you gave them. Do not give them a reason to take vengeance now."

"I suppose you're right. Forgive me, Orius." Argus frowned, licking the tea off his hand.

"We *all* need to watch what we say," said Orius. "This situation is delicate. Every one of you has an enemy in the vicinity." He sipped his tea. "Some of them have a friend who has died by your hands, and some of them have killed warriors from Torveg." A picture of himself killing Worgoth came to his mind, along with the thought of the animosity he had created in doing that. "We must learn to respect each other. If we cannot set aside our differences, we cannot survive. One of your enemies may save your life some day."

Kathair Vorhenin grunted. "I hope that dog Norlan of Lunevik doesn't save my life."

"Yeah, or that pig Egon of Haagenvaarder," Argus said with spit rolling from his lips.

Moreena rolled her eyes and shook her head. Culley muttered something and Orius sighed and sipped his tea.

Chief Condin of Skorva approached, and Orius's companions grew silent. A white wolf's head covered Condin's head, except for his face. He looked into everyone's eyes before he held out his hand to Orius. "Good morning, Father Candell. Skorva is ready to march."

Orius took Condin's hand and shook it firmly. "Skorva's name will endure in the heroic ballads of Cheltabria. Your time for vengeance is approaching."

Condin bowed his head, and the wolf's eyes stared into those of Orius. "You have returned the Light to our land. How could we not march with you? You have the Gift and we are members of your flock."

"And I could not march without the Wolf Riders of Skorva," Orius said. "Douse your fire and prepare to march."

He turned from Chief Condin and called out to the warriors gathered in the field. "Warriors of the North! Make ready!" He pointed his white-gauntleted hand to the east. "We march when the sun appears over the mountains!"

Loud cheers rose from the warriors as they put out their fires and gathered their belongings. Those with shields grabbed them and banged their axes or swords against them. A cacophony erupted in Ragnaar as a piece of the sun appeared over the eastern peaks and irradiated the opposite mountain's rocky face. The Chelts lined up along the road in two columns. They were a motley collection, dressed in hides, boiled leather, plaid, flaxen clothing, or buckskin. Burlap sacks contained their food and personal items. Two or three wineskins crisscrossed their bodies, hanging from leather straps or ropes. Barely half of the warriors had horses.

Orius, Moreena, Kathair, and Argus rode to the head of the army. Culley Magolin rode the length of the columns to ensure the army was prepared to march.

"They're ready," he said when he joined Orius.

"Good. Wait here."

Orius rode off to the side of the road and stopped at the halfway point down the warriors' columns. The Chelts were making much noise: talking, laughing, singing, and arguing. Orius removed a gauntlet and raised his right hand. An amber light appeared in the palm. It intensified until the faces of the warriors were illumined by its glow. The warriors on foot dropped to one knee, while the ones on horseback bowed their heads. Their voices faded away, and Orius commenced the Celebration of the Light:

> *Blessed be the body of Ghyo, the World.*
> *Blessed be His Light that manifests through the Gift.*
> *Blessed be the Cycle unbroken.*
> *Life perpetual.*

Orius released the light from his palm and spoke. "I see a great host before me! The entire Northern Valley is here to drive out the invaders!" Loud cheers echoed in the valley. "Let us remember this moment and how we put aside our differences! We march *together* in a Cause greater than any one village!" The warriors banged their weapons on their shields and roared again with approval.

Orius put on his gauntlet and returned to the head of the army. "Argus, signal the march."

Argus reached into one of his saddlebags and pulled out a bull's horn. He wrapped his lips around its end and blew a long, deep blast. The warriors moved out down the road, marching in groups, each representing a single village. Behind Orius and his companions from Torveg marched fifty warriors from Ragnaar, twenty from Haagenvaarder, twenty from Lunevik, and ten each from Skorva, Kyarna, Telstrand, and Tydorhagen. One hundred thirty in all, including thirty women, representing the best the Northern Valley had to offer.

By late afternoon, the column arrived at a clearing deep inside the Borvik Pass. Orius called for a halt. To his dismay, the warriors remained split up into their separate villages and set up camp as such.

Orius called for the leading warriors from each village to gather around him. *This will not be popular.* "Chief Condin," he said. "Take five warriors - two from Skorva, two from Kyarna, and one from Telstrand. Scout the pass ahead and find a spot to watch the road for the evening."

"As you wish, Father Orius," said Chief Condin.

Orius pointed to the forested slope of a mountain. "Tulbar of Lunevik, you are to scout the western slope and return before dark. Take a warrior from Telstrand, one from Lunevik, and one from Haagenvaarder with you."

Tulbar scoffed. "I can't rely on Chelts from other villages to guard my back."

"Your chief pledged your support to me," Orius told him. "Do you accept this charge, or do I find another to do this dangerous work?"

Tulbar's lips curled back from his teeth. "I accept."

Orius turned to face Jorga of Tydorhagen. "You will scout the eastern slope. Take one warrior each from Ragnaar, Haagenvaarder, and Tydorhagen. You are to return before dark, as well."

Jorga's mouth twisted with displeasure, but he grudgingly nodded his head.

"Work together," Orius ordered. "The Oruks do not favor one village over another."

He dismissed the warriors gathered around him and walked to where Culley sat building a fire. Argus skewered meat onto sharp sticks, and Moreena and Kathair tended to the horses. Orius placed his hands on his hips and watched the other campsites, searching for signs of trouble, or for signs of cooperation between the different villages. He saw nothing but scattered and separate campfires.

*They should be too tired to start any trouble tonight.* The Chelts were a hardy lot, but fatigue lined their faces. *We need more horses.* He sat on the ground.

"Well, how'd it go?" Culley asked.

"Except for Chief Condin, Ghyo bless him," said Orius, "the rest of them looked at me like I had been caught pissing in the village well, but they did what I told them to do."

Culley cackled and slapped his leg. "Good old Cheltan stubbornness. You did good, boy."

"We should run into Fayne and Alana in a few days," Orius said. "Hopefully, they will bring us some useful information." He crossed his arms and stared into the flickering flames of Culley's small fire.

"What bothers you, boy?" Culley asked.

Orius moved closer to the old Chelt. "Impatience," he whispered. "I do not like waiting for news. Much depends on what Fayne and Alana are able to tell us."

"Aye," Culley mused. "This'll be your first big test. Do not worry. I'll be beside you the whole time. I saw many battles when I was a mercenary in Fringia." Culley stoked the fire with a stick. "I've fought Kheldunii, Imbrians, Oruks, and bandits - the Vhantii, once. Hard fight."

Orius nodded. He had heard the stories many times. "Do not go over your credentials with me, old friend. You have taught me much of what I know about battle..." Orius abruptly stopped himself. "I mean you have taught me *everything* I know. It will be difficult to repay you."

Culley smiled warmly and grasped Orius's shoulder. "Your Ascension to the Azari throne will be my payment," he said quietly.

Argus sat next to Orius and Culley and handed each of them a skewer. "Moreena, Kathair - hurry up! I can't help myself." He held up two skewers, pretending to eat their share of the meat. Moreena and Kathair chuckled.

The Chelts drank wine, played cards, told stories, and rolled dice. The patrols returned from the mountain slopes with nothing to report. Chief Condin sent a rider to deliver food to the warriors who kept watch up the road. All was quiet.

The evening passed without incident. Orius and the army rose before sunrise and continued their uphill march. Hours after they left camp, they came to a narrow gorge with precipitous walls of granite rising hundreds of feet. The gorge was wide enough at the bottom for only one wagon to pass through, and it snaked around boulders and rough rock outcroppings for a mile. The gorge marked the highest point of the Borvik Pass.

Orius halted the column and turned to Kathair. "Select three mounted warriors from Ragnaar and scout the gorge. When you reach the end, send a rider back, but I want you to wait there for us."

Kathair raised a hand to his blonde brow. He called for the first three warriors to follow him and led them into the gorge.

Two hours later, one of the warriors returned and reported to Orius that the way was clear. Orius raised his arm, signaling the column to advance. It took a few hours for the army to move through the gorge. Orius emerged first and found Kathair standing on top of an immense boulder, surveying the land with a spyglass. Orius dismounted and climbed the boulder. From there, he could see how the narrow road ran for miles, descending gradually to the south.

"This is an excellent place to observe the pass," Kathair said.

"What have you to report?" Orius asked. The wind whipped at the bottom of his surcoat.

"Nothing," Kathair said. "I've seen no signs of movement along the road or among the trees. No dust clouds, either. Though, I admit I can only see so far with this device." He raised the spyglass to his eye and looked again. "I suggest sending a small patrol ahead of the main force. Scout out the pass. We can make contact sooner with Fayne and Alana that way."

"Sounds prudent," said Orius. "You will lead the scouts. Take Moreena with you and select five more warriors. Pick them from different villages. If you run into trouble, try to avoid getting tangled up in a fight and report back to me."

"As you wish, Orius." Kathair climbed down from the boulder and mounted his horse. He rode back through the column, gathered a party, and led them down the pass.

Orius waited for about a quarter of an hour, giving Kathair time to scout ahead. He then mounted his black gelding and led the army down the road until he ordered a halt for the day.

The next day, as the midday sun approached its highest point, Kathair spotted two green-clad horsemen riding toward him. He halted the patrol and ordered one of the warriors to ride back and tell Orius they had found Fayne and Alana. He then rode off with the others to meet his friends.

"Fayne!" Kathair shouted.

"Alana!" cried Moreena.

Their horses nearly collided as they met. Kathair offered a hand to Fayne.

"It's good to see you two again," said Fayne. "Where are the rest of the warriors?" His voice sounded concerned.

"A way back along the road," said Kathair.

"I'm glad you're both safe," Moreena said. "But you look exhausted." Her blue eyes displayed her worry.

"We haven't had a full night's rest in two days," Alana said. "In fact, I hardly slept at all last night." A troubled look appeared beneath her green bandana.

"Did you run into trouble?" asked Kathair.

"We never made it to Drenga," Fayne said. "I think we got within a day's ride from there." He bit his lower lip and glanced at Alana.

Kathair sat up straighter in his saddle. "Well, what happened?"

"There were Oruks in the middle of a valley..." Alana began.

Fayne interrupted her. "There were about a hundred of them camped near a stream." He then explained about the farm, the woman, and how the Oruks had discovered their presence.

"Bastards," exclaimed Moreena.

"Awful. Just, awful." Kathair's mouth and nose curled up in a sneer. "There will be retribution."

"Alana, you look as though you've aged ten years," Moreena said. "A young woman shouldn't have to see such evil...no one should have to see it."

"We couldn't have made it to Drenga," Fayne said. "And I believe there are many more Oruks in the area, in addition to those we saw."

"I agree," said Kathair. "A hundred Oruks couldn't have wiped out Drenga. Not even three hundred."

Fayne pointed to the south. "We have a spot up the road where we can wait for Orius. It's a good place to watch the road."

"We can do with a short rest and a bite to eat." Kathair turned in his saddle and ordered the patrol to follow him. The campsite was only a few hundred yards ahead.

Orius saw a Chelt in the distance. In a few minutes, the Chelt met up with him and the main body of the Cheltan army. He reared his horse next to Orius. Foaming sweat dropped from the horse's flanks.

"Easy, man," Culley complained. "You're going to kill that animal, riding uphill at that pace. Horses are hard to come by."

"What is your name?" asked Orius.

"Cathol of Kyarna, Father. I bring news from Kathair. He's found the two riders you sent ahead. He says he will rest the patrol and wait for you."

"How far ahead are they?" Orius asked.

"Five or six miles, Father Orius."

"Thank you, Cathol. You will remain with the rest of the army. Find your place in line."

"It's good to know they are still alive," Culley said. "Good kids. Smart, too."

"Yes, I cannot wait to hear what they have to say." Orius called over his shoulder, "Argus, join me here!"

The burly Chelt rode forward on his chestnut shire and plodded next Orius and Culley. "What's the matter? Is it good news or bad news?"

"Kathair found Fayne and Alana," Culley said.

"Argus, you and I will ride forward and meet up with our companions," Orius told him. He turned to Culley. "I want you to stay with the army."

"Are you taking any warriors with you?" he asked.

"No, it seems the road is clear. Kathair is only a few miles away. Argus and I will make good time riding downhill."

"Take care, boy."

Orius and Argus rode off down the road. As they left, Orius heard Culley shouting for the leading warriors to gather around him. *He takes command, like in the old days, just like my mother said he would.*

Running into the Oruks had been a complete surprise. When Kathair rode into the copse of spruces and pines where Fayne and Alana had camped, he rode over a short rise and found himself staring into the face of an Oruk, holding the reins of a stocky mountain pony. The Oruk dropped the reins and fumbled for the axe hanging from his belt, but Kathair had reacted faster. He reared his black shire and the horse kicked the Oruk with its massive hooves. The Oruk slammed against a pine tree, flopped onto the ground, and rolled onto his back. Kathair then leaped from his horse's back, drew his two-hander, and brought it down across the Oruk's stomach.

A shrill scream then caught Kathair's attention. A second Oruk had been nearby and he charged Kathair, holding a sword with both hands above his head. Kathair withdrew his sword from the dead Oruk and confronted the new adversary, but Moreena appeared from behind a pine. She hacked off the charging Oruk's head and an arm with a swipe of her two-hander.

Two other Oruks then suddenly bolted through the trees, mounted their ponies, and galloped across the field on the other side of the copse. Fayne, Alana, and two Chelts charged their horses through the trees and pursued the fleeing Oruks, but they only made it halfway across the field before they abruptly halted. Twenty horsemen were setting up camp on the field's far edge. The fleeing Oruks reined in their ponies next to their leader. They gestured wildly, pointing toward the trees across the field. The Oruk they spoke to sat up straight and looked in that direction. His sword then flashed in the afternoon sunlight, and he waved the blade left and right, screaming at the rest of the horsemen. The Oruks moved hastily and scrambled to their ponies. Fayne and the others raced back to the where Kathair stood beside the trunk of a pine.

"More riders!" Fayne had exclaimed, gasping for breath. "They're coming for us."

"Yes, I see them," Kathair said. He moved out of the trees where all the Chelts could see him. "We will defend this ground!" he had shouted. "Orius and the army will be here shortly. We have to hold. The Oruks must not get past us." The group roared with approval and those with shields banged their weapons against them.

"Those with bows pick a spot to loose from and drop a few before they arrive," Kathair had said, pointing with his sword. "The rest of you spread out in a line. Stick to the trees. They will slow their charge." He then thrust his sword into the air. "Show them that one Chelt is worth five Oruks!" Another roar came from the Chelts.

Across the field, the Oruk horsemen had lined up knee-to-knee and crossed the ground at a canter. The tips of their spears flashed in the sunlight. The Oruk with the sword rode out in front. He held his blade at his side, pointing upwards. A dull roaring sound of horse hooves washed over the Chelts in the copse. The noise had grown louder by the second.

When the Oruks had reached bow range, Alana loosed the first missile. It streaked through the air and struck the leader in the chest. He fell from the saddle and landed on the ground in a crumpled heap. The entire line of Oruks hesitated. A second later, Gorsod loosed an arrow, finding a mark among the packed riders. Another Oruk fell from the saddle. Fayne squeezed the trigger of his crossbow, and his bolt found a target, as well. The Oruks then suddenly halted their advance and routed for the far trees. A boisterous cheer rose up from the copse. The Chelts slapped each other on the back and congratulated the archers. The Oruks retreated down the road and disappeared into the woods.

"They were well-organized," old Turi had said. "I have never seen Oruks fight like that. Something isn't right." A hint of trepidation underscored his voice.

"I too noticed that," said Trohaarn, who was younger than Turi. "But never mind, they ran from a straight-up fight - like they normally do."

"Will they be back?" Moreena had asked.

"If they do return, we'll be ready for them," Kathair said.

A half-hour then passed. Finbar spotted movement along the road. Sunlight, reflecting off metal, winked through the forest. Fayne and Kathair dug out their spyglasses and scanned the trees. Fayne jerked his head back from his spyglass, blinking his eyes. Kathair's face lost some of its color. The Oruks had returned – lots of them.

Two columns of foot soldiers, marching in step, debouched from the woods across the field, clad in scraggly furs and well-worn woolen breeches. A rider, cloaked in black, rode at the head of the troops. He cantered his horse for a dozen paces, spun around, and motioned with his arms. The Oruk columns filed left and right, forming rows of a dozen soldiers, standing shoulder-to-shoulder four ranks deep. The Oruk horsemen had returned, too. They divided themselves into two groups and took up positions on opposite ends of the infantry formations. A pair of drummers stood behind the black-clad figure.

The Black Rider turned his horse and faced the trees across the field. He held a spyglass in his hand and raised it to his brow. He scanned the trees. His scouts told him they had attacked the grove, but fifty Chelts occupied it, so they did not drive them out. He knew that was a lie and the lack of dead bodies lying near the trees confirmed it.

"Scum!" he said loudly, from the darkened recess of his hood. The Black Rider counted only eight horses amongst the trees. He slammed the spyglass into the leather tube strapped to his saddle. He jerked at the reins, whipping his horse around, and shouted at his troops in Sytish. "Listen to me, you wretched dogs! There are no more than a dozen Chelts occupying those trees! We have ten times their number! You will advance and drive them out! If any of you should run, you will taste the cold steel of my blade." He drew his shining sword and pointed it at the drummers. "Sound the advance!"

The drummers snapped to attention and beat out the commands. *Ta-ta-ta-ta! Ta-ta-ta-ta! Tum!* The entire mass of Oruks advanced, keeping in step with the drums.

"They are coming again!" Kathair called out. He knelt behind a tree trunk, staring at the advancing Oruks. The exposed bowels of the dead one at his feet filled the air with an awful stink. To his right, Fayne knelt behind another tree, aiming his crossbow. Oisin and

Ewyn, of Ragnaar, knelt beside Fayne, armed with axes and round shields. To Kathair's left stood Moreena with her two-handed sword drawn and stained with blood, and Finbar, of Ragnaar, with his spear and shield. Alana stood beside Moreena, notching an arrow. Further to the left, Gorsod of Telstrand stood with his bow ready. Mathol of Lunevik, Turi of Kyarna, and Trohaarn of Haagenvaarder were on the far left, with their swords drawn and their shields ready.

*Tum! Tum! Ta-ta-ta-ta! Tum!*

Kathair clenched his jaw and turned toward Fayne, who was looking through his spyglass. "I think we can hold them off," he said, not sounding completely confident. "Orius has to be nearby."

Fayne lowered his spyglass and looked at Kathair. "Orius doesn't want us to fight the Oruks without the entire army present. We shouldn't disobey him."

*Tum! Tum! Ta-ta-ta-ta! Tum!*

"The situation has changed," said Kathair. "I was sent here to find you and wait for him. We can send another rider back to tell him to hurry. He and the army *have* to be nearby."

*Tum! Tum! Ta-ta-ta-ta! Tum!*

"Sending someone back will weaken us," Moreena said. "Ghyo help us if he doesn't find Father Orius in time. The Oruks will run over us like a flood."

*Tum! Tum! Ta-ta-ta-ta! Tum!*

"That's possible," said Kathair, "but the Oruks are a half-mile away. It'll be a quarter of an hour before they can attack us. There may be time if we send someone now."

Kathair stood up and pointed at a warrior. "Oisin, mount your horse and find Orius. Tell him we are being attacked by ten times our number. Tell him we hold a strong position and we can hold out until he arrives. But you *must* hurry!"

*Tum! Tum! Ta-ta-ta-ta! Tum!*

Oisin's eyes flashed with excitement. "Save some for me." He sprinted for his horse.

# Chapter 10

## Blood and Fire
### 11 Janoban, 229 A.G.S.

Worgoth's shining axe hung from a metal ring fastened to Orius's saddle. It bounced rhythmically as the horse trotted down the road. A two-hander hung in its scabbard from the saddle's left side. Orius scanned the countryside, looking for his friends. For nearly an hour, he and Argus had traveled at a brisk trot. It was a bright afternoon with a cloudless sky. The sun was an hour past its midday position and the day had become quite warm. A gentle breeze blew through the Borvik Pass, shifting directions as it swirled about the peaks. Orius and Argus entered the woods at the southern edge of the meadow they had just crossed.

Argus breathed in the piney air. "Ah," he sighed, "I love the scent of the forest. It reminds me of home."

Orius said nothing in return, but Argus's comments made his thoughts wander to Torveg, as well. Though it was not his true home, he had grown up there in hiding, living within the confines of an ancient keep, taking lessons from his mother, Culley, and Malagorn. Orius's childhood had been a source of great loneliness and bitterness for him.

They reached the end of the woods and halted. Orius and Argus sat their mounts for several minutes, observing the landscape. Before them stretched a long, undulating field of grass and wildflowers, with the ever-present mountains to the east and west. A copse of trees stood at the other end of the field, nearly two miles distant. Flashes of sunlight, reflecting off metal, winked at them from the base of the copse.

"There's someone in there," Argus said with his large hand shading his brow.

Orius retrieved his spyglass and scanned the field. "I do not see signs of anyone else to the east or west, and I cannot count how many people are in those trees." He strained his eyes, but it was no use.

"If they're our people," Argus said. "They aren't trying to hide themselves."

Orius returned his spyglass to the saddlebag. "I believe they are our friends. We have to be getting close to the road junction, but let us assume the enemy occupies..."

"Look there!" Argus exclaimed.

A lone rider appeared on the road, coming over a rise in the ground, disappearing, and then reappearing again. Orius reached for his saddlebag, but he stopped himself and instead placed his hand on the hilt of his sword. Argus pulled his double-bladed axe from the iron ring on his saddle. The rider was a mile away and Orius saw that he drove the horse at a furious pace. Small clouds of dust rose up behind it.

After a minute, Argus said, "It's a Chelt. I can see his shield. It is Cheltan."

Orius thought about the glinting metal beneath the trees. "Something is wrong. Fayne and the others would not give away their position so easily."

"Then they have drawn their weapons," said Argus.

Orius and Argus's horses blocked the road. The approaching Chelt reined his horse to a hasty stop, raising a cloud of dust that engulfed the two of them.

"Father Candell!" Oisin cried out. "Blessed I am by the Creator for granting me such good fortune." As the dust settled, Oisin looked into the woods past Orius. "There are only two of you?"

Orius coughed and spat dust from his mouth. "What is happening up there?"

"Yes," said Argus, wiping dirt from his blue eyes. "Explain yourself, you fool."

Oisin's eyes bulged and his face reddened. His lips curled back in a sneer and he pointed at Argus. "Watch your tongue. Your insults won't be forgotten."

"Enough of this!" Orius yelled. "Answer me. What is happening?"

"Oruks! We're being attacked by ten times our numbers." Oisin turned in his saddle and pointed across the field to the distant copse of trees. "There. We hold a strong position in those trees. They've yet to attack, but we need help. There are too many."

Orius's jaw dropped as he listened to Oisin. "Kathair was told not to engage the Oruks. There was to be no battle until the entire army had been gathered." One of Culley's lessons suddenly came to mind. *The tide of war continually shifts in unforeseen directions.* Orius took a deep breath. He cleared his mind of excessive emotion and put his thoughts in order.

"Father Orius, what are your orders? The Oruks will be inside the trees in minutes," Oisin said rapidly.

"Orius..." Argus began to speak.

But Orius cut him off and said to Oisin, "Ride north. Find Culley. Tell him to send Chief Condin and all of the mounted warriors here to our aid. Tell him to force the march of the rest of the army. I need all our warriors *here*." He pointed to the ground beneath him for emphasis. "Find him as quickly as possible - do not spare your horse."

"As you command," Oisin responded. He gave Argus a nasty look before he left and rode north through the woods.

"What now?" Argus asked.

"We have a battle to fight."

The Black Rider rode out in front of his advancing troops. His black horse calmly carried him across the field. He sat erect in the saddle, grasping the reins with his left hand and clutching his sword in his right. Despite the afternoon's warmth, he kept the cowl of his cloak pulled over his head. From the darkened recess, his yellow eyes stared at his objective. He studied the trees as he led his troops toward them. As he approached the halfway point across the field, he saw the bodies of the fallen Syts from earlier lying in crumpled heaps upon the grass. The Black Rider saw an arrow protruding from one of the bodies. He raised his hand. The Sytish drummers beat out the command to halt.

The Black Rider sat motionless in his saddle. The range and accuracy of the bowshots impressed him. *My life is too important to be squandered on that miserable clump of trees.* He turned the horse about and faced his soldiers. His voice issued forth from somewhere within his darkened cowl. Its sound seemed disembodied. "Grundish! Come forward!"

The Syt posted in front of the left hand formation of infantry jogged over. His ragged shirt of mail jiggled as he ran. He stopped a few paces from the Black Rider, held his round wooden shield at his side, and raised his spear in salute. "Captain Grundish reporting, sire."

"Grundish, now that someone has conveniently taken Shizak out of your way, I give *you* the great honor of leading this charge."

Grundish's eyes widened, and he fidgeted.

The Black Rider grew instantly agitated. "What is the matter? This is your chance to prove you are not just another Sytish pig, filling out the ranks of the army. At least show me some gratitude."

Grundish swallowed hard. "I...uh...thank you."

"Of course, should you fail, do not bother returning alive," the Black Rider added in a languid tone.

"Yes, sire," mumbled Grundish. He shook visibly as he spun around and faced the army.

The Black Rider spurred his horse past Grundish and met with the leaders of the cavalry squadrons, who had ridden to the army's center. The Black Rider wielded a terrible, unnatural influence over the Syts. They feared him more than they feared the Chelts waiting for them. He was one of the Outsiders who had come to the shores of Sytor, a decade before, arriving in a great black ship. They wielded strange powers and used powerful devices.

The commands for the cavalry leaders issued forth from the darkness of his black cowl. The words were icy, direct and deliberately redundant. "When the infantry charges *those* trees, the cavalry will ride around each flank of *those* trees and block off any chance of escape for the enemy occupying *those* trees. Show no mercy! Take no prisoners!" He dismissed them with a wave of his sword.

The cavalry commanders thumped their right hands to their breasts and hurried off on their stout ponies to either end of the line. The Black Rider guided his horse around the drummers and took up a position behind the line of infantry.

"Grun*dish*," his voice mocked from within the black cowl. "You may proceed."

"Prepare yourselves!" Kathair called out so everyone could hear him. His stomach quivered. The Oruks had paused just outside bow range. "Gorsod, Fayne, Alana - loose your missiles when they come into range. Aim for the leaders. Maybe some of them'll run if their leaders are down."

"What do make of that one riding the black horse?" Moreena asked Kathair.

"I'd say he is not an Oruk. He is too tall. Oruk legs are too short for horses."

"Maybe he is a *freak*!" young Ewyn shouted, cupping his hand to his mouth. His insult produced snickers and wry smiles from his comrades.

"If he is, he's a talented freak," old Turi said. Warriors his age had seen many fights.

"He seems to know what he's doing over there," Fayne added.

The drums quelled their talk. The Oruks stepped off again, marching to the drumbeats. A long minute passed. The Chelts waited quietly in the trees. The smell of their foe reached them first, both musty and ripe at the same time. Kathair's pounding heart echoed the Oruks' drums. *Ghyo grant me strength. Forgive me if I've poorly chosen this course I follow.* He wanted to pray aloud, but anxiety tightened his throat and took the moisture from him mouth. The Oruk army crept closer to the bodies lying in the field's center. As they began to step over and around the bodies, Alana's and Gorsod's bows creaked as they drew back.

Grundish's breathing was ragged. His arm muscles were taut with fear. He held up his shield, so that its top was just below his eyes. Only his groin, legs, and the top of his head were exposed. His spear was tucked under his armpit, the tip pointing toward the trees. The first arrow streaked past his head and buried itself in the ground. The second arrow struck his shield just above his arm, penetrating the wood by a couple of inches. Grundish gasped. If the arrow had struck any lower, it would have tacked his arm to the shield. His instincts told him to run for cover, but he looked over his shoulder into the darkness of the Black Rider's cowl. He felt the cold stare of the hidden eyes upon him. A dozen tortures and agonizing ways of dying flashed through his mind - if he ran. The thought of an arrow piercing his body perversely seemed the better choice. Grundish was still a couple hundred yards from the trees, but he screamed with all the courage he could muster.

"Follow me!" And he took off for the trees at a dead run.

A great roar erupted from the Syts. The formations of infantry lost their cohesion as the soldiers rushed forward. The leaders of the cavalry squadrons ordered their horns to blow, and they charged along with the infantry. The beating of the drums stopped as the charge began.

"No!" the Black Rider screamed as his battle plan unraveled. "Re-form ranks! Curse you all! Re-form your ranks!" But his orders were to no avail. He halted his horse and resigned himself to watching how the fighting would unfold. *Eo, take their souls.*

Alana stopped loosing arrows and shouted over the noise. "What're they doing? They're so far away."

Gorsod loosed another arrow. "Alana, don't stop!" He reached behind his ear and fetched another arrow.

"They're charging!" Turi yelled. "The horsemen are charging!"

"Kathair!" Moreena called out. "They're going to be on top us sooner than expected."

Kathair stood up and moved to where he could be seen by all of the Chelts. Fear stiffened his joints. "We'll stand and fight! We must buy time! Stick together! If we are too hard-pressed, withdraw to the horses!"

The Oruk infantry had closed half the distance to the trees when their charge slowed from a run to a jog. A few of them fell to arrows, but the rest continued. The Oruk horsemen had passed those on foot and headed for the opposite ends of the copse. A dark, sinking feeling filled Kathair's chest.

"We're being surrounded!" Fayne cried out. His blue eyes were wild looking.

"We must leave now if we wish to escape!" Turi shouted. Then...

The keening of a horn rose above the commotion of the Oruks' charge. All Cheltan eyes looked northward over their shoulders.

"Hold your places!" Kathair raced back in the direction of the sound to where their horses stood. Again, the horn keened. In the distance, he caught sight of two riders. One was conspicuously dressed in white. A third blast from the horn ripped through the air. Kathair's face lit up with elation. He ran wildly, back to his comrades.

"It's Orius! Thank the Creator, it's Orius!" he screamed. "Warriors of the North stand and fight!"

"Good man, Argus! Let them know we are coming!" Orius exclaimed.

Argus, with his face turning purple, unleashed a fourth blast from his horn. When he finished, he gasped, "I hope...we aren't ...too late."

A score of horsemen rounded the east and west sides of the copse. Orius brought his horse to a hasty stop. The Oruk horsemen did not turn to confront them.

He clenched his jaws. "I had hoped to find our companions before the Oruks engaged them, but circumstances are moving too quickly." He watched the horsemen close the net around his friends.

Orius dismounted. "Argus, you must protect me and help me back into the saddle." He handed the reins to Argus and walked a dozen paces ahead.

"What are you...?" Argus cut himself off before he finished his question.

A wave of thirty exhausted Oruks reached the grove. They were the fastest runners and had distanced themselves from rest of their soldiers. Despite their exhaustion, they threw themselves against the Chelts and a wild melee broke out along the edge of the trees. Metallic clanging blended with high-pitched screams from Oruk and Chelt alike, creating a terrific cacophony beneath the pines.

At five paces, Fayne loosed a final bolt, striking an Oruk in the stomach. He threw down his crossbow and drew his short sword and dagger. Three Oruks charged him. The first came at him with a spear clutched in both hands. Fayne swept away the spear thrust with his sword, slipped in close, and drove the point of his dagger through the Oruk's mouth. He withdrew the blade as the second Oruk came at him. This Oruk swung a Cheltan axe. Fayne evaded the blow and thrust his sword into the Oruk's stomach. But the third jabbed with his spear. The steel tip pierced Fayne's side, tearing open a gash the size of a fist. The Oruk twisted the spear and withdrew it. Fayne screamed in agony, but he wrapped his arm around the spear's shaft and slid his body down it. He lashed out with his dagger and sunk the tip into the Oruk's eye. The Oruk dropped the spear and clawed at his face with both hands. Fayne finished him with a sword thrust to the groin.

To Fayne's right, a trio of Oruks rushed Ewyn. He blocked a sword thrust with his shield and cleaved the Oruk's head with his axe. Blood and brains splattered onto the face of the Oruk behind Ewyn's victim. That Oruk dropped his axe and ran for the rear, screaming wildly and waving his hands above his head. The third Oruk fled too, but he was not fast enough. Ewyn buried his axe between his shoulder blades.

Kathair, Moreena, Alana, Finbar, and Gorsod held the center of the line as fourteen Oruks charged them. Alana and Gorsod positioned themselves behind the three fighters, felling one more Oruk each before the hacking and dying commenced along their part of the copse.

Two Oruks charged Kathair, who unleashed a ferocious howl and countercharged. Both Oruks hesitated as he bore down on them.

With his two-hander, Kathair split one from the shoulder to the middle of his torso. A gout of blood saturated Kathair. The other Oruk dropped his club and trembled with fear. Kathair smashed his fist into the Oruk's nose and the Oruk fell to the ground. He then rammed his foot into the midsection of the Oruk impaled on his sword and withdrew the blade.

An arrow zinged past his head and dove into the chest of an Oruk to his left. Kathair then stood on guard, with his hands held high by his left ear. Another Oruk, armed with a fire-hardened stake, lunged at his midriff. He parried the thrust to his left and stepped to the right. Blood was cast about as Kathair swung his two-hander. He completed a circle with his sword and brought it down upon the Oruk's shoulder. The sword came out below the armpit on the other side. The Oruk separated.

More blood now clung to the trees and Kathair's clothing. It flowed in small rivers from the wounded and lifeless bodies at his feet. Two more Oruks charged him. Another arrow zipped past and buried itself into one of them. The remaining Oruk held a crude axe in front of his body and made threatening jabs at Kathair. But Kathair lunged suddenly and jabbed the tip of his sword through the Oruk's face, provoking a sickening screech from his victim.

Alana saw that Kathair's charge had shifted the pace of the fighting in the Chelt's favor. But two Oruks had given him a wide berth and slipped around his left. She snapped her head in that direction and saw that the Oruks were running toward her. Their eyes were wide and their large, square teeth were bared. She raised a trembling hand behind her ear and fumbled for an arrow. She withdrew one and notched it. One of the Oruks had pulled ahead of the other. She drew the bowstring to her cheek as the leading Oruk raised a Cheltan axe above his head and screamed at her. Her arrow struck the Oruk in the center of his body, impaling him to the fletching. He jackknifed in the air and flopped onto the ground.

In a flash, the second Oruk swung a mace at her. Alana screamed and somehow blocked it with her bow, which snapped in two. The Oruk cocked his arms back and swung again, striking her right forearm. Alana stumbled backward, whimpering and cradling a broken arm. The Oruk smiled and raised his mace again.

"No!" Alana screeched as an arrow drove through the Oruk's throat. A frightful gurgling sound followed. The Oruk dropped the mace and clutched at his throat with his hands.

A second arrow struck him in the stomach and finished him. "Alana, get to your horse!" Gorsod yelled to her. He drew another arrow from his quiver.

Moreena, with her two-hander, and Finbar, with his spear and shield, were in front of Gorsod, keeping four Oruks at bay. Gorsod loosed an arrow, striking one of the Oruks in the forehead, which caused the others to flee. Moreena and Finbar pounced and made quick work of two of them.

On the far left, nine Oruks attacked Trohaarn, Turi, and Mathol. Three Oruks went for Mathol, who blocked a hammer blow from the first with his shield, hacked off the arm of the second, but the third speared him through the body. Meanwhile, Turi and Trohaarn fought side by side against the other six. They slowly yielded ground, blocking with their shields and parrying with their swords.

"Help us," Turi cried. "Mathol is down! The Oruks are breaking through!"

"Over here!" Trohaarn shouted. "Come to us, or we must retreat!"

Orius removed his gauntlets and tucked them into his belt. He cleared his mind of distractions. He focused on tapping the energy within the core of the world - the way Malagorn had taught him. He knelt and placed his left hand upon the ground. Immediately, an intense heat radiated from deep within the earth and transferred to his hand. Orius felt fire rush into his body. With practiced precision, he channeled the energy into the center of his chest and held it there for a moment.

He gazed across the gently rolling grass and selected his target, the body of horsemen on the right. He extended his right arm, pointed the palm toward them, and directed the energy within him through his arm. With a whoosh, a compact ball of fire discharged from his palm. Sweat broke out over his entire body and he became slightly disoriented. He struggled to focus on his target. The fireball rapidly closed the distance, and it grew in size the further it traveled. The horsemen were moving toward the left. Orius fought to keep his eye on them and to follow them with his hand. The fireball arced through the air, following the Oruks as if it knew where its creator wanted it to strike. It had expanded to the size of a man when it plowed into the horsemen, tearing a gaping hole in their formation. The fireball burst and sprayed liquid fire onto the Oruks. A shower of reddish flame and heat incinerated five ponies and their riders. Another five Oruks and their ponies, on the fringe of the blast, caught fire and were burned alive.

Orius switched his attention to the other group of riders who had stopped cold in their tracks when the fireball collided with their comrades. Some of them pointed towards Orius. He saw the group of horsemen turn to flee. With heaving chest, he drew more fire from the core of the world and held it within his breast. He struggled to maintain his focus - to keep his mind clear. The first channeling had not been too overwhelming, but the second channeling felt like he put a hundred pound weight on his chest. Sweat again poured from his skin.

The Oruk horsemen no longer rode in a tight group, but were strung out in a line. The faster steeds distanced themselves from the slower ones. Orius directed his palm toward the center of the line and unleashed Death from his hand. Another wave of sweat gushed forth as he released the energy. Dizzy and disoriented, he struggled to keep his arm pointed at the horsemen, but exhaustion forced his eyes shut. Orius dropped his arm and slumped to the ground. The fireball continued in a straight line and struck the Oruks near the end of the line, scorching two of them and their ponies, and setting three others alight. The survivors disappeared around the edges of the copse.

Less than a minute had passed since the first wave of Syts crashed against the trees. The Chelts' adroit swordsmanship had cut down most of them, and those Syts who ran away were greeted by fifty of the slower ones now approaching the grove, with Grundish leading them. Grundish had exhausted himself and so had his troops. He had watched in amazement as his enemy cut down the first wave. He cursed himself for panicking and starting the charge too soon. He hoped the Chelts were worn out, so he could lead his larger force into the trees and claim the victory.

To the right, he saw Sytish soldiers breaking into the woods. It was his opportunity for victory. Glory was near and he felt it. He would win favor with the Outsider, despite the botched charge.

"To the right!" Grundish screamed. "Follow me to the right! They are running!"

A great cheer arose from the advancing Syts who pressed forward. The entire mass followed Grundish. Like a wave of water, they approached the copse, when...

Red light flashed through the trees, accompanied by a fiery roar, followed by the screams of dying Syts and horses. The Sytish advance briefly faltered, but it regained its impetus. Grundish approached the trees. In ten paces, he and his troops would flood through the collapsing Cheltan line – when a terrible vision appeared. *A demon!* Grundish's mind screamed.

A screeching pony galloped through the trees. Its mane was singed and its flesh was torn and scorched. A flaming, screaming apparition rode in the saddle, leaving a wispy trail of smoke in its wake. Grundish realized how real the vision was as the burning pony careened into the advancing Syts. On the left, another flaming horseman appeared from the pines and plowed into the Syts there. The advance sputtered and then the thundering of hooves could be heard. In a few moments, Sytish horsemen came into view, fleeing for the rear. Panicked, pleading cries came from the riders.

"Conjurer!"

"They have a Conjurer!"

"Save yourselves!"

Grundish whipped his head around, his eyes now wide with terror. He was the first to run and his panic spread like wildfire. Within seconds, it infected every Syt on the field. The battle ended in a complete rout.

The Black Rider sat his horse, watching two plumes of black smoke rise from behind the grove. He watched his army, on the verge of winning the day, turn and run for their lives. A venomous hiss came from his cowl's darkened interior. He turned his horse and galloped down the road, disappearing into the woods.

# Chapter 11

## Devices and Contrivances
### 11 Janoban, 229 A.G.S.

R odrigo awoke a half-hour past dawn. A manservant held up a black silk tunic for him to slide his arms into. Rodrigo dressed and then strode down the hallway flanked by the Royal Family's apartments. His black boots thudded against the polished burgundy marble, with milky streaks flowing through it. The Eagle Guards stationed at the end of the hall snapped to attention as he passed. He walked down the palace's grand hallway, passing its huge tapestries and graceful sculptures. He marched to the entrance of the council chamber, and a guard opened the door.

Beltram sat on a chair beside the door and a secretary sat in his place in a corner. The windows were open and the heavy curtains drawn back. A warm breeze blew into the room. A stack of papers and letters sat on top of the map-table before Rodrigo's high-backed chair. A platter of food sat beside the papers.

Rodrigo took his seat. "You may commence, senyor," he told Beltram.

Rodrigo sipped herbal tea and ate a thick piece of toast with olive oil poured over it as Beltram went over the day's agenda. "If it pleases Your Majesty, we will begin with the signing of three Writs of Expenditures - one pertaining to repairs for the highway between Golandar and Vorencia; one for repairs to the Customs House of Vorencia, which was damaged by a fire; and one for twenty new horses for the Trackers. Later this morning, we have granted two audiences concerning the legal appeals of some minor lords from the valley of Ariandor. And after midday, Her Holiness the High Priestess has been granted an audience with Your Majesty. It appears she has a response from the Holy Tower."

Rodrigo stopped eating. "Very well, Beltram. That should leave us time to complete the plans for my departure." He continued to eat his breakfast, but he was dreading the meeting with Serophia. *What word will she bear from The Holy Tower?* Ghyo's Church always strove to increase its influence over the affairs of the nations of Iningia. During the past two centuries, the Church had lost much of its influence as kings chipped away at its power. The Church endlessly strove to reclaim its former glory. The result of this made dealing with it a difficult affair. The Church's decisions were often rash and bold, and the lack of predictability had only increased over the previous decade. The Holy Council, desperate to advance their policies, continually tapped their vast resources and riches.

Rodrigo finished eating and Beltram called for servants to clear the table. The secretary approached and placed a small wooden box in front of Rodrigo, containing an inkwell and a feather-pen. He read the writs, gave them approving nods, and scratched his name on them. When Rodrigo finished, the secretary gathered the papers, took them to his seat, and put them in the portable desk on his lap.

Rodrigo shuffled through the rest of the papers and selected a letter from Todu. It had been three days since the general and his army of seven thousand five hundred began their march south. Rodrigo broke the green sealing wax, indented with Todu's personal seal, and read the letter:

*To His Majesty, Gudor Valley, Morning of 10 Janoban, 229:*

*The weather is unbearably hot. We have marched for two days, and eighty men are lost to the heat. I fear the number will increase. As you are aware, a general makes calculations concerning attrition on the march, but it appears my figures will fall short of the actual losses on this march. Your Majesty, if this severe weather continues, I fear we may lose more than one in ten of our strength by the time we reach Spandel March. Furthermore, I estimate the army will require a week of rest and reorganizing at Spandel City, before we can undertake offensive operations. I look forward to seeing you soon.*

*With my compliments,*
*Todu Mazrio, High General of Soriazar*

Rodrigo folded the letter and placed it on the table. The contents disturbed him, but the events described did not surprise him. War was a strange beast and he understood that uncertainties were to be expected. He only hoped that the unforeseen things would not be ruinous to his plans. He had confidence in Todu Mazrio, who had been through far worse circumstances during his illustrious career, but the letter caused Rodrigo to feel a little uneasy about his plan for dealing with the Semotecs. The success of his design depended upon all parts working together. There simply was not much room for error or many casualties. The plan was bold, the risks were high, but so were the benefits - land. The Semotecs had invaded and overrun the Iduin coastal province called Apumium. The Iduin retreat left the territory undefended and ungoverned, and left a pretext for Rodrigo to use. To Azaris, the part of Apumium north of the River Boro was known as Galorica - the Lost Province of Soriazar.

Soriazar had lost Galorica to Idu in a war that lasted from the year 177 to the year 179. The war's cause was not complicated. Idu was landlocked and wanted a seaport on the western coast of Iningia, but a piece of Soriazar and Semotec stood in their way. The Iduin sent their legions across the Caroc Mountains and marched through the land, laying siege to the major towns and taking them one by one. They continued westward until they met an Azari army gathered astride the eastern road to the port of Morzon, led by the aging King Alonzo Mendio the Second. The ensuing Battle of Morzon ended in disaster for Soriazar. Their army was routed and it retreated to the port, where it was trapped and subjected to a month-long siege.

Memories from his childhood flooded Rodrigo's mind. He was only a boy of nine when Galorica was torn away from his grandfather's kingdom, and he could still hear the frightening sounds of the Battle of Morzon. He remembered the chaos of the Azari troops running for their lives. He felt his father's rough grip upon the collar of his tunic, as he had hauled Rodrigo up into the saddle, saving him from capture by the Iduin cavalry. Rodrigo remembered how two of his father's guardsmen gave their lives to cover their escape. He remembered the day he watched Morzon burn, from the deck of a ship, as the legions of Idu sacked the city. The people's cries still echoed to him across five decades, pleading for a chance to crowd onto the few remaining vessels in port. And Rodrigo remembered how the hardships of the campaign had taken their toll on King Alonzo and soon after sent him to his grave.

Rodrigo stared blankly at the lanterns hanging from the thick ceiling beams. The vivid scenes of the people leaping from the docks into the sea played out in his mind. Hundreds of people had drowned that terrible day. Their ghosts called out to him – "Save us! Save us!" *Fifty years is a long time to wait for vengeance, but patience is a kingly virtue.*

Rodrigo returned his attention to the present and opened a second message from Todu:

*To His Majesty, Gudor Valley, Afternoon of 10 Janoban, 229:*

*Masuf's Trackers are doing splendid work! He says the Semotecs are moving deeper into Spandel March. They advance in three columns - gathering food, burning homes, and leading prisoners south. One column moves along the coast, heading in the direction of Spandel. In the east, they have surrounded Orpresa. Nothing else is known of their fate. The third column is situated between the others and is fifty miles south of Turela.*

*The marquis has ordered all walled towns and villages to gather their food and families and seek shelter behind their defenses. There are to be no surrenders. Your cousin is a nervy one. We need more like him.*

*With my compliments,*
*Todu Mazrio, High General of Soriazar*

Rodrigo sighed and dropped the message onto the table. *We're being overrun, and Todu is confident.* He stood up, moved some of the wooden blocks across the map, and sat down again. A third message lay next to the other two. He did not want to read it, but he forced himself to pick it up. He broke the wax seal. The message was from Marquis Torenyo. It concerned the situation inside Apumium and spoke of the large numbers of Iduin refugees swarming into Spandel, but there was no news of the whereabouts of Idu's legions. Rodrigo had hoped at least for a tidbit concerning them.

"I wish to depart for Spandel in one week," Rodrigo said to Beltram. "I plan to leave Queen Khalia in charge of running the realm's daily affairs. She will occupy my seat on the council."

"Very well, Your Majesty," Beltram said. "And what will my instructions be?"

"You will not accompany me, old friend. Although Queen Khalia is competent, I need you to remain at your station in the palace. Keep me informed of what is going on here in Golandar."

"As you command, sire. How will Your Majesty be traveling? So I may begin the preparations."

"I wish to travel quickly, so I will not be going with the normal entourage. No wagons. I plan to sleep in an inn each night, or on the ground if necessary, until I reach Spandel."

Beltram sat up straighter, scratching his white beard. "I think fifty Trackers will be a sufficient escort. Not so many as to impede movement, but enough to afford His Majesty adequate protection." He paused. "May I presume His Majesty wishes to avoid the attention of others when he departs?"

"You presume correctly," said Rodrigo.

Beltram bowed his head. "Mistress Manda shall be informed of His Majesty's wishes."

Rodrigo had the audience chamber cleared upon receiving news of Serophia's arrival. He sat on his throne and waited for the High Priestess. Only he, Beltram, and a scribe remained in the room. Sunlight entered through the partitioned-glass ceiling, lighting the room in an amber hue. The sunlight raised the room's temperature. Although the room had been cleared of people, the ripe smell of sweating bodies mixed with perfumes lingered in the air.

Light footsteps clicked upon the marble floor of the hall outside the audience chamber. Rodrigo straightened his black tunic with a gold eagle embroidered upon the chest. Beltram moved into the hall and spoke to someone. He gestured for them to enter. Serophia appeared in the doorway at the end of the green carpet. As usual, she wore a white silk gown, flowing from her shoulders to her feet. Sunlight glittered off her golden tiara as she crossed the room. A priestess walked behind her. She, too, wore white silk, but the tiara circling her head was smooth and unadorned. The priestess was short of height with a slender frame. Her long, straight black hair contrasted with the white silk of her dress. Beneath the tiara, wide, apprehensive green eyes, the color of the sea, stared intently at Rodrigo – her father.

*Bitch!* Rodrigo cursed silently. *Fringian bitch! Serophia you have no shame, using my daughter as an advocate for the opposite party.* His outward demeanor changed little aside from the narrowing of his eyes, but his voice had an edge. "Holiness, what purpose does it serve to have my daughter, the princess, here representing the Church?"

"It serves my purposes, and those of the Church," Serophia said. "As you know, Drucilla has been assigned to the Holy Legate's Office. I felt her presence at this meeting would be a learning experience. She is here as an observer." Serophia smiled, ever so slightly. "She needs to know what it is like when a monarch seeks aid from the Church. Besides, her loyalties are now bound to the Creator. Native nationalism no longer applies."

Drucilla, with her head bowed to the floor, stood silently behind her mistress.

Rodrigo gripped the armrests. "And I suppose you, *Holiness*, no longer have loyalties to the Fringian crown. Considering, the Church has always been in bed with the Throne of Arshapel."

Serophia's nostrils flared and her neck reddened. Drucilla gave her father a wide-eyed stare.

Beltram opened the doors to the audience chamber and two servants appeared in the doorway, each carrying a chair. Rodrigo's eyes met Beltram's and he shook his head. Beltram quietly ordered the servants to leave, taking the chairs with them. Beltram shut the doors and returned to his place next to them.

"I am surprised by Her Holiness's forgetfulness. I recall requesting the assistance of some priests to travel with the army, and that is all. It was Her Holiness who brought up the subject of giving monetary support to our cause." Rodrigo stared at Drucilla, silently absolving himself of appearing to be a beggar in Serophia's presence. He switched his attention back to Serophia. "However, I am not going to dwell any longer upon your impertinence. What news do you bear from the Holy Tower?"

Serophia glanced over her shoulder as the servants departed. "I am surprised to see you have chosen to neglect your usual gracious hospitality."

"You will address me as Your Majesty," Rodrigo said.

"Of course." Serophia twisted her mouth as she bowed.

"Holiness," Rodrigo said in a flat tone, trying to maintain his dignity. "The Church and Soriazar have always found a way of working together. However, despite *your* position in Golandar, do not forget about *my* position in Golandar. Proceed."

"Your Majesty, the Holy Council has voted to appropriate one hundred thousand gold pieces for the purpose of hiring ships and sailors to operate along the coast of Semotec," Serophia said.

*One hundred thousand!* Rodrigo hardly believed her. *Enough coin to outfit five ships for a year.* "I am impressed by the Church's determination to punish the heathens. What stipulations are attached to the spending of this money?"

"The money will be transported to Vorencia by ship. From there, it will be escorted to Spandel by a contingent of the Order of Ilyas, who will then fight onboard ship with your men." Serophia raised her chin a little. "The Holy Council selected me to oversee the expenditure of the gold. Ships, flying Ghyo's flag beneath your Eagle, and crews, from your navy, will be hired in His name. An admiral of Your Majesty's choosing will lead the expedition, who will be accompanied by a representative of the Order of Ilyas, who shall be of equal rank. The two of them will share command."

Rodrigo snorted. The notion of a Black Hand in charge of his fleet turned his stomach. *Hang the Holy Council and their riches.* "The Church seems intent on changing a border war into a holy crusade. They also wish to put their hands on the running of this war. Having dual commanders creates a dangerous situation."

"King Rodrigo, the Holy Tower is always interested in punishing the heathens. Besides, the Azaris are religious, and fighting the Semotecs in His name will solidify their support of your war," Serophia said. "It *is* our money, which will finance this endeavor. But there are a few more stipulations, as you put it, that I must discuss with Your Majesty."

A sense of dread washed over Rodrigo. He was being entangled in an immense web. It did not surprise him that the Church would not be satisfied with simply burning a few Semotec towns and villages. They were determined to play a major role in the conduct of the fighting. Rodrigo sensed what was coming next would be difficult to accept. "What else does the Holy Council require?"

"The members of the Council are convinced that Your Majesty means to take back the land Soriazar lost to Idu half a century ago. They see the lack of a strong military response by Idu as a sign of weakness. They feel you may decide to take advantage of the situation, and the Holy Tower is always interested in the misfortunes of Idu."

Her statement caught him off guard. He was not ready to admit or reveal his long-ranged plans. "My concern is with defending the borders of this realm," Rodrigo lied. "There are tens of thousands of Semotec warriors occupying Apumium and Spandel March. At this time, we have not gathered an army large enough to defeat such a host."

"That is true," said Serophia. "But Your Majesty will have a large enough army gathered by this autumn, after the crops are out of the fields." Her voice suddenly softened. "Your Majesty, the Church and Soriazar have a common interest in the outcome of this situation. Both are aware that the real enemy is Idu. Campaigning against the Semotec heathens is not the final goal of your designs."

Rodrigo shifted in his seat. Drucilla's eyes widened again. "The Holy Council's presumptions amaze me," he said.

Serophia took a small step forward. "Your Majesty, Idu has committed wrongs against both parties. The Church is interested in punishing the Iduin for the expulsion of the knights of the Holy Order of Ilyas. The senate does not respect the Church, and it appoints its own priests without consulting the Holy Tower. They subject the Church's coffers to overwhelming tax burdens, far out of proportion to what is considered customary and reasonable. The Church has always opposed the flimsy pretext Idu used when they conquered Galorica. We feel Soriazar has the legitimate claim to the land, and we will support you in taking it back, should you openly commit to that course."

Rodrigo studied her for a few moments. The more he pondered this offer of assistance the more he disliked it. "Your offer is indeed generous, but what are the stipulations attached to *this* offer?"

Serophia answered quickly, "Your Majesty must allow a contingent of knights from the Order of Ilyas to ride with your army. They will be under orders from the Holy Tower to support your troops during the course of any pitched battles."

Rodrigo was dumbstruck. "And who are they responsible to in between the *pitched battles*."

Serophia lightly cleared her throat. She ran the tip of her tongue across her bottom lip. "They will have their own agenda."

*They'll have their own agenda*, Rodrigo silently repeated. He groaned with disgust. The tangled web Serophia was spinning had suddenly changed to a pool of quicksand, and it felt like it had sucked him in up to his knees and the muck pouring into his boots pulled him down faster. "Holiness, how many knights does the Holy Council intend to send into Soriazar?"

"I was told, five hundred and fifty."

Rodrigo's patience snapped. He could not bear the thought of having hundreds of the Black Hand marching through Soriazar. *They'll ravage the land.* "Holiness," he said tersely. "I will need time to consider all of this. When I have prepared my reply, you will be summoned to appear before me. You are dismissed."

Serophia bowed and turned to leave. Drucilla mirrored her and followed, but Rodrigo's voice stopped her.

"Drucilla, your mother and I would be pleased to have you accompany us for dinner this evening."

Drucilla glanced at Serophia, who nodded with approval. "Yes, Father. It will be my pleasure."

# Chapter 12

## The Webs of the Faith
## 11 Janoban, 229 A.G.S.

At the confluence of the rivers Rhodenum and Sorium stood Arshapel, Fringia's capital. Arshapel was a filthy but impressive city of bridges and walls, shops and marketplaces, and manors and hovels, linked together by a twisting network of cobblestone streets and dirt tracks. The rivers' courses gave the city a triangular shape, and stout stone walls and towers strengthened those natural barriers. A wall and fosse guarded the open eastern approaches and connected the rivers, turning the city into an island.

The Holy Tower stood at the triangle's apex. The waters of the rivers commingled at the feet of its white walls that cloistered it from the rest of the city. Inside the walls, the Sanctum of the Gift dominated the Holy Tower's compound. Its white marble walls supported a gold-plated dome known as the Second Sun that was visible from twenty miles away. Atop the dome sat a giant likeness of the sun, identical to the symbols on priestly vestments.

Four slender white towers, crowned with golden spires, flanked the sides of the sanctum. Buttresses linked them to its walls. The Morning Tower stood to the east, opposite the Evening Tower to the west. The Tower of Vigilance stood to the north, symbolizing the necessity for unending vigilance against the Hordes of Sytor, and the Sentinel Tower faced south, symbolizing the Church's unwavering commitment to watching over the nations of Iningia.

The Holy Council convened beneath the frescoes adorning the interior of the Second Sun. High gold curtains, hanging from iron rods imbedded into the massive columns supporting the roof, formed the Council's conclave. Pairs of knights of the Holy Order of Ilyas stood watch at the conclave's corners. Another pair stood where the curtains were raised, creating the entrance to the council area. In the center of the conclave, in the very heart of the Sanctum of the Gift, an ordinary granite rock protruded from the green marble floor. A golden railing encircled it.

The Holy Consistory sat in boxed pews along the long sides of the enclosure. They listened to a priest, standing on the rock, present his case to the Holy Council.

The five members of the Council sat atop a three-tiered oval dais, facing the rock. Archpriest Ignator occupied the loftiest seat.

In front of the dais, the Chief Prothonotary stood behind a long table and spoke in Tradespeak to the priest atop the stone. "Brother Kord, you stand upon the Rock of Ilyas, at the spot where the Creator handed down His Gift to the world. You stand before the Holy Council of His Church to give testimony to the matter at hand. Do you swear the testimony you are to render shall be the truth?"

The aging, white-haired priest responded, "I do."

"And should you perjure yourself, while standing upon the Rock of Ilyas, be forewarned - the punishments for such a crime are either imprisonment or pain of death. Do you acknowledge this as an affirmation of the Church's jurisdiction?"

"I do," replied Father Kord.

"Brother Kord, you may proceed." The prothonotary sat in his chair.

Father Kord removed his right hand from his breast and placed it on the railing before him. "Your Eminence and most holy members of the Council, I have traveled to Arshapel bearing news of the recent, untimely death of Baron Bror Drugen of Mytoria, and of the ascendancy of his brother, Hothar Drugen, to the Barony of Mytoria. Hothar's ascendancy has created great tension among the neighboring baronies."

Muffled voices broke out amongst the consistory's priests. Father Kord waited for their voices to subside. "His Holiness, High Priest Jurgan of Tonenbyrg, asks that the death of Baron Drugen be investigated by the Holy Tower. He feels it would enhance our reputation, and we would be seen as a moderating presence in a notoriously lawless region."

High Priest Ordbert, the Holy Exchequer, who sat upon the Archpriest's left, said, "Investigations cost money, a lot of money. Why should we not accept the death of the baron as a fact and accept the ascendancy of his brother?"

Father Kord kept a hand upon the gold railing, supporting his portly body. "Holiness, Baron Bror was a strong and healthy man. He was only twenty-five years of age. It is not natural for a man like him to simply die in his sleep. Besides that, Bror had no heirs and was not married, and Hothar expediently seized the throne for himself." Father Kord cocked his head. "The entire situation seems questionable."

High Priest Gaetan, the Holy Legate Plenipotentiary, sitting to the right of the Archpriest, interrupted Father Kord. His dry, flat voice issued from his indifferent face. "Members of the council and the consistory, I am in receipt of information concerning the recent political events in Mytoria, which will make an investigation there impractical and dangerous."

Again, muffled voices broke the silence of the conclave. The Chief Prothonotary banged his gavel on the table and called for order. The voices slowly died down.

Gaetan went on. "Baron Hothar is a devote follower of the Faith who has sworn fealty to Her Majesty, Queen Abella Fortyr of Fringia."

A loud, astonished gasp rose from the audience and from the members of the Holy Council, except Archpriest Ignator, who did not react to the announcement. Gaetan held up his hands, motioning for silence. "I spoke with the queen this morning about the baron's death, and I asked her what position Fringia may take. Her Majesty reacted to Hothar's sworn oath and the news of his ascendancy with great interest. She said she would discuss with her court advisers about what type of support she will send to her oath-sworn ally."

High Priestess Solayne, the Holy Steward, whose place was to the right of Gaetan, gave him a contemptuous look. "Brother Gaetan, your audacity knows no boundaries." She switched her attention to Ignator and softened her expression. "Your Eminence, the queen is not a member of the council, nor a member of the clergy. Brother Gaetan is steering us into this situation on the side of Fringia. He should have consulted with us before speaking with her."

Ignator looked down upon her from his higher seat. "I disagree, Sister Solayne. As my plenipotentiary, I feel Brother Gaetan acts within the bounds of his office. Hothar Drugen is a religious man." Gaetan gave Ignator a nod. "However, I do have a question for the good priest." Father Kord's eyes widened as he listened to the Voice of Ghyo's Church. "Why should the Holy Council investigate the death of a man who never showed support for the policies of the Church?"

Father Kord frowned. "Most Holy, Barons Otogard and Mandal are gathering swords to march against Mytoria. They had alliances with Bror, which kept the peace, and they wish to punish Hothar, for they believe he is responsible for Bror's death. But High Priest Jurgan fears the barons may defeat Hothar in battle and carve up his lands for themselves, which is a disturbing possibility. Otogard is a faithful follower of Ilyas's teachings, but Mandal is not. Baron Mandal is already powerful and he has designs on crowning himself as a king. His Holiness counsels that it would be prudent for the Church not to take sides in this conflict, but to send neutral emissaries to negotiate a settlement." The old priest breathed heavily, as he paused to catch his breath. "Of course, the settlement will be suited to our liking. For the good of Imbria, a war in the Mytor Pass must be avoided. And if Hothar is guilty of murder, that issue must be dealt with for the good of all."

"Not only the flock of Imbria would be affected," High Priestess Kalantha, the Holy Keeper of Artifacts, interjected from her seat on the bottom tier opposite Solayne. "A war in the Mytor Pass could easily involve Fringia. Much trade moves along its road."

"Fringia's involvement is foregone," High Priestess Solayne said. "Queen Abella has accepted Hothar's offer of fealty, and should the other barons press their issues, there will certainly be fighting. And thanks to Brother Gaetan, Church money and influence will support another war."

A lull came over the Holy Council. Only the scratching pens of the three prothonotaries could be heard.

Ignator broke the silence. "Father Kord, the council must discuss this matter. You may not return to Tonenbyrg until we have reached a decision."

Father Kord bowed graciously and stepped down from the rock. A priest drew back the curtains and Father Kord disappeared from sight.

High Priestess Raysa, a member of the Holy Consistory, rose from her seat and asked to address the council. She swept her eyes across the members of the conclave. "Your Eminence, it is clear that Brother Gaetan wishes to immerse the Holy Council into this quagmire in Northern Imbria. But Imbria is not Soriazar. There is no army of heathens to fight in Imbria. I understand it is the wish of this council to reinstate the Faith to its former greatness, but to do so by *any* means, including war and violence, is a stain not easily washed away."

A roar of approval rose from half of the high priests of the Holy Consistory. Raysa's comments won a smile from Sisters Solayne and Kalantha.

A shift in Gaetan's posture was the only sign of his reaction to Raysa's comments. His face remained indifferent, though his stare cut through her like an invisible knife. "Young Sister Raysa forgets that Queen Abella is a staunch supporter of the Church. Sister Raysa knows as well as everyone here, that the barons of Northern Imbria would like nothing more than to see the removal of the moral force of His Church from their lustful lives."

He rose from his chair and descended the dais. He stood behind the prothonotaries' table. "There *is* a pious baron ruling in the Mytor Pass, that vital artery of communication and commerce, and he is being threatened by forces hostile to him, because of his faith in Ghyo's Church." Gaetan thrust out his hand and pointed at the Rock of Ilyas. "I say we should – no, we must – support Queen Abella, should she send soldiers to Mytoria."

The other half of the consistory applauded as Gaetan returned to his seat. The Chief Prothonotary's gavel banged repeatedly.

When the sanctum quieted, Kalantha took another turn at speaking. "Once again, Brother Gaetan has delivered a convincing sounding speech." She smiled at the members of the consistory. "In fact, I am ready to don a sword and march off to save Imbria, myself. But have we forgotten the troubles with the Semotecs and the Iduin?"

Astonished gasps rose from the audience, accompanied by muted chuckling and whispering. Kalantha rose to her feet and threw back her shoulders. "I pose this question. How can His Church possibly fund another military expedition? The excursion to Soriazar has already ransacked the coffers of the Exchequer."

"And it has diluted the reserves of the knights," a voice interrupted the high priestess. It was Krotos, Grand Master of the Order of Ilyas.

"Master Krotos, please speak if you have anything to add," Kalantha said. She nodded to him and returned to her seat.

"I do, Holiness." Krotos rose from his place amongst the Holy Consistory. He wore a tight-fitting black tunic, trimmed with gold threadwork; his head was shaved to the scalp. "There is no question that my knights and I are ready and willing to serve His Church. But I feel I would be derelict if I did not inform the council of this one fact. Only two hundred knights remain of the five hundred I keep in Arshapel. Southern Cheltabria, Kheldune, and Imbria have already sent what knights they can spare, and those are marching toward Soriazar." Krotos then faced the Holy Council. "Your Eminence, I have little to offer to a campaign in Mytoria, without endangering the churches and property I am charged with protecting." He straightened his tunic and sat.

High Priest Ordbert answered Krotos's challenge. "The situation in Mytoria is as noble a cause as the one in Soriazar. Brother Gaetan has already received concessions from Queen Abella, should Hothar emerge victorious. In exchange for having the Knights of Ilyas patrol the Mytor Pass, the Church will be allowed to collect tolls from the caravans that traverse it. The war will pay for itself, and the Church will be seen as the protector of commerce and of peace. I move we support any Fringian decision to assist Mytoria, by auctioning some of the articles from the vast piles of treasure being hoarded by Sister Kalantha. Our gold pieces will be our soldiers."

Kalantha stood and faced Ordbert. "How can it possibly be suggested that we auction off the artifacts in my care? Those items have spiritual, artistic, and historical value. Those artifacts define the very nature of His Church. Some of them are enchanted, but we have no way of knowing. So much of the ancient arts of enchanting and conjuring are lost to us. No, Brother, it is not the responsibility of *my* office to fill the coffers of the Exchequer." She turned toward the Holy Consistory. "I say Brother Ordbert's suggestion is a sign that says we are overreaching ourselves."

Solayne rose to her feet. "I concur. Have we forgotten the ominous signs of the return of the Syts? Our properties in Northwestern Fringia and the lives of thousands of His followers will soon be threatened. If we send aid and knights to Imbria, we will have little left to defend against them."

Silence descended over the enclosure. No one else asked to address the council. The prothonotaries scratched their pens to their papers. They dabbed at the sweat on their foreheads, which darkened the sleeves of their white tunics.

At last Archpriest Ignator spoke. "The Holy Council will vote upon the issue of Mytoria at a later time to be determined by me. If there are no other issues to bring forth, I will adjourn this session."

High Priestess Solayne spoke up. "Your Eminence, there is one last matter I wish to address today. I would like to question Brother Gaetan about a heretic in Northern Cheltabria."

A mass of whispering filled the air. Gaetan looked down his nose at Solayne, sitting beneath him to his right. His face was blank, but the corner of his mouth curled.

"Brother Gaetan," Ignator said. "Please speak to us of this. I have not heard of this either."

Gaetan sighed. He looked up at Ignator. "Most Holy, over a week ago I received word from Sister Jurdana of Fallheim. There are rumors of a priest reviving the Faith among the villages of Northern Cheltabria."

The members of consistory again filled the enclosure with whispering. Archpriest Ignator shifted in his seat and leaned toward Gaetan. The prothonotaries ceased writing, but only for a moment. Solayne smiled slightly.

"I was not aware of any missions sent to that most frigid region of Iningia," said Ignator.

"Eminence, we have sent no missions to the Northern Valley," Gaetan said.

"Then who could possibly be spreading the Faith?"

"Some miscreant, or rogue priest. I have ordered Sister Jurdana to investigate the rumors."

"Do we know the name of this person?" Ignator asked.

Gaetan quietly cleared his throat. "Your Eminence, I was awaiting for more credible information. As I said, it is only a rumor, and I did not wish for it to be a distraction to the larger issues facing the Church." Gaetan's eyes moved across the dozens of faces fixed upon him. "His name is Orius Candell. There is no record in the Holy Tower of a priest by that name."

"Brother Gaetan," Solayne said. "Should this Orius Candell turn out to be a priest, spreading the Faith is not heresy. What makes him a heretic?"

There was a pause before Gaetan answered. "You are correct, Sister Solayne. But it *is* heresy to be a priest and to rule at the same time. This Orius Candell is said to be gathering warriors, and he claims to hold the title of Chief of the Northern Valley."

The Holy Council and the Consistory sat in silence for nearly a minute, until the roar of dozens of voices ripped apart the silence.

# Chapter 13

## The Past Haunts No More
### 11 Janoban, 229 A.G.S.

The sun reddened as it descended behind the peaks of the Blancuros, casting ragged shadows across the Gudor Valley. Its departure would bring a welcome relief from the day's heat. The fieldwork was complete, and families in the countryside settled down for the evening. But inside the walls of Golandar, the streets remained alive. Nightfall did not bring respite from the noise and bustle. The pace on the streets did not slacken. Shopping, working, and business dealings gave way to eating, drinking, and gathering with friends and family. Strains of music filled the air as troubadours, minstrels, and balladeers commenced their performances in the inns and taverns. Later, drinking songs would become more frequent, as the crowds became drunk and boisterous. Near the docks, the brothels would grow busier as the shadows darkened. The City Guard would be out in force, and Golandar's jails would be packed by dawn and half-empty by noon, as the magistrates branded the thieves and released the drunks and rabble-rousers. It was an ordinary night in the city, despite the troubles facing the nation, and the people lived it in the traditional Azari manner – live for the day.

Rodrigo stood atop the Alcazar's western tower. His perch was five hundred feet above the valley floor. With his eyes, he followed the northerly course of the Gudor River, which resembled a fat brown snake. To the east, the half-moon hung just above the Yunar Mountains, and one by one, stars flickered into life. In the northern sky, the star Janoban had passed halfway through its calendar cycle. To the west of Janoban, Gastus, the first star of autumn, approached the spot where the new month would begin in nine days.

Beside Rodrigo stood a metallic pole with a small hoop fixed to the top of it, set into the stone of the tower's roof. Astronomers used it to plot the position of the Calendar Stars. A precisely crafted pole existed for each of the eighteen months of the year. At midnight of the first day of each month, the new star would pass through the center of the circle. Rodrigo's astronomers would record the event's passing, ensuring the accurate passage of time, which regulated the flow of information and trade between nations.

Beltram accompanied Rodrigo. Between them stood a small wooden table, with a crystal flagon of brandy and three glasses on it. A lantern on the parapet lit the area around them.

Rodrigo poured brandy into two of the glasses. He handed one to Beltram. "Will you drink with me, old friend?"

"You flatter me, sire," said Beltram. "I am but a humble servant. I should be pouring for you." Music and laughter drifted up from the streets below.

A thin smile came to Rodrigo's lips. "Pouring a drink for a friend is not service."

Beltram raised his glass. "May you rule another thirty years." He sipped the fiery liquid.

"Thank you, senyor, but I will be happy if I survive this year." *Considering Serophia's proposals.* "Tell me, should I accept the gift of money from the Church?"

Beltram took another sip of brandy. He shook his head. "No. But I cannot see how we can refuse them."

"You waver in your counsel. One hundred thousand gold pieces is a substantial sum of money."

"Under their terms, accepting the money acknowledges the Church as being equal to your Majesty," Beltram said. "They will use any success in the campaign as an affirmation of their power and a testament to our weakness. I can already hear the Holy Council crowing about their victory against the heathens and how we needed assistance in defending our borders and how they saved us." Beltram exhaled and ran his hand through his gray hair. "But if you refuse them, they will certainly use knowledge of your first wife against you. They will soil your name and bring disgrace to your crown. It could mean civil war here at home."

Bitter memories of his first marriage returned to Rodrigo. The marriage had lasted scarcely a year before he had ended it and took Khalia for his bride. At the time, he had been embroiled in the war with Kheldune, and Khalia's father was the powerful Duke of Ariandor, with thousands of soldiers at his disposal.

Rodrigo looked into his glass and swirled his brandy. His first marriage had broken with tradition. His wife had been Damiana, the High Priestess of Golandar, whom he had loved deeply and married against his councilors' advice. And she had married Rodrigo against the canons of Ghyo's Church. Azari tradition stated that the monarch should marry someone of Sori blood, to symbolize the bond between the Sori and Azari people, forged when the country was united after driving out the Muorii from western Soriazar. And Church canon forbade the clergy from holding temporal titles, which governed the earthly affairs of people.

Rodrigo considered the end of his first marriage the greatest mistake of his life, and it saddened him when the memories surfaced. His wife had disappeared soon after the marriage's annulment, and it was rumored the jealous Khalia expedited Damiana's removal from her seat in the temple of Golandar.

"If we fail," Rodrigo told Beltram, "the blame will rest on our shoulders. The Holy Tower will talk of how we squandered their resources and misused their troops. Ghyo's Church has little to lose and everything to gain by aiding us, and we have much to gain, but win or lose, what will be the cost to our prestige?"

Rodrigo looked down upon the city. Shadows enveloped the streets. Lights from lanterns carried by people danced about the streets like fireflies. Rodrigo sipped his brandy. "One thing disturbs me about the offer. They are sending five hundred and fifty Black Hands into the fight. I did not know they had so many to spare. They would not send them all, would they?"

"There are plans unfolding which we cannot see," said Beltram. "It appears the Holy Council is genuinely concerned with the success of our campaign against the Semotecs, but their conditions about who will command are ludicrous."

"The offer *is* generous," Rodrigo said, "but the conditions are unacceptable. Why would they make an offer like that to us?"

Beltram finished his brandy and set the glass down with a sharp thud. "Sire, the Holy Council is desperate. They seek power and glory. They see the situation with the Semotecs as an opportunity to enhance their reputation." His pause was conspicuous. "Your first wife is the one secret the Church and we have guarded best, and they must surely know of your wife's location and of the child's - if one exists. That is why they gave us such a preposterous offer. That is why we cannot refuse them. As in the past, we must find some way to deal with them."

"No! No more deals!" Rodrigo glanced at the pair of Eagle Guards standing beside the stairs and lowered his voice. "The rumor of the child has never been proven. Damiana disappeared shortly after returning to Arshapel. If they found her, we would have heard something, especially if there was a child born of our union. The child would be my heir. Something like that causes tongues to waggle. No, they would have already used my legitimate firstborn against me."

Rodrigo set his glass down and fixed his dark eyes on Beltram. "I am tired of giving into them. I allowed them to place a Fringian spy upon the High Priest's throne in Golandar. I said yes to Khalia and allowed my daughter to take the Trial of Ghyo, who they now use against me. Beltram, we shall fight our enemies alone, and we shall deal with whatever nightmares the Church dredges up from the past." He moved closer, placed a hand on Beltram's elbow, and hissed into his ear. "And if they blackmail us, I will expel their priests and appoint others to their places." His thoughts flashed to Todu's new army.

Beltram's eyes widened and he jerked back his head. "Sire, the other nations will not tolerate an attack against the Church."

"The other nations have as many issues, or more, with the Church as we do."

"But our people love the Church."

"The Azari people love their country more than they love their Church."

One of the guards by the stairwell spoke. "Your Majesty - Duke Borto Camidor."

Borto emerged from the stairs and strolled to where Rodrigo and Beltram stood. He bowed deeply. "Your Majesty, please forgive me for coming so late."

"Rise, Borto," Rodrigo said. "What has kept you from seeing your king?"

Borto straightened. His eyes found the flagon, but he quickly averted them to Rodrigo. "Your Majesty, I finished my business by early afternoon and was on my way to the Alcazar, when I received word from one of my people, who wished to relay something urgent to me. So I met with the man, and he took me to a whorehouse near the docks."

"Get on with it Borto," Rodrigo said with impatience.

Borto placed his arms behind his back. "He took me upstairs to speak to the prostitute he had rented this morning, who had slept with one of my competitors last evening. While my man was conducting *his* business, he asked the girl how was *her* business. If Your Majesty follows me." Rodrigo rolled his eyes and bid Borto continue. "She then spoke to me of what my competitor bragged about to her. It seems the man is scheming against Your Majesty."

Rodrigo's eyes had grown heavy listening to Borto, but they suddenly perked up. "What type of plot?"

"The prostitute knew nothing specific," said Borto. "She simply said that the merchant was very drunk and was ranting about His Majesty's latest decree, concerning prices and commerce, etcetera. He also told the girl that the king would regret his policies and would pay for his tyranny."

Rodrigo raised a hand to his forehead and massaged his temple. "Beltram, pour our fine duke a drink." He turned and placed his hands on the parapet. A sliver of sunlight still shone over the tops of the Blancuros. "Borto, who was this other merchant?"

"It was Prosporo," Borto said, as Beltram handed him a glass. "He frequents that particular whorehouse; the girl is his favorite lay. I did ask her to work harder next time she slept with him. I also paid her well and threatened her great bodily harm if she dared speak of our meeting."

"Spying is such nasty business," said Beltram. "How does His Majesty wish to deal with the traitor?"

Rodrigo did not answer. He faced westward and watched the sun disappear. Points of light appeared in the windows of the manors and farmhouses on the valley's western side. He stood motionless for several minutes, pondering different courses of action and their possible consequences. When he turned to face Beltram and Borto, he was somber. "We will do nothing." Beltram and Borto glanced at each other. "I do not want Prosporo Rabago arrested. There are others involved, and I do not want the rats to scatter. When I make my move, I want them all. You have done well, Duke Borto. I will pay you handsomely for this information."

Beltram bowed, acknowledging Rodrigo's wishes, and Borto mirrored him.

"Please, sire," said Borto. "I cannot accept compensation for this. My payment will come when my competitors are out of the way." He kneaded his hands together and a wicked smile appeared on his lips. "I will be a *very* rich man."

"You are already a rich man," Rodrigo said. "You will be a richer man."

Borto laughed heartily, but quickly stifled it. "Sire, I have two men watching the whorehouse, one in the front and the other in back. I will let Your Majesty know if we learn anything else." He downed his brandy in one gulp.

Borto's efficiency impressed Rodrigo. He maintained an extensive network of informants and spies around the city and inside other cities. He ruthlessly used his position as duke to maintain an edge over the other merchant houses.

"Tell your people to be discreet," said Rodrigo. "I want no mistakes. The conspirators must not know we are on to them. You are dismissed."

Borto set his glass upon the table, bowed at the waist, and descended the stairs.

When Borto was out of sight, Rodrigo motioned Beltram to come nearer. "Summon Rufina. I have some special work for the Trackers."

"As you command, sire."

Rodrigo turned his back on Beltram and peered over the parapet at the city. "I feel like getting more fresh air. We are finished. Send word when the princess arrives."

"Yes, sire." Beltram bowed and left.

A gilded coach stopped in front of the Temple of Ghyo. It arrived promptly at sunset. The driver stepped down from his seat and opened the door. Drucilla raised her white dress and climbed the little ladder fixed to the coach's bottom. Inside, the red velvet cushions drew her into their softness. Sitting in the coach brought back memories from before she was sent to live and study in the temple. And they were sad memories. As a priestess, she did not have the amenities of her royal status.

Drucilla fought back a tear and scolded herself for being sentimental. She was an ordained member of the clergy and she wielded the Gift. She had become much more than a princess. She was not to be a political tool to be used by her father. She would not be married to some Muori noble who would never truly love her. But she did miss dining upon sumptuous foods and having clothes of the finest silks, damasks, and black-works. There were no rubies, diamonds, sapphires, or emeralds adorning her ears, neck, and fingers. There were no handsome young gentlemen waiting for the next dance. There were only books, studying, meetings, training, and prayers.

The coach hit a rough spot in the street. The jolt woke Drucilla from her daydream. People crowded the street, entering and exiting shops and taverns. The air was still heavy from the heat of the day and filled with the smells of evening meals, mixed with the stench of manure and garbage in the streets.

Drucilla returned to her thoughts. She recalled the day her mother told her she had selected her to attend the Ecclesiastical School. Drucilla remembered how she had spent that night crying, because she would not attend the university at Ariandor, like her siblings and her parents. A life with the Church had no appeal to a ten-year old, and at that time, she had been unable to understand the stakes involved. She then recalled the day when Khalia explained the importance of having a member of the Royal Family in the clergy, and how proud it would make her father if she passed the Trial of Ghyo, but that turned out to be false.

Drucilla let go of her thoughts as the coach began its slow ascent up the Alcazar's winding road. Iron braziers illuminated the path, marking its edge. Through the coach's window, she watched the vista of dark cobblestone streets, running between the rows of houses and shops and lit at random by yellow glows radiating from windows. People in the streets passed from light to shadow to light, like ghosts.

The coach passed through the Alcazar's gates and halted in the courtyard by the stables. A female servant waited to take her through the gardens. The servant held a lantern as she led the way along the brick paths to the palace. She took Drucilla to Khalia's parlor at the end of the corridor that formed the royal family's private chambers.

Khalia had spent lavishly on the decorations for her parlor. The finest Sori craftsmen from Ariandor had completed the work. A prismatic Muori carpet, displaying intricate, repetitive floral patterns, dominated the parlor's center. Two settees and a low, ornate wooden table were situated atop the carpet. Slender, gray-veined marble columns, connected by horseshoe arches, formed a cordon around the settees. Repetitive, bas-relief floral moldings decorated the walls.

Khalia sat on the forest-green settee that faced the large paintings of her father and mother mounted on the left-hand wall. Her hands rested in her lap. A silver tea set sat atop the table, wisps of steam rising from its spout. Khalia wore a deep blue velvet dress and her long red hair was tied into a complicated braid. A gold tiara crowned her head, with a massive sapphire fixed to the front of it.

As the door opened, Khalia rose and embraced Drucilla. She released her hug, but held onto Drucilla's shoulders and looked into her eyes. Drucilla had Khalia's green eyes and face, the exception being her black hair, an Azari trait from her father's side.

"Mother, why have you summoned me here, alone?" Drucilla asked.

Khalia seemed taken aback. "Because I wish to spend time with a daughter whom I have seldom seen in the past decade. Please sit." Drucilla chose the opposite settee. "You used to sit next to me when we had tea," Khalia said. "Now you take an opposing seat."

"I am sorry, Mother, but father has not invited me here to be social. He wants something. I guess I chose this seat, because I no longer feel comfortable in the palace."

Khalia sighed. "I know you have never forgiven me for sending you through such a rigorous school. But I still hold hope in my heart that I will receive your forgiveness." She poured tea for them.

Drucilla picked up a teacup and sipped the hot brew. The minty flavor made her tongue tingle. *She poured for me – she wants something too. There are no servants here.* "Mother, that no longer has significance in my life. Ghyo's power fills my heart with compassion. Forgiveness is my nature. Any anger I held for you was washed away upon the day of my Ordainment. So, I ask again. What does father want?"

"Your father has not confided in me his reasons for asking you to dinner."

Drucilla felt embarrassed by her harsh questioning. Her mother deserved respect, but something told her she was not being honest. Khalia was known for her shrewdness. Drucilla's thoughts jumped to the meeting between Serophia and Rodrigo. *The Church is powerful and influential, and kings come calling when they need assistance. Maybe the same applies to queens.*

"Thank you," Drucilla said raising her teacup. "What is bothering you, mother? I see restlessness in your eyes."

Khalia smiled wanly. "Your training has made you perceptive. I must be getting old and can no longer remain impassive. Do you enjoy the position you hold in the Church?"

Drucilla shrugged. The directness of the question surprised her a little. Khalia had to know the answer. "Yes, I find the work interesting. I am learning much about how the world works. Thank you for arranging to have me placed in the Legate's Office."

"Excellent, I am happy for you. Every person needs to feel their occupation is of value and substance. Any other position is beneath your standing."

"I...would have been pleased to hold any position in His Church. Arrogance is not becoming for a priestess."

"No, but you were a princess before becoming a priestess," Khalia said. "And you are still a member of the Mendio family."

Her mother's attitude perturbed her. It had been Khalia's decision to send Drucilla to study at the temple, and receiving the Gift was not Drucilla's doing. She was one of the rare people pious enough to wield the Gift. She now owed loyalty to the Church, and she had sworn an oath, which superseded temporal oaths, including any that she owed her family.

"Mother, I find it awkward to listen to you remind me of my heritage. How could I possibly forget that?"

"I do not doubt you have forgotten," said Khalia. "It seems you have chosen to ignore it."

"When I received the Gift, the decision was made for me."

Khalia chuckled and covered her mouth with her hand. "*Ojala!* You must pardon me." She looked at Drucilla and shook her head.

Drucilla became angry. "Mother, I am a priestess and a member of the Holy Legation. I do not have to remain here and listen to your condescending remarks."

Khalia regained her composure. "My dear, you have much to learn. Already, I see you are fast becoming a pawn of the Church. Your loyalty to the Creator is something no one will ever question. You are, and will always be, revered for that."

Khalia stood and sat beside Drucilla, who looked away. Khalia grabbed Drucilla's chin, and with a gentle pull, turned her head until their eyes met. Drucilla's jaw was clenched. Her eyes glistened with tears.

"What people *will* and *do* question," Khalia said, "is blind loyalty to an institution which is a creation of humankind."

Khalia's blasphemy shocked her. Was she not the one who had insisted on a religious education? "That...that is a lie," said Drucilla. "The Creator Himself guided Ilyas during his wanderings. Ilyas established the Faith according to Ghyo's instructions. The Creator spoke to him."

Khalia released her hold of Drucilla's chin. "That is true, except Ghyo did not invent the Church. There is a difference between the two, which is certainly a matter of opinion, but it happens to be the opinion of this family." Khalia rose and walked to the portrait of her father. "The Church often strays far from the ideals preached by Ilyas. They immerse themselves in the affairs of nations. They use their gold to assert their policies. Their priests are not allowed to use violence, but still they fund wars. A few centuries ago, they invented the Black Hand to do their dirty work." Khalia's pause was abrupt. "What is your opinion on those facts?"

"It is for survival," answered Drucilla. "The Church struggles to elude the grasp of greedy monarchs."

Khalia waved her hand. "Let us no longer argue. I wish to get to my point."

"Please do so," Drucilla said. The conversation was draining her strength, and she had already completed a busy day.

"I do not wish for you to forsake your vows to the *Creator*." Khalia's emphasis on the last word was obvious. "I want you to remember your duty to your family – a royal family."

Drucilla turned her head from her mother, but gave her a sideways glance as she did.

Khalia continued. "The Church is the keeper of many secrets, especially the damaging kind. You are in an excellent position to keep your family informed of things pertaining to your country. Try not to think only of our welfare, because our welfare is the welfare of the Azari people."

The servant's knock ended the conversation. Rodrigo awaited them.

# Chapter 14

## Myths Betrayed
### 9–11 Janoban, 229 A.G.S.

Tarik kept his good arm on the chariot's railing. He watched the forests of chestnuts, black gums, and oaks whirl by in a green blur. The wheels clattered against the cobblestone road. Bone-numbing vibrations reverberated though his legs and up to his aching shoulder. Tarik's gelding trotted behind them, tied to a tether.

"I do not care if this is faster," Tarik said in Tradespeak. "This rattling is unbearable."

"Keep your knees bent a little," Murius said. The horsehair of his helmet fluttered in the wind. He paced the horses. Tarik could tell Murius had made the journey several times.

"I fear I will not be in a proper condition to meet with the Senate," Tarik said.

"I promise, you will have a hot meal and a soft bed tonight," said Murius. "I will get you to Roda in fine shape."

When Tarik arose the next morning, he found Murius waiting for him in front of the inn. The horses were frisky from their oats. Murius was blowing kisses to a young woman who waved goodbye to him from a window.

"I love traveling to the capital," Murius said. "I must thank my father when I return."

Another woman appeared in the window and flung open her shawl. She cupped her large breasts. "I will retire these until you return to me, foreigner," she said in Iduin. Murius interpreted for Tarik, who rolled his eyes.

"I thought you were exhausted last night." Murius grinned.

"I found the motivation," Tarik answered.

Murius laughed and shook his head. His cropped black hair contrasted with his green eyes and the light complexion of his shaven face. Tarik thought Murius looked every bit the soldier he was. His lean, hard body reflected rigorous training. Murius's shining cuirass of banded metal completed the picture.

Tarik wore his green tunic and breeches. During the night, the mud of the Iluta Pass had been scrubbed from his clothing. His sword dangled from his hip at the end of his baldric. A morion covered his head.

The two of them grew accustomed to each other's company. Their talking passed away the hours spent on the road. They discovered they had similar interests - hunting, riding, and womanizing - though Tarik explained he had little time to enjoy those pleasures, and he did not speak of Aida. His feelings for the innkeeper's daughter had stopped him. He did not think it was love, but he knew his feelings ran deeper than lust.

Murius asked many questions about Tarik's life and adventures, but it seemed that his real interest lay elsewhere. Tarik sensed Murius was working his way toward something specific. After the first day, it was obvious Cuentis had instructed Murius to question Tarik about the message.

Tarik let Murius spend three days coming up with different ways of asking the same question, but Murius could not pry open a crack in Tarik's defenses. Tarik would only say he was to personally hand the letter to the Presiding Senator of Idu and knew nothing of the contents.

But Tarik decided he liked Murius. He admired the younger man's loyalty and dedication to his duty, though he did not believe he had an equal knowledge of politics and worldly affairs. Not that Tarik knew everything, but being a Royal Messenger, and the third son of the Marquis of Spandel, gave him a rare insight into the dealings of royalty. Tarik enjoyed being privy to things most people were not, but he also realized that having such knowledge brought about dangers most people would never face in their lifetimes.

The chariot wheels clattered against the road. Tarik could see for miles across the central plains of Idu. Its wide, undulating spaces were nearly devoid of trees. Before the War of the Schism, the central plain had been the breadbasket of the imperial lands south of the Buleyn Mountains. The famous black Iduin soil was bountiful, and Tarik saw the truth in the stories that Idu seldom knew starvation.

At one point, Murius had to pull the chariot off the road to allow an entire legion to march past them in the opposite direction. For hours, Tarik watched thousands of infantry, wagons, ballistae, catapults, and camp followers move westward.

The road continued for miles. Through the glare of the noon sun, Tarik could just see how the road skirted the northern end of a large hill-mass, which rose sharply from the plains. An immense field of barley grew to the left of the road, rolling with the wind like the waves of the sea. Long rows of grapevines grew on the right, their fruits ripening as the summer wore on. Tarik thought it nearly impossible to harvest all of the produce before each winter. But he suddenly remembered why the Iduin were able to harvest so much produce - Bondage.

The hill loomed larger and larger. It was miles in length, running north to south and topped by three peaks. Its western draws and spurs were covered with olive trees, planted in grid-like patterns.

Idu was famous for its paved roads, a marvel of engineering made of cobblestones and flagstones. Seeing them and traveling them piqued Tarik's excitement about catching his first glimpse of the mighty capital of Idu. The traffic on the road had become heavier. Murius had to weave around merchant wagons loaded with goods. The horses' hooves clattered rhythmically against the road, vibrations rattled the chariot. They skirted the hill's northern face, and as they passed to the eastern side, the road straightened and descended into the Roda Valley.

The valley floor was filled with fields of cotton and wheat. To the north were long rows of almond trees, stretching two miles to the feet of the large hill, which formed the valley's northern edge. To the east, the sprawling city of Roda lay behind a wall of sandstone blocks.

The road led to Roda's northwest gate. Tarik could only see the city's western portion. The rest was blocked by a hill, crammed with dingy looking apartments, all of which leaned at odd angles. His first sight of Roda dashed all the images he had formed in his mind, from the tales he had heard since his childhood. There was no gleaming capital to be seen. There was only squalor looking no better than the poorest sections of Spandel.

The road's last five miles ran between rows of oak trees. Statues stood beside every tenth tree. They were lifelike renderings of heroic figures in armor, of athletes throwing javelins, of mythical beasts, snarling and clawing at the air, and of Iduin statesman, dressed in togas, with one arm stretched toward the travelers on the road.

"This promenade is beautiful," said Tarik. But he wrinkled his nose as they passed through the stench of decaying bodies. "Ugh! But that smell spoils the beauty of it."

Murius pointed toward the north at the many white marble mausoleums, adorned with statues and columns. "The Rodii house their dead over there. The mausoleums belong to the richest families of Roda. The cremated remains of their dead are housed inside. But the stench comes from the many openings in the southern slope of that hill."

"Are those catacombs for the common citizens?" Tarik asked.

"Yes," Murius told him. "Cremation is a sign of wealth."

Tarik and Murius emerged from the shade of the oak trees within extreme bowshot of the city walls. Merchant tents were pitched in the untilled fields surrounding Roda's walls, forming a colorful canvas city, which bustled with a carnival-like activity.

Roda sprawled out for miles to either side of the road. As they stopped at the gate, Murius showed his signet ring to the guards, who quickly waved him through. They were more interested in monitoring the merchants and civilians entering and exiting the city. Once Tarik and Murius were inside the walls, a noxious mixture of manure, garbage, sweating bodies, roasting meats, and baking bread greeted them. The road curved to the right and followed the course of the city's western wall. The street was lined with one and two-story shops all of kinds, constructed from wood and sun-baked mud bricks. Well and poorly dressed merchants, sweating artisans, shoppers, and scores of dirty children darted in and out of the shops and weaved through the crammed street.

The people made way for the chariot. As they did, their eyes fixed upon the stranger with the morion on his head, riding beside the army officer. Tarik gazed down innumerable alleys and narrow side streets. Most of them were veiled in the shadows and seemed like dangerous places to be, even during daylight. As they rode along, Tarik caught bits of conversations in Tradespeak, but other than that, the rest of the talk was babble to him.

They rode for a mile until they reached a large intersection. There the street ran a little ways further, until it ended at Roda's southeastern gate, but the east fork led to the Roda River and the rest of the city. Murius turned that way, and it was not long before Tarik glimpsed the Senate building's gleaming white marble, which rose above the rooftops to the northeast. More of the Capitol came into view the closer they got to the river. Tarik stared in wonder as the splendors of legendary Roda unfolded before his eyes. To the east, he saw how the Rodii had leveled off a hill to accommodate the manses of the rich. The Temple of Ghyo stood to the north of the Capitol's hill, atop the smallest of the city's five hills. It did not stand as high as the temple in Golandar, but its clean white walls and spires were nonetheless breathtaking. He reminded himself he must pray there before he left for home.

They reached the southern bridge, spanning the Roda River. Running away to the north, a wide street ran alongside each bank. The conditions of the buildings on the opposing banks of the river emphasized the city's dichotomy. They were night and day, black and white, divided by the river's endless, slow current.

Tarik's awed expression brought a smile to Murius's lips as he drove the chariot and the tethered gelding forward. They crossed the bridge and followed the road along the opposite bank, until they turned up the street leading to the top of the Capitol's hill.

They halted near the bottom of the steps to the Senate building. A man dressed in a plain white toga descended the stairs and took hold of the reins. Murius bid Tarik to follow and they marched up to the entrance, passing between two of the eight columns of the building's colonnade. Inside, a gray-haired secretary, wearing a white toga, sat behind a table covered with papers and an inkwell. Two soldiers wearing banded metal cuirasses flanked the table. Behind them, the doors to the Senate chamber stood open. Through the doors, a balding senator adjusted his gold trimmed toga as he spoke to the Senate. His voice echoed off the polished marble floor and walls.

Murius introduced himself in Tradespeak. The secretary glanced up from his work, unimpressed. "So, Murius, son of Cuentis Attalus, what business do you bring to the Illustrious Senate of Idu?"

Tarik spoke before Murius could respond. "He was my escort," he said . "I am Tarik Torenyo, Royal Messenger of the His Majesty, King Rodrigo Mendio of Soriazar. I bear a message from His Majesty addressed to the Presiding Senator of Idu."

Although Tarik did not speak loudly, his voice carried to some people nearby, waiting their turn to be called onto the Senate floor. Tarik felt their eyes upon him.

The secretary pursed his lips and checked the agenda, on which he had been working. "There will be no opportunity to present your message today. You arrived too late. The senators will be adjourning soon. You will have to wait for the morning."

Tarik frowned. From his training, he knew it was proper to respect the protocol of other cultures, but Rodrigo had been clear in his instructions. The letter was of great importance, and His Majesty said it was best to deliver it immediately. Tarik grew impatient.

"Sir, I insist I be allowed to deliver this correspondence now. I have traveled far and under great hardship." Tarik gestured to his arm. "But more important than my humble problems, His Majesty ordered me to personally hand this to the Presiding Senator upon my arrival."

The secretary leaned back in his seat. His expression had not changed. He then leaned forward and looked over the agenda again. He slowly rearranged a few papers, signed one, and then stacked them into a neat pile off to one side.

Tarik's heart thumped as his impatience turned to anger. He glanced around at the faces watching him. Each of those people held a scroll, or a bundle of papers. Tarik returned his attention to the secretary. "I carry a letter of great importance. A letter that pertains to the security of not only our nation, but yours as well."

The secretary ignored him. Tarik lost his patience. He pointed toward the open doors leading to the Senate chamber. "Do you mean to tell me the Presiding Senator allows his *doorman* to control the fate of his nation?"

The secretary looked up again. His expression was the same, but his eyes had grown cold. In the chamber, the senator who was standing in the middle of the floor stopped his speech and looked through the doors.

The secretary's nostrils flared; his face reddened. "Aristus," he said, as his eyes remained fixed upon Tarik.

A young man trotted up to the secretary, adjusting his plain toga. "You summoned me, Master Fulvio?"

"Please inform the Honorable Pavilius Bulbius that there is a messenger from the king of the Azaris here," Master Fulvio said, jerking his head toward Tarik, "bearing an urgent correspondence."

"Right away, master," Aristus answered. He walked quickly through the doors.

"For your sake, you better pray he wishes to see you," Fulvio told Tarik, nodding toward the guard standing next to the table.

A minute later Aristus returned. "The Senate bids him come forward and present himself."

Fulvio grunted, snatched a feather pen, and dipped it into an inkwell. "Wait," he said. He scratched something onto a blank sheet of paper. He then pressed a stamp into the paper's bottom. "This is your summons. Present this to the secretaries seated upon the podium."

Tarik took the paper from Fulvio and shook his head at the ridiculousness of Idu's bureaucracy. He reached inside his tunic and pulled out the leather tube containing Rodrigo's message. Murius held his sword for him, and Tarik walked around Fulvio's table and followed Aristus. Murius positioned himself beside the doorway. A few of the others who had been waiting their turn to speak to the Senate joined him there. Even Fulvio left his station to watch.

Aristus halted a few steps before the black marble podium, with milky veins running through it. Tarik did likewise. Seven secretaries sat behind the wall of the podium's lower tier. The middle secretary rose and banged a gavel, until the sounds of the senator's voices fell to a dull roar. The secretary's voice echoed across the hall in Tradespeak. "Silence, please. The Illustrious Senate of Idu shall now hear the petition of Rodrigo Mendio, Sovereign of Soriazar. His envoy, Tarik Torenyo, appears before the ruling body of Idu. Come forward, sir, so you may be seen and heard by the honorable members of this Senate, the eyes and ears of the Republic."

Silence filled the hall. Aristus motioned Tarik to approach the podium. Tarik straightened and tried to look dignified, despite having his arm in a sling. Three hundred sets of eyes followed him as he crossed the floor. There was no noise except the sound of his boots against the marble. The senators, mainly older men with balding heads or graying hair, occupied chairs on three ascending tiers, running along the rectangular hall's sides.

Tarik halted a dozen paces from the podium. He tucked the leather tube into his sling, reached up and removed his helmet, and placed it on the floor beside his feet. He then retrieved the tube from his sling. "I bear a message from His Majesty to the Presiding Senator," he announced, looking up at the man standing alone on the top level of the podium. "I was instructed by His Majesty to deliver this to you in person. I was also instructed to inform you that I know nothing of the contents of this message, and at the request of His Majesty, my distant cousin, I am not to be harmed, nor detained, in any manner."

The silence was shattered. The senators spoke amongst themselves, except Pavilius, who remained silent. The secretary banged his gavel and called for order. For a few minutes, his calls went unheeded. The commotion finally ceased when Pavilius raised his hands and motioned for silence. He looked down at Tarik, his faced etched with concern. He straightened his green-bordered toga and scanned the room. The senators waited for him to speak.

"Bring the message to me," Pavilius said. "I must state, sir, I do not like your tone, nor do I like the tone of your master. We shall have to see about these requests."

Tarik marched up to the podium and handed the tube and the summons to the secretary, who in turn handed them up to Pavilius. Hushed voices could be heard as Pavilius opened the container and broke the seal on the message. He read the parchment, which was written in Tradespeak. The color drained from is face, then it returned - red with anger.

"This is an outrage!" Pavilius roared. "Never in my political life have I ever been the recipient of such naked ambition and shameless aggression."

A shout came from the hall. "What is it? Tell us!"

"Is it war? Oh, merciful Creator, let it not be so!" another voice cried out.

"Tell us, Pavilius," a third voice echoed off the stone walls and floor.

The collapse of Pavilius's dignity worried Tarik. Sweat ran down his back.

Pavilius dramatically placed the letter atop the podium's wall. He pointed at Tarik. "Your king is no better than a common thug and a thief. He is not fit to rule a gang of Muori pirates, which is what he is."

Tarik's eyes widened and his jaw dropped. Gasps and laughter came from the senators and the crowd by the door. Pavilius's voice then rose above the confusion. "Your king wishes for you to remain in Roda until the senate has drafted its reply. We shall honor that request." He picked up the letter and pointed it at Tarik. "I, Pavilius Bulbius, presiding over the Illustrious Senate of Idu, do judge this document to be evidence of a crime about to be committed. Seize him!"

# Chapter 15

Contradiction's Icon
12 Janoben, 229 A.G.S.

Before they lit the pyres, Orius gave the dead the Obsequies of the Faith:

*The Spirit returns to the Creator, from whence it came.*
*His will returns it from the earth, may its form be a blessing to us.*
*The Cycle unbroken.*
*Life perpetual.*

When he completed the rites, he said, "Let the Oruks see we have not left. Let our smoke be a warning. Let them know we are coming." The warriors made no sound until the fires were lit.

Five pillars of smoke snaked upward and mingled above the peaks of the Borvik Pass. The pyres roared and Orius watched Alana weep inconsolably as the flames licked at Fayne's body. Lank strands of blond hair hung from her forehead and stuck to her face; a sling supported her right arm. She tried to hold back her grief, but she was not successful. It was against custom for warriors to weep for fallen comrades as the flames consumed their remains. Weeping was a private matter, but Orius noticed that the warriors quietly ignored the breach of tradition. Mathol's body accompanied Fayne's upon the pyre. The warriors from Lunevik stood close by, chanting a dirge in his honor. Pyres for the Oruks crackled nearby as well. But the Chelts had sloppily heaped their bodies and set them ablaze.

When Orius had recovered his strength after the fight, his first thoughts had been for the wounded, and he sought them out. But Fayne had bled to death, while Orius was incapacitated. The news of Fayne's death was a heavy blow to him. He had known Fayne and his other companions for nine months. They had become like the siblings he never had.

"Culley, show me his body," Orius had said.

Culley had led him through the copse of pines. Orius knelt upon seeing the body and placed a hand on Fayne's cold chest. "If I had used my strength to save life instead of taking it...it is my fault. His wound was serious, but not immediately life threatening. I raised my hand in violence and Ghyo has punished me."

Argus had followed Orius and Culley. "Don't cry for him," he had said. "Fayne knew the risks of battle. We'll later mourn for him together."

Orius then rose. "You Chelts are a hard people. Compassion is a trait within you that needs nurturing."

"Your fireballs turned the battle and saved everyone else from death," Argus had told him. He then quoted one of Orius's sermons. "Perfect only are Ghyo and the wisdom of the ways of Ilyas."

Orius's grief changed to anger. "Summon Kathair. I will know why my orders were disobeyed."

When Kathair appeared before him, the sight of his blood-encrusted face, hair, and clothing had shocked Orius. Kathair's condition spoke of the savageness of the melee. Orius checked his anger as Kathair explained his actions. *Battles are uncertain. Savor the victories,* one of Culley's maxims came back to him.

Culley then shook Kathair's hand and slapped him on the back. "You fought well."

"Father Orius," Kathair had said, humbly. "My actions killed Fayne. How can I face his family? His sister?"

Orius placed a hand on Kathair's shoulder. "Ghyo will show you a way. Open your heart to Him and the answer will appear. The you can pay Him any penance."

The sun was past its midday point when the pyres died out. The funeral rituals had taken most of the morning, but Orius felt it had been fitting to honor their fallen comrades. He gave orders for the army to eat and prepare for the march to Drenga. A Wolf Rider, sent by Chief Condin, reported that the Oruks had fled down the Drenga road and did not occupy the woods around the crossroads. But they were camped in the valley that Fayne and Alana had scouted a few days before, and hundreds more had joined the ones Kathair's party had defeated.

As the warriors formed up along the road, Culley and Orius rode a short distance away. "You surely made an impression on the Oruks, my boy," Culley said. "I wager they'll turn and run for the border when they see us again."

Orius raised an eyebrow. "Maybe, probably...but they hold Drenga and may wish to keep it. The will of the Oruks' commander holds the answer to that. Who do you believe him to be?"

"A mercenary, perhaps," Culley answered.

"Have you ever heard of a Sytish-speaking mercenary?"

"No, I haven't. But there could be someone out there who speaks that nasty sounding tongue."

"A Sytish-speaking mercenary," Orius mused. "Where could he have come from?"

"A mercenary wouldn't fight without pay. Especially when there is so much to be made in Imbria. I have never known the Oruks to use gold or any other type of currency," Culley said. "They're trade and barter folks."

"Could he be a rebellious Fringian?" Orius asked. "I could see a Fringian speaking Sytish."

"No." Culley cut him off. "It really doesn't matter who he is. What matters is, who's paying him and equipping those soldiers. Only a very wealthy person or a king can afford to raise an army. But Fringia's always at the mercy of the Oruk hordes, like Cheltabria. Arshapel wouldn't aid the Oruks."

Orius's stomach instantly tightened at a horrible thought. *It couldn't be that. That makes no sense.* "The Church has that kind of money, but why would they support disbelievers?"

"Missionary priests do learn the native tongues..."

"A Black Hand," they said in unison.

"Hopefully, the answer is in Drenga," said Orius. "The Black Rider's presence is an unforeseen obstacle. He greatly desires to conceal his identity." He shook the thoughts from his head. "It is never wise to speculate without better proof."

"If the answer is in Drenga," Culley said, "I hope it doesn't kill us."

Orius smirked, but blushed at the same time. "Your pessimism should not affect me this way. I should handle myself with more dignity. I am a priest and killing with my own hands is a sin. War itself is disruptive to the Cycling of Souls. I can only pray that our cause is just in Ghyo's eyes." *Evil breeds evil.*

"Don't fret, my boy. The Oruks forced this violence upon us. Act like a general or chief around the rest of them, but be yourself when we're alone. Command is a lonely position, but you're still a man."

Worry etched the edges of Orius's dark eyes. "I am a man ordained by the Creator. Each day my legacy wrestles with my faith. I cast aside the Tenets when it benefits me to do so, which is sinful. But I can find no other way. It is cheap to blame my enemies for my actions, but they force my hand. I either pursue my legacy, or I live in isolation until the Holy Tower finds my mother and me."

"This is a good fight," said Culley. "You use your powers to save people. Ghyo will take that into account. He knows your heart."

Culley's reassurance did little to ease Orius's mind. "Murder is evil. That is clear. But war is a hazy matter. Each side prays to the Creator for strength and guidance. And each side believes their cause is right." He turned to Culley. "But the truth of war lies with Ghyo. And there lies the mystery."

The two of them sat their mounts for a few more minutes. "What a lovely day," Orius said at last. "It is a pity to have had a funeral."

"What're you going to do with Alana?" Culley asked.

"She will return to Ragnaar, so she can recover. Her arm will not have strength for at least a week."

"It'll be difficult for her to stay out of the fighting," Culley growled. "She's young, but she understands the risks. And she wants vengeance."

"I will tell her to return in two weeks, but I will task her with gathering more warriors while she convalesces. We may need them."

"Orius, you did well yesterday, but you must always expect to lose someone each time we fight. You gained much respect from the warriors."

Orius nodded sullenly. "I know, but I do not have to get used to losing people. I *am* a priest."

"And a Conjurer," Culley said. His eyes widened and he raised his gray eyebrows.

"I would rather be remembered for my faith." Orius slapped a fist into his palm. "I did not want to reveal my conjuring ability like that. Word will spread as soon as these warriors meet others. It will attract unwanted attention."

"It had to happen some time," said Culley. "You can't expect to keep something like that quiet forever. Especially, since we're no longer hiding in Malagorn's keep. Besides, what you have'll strike terror into the hearts of your enemies."

Orius snorted and shook his head. "*Terror.* The word leaves a bad taste in my mouth. When my enemies discover I cannot conjure fire without shitting my breeches, they will find a way to use that against me. Malagorn was right. I began the training too late. If I was six, instead of eighteen, I would have developed better control and would be able to channel larger amounts of energy without fainting like an old woman."

Culley chuckled. "Let me worry about protecting you. If one of your fireballs saves my life, I'll personally wipe your unconscious ass." He guffawed at his own joke.

"You have more confidence in my abilities than I do, and I do not share your humor. Besides, I do not want this army to become reliant on my conjuring. They must know they can win without it."

Culley wiped a tear from his eye and became serious. "They know they can win without the power of the elements. They've been doing that for generations."

Orius looked over his shoulder. The army was lined up on the road, waiting for his orders. He called for the Wolf Rider that Chief

Condin had sent back and sent him ahead to let Condin know the army was on the move.

# Chapter 16

## Ghyo's Sword
### 13 Janoben, 229 A.G.S.

The Oruks had remained in the valley. Their camp was less than two miles from where the Cheltan Army camped by the edge of the woods. Orius had sent Chief Condin and the Wolf Riders to scout them before the sun rose over the mountains. Condin's scouts had counted over three hundred Oruks, more than twice the number Orius could put in the field. They returned and reported what they had seen.

"So be it, they shall have their fight," Orius told Condin.

Orius fed his warriors and formed them up along the road. He ordered the army to advance, while he and Culley rode ahead to scout the Oruks for themselves, taking the twenty-five mounted warriors of Ragnaar with them. A stiff wind blew in from the west. This part of the undulating valley was devoid of trees, but weatherworn boulders protruded from the ground here and there.

A mile and a half up the road, Orius found a spot where the ground rose sharply, forming a squat, rounded mound running north to south. The road to Drenga ran up and over the rise, cutting a notch into the crest. Five Oruk scouts sat their ponies atop the mound, facing east.

Orius's column thundered toward them and the Oruks scattered, disappearing behind the mound. *We no longer have surprise on our side. I should've advanced the entire army behind Condin's scouts. But I half-expected them to be gone.*

Orius drew his two-hander and spurred his horse forward. Culley and the others charged after him. As he approached the mound, he veered to the left of the road and galloped to the top. He broke over the crest and reined his brown mare to a halt. Before him, the ground sloped away toward a dry gully, a natural obstacle, fronting the Oruk's camp not two hundred yards away. The Oruk scouts disappeared into the gully and popped back up again on the opposite side. Orius watched them ride up to their commander – the rider cloaked in black. Orius sheathed his sword, as Culley and the warriors from Ragnaar joined him along the crest. Across the field, dozens of cook fires were lit and the Oruks milled about them, eating their breakfast.

Orius counted three picket lines of horses and figured there were twenty shaggy ponies tied to each.

The Oruk commander motioned with his arms. Drum rolls filled the air, and the Oruk camp became an anthill of activity. There was frantic movement along the top of the gully as the Oruks lined up along it. Orius studied their dispositions. Four formations of infantry lined up on either side of the road, two in front and two in back. A group of archers formed up on the road in the middle of the infantry. To the left and right, about a hundred yards from the road, bodies of cavalry and archers took up positions on the flanks. In the center, another group of cavalry lined up behind the infantry and archers.

Orius smiled. *This will do.*

The Black Rider rode his stallion to the gully's edge and raised his spyglass to the darkened interior of his hood. Orius saw him looking in his direction and *sensed* he was looking directly at him.

Orius found his eyes were glued to the black figure. The sight of him produced an aching sensation in his bones, a slick, diseased sensation that he had never felt before. Cool sweat trickled down his back and his insides became queasy. His eyes widened and the corners of his mouth drew in. His body trembled. *What's wrong with me? I...I sense fear and doom when I look upon him. It...it's difficult to concentrate.*

Culley said, "Their commander is clever. They occupy a good position."

Culley's voice sounded distant to Orius. He heard his old friend, but it was difficult to pry his eyes from the Black Rider. He snapped his head away. "Yes," he answered almost unconsciously and returned to staring at the figure on the black horse.

Culley moved his horse in front of Orius, blocking his view of the Oruk army. "What do you see over there that affects you so?" he asked quietly.

Orius blinked a few times. "It is not what I see. It is what I feel. I sense their commander wields Power. Something different from anything I have known. I can feel his presence when I look upon him. He projects *fear*."

Culley made a shushing noise. The Chelts of Ragnaar were nearby chatting about the size of the Oruk's army. Culley moved closer to Orius. "What do you mean he has Power?"

"He commands something not of the Light of Ghyo." Orius could again see the dark figure. The hidden eyes were still upon him. Feelings of dread and hopelessness accompanied the stare of the invisible eyes. "I sense..." Orius stared across the field into the dark void of the hood and searched for the words to explain himself. "Something...ancient, corrupt..." He gasped and the color drained from his face. He tore his eyes away from the Rider's hood. It was easier to do this time. His clenched his jaws. "He is not a knight of the Black Hand, nor is he a priest of the Faith. He is...evil...opposite of what I am."

Orius shuddered and rubbed his eyes. He suddenly thrust his arms in front of him and called out to his warriors. "Before us has gathered the vanguard of the forces of Darkness! The antithesis of everything that walks in the Light! They are the minions of Eo, the Soul Stealer! We must fight them!"

The Chelts whispered to each other.

"Orius, I don't pretend to understand what you're talking about," Culley growled quietly. "But your words can damage morale. Chelts're superstitious."

Orius gave Culley a hard stare. "Old friend," he said. "Evil is before us. My mother taught me of the exiled followers of the Stillborn Child. I see one now. Never before have I known or felt anything more plainly. After a thousand years, they have returned to Iningia. We will attack them and they shall be destroyed!"

The Cheltan warriors ceased their whispering. One of them raised his sword and cheered loudly. Others drew their weapons and joined him, until they all roared and waved their weapons.

Culley shook his head. "Have I taught you nothing practical about war throughout these years?"

Orius's tone was respectful, but filled with conviction. "Today, I will use the things you have taught me."

Culley exhaled with exasperation. "Attacking twice your numbers across open ground is never wise policy. They've more archers than we, and our warriors'll be cut to pieces."

"You are as keen as ever, old friend. I agree the ground is open, but this mound will hide our forces. The ground between the armies is dry and half our force is mounted. We will cross it rapidly." With his head, he gestured to the rear. "When we attack, the sun will be at our backs and in their faces."

Culley spun his horse around and faced west toward the enemy. "Our foe is being cautious. He's chosen a good defensive position and keeps a strong reserve." He looked at Orius and raised his eyebrows. "I wager you'll attack a flank and overwhelm it."

"We shall hit them on both flanks simultaneously."

Culley rolled his eyes, but he admitted, "Your plan is bold, and it could work. Who'll command the wings?"

"I will place Chief Condin on the left, and Kathair on the right."

"And where shall I be posted?"

"Next to me in the center, with the reserve." Orius leaned forward and said quietly, "Where I need you."

Within a quarter of an hour, the remainder of Orius's army arrived. He gathered his companions, the leading warriors, and Chief Condin on the road behind the mound. A few warriors from Ragnaar remained along the crest, observing the Oruks. The rest of the warriors waited. Orius gave his orders, and then he called for the entire force to gather around him.

"Warriors of the North, across a short distance our foe waits for us to attack him. And we will. Smash his flanks and meet me in the middle." Orius swept his hand across the Chelts. "Should your leaders fall, do not stop. Every man and woman here today is a leader. The eyes of your villages are watching you." He drew his sword and thrust it into the ground. "The Rape of Cheltabria ends here!"

The entire host unleashed a cheer and banged their weapons against their shields, or against the weapons of the warriors beside them. Orius removed the white gauntlet from his right hand and raised it above his head. The palm glowed with an amber light. The warriors grew silent and dropped to one knee. Orius conducted the Celebration of the Light:

> *Blessed be the body of Ghyo, the world.*
> *Blessed be His Light that manifests through His Gift.*
> *Blessed be the Cycle unbroken.*
> *Life perpetual.*

Afterwards, Culley ordered the warriors to their positions and the army dispersed. Kathair led the mounted and dismounted warriors of Ragnaar, numbering fifty in all, to the far right of the mound. The dismounted warriors of Tydorhagen and Telstrand, led by Argus, lined up to the left of the road; while the warriors of Kyarna and Lunevik, led by Moreena, lined up on the road's right side. Their commands each numbered twenty-three, and both groups lay on their stomachs near the crest of the mound. To the rear of Orius's center stood the ten dismounted warriors from Haagenvaarder, led by Egon, a massive Chelt with arms the size of most people's legs. Behind Egon's warriors were twenty mounted warriors from Telstrand, Kyarna, Lunevik, and Tydorhagen and the mounted archers from Lunevik. Chief Condin rode to the left and divided his warriors into two lines. The mounted archers from Kyarna, Telstrand, Tydorhagen, and Haagenvaarder, numbering twelve, made up the first line. His second line consisted of the Wolf Riders and the mounted warriors of Haagenvaarder, fifteen all told.

Orius sat his horse at the crest of the mound, in the middle of the road, and peered through his spyglass. The appearance of the Chelts had interrupted the Oruks' breakfasts. *Hopefully, they didn't have time to finish.* It had been two hours since the Oruks were called to arms. Orius smiled as he watched dozens of them drop their breeches, and empty their bowels and bladders where they stood. *Wish it were hotter.*

The Cheltan army quietly sat their horses or lay on the ground. They were rested and fed and had time to relieve themselves. They waited for the order to charge the enemy they had defeated two days earlier.

Orius stared at the Black Rider. The uneasy feelings returned. *Can he sense me, like I sense him?* He pulled his eyes from his spyglass and bowed his head in prayer. *Ghyo, I pray the lives I am about to sacrifice further your glory. I pray that the dead souls do not return to poison the world. I place myself in your loving hands. Life Perpetual.* Culley rode up next to him.

"We shouldn't wait much longer. Our warriors grow impatient. They need to wet their steel." Culley raised a hand to his brow. "I see they're restless. I wager they grow tired of smelling their own shit." He glanced over his shoulder toward the morning sun. "Wish it were hotter."

Orius, too, looked back at the sun, noting its position in the sky. "It is time." He jammed his spyglass into a saddlebag.

He turned his horse and trotted down the road with Culley behind him. He rode a short distance and stopped at a spot where Kathair and Condin could see him. He removed the gauntlet from his hand and raised it above his head. His palm glowed brightly, signaling the attack to begin. A resounding cheer came on the heels of the signal. Orius extinguished the light and stuffed his hand into the gauntlet. Then he and Culley spurred their horses back up the mound where they could observe the battle.

Excitement rose within Orius. "Argus, Moreena - bring your warriors to the top of hill. I want them to see you, so they will have to keep troops to hold their center."

To the right, cheerful shouts filled the air as Kathair led his command over the top of the rise. He rode in front of the dismounted warriors, who jogged behind him. The archers from Ragnaar, all of whom were mounted, trotted behind the infantry, slowly loosing arrows in the direction of the Oruk cavalry on that flank. The mounted warriors of Ragnaar followed the archers and gradually veered to the right.

On the left, Chief Condin followed his mounted archers to the top of the mound where he halted and watched them gallop toward the Oruks, loosing arrows as they rode forward.

There was a reaction within the ranks of the enemy. The Oruk horsemen on both flanks raised their wooden shields to protect themselves from the arrows pelting their formations. Not all of the arrows found a mark, but a pony or two reared up inside both formations. On the right, an Oruk horseman fell from his mount and flopped into the gully.

A score of Oruk archers weaved their way through and around the cavalry on the flanks and took up positions along the steep edge of the gully. They drew their bows and released the strings. Black streaks arced through the air toward the advancing Chelts on the flanks.

The Chelts from Ragnaar, with shields raised above their heads, jogged forward. Most of the Oruk arrows missed and sunk into the ground, but two Chelts staggered and rolled onto the grass. Their fellow warriors did not stop to give them aid, but hopped over and around them.

On the left, the mounted archers closed the distance between the armies. They galloped across the field, loosing arrows into the Oruks. These Chelts, too, found themselves the target of Oruk archers. Arrows struck two of their horses, causing them to rear and nearly throw their riders. A Chelt caught an arrow through her face, killing her instantly. But her horse continued to gallop toward the gully with its dead rider bouncing lifelessly against its rump.

But the remaining Cheltan archers rode on, loosing more arrows and causing an Oruk archer to career into the gully and a pony to rear in pain. When they got within fifty yards of the Oruk line, the Chelts whipped their horses to the right; each warrior loosed a missile over his shoulder and spurred their mounts toward friendly lines. Then, the entire group wheeled around and charged the Oruks again. Their aim was better on this charge. An Oruk archer fell; then a horseman caught an arrow in the chest. The Oruk's mount collided with the pony next to it, causing much commotion among the horsemen. Again, the Cheltan archers veered away and loosed arrows. As they fled, another Oruk archer dropped into the gully.

Suddenly, the entire body of Oruk ponies rushed forward, knocking several archers into the gully. The Oruk cavalry emerged from the gully in a ragged line. Sunlight reflected off the tips of their spears. Once on level ground, they picked up momentum and pursued the fleeing Chelts who twisted around and sent arrows over their shoulders.

From the center, Orius watched the Oruk cavalry leave their positions and charge into the field between the armies. It did not take them long to cover half the distance, and he looked to his left and saw Chief Condin signaling with his arms. *Do it, Chief. Take them.*

The Cheltan archers reached the top of the mound ahead of the Oruks. They wheeled around and sent more missiles toward their enemy. The Oruks charged onward. Meanwhile, the Wolf Riders and the mounted warriors of Haagenvaarder rounded the far left of the mound and wheeled into the flank of the charging Oruks.

Orius heard the Wolf Riders howling and snarling. The entire mass of Oruk horsemen halted. Arrows rained into them from the archers on the mound. Five of them wheeled their ponies to the right, lowered their spears, and counter-charged the Wolf Riders and Haagenvaardars. But the charging Chelts were three times their number and flowed around them like a stream around a rock. A sharp melee ensued. An Oruk speared a Wolf Rider through the stomach, but a Haagenvaardar buried an axe into his chest. The other four were already writhing on the ground, their blood draining into the grassy field.

The remaining Oruk horsemen broke. Sunlight flashed off Cheltan swords and axes as weapons rose and fell, taking life and hewing limb. Three of the Oruks fought their way out of the trap and fled toward the gully, furiously whipping their stout ponies. Chief Condin, the archers, the Haagenvaardars, and the Wolf Riders pursued them. The stubby mountain ponies did not carry the Oruks far. The Chelts overtook them, slaughtered them, and rode onward. Only a handful of archers remained on that flank to defend against the Cheltan charge.

A pernicious smile came to Orius's lips as he watched the destruction of the Oruk cavalry. He switched his attention to events on the right, where the fight was developing much more slowly. Kathair's formations were intact and closing in on the gully. Five bodies dotted the field behind them. The Oruk archers continued sending arrows into the warriors from Ragnaar, but there were fewer of them. The Cheltan archers had taken their toll, too.

Orius looked for Kathair, who had been riding in front, but he was no longer there. A tightness gripped Orius's throat and his heart beat faster. From that distance, he could not tell if Kathair was one the bodies lying in the grass. The horseman of Ragnaar drove their mounts to the right and charged ahead. In a few seconds, the Chelts on foot disappeared into the gully. The Oruk archers bolted to the rear and ran through the ranks of their cavalry, breaking up the horsemen's formation.

The Cheltan infantry scrambled up the gully's steep wall and threw themselves at the Oruk cavalry. To the right, the Cheltan horsemen rode out of the gully, wheeled left, and charged. The Oruk cavalry melted away and fled west. The Cheltan archers loosed arrows into the backs of the routing Oruks, dropping a few from the saddle. And the Cheltan horses overtook the rest.

Orius slammed a fist into his hand. He turned his horse about and shouted, "Argus, Moreena, Egon! Take the center forward and drive them from the field! Horsemen and archers will follow the infantry. Now forward!"

The Chelts gave a lusty cheer and advanced toward the Oruks' center.

Orius turned to Culley. "We are reaching the climax of this thing. I figure there are three hundred in the center."

"Aye, boy," said Culley. "This is where it can get messy."

Across the field, enemy movement caught Orius's eye. A body of infantry was moving to the left, and another marched to the right. "He is shifting his reserves." He pointed. "There."

"It looks to be over fifty in each formation," Culley said. "I figure we have twenty remaining on the left, less than fifty on the right, and around fifty advancing against the center. We can still lose this fight."

Orius furled his eyebrows. It was possible his warriors would not carry the field. He knew the Chelts were a proud race. And he had gained their respect when he slew Worgoth with an axe. *Will I keep their respect if I resort to using my powers in each fight?* He watched the Oruk infantry march toward the flanks. *If I use my powers, do I take away their honor?*

"Culley, I am giving you command of the battle. Our objective is to reach Drenga. We cannot afford to suffer heavy losses here."

Orius jumped off his horse and removed his leather gauntlets. He knelt down and placed his left hand on the ground. He breathed deeply and focused on the energy, deep within the earth. Like a siphon, he drew in the earth's Power. Energy surged through his arm and collected within his chest. He sent it flowing down his other arm, to where his palm pointed at the right-hand formation of Oruk infantry. He felt a physical release as he expelled the energy he had conjured. Sweat gushed from his body. A tight ball of swirling fire streaked through the air. He focused on the slow moving infantry, guiding the fireball to them. It covered the distance in seconds and slammed into the rows of footmen. Fire rippled through the formation. A score of Oruks screamed as their clothing and skin burst into flames.

Panting, Orius pointed his hand at the group on the left. Again, he drew fire from the earth and sent it hurling toward his foes. A new wave of sweat drenched his body and he started to faint. But he fought to keep his eyes on the target. Seconds passed like minutes, but he held on until the fireball struck the Oruks. Then he collapsed.

When the Chelts had first appeared over the rise, the Black Rider recognized the golden sunburst upon the white surcoat. The priest of Ghyo projected a powerful aura of Goodness and Kindness. The Black Rider envisioned himself walking up to the priest and sliding his sword deep into the priest's chest. The thought brought him comfort.

He recited his sworn Creed:

> *Death to all things that walk in the Light of Ghyo.*
> *Death to the white-cloaked Healers of the sick and the Keepers of*
> *     the Light.*

The pacifistic clergy of Ghyo were sworn never to handle weapons or harm another human being. But he had to pull his eyes away from the priest to search for the conjurer. So it was an utter shock, when streaks of rippling flame issued forth from the priest. The Black Rider was stupefied, but he could not doubt what he had seen. The priest drew Power from the earth and sent it into his soldiers. The fireballs had torn wicked gaps in his infantry. The Black Rider now watched the burning bodies writhe upon the ground and the survivors flee pell-mell to the west.

The Black Rider watched his army disintegrate, and it did not anger him. *I cannot counter such power. The lives I spend now buy the Master another day.*

He rode west, taking the remaining cavalry with him. The road to Drenga was already clogged with the fugitives of the Oruk army. The Black Rider and the cavalry galloped through the terrified survivors, who clambered around them and begged to be picked up and taken to safety. He drew his broadsword and hacked at the grasping arms. "Make way, you scum, you animals." The Oruk cavalry mimicked their leader and cut their way through the crowd, as well.

A fleeing Oruk in a mail shirt caught the Black Rider's attention. He spurred his horse in that direction. "Grundish!" he roared. "Why do you live again?"

Grundish held his hands before his burned face and cried out. The Black Rider cocked back his sword arm, but a new wave of shouting and screaming drew away his attention from Grundish. He whipped his head around and saw Cheltan horsemen drawing near. A loud hiss issued from within his cowl and he galloped off to the west. Grundish disappeared into the chaos.

# Chapter 17

## Duty Questioned
### 12 Janoban, 229 A.G.S.

The odor of damp straw and human waste made the air sticky and heavy. Tarik's back ached from sleeping on the thin layer of straw, which covered the jail's bumpy stone floor. The cell was crowded; ten others shared it with him. A grown man could just stand upright at the apex of the rounded ceiling. A shaft of light passed through the window outside the cell and lit the jail's interior. A crude wooden bucket sat on the floor by the cell's entrance. Its ill-fitting lid could not contain the odor of feces and urine.

By Tarik's estimate, it was morning. But the dim light made it impossible to be certain. The noises of people in the street outside the window had awakened him. He was surprised he had slept at all. He had laid awake most of the night, keeping an eye on the ruffians who shared the cell with him.

A heavy door banged somewhere to the right. The noise was followed by harsh voices, footsteps, and weird sloshing sounds. More voices joined in on the racket. The prisoners in the cells closest to the door rattled the bars of their cells. The prisoners in Tarik's cell sat up and stretched.

Tarik sat with his back against the wall and removed the sling from his shoulder. The pain of his injury ached slightly. Slowly, he rotated his arm, testing the muscles and ligaments. They felt stiff at first, but the more he moved, the looser they became. His arm's strength was returning. He breathed a sigh of relief and silently thanked Father Grigorio for his skill. At least he had the use of both his hands to defend himself, should any of the prisoners give him trouble.

Beside Tarik sat a man with his legs crossed. The man's skin was bronzed from the sun, and his hair was black and tied into a stubby ponytail. He wore a loose-fitting tan coat with a half dozen metal hooks running down the front. He resembled sailors Tarik had seen disembarking from Terghui merchant ships, docking at Spandel's port. He guessed he was part of an overland caravan from Terghu.

"Time to eat," the man said to Tarik in Tradespeak. "My name is Feng. And yours, my Azari friend?"

Tarik touched the gold-embroidered eagle upon his breast. "I am called Tarik. How long have you been in here?"

"Six days, I think," said Feng. "You speak the language of commerce well."

"It was part of my upbringing. What did you do to get sent here?"

A slimy smile crossed Feng's face. "I was jailed for having sex with a very young female. I guess it is against the law to have sex in Roda. She gave herself to me willingly. Well, mostly that is."

Something in the back of Tarik's mind put him on guard against Feng's character. "I would not know about that. I only arrived in Roda yesterday."

Feng chuckled. "The Iduin cannot take a shit without checking their law books." He rubbed his face thoughtfully. "I have been in Roda four times and never got arrested. These Rodi women look older than they actually are. Well anyway, how can a man wearing the emblem of his king get himself arrested the same day he arrives?"

Tarik looked at the other prisoners, gathering near the cell bars, and wondered if any of them understood Tradespeak. "I am not going to say," he told Feng.

Feng's eyebrows rose and he pursed his lips. "You are not like the rest of us. Your clothes are too fine." His eyes wandered to Tarik's legs. "Nice boots." He showed Tarik a pair of gold teeth. "Trade you for these. Gold for leather." He nodded and winked.

Tarik snorted. "I do not need gold."

Feng whistled quietly. "You have no need for gold?"

A couple of the prisoners turned their heads toward Tarik and stared in silence. They then looked away and moved closer to the cell's bars.

"I need to escape," Tarik said, feeling the cell's closeness. "I do not belong here."

Feng laughed. "None of us belongs here! We are all innocent!"

Tarik shook his head and looked at the floor. *It was foolish to say that.* He had never been in jail before, and he was sure Feng could sense it. *Criminals seldom acknowledge their wrongdoing.*

Feng stifled his laughter. "What happened to your arm? Did they beat you? Dirty bastards. They always beat you on the way to jail. Did you fight back?"

Feng's rapid questions made his head spin. "Nothing so spectacular," Tarik said. "I hurt it in a fall."

"You must be a burglar, but not a very good one. A man cannot climb walls with boots like those." Feng pointed to his own black, flat-soled slippers. "These are better for climbing. The bottom is flexible, so you can use yours toes to help keep your grip. I will add these to the bargain for your boots."

"There is no bargain," Tarik said. "So stop making offers."

"Everything has a price, my friend. Everything. Everyone has a price, too."

"Are you saying a man's beliefs have a price?" Tarik asked.

Feng nodded slowly, as though he were the keeper of some great wisdom. "I have to answer yes to that. I have yet to meet a man who does not have a price. And if the man does not know his price, it is because no one has offered him the right price."

Tarik looked away, hoping Feng would realize he was not interested in continuing their talk. He knew many Azaris who worked to support the Crown and gained satisfaction from service to their country for little money. People who knew they would never get rich. But Tarik knew some corrupt Azaris as well, though he knew many more forthright ones. At least he thought he did.

*What's Aida doing now?* he asked himself. *Is she safe? Has the war come to Turela? Has it touched her, like it touches me?* Tarik observed the cell with disgust and cursed Senator Bulbius. Jailing an official messenger breached the protocols of the treatment of foreign ambassadors and the like. In front of the entire Senate, Iduin soldiers had laid their hands on him and led him away. The sovereignty of Rodrigo Mendio had been publicly ignored and disgraced. *What did the letter say?* All Tarik knew was that his association with the letter had rendered him to be found guilty of a crime.

*I'm the third son of the Marquis of Spandel, the king's first cousin. I'm not some commoner's son who filched a bauble from a lady's hand. And yet here I sit, in this filth, with these wretches.*

Across the cell, a sick prisoner unleashed a wracking cough. The man had hacked and wheezed the entire night. Another one, with a jagged scar where one eye should have been, sat beside the sick man. Beside them sat three other prisoners, each with a letter branded into his face. Tarik guessed it was the initial of the Iduin word for thief.

A burly, bare-chested jailer, with more hair on his wide back than on his head, came into view beyond the cell bars. He croaked something in Iduin, and the prisoners in Tarik's cell held out their hands. Two other jailers, carrying a large black kettle between them, joined the burly jailer. One of them raised the kettle's lid and stirred the contents with a ladle. The scent of boiled barley and millet wafted from inside. The second man reached into the large burlap sack he held and pulled out a wooden bowl. A runny soup was slopped into it and handed to one of the prisoners. The man cupped the bowl in both hands and hungrily slurped down the soup. The bland soup was served to each prisoner. Tarik was amazed that no one fought to be the first in line. He expected it after hearing the frenzy in the other cells. The jailers returned a short time later, picked up the bowls, and counted them. The rest of the morning passed by slowly. The other prisoners talked quietly or slept. Screaming occasionally erupted from another cell, followed by the sound of fists smacking flesh.

In the afternoon, the door to the cellblock banged against the wall. A furious howling drowned out the other noises of the jail. Prisoners in the cells closer to the entrance shouted and rattled their cell bars. The burly jailer had returned. Tarik could hear his harsh voice. Two other jailers were with him. They were larger than the two who had served the morning meal and they dragged a shackled man between them. A sinewy man, with long, matted brown hair, thrashed about wildly. Spit and threats flew from his lips. The burly jailer stopped in front of Tarik's cell and began unlocking the door. The shackled man stopped his screaming and spit a glob of phlegm on the back of the burly jailer's head. The jailer calmly pulled the key from the lock and said something to the men holding the prisoner. They held him up straight and the burly jailer smashed his fist into the prisoner's face. The shackled man fell limp. The jailer turned around and opened the cell door, barking orders and gesturing as he did so. The prisoners backed away as the shackled man was dumped face first onto the straw-covered floor. The jailers removed the shackles and left.

After a few hours, the new prisoner rose to his knees. He rubbed and probed the large red swelling on his jaw, wincing as he did. He stuck a finger into his mouth and checked his teeth. He narrowed his eyes and a scowl tightened the corners of his mouth. He moved his gaze from prisoner to prisoner. When his eyes moved across Tarik, Tarik could see the eyes were cold and lifeless. The prisoner studied him and the others like a wolf searching for a lame sheep to separate from the herd.

The prisoner finished his scrutiny and moved over to the one-eyed man. He kicked the man's legs aside and said something in Iduin. Tarik did not understand, but the tone was intimidating. The one-eyed man jumped to his feet and thrust out his chest. The new prisoner struck him in the face with the palm of his hand, pushing him backward. The one-eyed man's head snapped back and banged against the stone blocks of the wall. He slid to the floor and lay in a crumpled heap.

The other prisoners ignored what was happening. The new prisoner dragged the one-eyed man away from the wall and sat down in the spot he had cleared for himself. He leaned his head back, raised his knees to his chest, and closed his eyes.

Feng leaned close to Tarik. "That is the problem with jail. One never knows who will be your roommate."

"The others appear to know him. What is his name?" Tarik asked.

Feng spoke quietly to the prisoner on his left. The prisoner answered and Feng turned back to Tarik. "He is called Carcero. A very violent man, so the fellow next to me claims."

The afternoon wore on. Feng talked, talked, and kept talking, though Tarik ignored most of what he said. Carcero napped most of the afternoon, but occasionally opened his eyes and stared at Tarik, who met the man's stares with a blank expression. Tarik was determined to not attract Carcero's attention or to provoke him. He assumed Carcero had nothing to lose, and risking injury, or worse, would not get him back to Soriazar.

As Feng chattered away, Tarik's mind left the jail cell. He remembered a time when Aida's long hair brushed against his face and her soft hip bumped his arm as she spun around and headed for the inn's kitchen. Thinking about her gave him comfort. An empty spot opened up within him and it widened the longer he dwelt on her. Sadness then filled the void and Tarik grew sullen. Something was missing in his life. Something his service to Rodrigo could not satisfy, but he dared not explore those feelings too deeply. Each time they surfaced, he dismissed them as being sentimental – unmanly. He wondered if other men felt as he did about a woman.

His thoughts switched to the message he had delivered. He had assumed it was one of conciliation, a burying of the old, bad blood between Soriazar and Idu. *What else could the message contain?* Spandel, Turela, and Orpresa were in danger of being razed, and it would be months before enough militia could be gathered to throw out the Semotecs. Winter would have arrived by then, and the people of Spandel March would be starving due to the ruined harvests. To Tarik, the solution seemed obvious. Soriazar and Idu needed each other, but the unknown content of the letter and the reaction of Senator Bulbius told him Rodrigo had chosen a different course. The letter did not ask for nor offer help. A letter such as that would not have brought about Tarik's arrest, but a letter of belligerency would.

Tarik's cheeks and ears flushed hot with anger. He had done his duty faithfully and had served Rodrigo honorably. He had traveled a great distance and bore an injury in reaching Roda, always continuing onward. And a stinking jail cell was his reward. Soriazar held no embassy in Roda. He was on his own.

*What did the letter contain?* Tarik fought the notion of being expendable, of being a tool in the game of policy. He was more than that. He was the son of Rodrigo's cousin. *What've I done to deserve this? No!* He stopped his self-abasing. *The king didn't hang me out like a piece of bait. Senator Bulbius has overstepped his authority. Nations are supposed to respect foreign emissaries. Diplomacy can't function without that rule. I must keep faith with Rodrigo. I must smooth over relations between our country and Idu. At least, I'm in a position to try. I've received training in this.*

Tarik halted his racing thoughts. He calmed himself. *What if the letter was conciliatory, and the Senate of Idu has already embarked on another course? Something that is so far advanced that they are past the point of recall.* He considered that. The Iduin had taken a beating from the Semotecs. It was rumored they lost an entire legion trying to keep them from crossing the border. *An Iduin legion numbers about five thousand, and they're among the toughest and most disciplined troops in Iningia. But what could five thousand do against one hundred fifty thousand? Only delay and delay, and eventually withdraw from the province or die. Rumor says the latter happened. Have the Iduin recovered from the blow? Are they ready to strike back by themselves? I saw two legions marching westward.* Tarik shook his head with frustration. *But if the letter was peaceful, why jail me?*

He gave up looking at the situation from the Iduin angle. Speculation was never good and guessing was even worse. He thought about the situation from the Azari perspective. *What does Rodrigo need or want from the Iduin? He's moving General Mazrio's royal troops to Spandel, and there's yet to be a major battle, as far as I know. Spandel's local militias have done well in sticking to their walls and making sorties against the Semotecs.*

He pictured a map of Spandel March and the Iduin province of Apumium. *If Rodrigo had offered an alliance with Idu, then the military situation would be a good one. The Iduin could sally from the passes of the Caroc Mountains and attack the Semotecs in the flank, while Azari forces pushed them from the north. Together they'd drive them into the ocean.* But there were plans unraveling. Unseen plans with unseen goals – belligerent goals. Tarik was certain of it.

*What kind of opportunity has caught the king's eye?* He could not picture anything positive about the Azari position. *King Mendio has reigned thirty years. Could he be slipping? No, Beltram Zepio wouldn't allow that. He would sense that happening. Or was he past his prime, too?* Tarik cursed aloud, breaking his silent contemplation.

He looked around. No one had paid him any notice. Even Carcero slept. Tarik was close to those who made policy, but seldom was he privileged to know their reasoning. And now he sat in an Iduin jail, smothered by the thing that was always so close to him, yet never within his grasp.

Carcero's voice broke his concentration. Tarik could not understand him, but he knew Carcero spoke to him. He gave him a questioning look, and Carcero repeated himself in the choppy, hard Iduin tongue.

"That man is talking to me. What is he saying?" Tarik asked Feng.

Feng asked Carcero what he wanted. The man uttered something back. "My Azari friend, he says you have nice boots."

Tarik's belly quivered. The last time Carcero wanted something he took it. He kept his eyes on Carcero and tilted his head toward Feng. "Tell him thank you." Feng translated.

Carcero scooted away from the wall, until the bottom of his sandal touched the sole of Tarik's boot. To Tarik's dismay, their feet were the same length. Carcero nodded, smiled, and spoke again. His voice was calm and confident, but his eyes were dark and lifeless.

Feng translated. "Give me those boots, he says."

Tarik slowly shook his head. Sweat beaded in the palms of his hands and his heart pounded. "Tell him I need my boots. I have a long journey home."

Feng translated and Carcero jumped to his feet. In a flash, his demeanor switched from relaxed to menacing. Through the sneer on his face, Carcero hissed as he spoke to Tarik. Veins bulged from his neck and forehead.

Feng spoke to Tarik in Tradespeak. "He says he will take your boots and *maybe* spare your life."

Tarik's voice took a hard edge. "I do not think he understood me. They are mine." He stood up during the time it took Feng to translate.

As Tarik got to his feet, the other prisoners in the cell slid away. Carcero hardly waited for Feng to finish speaking, he lunged at Tarik.

Tarik ducked and moved quickly. He slipped to the left and wrapped his arm around the back of Carcero's neck. With his left hand, he reached between Carcero's buttocks and grabbed his testicles. The Iduin froze and yelped. Tarik used Carcero's momentum and flipped him over his hip. Carcero landed on his head and rolled onto his side. He cradled his groin and the bleeding lump growing on the top of his head. Cheering and laughter filled the cell.

Tarik's training told him to choke his man out, but he resisted and backed off. Fighting for real was not as exhilarating as for fun. "Tell him this is over," Tarik said. "Tell him to stop, or I will finish him off."

Feng translated, but his words fell on uncaring ears. Carcero got back on his feet. Blood ran into his eyes and he wiped it away with one hand and then the other. His lifeless eyes showed only rage.

Carcero rushed Tarik again. He feinted with one hand and punched Tarik with the other. The prisoners cried out as Carcero landed his blow. A cut opened on the inside of Tarik's mouth. He fell back, but he grabbed Carcero's shirt as did and pulled him down with him. Tarik rammed the heel of his boot into Carcero's belly and flipped him through the air. He landed with a bone-crunching thud. The prisoners howled lustily.

Tarik rolled over, spat blood from his mouth, and lifted himself to his feet. Carcero got up much more slowly. He rolled over and raised himself up to his hands and knees. *Finish him*, Tarik's training told him. He landed a kick to Carcero's nose. Blood gushed from his face as he screamed and cupped his nose with his hands. Carcero curled up into a ball on the floor.

The other prisoners suddenly stopped cheering. They formed a circle around Carcero, and blow after blow struck him until his cries turned into whimpers and then to silence.

The main door to the cellblock banged against the wall. The burly jailer had returned. His gruff voice echoed off the walls. He sounded angry again. The prisoners grew silent. The burly jailer stood in front of the bars of Tarik's cell, said something in Iduin, and pointed at Carcero. The jailer's face showed contempt. A couple of prisoners answered his questions. Tarik watched them make falling gestures as they spoke. The burly jailer scoffed, but he did not pursue the matter. He produced the keys to the cell and unlocked the door. He stared at Tarik and motioned to him with a hairy hand. Tarik was unsure what to do, but he reluctantly moved toward the door. The burly jailer barked something in Iduin.

"He says you are being taken away," Feng said. "You need to hurry."

"Did he say where I am going?" Tarik asked.

Feng shrugged. "He did not say. But if you return, should you need bribe money or something, my offer for your boots is still good." He smiled mischievously and waved goodbye.

Tarik's mouth went dry as he turned away from Feng. The coppery taste of blood clung to his tongue. An image of himself standing before a magistrate flashed in his mind. He followed the burly jailer down the cellblock, silently preparing his defense to his charges. He hoped the magistrate would be reasonable and see the injustice of his arrest. A magistrate would know the law and the customs governing relations between nations, customs dating back to the Iningian Empire.

Tarik and the burly jailer passed through the metal door to the cellblock. They walked down the hall to the right, past other doors leading to other cellblocks, to a stout metal door at the end of the hall. The burly jailer banged on the door and someone on the other side opened it. Tarik passed through and entered an office. Murius waited for him, dressed in his complete panoply.

A big smile split Murius's face. "Come along, it is time for you to leave."

# Chapter 18

## Justification
### 13 Janoben, 229 A.G.S.

Two-dozen lammergeyers floated on the winds amidst the valley's high walls, revolving in endless circles, as if performing a complicated dance. The first bird appeared shortly after the fighting had ceased, and gradually another arrived, and then another, and still another. From the sky, the cluster of dead Oruks resembled an elongated teardrop, the tail of which pointed to the west. Trails of blood flowed from the bodies' distorted postures, pooling in the ground's indentations. Here and there, a vulture had descended on a corpse and picked away at the lifeless flesh, tearing it off in thin red strips.

The air was rife with the stench of burnt flesh. Burnt corpses lay on top of two blackened circles, scorched into the ground. Wispy fingers of smoke curled up from the bodies. Between the burned areas, the Oruk infantry in the center had remained to face the Chelts. They had stood alone, abandoned by their commander, cavalry, and archers, and they were slaughtered. When the mounted Chelts on the flanks had charged their rear, only a handful resisted. The others fled and were ridden down somewhere along the road. Bits of armor, shields, and weapons littered the field. To their vexation, the Chelts discovered that many of the Oruks wielded weapons of Cheltan design.

The Oruks had left three hundred dead in the valley, while only five Chelts were counted dead and thirty wounded. The older warriors could not recall a story of such a complete victory, considering the numbers involved. Nor could they remember a story of such a large battle where so many villages had joined together. The victory seemed even greater than any battle fought by King Kirkvold, when Cheltabria was a whole nation. The warriors of the North had clapped each other on the back, shook the hands of those from rival villages, and cheered loudly.

But a rumor circled. Father Orius had collapsed during the fight. The news sapped away some of the Chelts' merriment. Twice his conjuring had overcome him and rendered him useless during battle. Doubts surfaced of his physical prowess and of his ability to be a strong leader.

Egon of Haagenvaarder spread the rumor saying the Creator had punished Orius, for raising his hand in violence. "What else has Father Orius forsaken to gain the ability to conjure?" he asked his fellow Chelts. "Despite his slaying of Worgoth, could it be Father Orius was simply lucky in that contest, or did he use something sinister to gain an advantage?"

Egon had been near him, leading the Haagenvaardars across the field, when Orius unleashed his Power upon the enemy. He had seen Orius collapse after releasing the fireballs.

Like all of the cultures of Iningia, the Chelts knew of the legends of the great conjurers of the Tolorium Wars, and of how they cast their powers across the battlefields of that terrible struggle, killing their foes by the hundred. But there had not been one on the battlefield in a thousand years. "Father Orius dabbles in Powers forbidden to him," Egon said. "He's weak and his lust for power consumes him."

After Orius had recovered from his exhaustion, he laid hands upon the wounded. He was strong of Spirit, the source of the Gift. Though he had been pale and weak, he had worked his way through the wounded, where they had gathered near the notch in the top of the mound. He healed them all, but ten required a few days' rest before they would be fit again for battle. They would have to be left behind. The remainder would march on the next morning.

By itself, the Gift was not remedy to all injuries and ailments, though it instantly sealed open wounds and the ends of amputated limbs. The real Miracle of the Gift was in the ability to speed up the body's healing process. Combined with food and rest, the most serious injuries, which might normally require months or even a year to heal, took only weeks to mend, though that depended upon the strength of Spirit of the healer.

The sun was near its midday position. The day was warm and a light breeze blew in from the west, carrying with it the smell of the battle's aftermath. Orius rose from where he knelt next to the last Chelt he had healed. His white surcoat was soiled with dirt and blood. His army rested beneath the late summer sun, spread out across the length of the mound. A number of cooking fires had been lit and the last of the army's meat was roasting.

He pondered the wreckage of the Oruk army and the injuries inflicted on his warriors. *So many have died, or bear wounds. When will it end?*

His body ached and his chest felt as though it had received a great blow. His eyes were heavy with exhaustion and fatigue fogged his mind. He ran his dry tongue over his dry lips. Although he had not swung his sword in the battle, he felt like he had been in the front rank. Each time he tapped the earth's energy, it took a toll on him.

Kathair had emerged from the fighting with hardly a scratch, which brought Orius relief. He was not prepared to lose another close friend. For years, Culley had taught him of war. *Leading people sometimes means harming them*, he would say, instilling that into Orius's psyche. And Orius's mother had taught him about Ilyas and his wanderings. But Ilyas's teachings ran contrary to war and to his mother's ambitions for him. And that made Orius struggle with understanding his true nature and purpose. *I've the power to take and give life. How will I find a balance between war and faith?*

His mother's voice broke into his thoughts and said, *Take what is owed you, my son. Justice is the way of Ghyo. The use of violence is sometimes necessary to serve that end.*

Orius placed the heel of his hand to his forehead. The Tenets of the Faith spoke of Justice and Civility, Kindness and Charity, Love and Compassion. *But there's a dearth of such things in this world. Jealousy and Hatred, Vengeance and Cruelty sent us into hiding. Mother says I must use the traits of my enemies against them. And she knows that's heresy in the Church's eye.*

On the day of his Touching, while his mother conducted the ceremony, she had turned to an open window, facing to the south, and spoke as though she announced the event to the world. "Behold the Instrument of Change. Vehicle of Ghyo's Power, Protector of the Weak, Defender of the Faith, Righter of Wrongs." She then turned and raised her hand. "Rise, Father Candell."

"Priest!"

The voice shattered Orius's thoughts. Egon and seven Chelts walked toward him. They stopped a few paces off. Egon was slightly taller than Orius, but his frame was twice that of Orius's. Long blond hair hung to Egon's shoulders and a leather band circled his head to keep it out of his face. "Priest, I want a word with you," he said.

Orius rubbed his hands together, scraping dried blood from his palms. There was tension in the faces of the Chelts before him. Their eyes darted about. They licked their lips and flexed their fingers.

"Are you wounded?" Orius asked eyeing the bloody bandage wrapped around Egon's forearm.

"My wound isn't the reason I have come," he said. "The last of our meat is being eaten. The Oruks have been defeated. We've crops to tend and families to care for. And still you order us on to Drenga."

Orius shook his head and placed his hands on his hips. "The Oruks have not been defeated. There are more of them around Drenga."

Egon jeered at him. "How can you be sure? Your scout Fayne is dead and his luscious sister has been sent north." He grabbed his crotch and smiled at the Chelts behind him. "I hope she returns soon."

Orius's heart pounded. His limbs trembled and his neck muscles tightened at the mockery of Fayne's death and the jibe at Alana. "If you had any military sense, you would look at the ground on which we just fought. There is nothing here worth gambling an entire army on. The Oruks were buying time."

Egon puffed out his chest. His nostrils flared and his smile changed to a scowl. The Chelts behind him chuckled. "That matters not. We should return to our valley and protect our villages. Drenga is gone. It's of no use to us."

A crowd gathered around them. Orius paid them no notice. He was exhausted from the battle and now his authority as Chief was being challenged. *I need my strength. I must lay hands and take away my fatigue.* But he did not do it. *The warriors'll see no honor in that.*

"There are answers to be found in Drenga," Orius told him. "I know what has stirred the Oruks into action. It explains the way in which they fight."

"We're running out of food." Egon pointed to the west. "There's no telling how many *more* are waiting for us behind the mountain. They get stronger each time we meet them and we get weaker!"

There were grunts of approval not only from the group of Chelts with Egon, but also from the others who had gathered around. Orius took notice of the crowd; faces stared at him intently. The smell of sweating bodies and blood tainted the air. Orius kept his hands on his hips. "We have gathered the strongest Cheltan army in generations. The threat lies to the west. Ghyo fights for us. He has given me abilities that make up for our numbers. We must strike again before our enemy regains his balance."

"The Creator's blessed you with the Gift, but you use powers forbidden to you." Many Chelts openly agreed with Egon. "You see. I speak for many of us."

Orius appealed to the crowd. "The Elemental powers have been declared forbidden by the Church of Arshapel. A church created by humankind, not by the Creator. Their Canons are issued by the same people." *The Chelts don't know that the Elements and the Gift derive from the same source. The Church will never admit it.*

"We don't believe you," came a voice from the crowd. "You're cursed and don't know it."

"Cursed!"

"Heretic!"

"Misguided!"

"Egon, you pig!" Argus roared. He shoved his way through the crowd and stood in the small space around Orius. "Draw your weapon. Your disrespect will cost you your life."

Egon's upper lip drew back in a snarl, exposing clenched teeth. "Are you here to defend your priest, or your sister's youth? She gave it to me willingly, you know. Again and again." He chuckled at his own joke, and the laughter of others accompanied his.

Orius saw the back of Argus's neck turn purple. Tendons and veins bulged from his skin. He placed his hand on Argus's thick shoulder. "No. There will be no bloodshed over this. Enough has been spilled. I forbid the resolving of personal scores until this Oruk business is over."

"It's already over," Egon said. "We'll follow you no further." Half of the Chelts nodded their heads.

"Father Orius speaks the truth." Chief Condin's voice rose above the noise of the crowd as he moved into the center where he could be seen. "Skorva lies in ashes. Other villages will follow. We cannot defeat the Oruks individually."

"Candell is a foreigner! He's cursed!" Egon shouted. "How can we trust him?"

"We have to trust him," answered Condin. "He is our chief. I stand beside him and I oppose you. Father Orius wears white, like me." He patted the yellowing, blood stained pelt he wore. "It was Fate when I returned from my Seeking with this white pelt, and like that, Orius's coming to the Northern Valley was a sign of good things to come, a sign of change. I and the other chiefs recognized this and raised him to lead all of the tribes."

Culley, Moreena, and Kathair emerged from the circle of Chelts. They, too, stood next to Orius. Culley moved his hand to his sword hilt. Kathair and Moreena held their two-handers propped against their shoulders.

"Egon, we must continue westward," Orius said. "For the sake of the lives of your children at home, this threat must end."

"Orius, let me kill him," Argus said. Egon took a step back and raised his axe.

The crowd held its breath. The whispering and talking stopped. The seven Chelts standing with Egon loosened their swords, or held up their maces and axes. Eyes widened. Sweat trickled down foreheads. The Chelts waited for someone to make the first move. Then...

Orius compromised. "Egon of Haagenvaarder, I release you from service on this campaign. Return to your home and your crops. You have fought bravely on this field and risked as much as anyone." His voice then took a commanding tone. "But remember this, I will again call upon your axe to render service to the Northern Valley. You owe me such. Now, swear homage to me and depart."

The grim look on Egon's face melted away and a perplexed expression replaced it. He breathed in deeply through his nose, expanding his thick, solid chest. He exhaled slowly, nodding his head as if he had come to a decision. "I'll not swear homage to a heretic, or a foreigner. By Rite of Combat, I challenge you for the seat of Chief of the Northern Valley."

The crowd gasped. The air buzzed with the din of anxious voices. The warriors standing behind Egon backed away from him.

"Father Candell, let me fight for you," Chief Condin said.

"This is outrageous!" Culley exclaimed. "Withdraw your challenge. Orius has brought us a victory."

"It's my right as a warrior to challenge the chief," Egon said.

"Bastard!" screamed Moreena. "You cowardly bastard. You wish to tuck your tail and flee north, but you can't even muster the courage to admit it. You have no honor."

"You selfish pig!" Argus roared. "With your challenge, you piss on the warriors who died here today." He spat at Egon's feet.

Orius's head and shoulders slouched, more from exasperation than from exhaustion. Then he straightened and raised his hands, motioning for silence. The crowd noise abated. Egon had the right to challenge him. The challenge was deeply ingrained into Cheltan culture. It was something he could not avoid, unless he was crowned King of Cheltabria. A king is above such challenges.

Orius raised his right hand. An amber light appeared in the center of his palm and slowly grew in intensity. The crowd gasped again and backed away in unison. "Egon of Haagenvaarder, may Ghyo forgive you for your vanity and pride." He closed his hand and extinguished the Light. "As Chief, I select this spot for the contest. We shall meet on the morrow as the dawn breaks over the eastern peaks." *Now, I gamble for the sake of keeping the respect of the others.* "I forego my right of choosing the weapon. Bring what you wish."

Orius turned his back on Egon and nudged his way through the crowd. His companions followed him, along with Chief Condin. Egon remained where he stood, wearing a smug smile.

# Chapter 19

## Wine, Olives, and Intrigue
### 13 Janoban, 229 A.G.S.

Aurelo Irigo stood behind the long wooden bar of the Oaken Cask. He wore a yellow doublet with red and yellow striped sleeves tailored to support his paunchy, pear-shaped torso. Sweat glistened on his balding forehead, which he dabbed at with a white kerchief. Wine dripped onto the cuff of his sleeve as he waved his cup while he spoke. He set the cup on the bar's worn surface and stroked his black goatee with his fingers.

The Oaken Cask tavern was a typical Azari building. Its walls, inside and out, were built of brick covered with whitewashed stucco, and the ground floor was made of cobblestones. Exposed wooden beams lined the ceiling, supporting the floorboards of the upper floor.

Four large wine casks rested on stout wooden racks along the wall behind Aurelo. His family's emblem was branded onto the casks. The Irigo's brand could be found nearly anywhere in Soriazar, and as far north as Harluer.

Porfiro Jorez, the owner of the Oaken Cask, stood beside Aurelo. A crisp white apron rounded his girth. It was a hot evening and the tavern's great room was crowded with shopkeepers and merchants who had come for their nightly drink and a bite to eat, before heading home for dinner with their families. Four assistants worked behind the bar, while three others worked in the kitchen.

"I require my usual room," Aurelo told Porfiro. "I am hosting a card game."

"Of course, senyor," Porfiro replied. "How many will there be for me to serve?"

Aurelo eyed the three people on the other side of the bar, who were absorbed in their own conversations about the day's business. "Four," he said quietly.

"I shall have Sancho prepare a little something from the kitchen for you and the other card players." Porfiro snapped his fingers and whistled. "Pepe!" He waved at the old man working behind the bar. Pepe nudged his way past Paco, Porfiro's oldest son, who was pouring a two-foot stream of sherry wine into a pair of glasses from a silver dipper attached to the end of a slender rod. "Master Aurelo requires some privacy," Porfiro told Pepe. "Prepare a room for him."

Pepe begged a pardon from Aurelo as he slid past him and rounded the bar. He crossed the tavern and climbed the wooden stairs leading to the second floor.

Aurelo sipped his wine. He watched Porfiro's son pour two more glasses from the dipper. "That's it," he grinned. "Pour it in a good long stream. Let the air at it. The wine needs to breathe." He took a deep breath and waved a hand in front of his nose.

Paco smiled, handed one of the glasses to Aurelo, and handed the other one to a man waiting on the other side of the bar. "Master Aurelo, please taste the sherry and let me know if I honor your brand." Paco dipped the silver dipper into the hole in the top of one of the casks, filled another glass, and gave it to the waiting man.

Aurelo sipped the yellow wine and raised his glass to Paco. "Excellent, this was a good vintage. Please allow me to pay for taking that man's wine." The customer bowed his head to Aurelo, thanking him.

Aurelo continued chatting with Porfiro. His voice turned mournful. "The last word I received from home was that the Semotecs ravaged my prized vineyard and burned the buildings. They told me *rivers* of sherry ran from the broken casks. Three hundred years of winemaking - lost."

"Master Irigo," Porfiro said. "I am...speechless at your loss."

"I will be fine, senyor. Thank you." Aurelo dabbed his forehead with the kerchief. "The summer heat makes one tired and fuels ones emotions."

"Perhaps you are hungry," Porfiro said. "I will have Blas bring you some olives, bread, and cheese."

Porfiro walked to the kitchen doorway and called for food. A man at the bar waved at him. Porfiro reached for the square piece of slate and the piece of white chalk lying on the bar. He counted on his fingers, scribbled down some numbers on the slate, and showed it to the man. The customer placed some coins onto the bar and left.

A boy appeared from the kitchen with a wooden trencher, holding a wedge of cheese, a hunk of warm dark bread, and a small glazed earthenware dish containing olives. The boy set the trencher on the bar beside Aurelo and bowed to the winemaker.

Aurelo popped an olive into his mouth and reached for another, but he found someone else's fingers in the dish. He looked up with a start and saw Uroyo Senen, a short, nervous, middle-aged man dressed in a supple leather doublet. Uroyo had all of his black hair, though it was heavily peppered with gray. A grin widened his tight mouth and stretched his neatly trimmed, but equally peppered beard.

"Good, aren't they?" Uroyo said, referring to the olives. "These're mine."

"Yours?" Aurelo asked.

Uroyo smiled weakly. "Yes. One can taste the rosemary and basil I put in the mix. I wager there's a Senen family jar in Porfiro's kitchen." He put an olive into his mouth and licked the garlicky juice from his fingers.

Aurelo chuckled and reached into his pocket. He slammed five large gold coins onto the bar. "We will commence the night's wagering." Again, he dabbed sweat on his forehead.

Uroyo snapped his fingers. "Senyor Porfiro, we have a wager here." Porfiro wiped his hands on his apron and approached. "Senyor Aurelo believes all olives taste the same. I tell him that's false, and I know the taste of my product." He gestured to the coins on the bar. "He's so confident he bets five *doblays*. I tell him there's a Senen family jar in your kitchen."

Three wide-eyed patrons, standing nearby, leaned closer to eavesdrop on the bantering. Their plain dress said they were minor shopkeepers, having a drink in a place above their class. Five *doblays* equaled what they took home at the end of a good day.

"Senyor Uroyo is correct." Porfiro's cheeks reddened as he informed Aurelo he would be losing his money. "I cracked the clay jar this morning. A Senen jar."

Aurelo groaned and thumped his fist on the bar. Uroyo chuckled and gathered his winnings.

At that moment, haughty Prosporo Rabago, dressed in a shiny white silk doublet, trimmed with silver stitching at the wrists and collar, appeared at the Oaken Cask's entrance. He surveyed the crowded tavern, hesitating briefly when he saw Aurelo and Uroyo. The pause was so slight, only someone watching closely would have perceived it.

A young woman, with smooth, fair skin, glided across the floor toward Prosporo. Her tight brocaded bodice was stuffed with her pert breasts. She smiled as she greeted him and offered her hand. Prosporo took it and lightly kissed the back of it. A ruby blush formed on the woman's cheeks. She gestured toward two women across the room. "Will you join my friends and I at the bar, senyor?"

Prosporo smiled and nodded to the two women at the bar. "I apologize, senyora. I have other plans."

A dejected look spoiled the woman's smile. The women at the bar returned to their chatting, though they kept a discreet eye on Prosporo.

"Perhaps another time." Prosporo excused himself and headed upstairs.

Uroyo placed a piece of cheese on his tongue, chewed it anxiously, and glanced at Aurelo. Uroyo emptied the remainder of his wine glass and wiped his beard with the back of his shaking hand. Then he too, climbed the stairs.

Aurelo leaned close to Porfiro's ear. "Please ensure we are not interrupted. There will be extra in it for you."

"You have nothing to fear, senyor. I will take care of it," Porfiro said.

The upper floor of the Oaken Cask had been converted from bedrooms into sitting rooms. Merchants and the wealthy paid well for quiet places to conduct their affairs - business, sexual, or otherwise. The second story was split into two by a hallway. A thick Muori carpet ran the length of it, displaying a finely stitched pattern of blue six-pointed stars on square white backgrounds, in parallel rows.

Behind the second door on the right, Aurelo, Prosporo, and Uroyo sat around a square table covered with rawhide secured by metal rivets. Above them, the candles of a small crystal chandelier illuminated the room. The flames cast dancing shadows on the stucco walls. The heavy black curtains were drawn. The air was heavy from the day's heat. A deck of cards was the only object on the table.

"Faquezia will not make it tonight," Prosporo said. "She has left the city."

Uroyo's voice quavered. "Are we betrayed?"

Aurelo showed no emotion, aside from pressing his face into his hands.

Prosporo slowly shook his head. His dark eyes were gloomy. "I do not think so. Borto's hounds would have picked us up by now."

"Then where did she go?" Aurelo asked speaking through his hands. "My understanding was that she planned to remain in Golandar another month."

"Maybe she got called away for an emergency," Uroyo said, sounding hopeful. "Family business or something."

"No, Faquezia does not move without a purpose and not without planning," said Prosporo.

Uroyo kneaded his hands together. "Harvest time's a month away. Her fields've yet to fully ripen. Why would she leave?"

"She did leave in a hurry," Prosporo continued. "And without her usual baggage. No carriages, wagons, or trunks crammed with her personal affects. Only herself and two escorts."

"She must be taking a short trip," Aurelo said lifting his face from his hands.

"Or, she wanted to leave unnoticed. We're betrayed." Uroyo moaned as he spoke.

Prosporo grit his teeth as he looked at Uroyo.

"She could've been arrested and collaborated with the king," Uroyo said. "She could've made a deal with him to betray us."

Prosporo's face reddened. "Stop guessing! You sound like a fool." He glared at Uroyo and Aurelo. "If neither of you have said anything to anyone else, then we have no problem. Besides, the Letios are not pro-monarchy. They do not fight. They pay the military tax as readily as we do."

Aurelo's mouth tightened. "Prosporo, have you said anything to anyone?"

"Bah! Do you take me for a fool? Of course, I have not."

"He had to ask," Uroyo said. "You practically accused *us* of doing so."

"I did not," said Prosporo. "I merely raised a valid issue."

A knock at the door quelled the argument, like a douse of cold water.

"Deal the cards," Prosporo said. He stuffed his hand into the leather pouch on his belt, dug out some coins, and dumped them onto the table.

Uroyo fumbled with the deck of cards and sloppily dealt them to the other two men, forgetting to deal himself in. Aurelo threw money onto the table, with a loud jingle. Then he approached the door to ask who was there.

A voice came through the door. "It is Pepe. I have brought the refreshments, senyor."

Aurelo heaved a sigh of relief and opened the door. Pepe entered, carrying a silver tray with a decanter of wine and four crystal goblets. A kitchen boy followed him and set a tray of food down on the table.

"Senyors, please ring the bell if you need anything else," Pepe said. He bowed his graying head and left.

Aurelo shut the door and took his seat at the table. "Bickering will not help us. I think this should be our last meeting, for a while at least."

"Agreed," Uroyo said with relief. "We can send word and arrange another meeting in the future, when the right situation comes about."

Prosporo poured himself a glass of wine. "Very well, now let us get on with this one."

"We are not the only merchants losing money," said Aurelo. "We have a right to charge a fair price and profit from the sale. This war is disrupting business. It has already destroyed my business. I cannot recover my losses with the king's decree in affect. I cannot save my business."

Uroyo put his cards on the table. "There'll be a great shortage of olives, too. Half of my groves have been ravaged. My competitors will bury me."

"My business has not been hit as hard as either of yours, but the people are worried and they are stocking up on goods like cloth," Prosporo said. "They are buying my cloth faster than I can bring more to market. I could easily double my prices and still sell it all. But I am losing profits on these sales, because of King Mendio's price decree. I pay a fortune to import the finest silks from Terghu and wools from Fringia." His voice hardened. "King Rodrigo has overstepped himself."

"That may be, but there's no law stopping him from issuing the decree," Uroyo said.

"Not yet," said Prosporo. "Things can change, however, and there are people willing to make those changes."

Aurelo's face was grim. "The nobles and the merchants. Rodrigo has always been heavy-handed. He picked up that bad habit early in his reign. He does not have all of the nobles on his side and even fewer merchants."

"War shaped him," said Prosporo. "It hardened him. It got him used to absolute authority."

Aurelo nodded. "Appointing Mazrio as High-General certainly did not win him friends among the nobility."

"He has been paying for that decision for the last twenty years," Prosporo said. "All his dealings and granting of favors have left many a noble insulted."

"Only a privileged few are called upon to be guests at Rodrigo's table," said Aurelo. "I have yet to be invited, and my wine is a favorite of his. It flows like a stream from the Alcazar's dining hall."

"He would not even bargain with us last week," Prosporo said with disgust. "He hardly let us speak. He simply spoke down at us from his raised seat, flexing his authority in our faces."

Uroyo nervously worked his lips. "What does he gain from the decree? It has nothing to do with gaining more support from the merchants. In fact, he alienates us."

"Or the nobles," said Aurelo. "Many nobles have mercantile interests, aside from ruling the duchies and the counties. Those nobles may be sympathetic to us."

The conversation paused. They sat in silence around the table. Laughter and voices from the great room filtered through the floorboards. They sipped their wine and picked at the bread, cheese, and slices of meat on the tray.

Prosporo broke the silence. "Only commoners benefit from the price decree. What could he possibly want with more support from the low-born?"

"Conscripts," Aurelo said. "He needs troops to drive out the Semotecs."

Uroyo furled his eyebrows. "But he's already sent the royal troops, and the marquis has mustered his militia to defend Spandel. He hasn't called for additional levies. There must be another reason."

"It is always like this with the king," said Prosporo. "The objectives of his plans are always masked in some way. The trick is to determine what is happening behind all the diversions."

"Let's stop guessing," said Uroyo. "It's useless, until we get better information."

"A defeat of the royal troops would be enough to start something." Aurelo walked over to the window and cracked open the curtain with a finger. The temple of Ghyo was visible across the street. "The nobles would call for Mazrio to be replaced as High-General. Much of Rodrigo's power is based on him."

Prosporo's face brightened. "Rodrigo's position would be severely weakened. If the humiliation were great enough, the nobles could be convinced to demand Rodrigo's abdication."

Uroyo's mood picked up, too. "Yes, then Sandovar would ascend to the throne. The nobles and the merchants can apply pressure to Sandovar. Bend him to our influence. He isn't made of as stout a material as his father. Masuf got that trait."

"Beltram Zepio must be thrown out of power, too." Aurelo said. "Sandovar hates him almost as much as he hates Mazrio."

Prosporo said, "We must help the army to fail, but we do not want a complete disaster, either. We can make arrangements to delay the supplies being sent to Todu's army, or deny them supplies entirely."

"We must speak to the other merchant houses. Find out who is supplying what to the army," Aurelo said. "Convince them to see the injustice Rodrigo has placed on us."

"The king has reigned for three decades and not expanded Azari territory, or influence," said Prosporo. "Sandovar will change that. He is aggressive and seeks glory."

"War is good only when it isn't on your land," said Uroyo. "Our profits will increase, supplying more war. Sandovar can overturn his father's decree, and we can rebuild our livelihoods."

"Rodrigo has fixed the prices so he can cheaply supply his army!" Aurelo suddenly exclaimed. "That's the reason for the decree."

Prosporo nodded. "He is using his decree to fix the mess he is responsible for making. Spandel was not properly defended."

"Many merchants are as wealthy, or wealthier than most of the nobles," Uroyo said.

"We will be heard. Our money gives us the right to wield more influence," said Aurelo. "The king is stubborn, but we will get what is ours."

"Our fortunes are made by us, from our hard work and ingenuity. Our income is not perpetual, like the nobles who have it handed down to them – land and title," Prosporo said, bitterly. "They simply have to worry about not squandering it. But unfortunately, we need some of them to affect a change."

"Our next step should be to learn the positions of the other merchant families," Uroyo said. "But we must be careful."

"Yes," agreed Prosporo. "Treason is deadly business."

"Our borders should have been better guarded," Aurelo said angrily. "It was *his* fault the Semotecs invaded so easily. And we pay for his mistakes. My *family* pays for his mistakes!"

# Chapter 20

## Pawn of the Faith
### 13 Janoben, 229 A.G.S.

Jurdana stood in the flickering light beside the bronze brazier at the edge of the dais, reading the message she had deciphered. A raven had arrived with it scarcely half an hour before.

Below her tiara's golden sunburst, Jurdana wrinkled her eyebrows with concern as she moved her eyes across the paper. Brother Gaetan had personally penned the original message. She knew it had to have been his writing. It was not the practiced and polished hand of a scribe. Gaetan only wrote his own correspondences when secrecy was his aim.

His message was brief. It instructed her to be by the sphere at one hour past midnight, on fourteen Janoben, not four hours away. Gaetan had drafted the message in the evening hours of the eleventh. The bird had made the journey from Arshapel to Fallheim in less than two days. Gaetan conveyed his urgency to Jurdana by gambling on the bird arriving at the earliest possible time.

Jurdana folded the paper and placed it into the brazier. The edges caught fire and the letter rapidly curled up into blackened ashes. She stepped over to her seat and smoothed out the back of her dress before sitting. She leaned back in the chair and curled her fingers around the armrest's smooth, curved ends. She no longer wrinkled her eyebrows, but her face was somber. Two messages had arrived from the Holy Tower that day, and Jurdana sensed their arrival had not been a coincidence. Though Gaetan's message did not reveal his reason for having such a late meeting, she had a distinct feeling that Orius Candell would be the chief matter discussed. *The power struggle within the Holy Council has moved its focus to Cheltabria.*

Jurdana considered the message that had arrived that afternoon. A scribe had not penned that one, either. The message had read:

*11 Janoben, 229 – Fifth hour after noon*

*Find out who is the heretic in Northern Cheltabria. If he is a priest, find out where his politics lie. Report any information about this. Remember your debt to me.*

*Sister Solayne*

Jurdana closed her eyes and breathed deeply, allowing her anxieties to drain away. She was in a difficult position. By the laws of the Holy Tower, she owed loyalty to the Holy Legate, her immediate superior, but she also owed a silent, unwritten loyalty to those who had aided her Ascendancy to the High Priesthood. Oftentimes, that loyalty held more influence, which Jurdana had known at the time she made her bid for power. And then she became a pawn in the schemes of others. Her fate had been bound to the fate of her supporters. A power shift within the Holy Tower, or a scandal, would remove her from her post in Fallheim.

But her main duty was to advance the Faith by bringing more people into the flock and to administrate the churches under her charge, but she spent more time than she cared to admit assisting in advancing the agendas of others. *There needs to be change. The system is corrupt. I must find the strength to finish what is started. I am so tired.*

Jurdana clenched her hands and raised them to her brow. She was fatigued from a long day, but it was only going to last longer. The Holy Council's machinations had drained her energy. She cursed herself for telling Gaetan about Orius Candell in the first place, but that had been unavoidable. Her knowing about happenings in the North was part of her portfolio. Gaetan would have found out some other way and confronted her about it. Then he would have used her failure in knowing about Orius Candell to damage her reputation with the Holy Council.

But she also had to deal with the demands of Sister Solayne, who no doubt had Sister Kalantha standing next to her when she had signed her letter. *But what is her aim? Gaetan will crush this heresy. That's his responsibility. Orius Candell has awakened the Holy Council, and they smell the stench of heresy in the North.*

Jurdana sat in silence. Ideas about dealing with the messages came to her and left as others took their places. She measured each one's value, weighing the positives against the negatives, looking for a way that would benefit her most and cost her least. But her thoughts were soon locked in a conundrum and her head ached.

She set aside the problem and called for an acolyte who appeared from a side entrance. She instructed him to summon Father Laigren. The priest had returned that afternoon from inspecting church properties in the eastern part of Southern Cheltabria and delivering items to be stored there. Jurdana hoped Laigren's report would be favorable, so much depended upon it.

The acolyte glided across the floor, white robe rippling behind him, and opened the doors opposite the dais. Father Laigren slowly appeared out of the darkness and lumbered into the brazier's flickering glow. He was of average height, with a large rounded stomach, balding head, and meaty arms and legs. His portly face was perpetually pink and walking made him breathe heavily. He wore a full-length white habit with an embroidered sunburst upon its breast.

Jurdana watched as he crossed the blue carpet's trail. It always amazed her when Father Laigren returned from an errand. In spite of his size, he had tremendous energy and always completed his assignments.

Father Laigren halted and bowed as deeply as his girth allowed. "May the Light of Ghyo guide you through the darkness," he said, breathing heavily through his nostrils.

"And to you as well, Good Father," Jurdana replied. "How was your journey back?"

"A month in length, Holiness. It rained much. Very hard on the mules." His heavy breathing replaced the sound of his voice. "But everything is secure in the east."

"I worry for your health Father Laigren. The efforts you exert in the service of His Church are incomparable."

Laigren shook his head. "I am but a tool in the hands of Ghyo. My toils and suffering are of no consequence. The work must be completed."

Pride for him welled up inside Jurdana. *How can I be blessed with such freely given dedication?* she asked herself - or maybe she asked the Creator. She then thought of the arrangements she had made, which led to her Ascendancy, and some of her pride slipped away. She thought about the loyalty she had promised to those who would use her to satisfy their own means. Gold and Ghyo's throne in Fallheim had secured her loyalty to them. She then thought about Father Laigren's position in the Church. He was a common priest blessed by the Gift and forever giving thanks to the Creator for the ability to ease suffering and heal wounds. *Am I using you, Good Father, as those above me use me?* Her conscience moved her to send someone else on the next assignment. *You've sacrificed too much.*

"Father Laigren," she said. "I intended to send you on another errand. However, I have already asked too much of you. You shall have a rest."

Laigren cocked his head. "Holiness, I tell you it would be a great insult to me if you chose someone else to do my work. We have come a long way together. A change would not be good at this time. Besides Holiness - there is no one else we can trust."

Jurdana sat rigidly in her chair and studied Father Laigren. His opposition surprised her, but he was right.

"Very well, I shall send you," she said. "In the morning, you will prepare to travel northward. It is time we established contact with Orius Candell."

"As you command, Holiness." Laigren bowed once again. "I thank you for your confidence in me."

"You may leave, Good Father."

The priest slowly turned and lumbered toward the doors. With every other step he took, his joints creaked beneath his heavy weight.

*I'm not like Gaetan and the rest,* Jurdana told herself. *Father Laigren serves me of his own free will. He asks no gold to secure his loyalty. We all use others to pursue our plans, but that's where our similarities end.*

An oil lamp cast stark shadows upon the many nooks and corners of the bookshelves. An hour past midnight came quickly. Jurdana sat in a cushioned chair in the corner of her small library beneath the temple. She forced herself to sit upright to fight off her drowsiness, but the solitude of the tiny library and the comfort of the chair's cushions beckoned her to shut her eyes.

All she heard was the sound of her own breathing. No noises from above penetrated the thirty feet of earth separating the library from the rest of the temple, which provided her a refuge from her priestly duties. Reading relaxed her. She most enjoyed books about Cheltan history.

Like few others in the Church's hierarchy, Jurdana had received special training in the use of the spheres. The trials taken in becoming a High Priest subtly determined who had the ability to use the spheres. Only the innermost circles of the Faith knew of them, and the Holy Council publicly denied their existence. The spheres had no special names except "The Devices." Having no certain names preserved secrecy. For the spheres were not of the Power of Ghyo, they were of the realm of the Elemental powers, wielded by the outlawed conjurers.

The crystal sphere sat on the table before her, two feet in diameter. A tiny blue light winked in the sphere's center. It grew in size and intensity as it filled the crystal and illuminated the darkened recesses of the small room. A milky mist swirled around the light, and slowly a face appeared amid the mist's wispy strands.

Jurdana had dozed off. Her head lolled awkwardly against her shoulder and she dreamt. In her dream, she stood on the highest balcony of the Tower of Vigilance, watching a light appear in the northern sky. It was beautiful to behold, like dawn's first light. The sight of it brought her a sense of warmth and security. *The light contains Hope.*

"Am I disturbing you, Sister Jurdana?" a familiar voice said.

She sat up with a start, rubbed her eyes, and ran her hands through her blond hair.

"I know it is quite late to have a meeting," Gaetan said. "Please, take your time." His last phrase was imbued with sarcasm.

"I...apologize for my appearance, Brother Gaetan," Jurdana said. "It has been a long day."

"And it will not be the last one for you for quite some time," Gaetan retorted. He held his arms to either side of the sphere at his end of the link. "Whenever you are ready, Sister."

Jurdana was embarrassed and silently cursed herself for dozing off. She knew Gaetan had been up since sunrise, too; but he never, in her recollection, showed signs of fatigue. *He has others take away his fatigue, but that only goes so far.* She knew he enjoyed putting her down and reminding her of her place. Her cheeks flushed with anger. "I have answered your summons," she said. "What service may I be to the Council?"

"News of Orius Candell has reached Arshapel. The subject was brought up inside the conclave. This heretic has aroused the attention of the Holy Council, whether he wants that attention or not," Gaetan said. "Tell me, Sister, have you heard anything new about this?"

Jurdana folded her hands in her lap. "I have no more information for you."

Gaetan did not hide his disappointment. "I was expecting to find out you had already sent someone north, but I see that I was mistaken."

"I understand your concern, Brother. I was unable to assign someone trustworthy enough to make the journey north, until this evening. My most trusted priest has returned. He will be leaving in a day or so."

"The Arch Priest is concerned by the possibility that one of our own is leading troops into battle. This is heresy of a most serious nature."

"I agree, Brother," said Jurdana. "His presence can damage our delicate relations with the Royal Houses of Iningia."

"I am glad you are of the proper opinion on this matter. The kings are always suspicious of militant moves by members of the Clergy,"

Gaetan said. "They have a difficult enough time accepting our explanations for the maintenance of the Order of Ilyas."

"Of course the kings have nothing to fear from the Faith," Jurdana said. *Or need they have fear, Brother?*

"The Faith exists to serve all. Now, I have had enough of the for-
malities. The priest whom you intend to send north, is he experienced
in dangerous assignments?"

"He is."

"I hope so. Because I am tasking your temple with the arrest of
the heretic, Orius Candell."

*Arrest.* The word struck like a slap. *No!* she nearly blurted out.
She blinked her eyes several times and felt light-headed. She needed
time to speak with Orius Candell. Learn about what drove him to
take the course he followed. And she had to satisfy Solayne and
Kalantha's wishes. She had to change Gaetan's mind.

"B-Brother," she sputtered, "it is said this Orius fellow has united
the Northern Tribes in the name of Ghyo." Her thoughts raced ahead
of her. She paused briefly to slow them and sort them out. "Admit-
tedly, his methods of uniting the northern Chelts are heretical, but I
believe arresting him will be a mistake and turn thousands away
from the Faith, whom the Church has ignored for centuries."

Gaetan's nostrils flared. Jurdana had struck a nerve. The High
Priest's hazel eyes narrowed and his voice took on a harder edge.
"*Sister* Jurdana, I understand your Cheltan heritage skews your view
of this issue. I do not have to remind you that it has taken the Faith
two hundred years to rebuild itself from the disaster of the Schism.
And we still have a long ways to go. But since that time, our reputation among the Royal Houses has never been more secure. The arrest
of Orius Candell is in agreement with the wishes of the Arch Priest.
His arrest will benefit the Faith."

*There's no way out of this dilemma. I have to order the arrest of
Orius Candell.* "I will make the arrangements," she murmured.

"Yes, I am sure you will. However, I have already made arrangements. A message should be arriving there within a day, instructing
the captain of the Order of Ilyas in Fallheim to send a group of
knights to accompany your priest. Since, I believe, the heretic is well-
guarded."

"And what shall I do with Orius when they return with him?" she
asked.

"Duke Malcomb will have a place reserved for Orius Candell in
the dungeon of Fallheim. That is all I have to discuss with you, Sister. Good night."

Gaetan dropped his arms and his image disappeared in a blink.
Darkness enveloped the room, though the lantern's soft light fought

against it. As Jurdana sat in her chair, her plans dissolved before her. Anger seethed within her. *Gaetan has again used his influence over the Arch Priest to further his goals.* She felt powerless to oppose him. *But Gaetan's moving quickly to conclude the issue of Orius Candell. Why?* The question added to her frustration. She made a fist and struck the armrest. Her post in Fallheim was too far removed from the Holy Tower. Getting news of the Holy Council's dealings took time, and her contacts in the tower had to use caution when they sent word to her. They had their reputations to look after as well.

Jurdana sat for some time in the semidarkness, mulling over her ruined plans, but she was determined to not give up. *I'll advance my plans despite you, Gaetan.* She would delay the departure of Father Laigren and the knights for a day. *I'll steal a march on you, but I have to find someone adventurous and arrogant enough to do the work - and it can't be a priest.* She had to make a choice by dawn, because a bird would soon arrive with the message for Captain Bilayr Argamone.

# Chapter 21

## Tradition's Sin
## 14 Janoban, 229 A.G.S.

A cool wind had picked up during the night. It blew in continu-
ously from the west, carrying a hint of moisture on its currents. Far to the west, below the horizon, heavy, dark clouds
moved toward Cheltabria. In the east, just above the mountain
peaks, the sun hung fat and yellow.

Small groups of Chelts dotted the valley floor. They had risen at
daybreak and eaten their meager breakfast of air-cured meat and
cheese. The warriors had taken rations with them to last a week,
enough time to reach Drenga from Ragnaar, but delays had occurred.
Two days had been lost recovering from the fights with the Oruks.
Tired warriors are hungry warriors, and after the previous day's fighting, they consumed double what they should have.

No one could have, or rather would have, dreamt of the Oruks
possessing the knowledge or the ability to fight as *civilized* armies
did, using tactics, reserves, and communicating during the battle.
But the Chelts had witnessed the reality of it. The Hordes of Sytor
had marched in great numbers to a single drum, under a single master, and fought shoulder-to-shoulder, as humans did. Although they
had been victorious, the Chelts knew next time could be different.

Egon had slept alone. His fellow Haagenvaardars had kept their
distance from him. Orius had not slept at all. And he, too, had spent
the evening away from his friends. But Culley had told him not to
wander far from the firelight's edge, so his companions could keep an
eye on him.

"Orius, please," Argus said. "Let me take your place. Egon's dishonored me as much as you."

Orius spoke calmly, "Thank you, but your injury is not worth the
taking of a life."

Argus stomped his foot and stormed off.

Chief Condin said, "Orius, being Chief of the Northern Tribes is
practically like being King of the Northern Valley. You could refuse to
take the Challenge on those grounds."

Orius shook his head. "There is a specific coronation ceremony
established by Kirkvold. Without the legitimacy of such a ceremony, I
would look like a coward, hiding behind a hastily set up law to save

my own skin. I must meet this Challenge in the old way, because our position here is precarious. We must pursue our enemy, because we cannot remain here longer for want of food. The army cannot be allowed to break up. I intend to settle this matter and go to Drenga."

Orius's companions averted their eyes. They knew he had to accept the Challenge, or lose his credibility as chief.

Orius laid his hands upon himself to use the Gift to drain away the fatigue of his sleepless night. But he stopped and did not take that luxury. His duel must appear legitimate, and he could not conjure fire to kill Egon, even if it meant costing him his life. He knelt and unrolled the rigid blanket roll he never used and removed two items from it – a cup-hilted rapier and a long, matching dagger.

Culley sat nearby, gnawing on a tough piece of cured ham. "You'll make your fight with that? I rather thought you'd select your two-hander."

Orius slid the rapier's slender blade from its stiff leather sheath, only the point and a third of the blade were sharpened. A touch of sorrow tainted his voice as the thought of killing someone entered his mind. "No, I am better with this. I am counting on Egon to use *his* two-hander."

Chief Condin pricked his finger on the rapier's tip. "He will not be expecting this. I have seen a sword such as this only a few times. That merchant from Fallheim, Pendros, he carries such a blade."

"I doubt that," Culley croaked. "That's an Azari blade. Azaris beat out the finest rapiers and cut-and-thrust swords in Iningia. His mother gave it to the boy when he was twelve. She charged me with his training."

Orius smiled affectionately at Culley. "Hard to believe an old warhorse like you can handle a blade like this."

"I may be a Chelt, but I cut my teeth on the battlefields of Fringia. A mercenary has to learn to use different weapons, or die." To Condin he said, "Actually, the boy's mother taught him the finer points of using that blade."

"Your mother?" Condin was surprised.

Orius's eyes drifted to the ground. "Yes. She has many talents. She was very active when she was younger, almost athletic. That was one of the reasons my father loved her."

Chief Condin nodded. "So, the mother of the Chief of the Northern Valley is Azari?"

Orius raised his eyes. "No, my mother is Fringian." His tone sounded as though it had been rude for Condin to ask.

"Please tell me if I offended you, Father Candell," Condin said, bowing.

Orius shook his head. "It was natural to ask. I will not blame ordinary curiosity."

"Thank you, Great Chief."

Culley's gruff voice cracked the air. "Remember, boy, Egon's speed with his two-hander lies around the edge of his range. Be quick on your feet and get inside it. He'll then have a serious problem."

Kathair rose from where sat cross-legged next to Moreena. "He's dangerous in a fight, Orius, like a cornered bear. Scared and enraged at the same time, interested only in survival. I was there when Argus gave him his scar. If Argus is a bull, then Egon is certainly a bear."

Moreena chimed in from where she sat. "It happened at the Summer Festival last year. Egon and Argus were the final combatants in the tournament. The prize was ten Fringian ducats. Egon knocked Argus backward. Their wooden swords cracked like thunderclaps. I can still hear the noise and see the rage in Egon's eyes. Spit running from his mouth. Argus's heel struck the root of the tree Egon was backing him into. As Argus fell, Egon swung his wooden sword so hard he snapped off a quarter of Argus's blade. Argus counterattacked and thrust the splintered end of his sword into the bottom of Egon's throat, tearing a gash where the shoulder meets the neck. The Chiefs judging the match declared Argus the victor. The object wasn't to draw blood, but to score hits that were lethal with normal blades. The Chiefs said Argus's hit was a killing blow."

Kathair went on. "While Egon laid on the ground, stopping the blood with the palm of his hand, he motioned Argus to approach. That's when he said to him, 'You took my prize money, but I got your sister.' Argus didn't realize what Egon was saying and paid it no great attention. You know Argus *is* a little dense, but after his sister's belly began to swell, Argus remembered what Egon had said, and Selma admitted to lying with Egon during the festival. Argus then traveled to Haagenvaarder last spring, to speak with Egon about caring for his sister and the child. He took with him half of the prize money to persuade Egon, but Egon laughed in his face, patted the scar on his neck, and told him, 'Give me the money, and I'll take them in.' You know about Argus. He gave Egon the money and went home to bring back his sister. When the two them returned, Egon and a couple of his companions met them outside the village. He told Argus he wasn't the child's father, and he and his friends would kill Argus and his sister if they didn't leave. Argus had no choice but to leave, though he told Egon the matter was not settled. Last spring, Selma began having the Pains."

In a quiet voice, Moreena said, "Selma and the baby died during childbirth. Egon's a big man and...well, she was so small and the baby was too large."

For an instant, Orius decided to give Argus permission to take his place for the Challenge, but the notion melted away as quickly as it came. The future of the tribes and his position as chief had consequences far more reaching. It made Orius uncomfortable to think that way. He was still not used to using others to further his ends.

"I will speak with Argus, should I survive this contest," said Orius. "I will pray with him, for his sister and her child. He must know their souls have returned to Ghyo and the Cycle is complete."

Orius peered toward the eastern peaks of the mountains. The sun was climbing higher in the sky. Across the field, he watched Egon wiping his sword blade with an oily cloth. The Challenge needed to be settled. The army had to get moving, but first, Orius had to kill again.

He slammed the rapier into its sheath and handed it and the dagger to Kathair. "Prolonging the wait is useless. My foe waits for me."

Orius dropped his white gauntlets to the ground. He reached behind his neck, unbuckled the straps of his studded-leather gorget, and let it fall to the ground as well. He undid his belt and pulled his bloodstained, dirty surcoat over his head. He removed his boiled leather cuirass and peeled off his sweat-stained shirt.

Stripped to the waist, he retrieved his sword and dagger and marched across the camp. Culley, Kathair, Moreena, and Chief Condin followed him. The Chelts he passed bent a knee to him. He cradled the rapier and dagger in the crook of his left elbow and raised his other hand above his head. The Light of Ghyo radiated from his palm and the glow shone upon the faces of those he passed.

"May the Light of Ghyo guide you through the Darkness," Orius said as he walked. "Stand by the Light, and your families and homes will live on. Turn your back on Ghyo and Darkness from the west will flood our valleys and drown us all."

Egon stood silhouetted against the rising sun. He was stripped to the waist as well; his blond hair was tied back in a thick braid. His pale blue eyes contrasted with the sunburned skin of his face. His two-handed sword was propped over his shoulder, beside the jagged pink scar Argus had given him. A cocky smile split his face.

Dozens of Chelts had gathered around Egon, but the crowd was ominously silent. A warrior had the right to challenge a chief. That was the way it had always been in Cheltabria. It was the price of leadership. The end was always deadly.

Orius closed his hand and extinguished the Light. The crowd merged into a large circle.

Egon's smile angered him. "The Oruks are probably watching us from the slopes of the mountain," Orius said, pointing to the peak at the valley's western end. "By pursuing this madness, we show our weakness to them. We only encourage them to continue resisting."

Egon laughed. "You're wrong foreigner. The Challenge shows our enemies we always have the strongest warrior leading us. You're afraid to defend your position as chief."

"You are a man of great pride, but of no honor," said Orius. "Your show of bravado does not fool me, nor the others gathered here. You are unwilling to set aside your personal safety for the good of all the tribes. This you proved yesterday when you swore no homage to me. Your love of yourself is your flaw."

Egon's eyes bulged. "Draw that bee stinger. My blade'll snap it like a twig!"

Orius pulled the rapier from its sheath; then he drew the dagger and handed both sheaths to Culley. To Egon, he said, "For one so interested in exercising his rights, you forget there is a certain way of conducting a Challenge, a traditional way. I am a foreigner and *I* know these things. I find it hard to believe you could be an effective chief – should you kill me, of course."

Egon snarled, grit his teeth, and recited the traditional lines. "I have come to the appointed place. I wield a weapon, matching your wishes. I am bared to the waist to show I wear no armor."

Orius responded. "I have come to meet the Challenge. I wield a weapon, matching my wishes. I am bared to the waist to show I wear no armor." He raised the rapier in his right hand and the dagger in his left, directing the points at Egon. He adjusted his feet and led with the right.

Egon hefted the stout sword from his shoulder, holding it in both hands and tucked against his right hip. He placed his left foot ahead of the other.

Silence hung over the crowd. They waited for either fighter to make a move.

Orius lunged forward, thrusting the rapier at Egon's chest. Egon was almost too slow, but he knocked Orius's blade away. He deflected the tip an inch from his flesh. But Egon countered and slid his sword along the rapier, aiming a cut at Orius's head and neck. Orius trapped Egon's sword between the cups and quillons of his rapier and dagger. He then pushed aside the blade and slammed a foot into Egon's groin. Egon yelped and staggered back. A boisterous cheer rose from the crowd.

Egon recovered and tucked his two-hander beside his left hip and placed his right foot forward. Orius regained his on-guard stance, keeping the dual tips pointing at Egon. He studied Egon's stance, searching for a weakness. There was a lull in the noise from the gathered warriors.

Orius closed the distance, thrusting the rapier at the center of Egon's body. Egon parried to the right, and with startling speed, swung the two-hander left in a tight arc to take Orius's leading leg. Orius shifted his quicker, lighter blade to the right and deflected Egon's blow. But instead of stepping back, he advanced and stabbed with the dagger at Egon's neck. Egon's eyes widened and he threw up his shoulder. Orius's dagger sank into his thick shoulder. Orius hopped backwards, withdrawing the dagger and simultaneously slicing the rapier's tip across Egon's thigh, leaving a cut across his skin and breeches. The Chelts howled with approval.

Egon cried out in pain and anger. He made a sloppy horizontal slash, but Orius skipped back and returned to his on-guard stance. Egon recovered his sword and held it again near his right hip. Blood flowed down his arm and leg.

Orius circled Egon, allowing time for blood loss to weaken him. But Egon's stance remained rock solid, though he breathed heavily through his nose and mouth. Orius lunged. He aimed the rapier at Egon's face. Egon's wounds slowed his reflexes, but he raised the two-hander to his forehead and barely knocked the rapier high. He groaned as he blocked the attack and fresh blood streamed from his shoulder.

Egon swung his heavy sword in an arc to his right. Orius drew back the rapier and parried to his left. Egon's heavier blade collided with the rapier, sending a shock wave from Orius's fingers to his shoulder. The cut's force carried the rapier with it and slammed into Orius's thigh. Only the thin rapier saved his leg. Orius cried out as the blow knocked him off balance. The crowd gasped. He struggled to keep the rapier and dagger pointing at Egon. The crowd murmured about how the blade had not snapped. Orius silently praised the forger for the fine work.

Egon recovered his blade to his right hip and suddenly lunged, thrusting his sword with both hands. Orius's eyes widened at the speed of the desperate attack. For an instant, he admired Egon's strength, stamina, and courage, but his admiration winked out. As Egon extended his arms, Orius stepped to the right, parried high and left with the dagger. He then flicked his wrist and trapped Egon's blade between the dagger's cup and quillon. All he needed was that instant. He slid the rapier's point through Egon's muscled chest and several inches out his back.

Egon's blue eyes bulged and his jaw dropped. He unleashed a high-pitched cry as Orius withdrew the rapier. His arms dropped to his side and his sword fell to the ground with a dull thud. He sank to his knees and flopped onto his face.

# Chapter 22

The Eagle and the Sunburst
14 Janoben, 229 A.G.S.

Rodrigo strolled the brickwork path of the Alcazar's parterre gardens. The twittering of birds filled the air, along with the wind rustling through the beech trees' boughs. Rodrigo loved the gardens' serenity. They were the ideal spot for him to be alone and think. Over the course of his thirty-year reign, he had made most of his important decisions while strolling the gardens' paths. It was in the gardens that he made the painful decision to annul his first marriage in favor of a political union with the Duke of Ariandor. During the darkest days of the war with Kheldune, the Trackers had come into existence here, while he sat on the ground leaning against the trunk of a tree. Rodrigo had given his concession to place Serophia on the throne of Ghyo's temple in Golandar while he stared at his reflection in the waters of the Muori fountain and cursed himself for not having the strength to deny them.

Now, solemn faced, he clasped his hands behind his back as he walked up to Beltram, who waited for him beside the fountain. Rodrigo wore a green silk tunic with a gold silk sash, running from his shoulder to his hip. His short black hair, sprinkled with gray, contrasted with his neatly trimmed black goatee. Beltram wore the black robe of his office and held his silver staff between his hands, supporting his aging body. For two days, Rodrigo had pondered the proper course to take, concerning the Church's offer. He had decided upon his answer to the offer that morning. Rodrigo knew he had made the *right* choice – but now, to Beltram's relief, he had changed his mind.

A palace footman rapidly approached. He stopped next to Beltram and whispered something into his ear. He nodded and waved the servant away. "She is here. And your daughter is with her."

Serophia marched through the arch cut through the evergreen hedge, bordering the stables' courtyard. Her silken shoes clicked against the bricks. Sunlight glinted off the golden sunburst covering her forehead. She resembled an apparition, riding a wind that whipped up the delicate silk of her gown. Rodrigo grudgingly admitted there was a beauty to the woman, and a sense of power surrounded her as well. Drucilla walked behind her.

The women stopped a few paces from the men and bowed their heads slightly. "Good morning to you, Your Majesty," Serophia said formally.

"Good morning, Holiness," Rodrigo responded.

"Good morning, Father," Drucilla said quietly.

"Good morning, *Princess*," Rodrigo said.

"I have answered Your Majesty's summons," Serophia said. "I can assure you the Holy Council eagerly awaits your approval. The money and knights have already been dispatched."

Rodrigo flinched. He rarely showed emotion while conducting royal business. "Why are they already on the move? I have not given the Church my response."

Serophia licked her lips, glanced over her shoulder at Drucilla, and returned her attention to Rodrigo. "For the sake of timeliness, the Holy Tower dispatched the money and the knights over two weeks ago. I cannot presume to know the thoughts of the Holy Council, nor control their actions. I can only guess they saw the situation here as severe, and they felt sure you would not reject such a generous offer of assistance."

Rodrigo turned his back on the High Priestess. His face reddened. He looked down at his feet and shook his head slowly. He faced Serophia again and stared coldly into her eyes. He would not allow the meeting to last much longer. He hated Serophia for all that she was and what she stood for. His chest fluttered and the sensation tightened into sharp pain about his heart. In a flash, he changed his mind back to the *right* choice. *Now's the time to give her my answer.* "The Holy Council throws around such large amounts of money and soldiery without assurances. I believe Your Holiness has assured them too much. The Eagle of Soriazar rejects your offer."

Serophia gasped and placed a hand to her mouth. Drucilla's jaw fell slack, and her eyes were white circles.

Beltram spluttered, "S-sire, I thought we decided on..."

"Silence, old friend," Rodrigo snapped. He kept staring into Serophia's eyes. "The king has spoken."

Serophia became pale and seemed on the verge of becoming ill. She wrapped her arms around her stomach.

Rodrigo smiled with satisfaction at her reaction. The pain in his chest lessened. "You seem surprised, Holiness. I wager you were counting on leading a successful expedition against the coastal towns of Semotec. You saw a chance for personal glory and a seat on the Holy Consistory. I also wager you made promises that are now impossible to keep. No, Holiness, my reasons for refusing the Church's assistance go far beyond the petty differences between you and I, but *your* troubles happen to be to my advantage."

Serophia's lips wriggled. "The council will be most displeased," she said, feebly. "If you think your refusal will result in my removal from Ghyo's throne here in Golandar, you are mistaken." Nervously, she smoothed the wrinkles in her gown. She breathed deeply, and then spoke with more confidence. "Since you have refused us, I must carry out the instructions given to me by the Holy Legate. Brother Gaetan said to remind Your Majesty of the debt he owes the Church for keeping silent. He said you would know what that meant."

*Indeed, I know what that means.* Rodrigo was certain he had chosen the right course. The Holy Legate coerced people into bending to his wishes. It was his best tactic. *A line's been drawn, and the next step is squarely in their hands. Information is power, but so is the sword. I'll not bend to the will of the Holy Council. The Azari people aren't a tool to be used for the aggrandizement of the Church of Ghyo. The Holy Tower was planning to make war pay for war.* Soriazar would have born the scars of the fighting, and the country and his coffers would have missed out on much of their rightful claim to the spoils of war.

"I shall send my refusal directly to the Holy Council. I am sure you will be sending a message as well," Rodrigo said. "Make sure you tell them, no foreign soldiers will march unopposed upon Azari soil. Tell them we do not require Fringian gold to finance our ships, or foreign mercenaries to fight our battles. Tell them they have misjudged the soul of the Azari people and the will of their king. Tell them, the Azaris love their land more than they love their Church."

Serophia stared mutely at Rodrigo. She turned to Drucilla. "There is nothing more for us to do here. He has chosen to suffer through what will surely come. We are leaving." Drucilla dutifully bowed to her mistress and followed Serophia down the brick path, but Rodrigo's voice stopped her.

"Drucilla, my child. Stay here with your family."

Drucilla turned and faced her father. Her eyes glistened with tears. "It saddens me to know my father has such contempt for the Faith."

"You do not know what you speak of," Rodrigo said. "You serve the enemy of your family. Stay with us and renounce your loyalty to the Church. Everything will be explained to you in time. You can continue with your priestly duties here in the palace. You will remain faithful, but you will serve Ghyo and not the Holy Tower."

"Child," Beltram said. "Listen to your father. He speaks to you truly. You know I have never lied to you."

Drucilla stared at her father. "I will learn of what is happening from whomever I stay with. I will then decide which version of the truth is *the* truth. What troubles me is I never expected to have my entire future turn upon the outcome of a single meeting." A tear ran down her cheek, but a wan smile came to her lips. "It would be easy for me to remain with my family, behind the high walls and atop the cliffs of the Alcazar. Mother Serophia is powerless to stop me." The breeze rippled Drucilla's gown.

"You must decide what is best for you," Rodrigo told her. "Not for your Church or your family, but for you."

Tears flowed steadily down Drucilla's cheeks now. She slowly walked toward Rodrigo and held out her hands to him. Rodrigo stepped into her embrace and pressed her to his breast. Her body shook as she sobbed.

"A piece of me...is being ripped away," she said with her face in his chest. "Half my life...has been devoted to the Church, and the other half...to my family."

Rodrigo felt her release the embrace. She took a step back. The tears still ran down her cheeks, but her sobbing had ended. "I am sorry, Father," she said.

Rodrigo watched in horror as his daughter slowly raised her right hand. The palm radiated an amber light that grew in intensity, until Rodrigo had to squint to see her.

"Blessed be the Light of the Creator. May it guide you through the darkness that lies ahead." The light faded as Drucilla closed her hand. She turned and walked to where Serophia was waiting. The High Priestess's face beamed with a triumphant smile. "I am ready to leave, Holiness."

Serophia placed her arm around Drucilla's shoulder, and the two of them walked down the path through the arch carved in the hedge.

Rodrigo shut his eyes and slumped his shoulders. His arms hung listlessly at his sides. "I have lost a piece of my family."

Beltram stepped closer to Rodrigo, his staff made a metallic clunk on the bricks as he did. "She may eventually see things as they really are. The allure of the Faith is powerful, and the Gift is a rare thing. She has something no king can give her, and she believes she wields a power greater than any king could possibly have. Drucilla is your brightest offspring, but she understands she is the fourth child of a king, destined to be married, to serve the best interests of her family. And she does not want that."

Rodrigo nodded. "You are right about her being my brightest hope, old friend. She may be my most intelligent child, but that alone does not produce wisdom. We shall see how long she stays there." He shook his head to clear his thoughts. He was the king again. "Summon Mistress Manda," he ordered. "We have preparations to make, orders to draft. The Black Hand marches at this very moment."

Beltram bowed. "As you command, sire." He headed down the path to the palace, but before he could leave, Rodrigo grabbed the sleeve of his robe.

"Send a rider to Olantaro. I am calling out the rest of the banners."

"As you command, sire."

Rodrigo remained beside the fountain until Beltram was out of sight. His face was sullen as he sat down on the fountain's edge. He pulled a linen kerchief from the sleeve of his tunic and dipped it in the cool water. He wrung the excess from the cloth and wiped his face and neck. She was his favorite. Drucilla had wounded him. She was not ill tempered like Sandovar, who reveled in the fact that he was heir to the throne, or garish like her sister Caermela, who was scandalously indiscreet about her private liaisons. She was not rough and unrefined like Masuf, whom Rodrigo loved second to her, or pampered like Javior, the baby of the family. His plan for Drucilla had been to have her receive one of the finest educations available. Then, she was to have become the First Wife of a suitable Muori prince, where she would have lived in extravagant luxury. Her marriage would have secured safe passage for Azari merchants sailing between Soriazar and the continent of Goria to the west of the Muoria Archipelago. It was to have been a great gift to his favorite child and to his country. It would have solidified the legacy of his long reign. It would have brought wealth to his coffers. But, with a single stroke, Drucilla's rejection of her family, of her obligations to Soriazar, had wrecked his plans.

Rodrigo envisioned the sickening smile across Serophia's lips as she had placed her arm around Drucilla. It was a mockery of his manhood and his kingship. Serophia was powerful, ruthless, and unscrupulous. She was a queen in all but name. *But how sturdy is the foundation of that power?*

"She will return to us," Rodrigo said aloud as he looked down the pathway leading to the arch through the hedge. He cared not at all if someone overheard. He ran his fingers over the golden eagle clasping the sash at his waist. "The king wills it."

# Chapter 23

## Designs Unraveled
## 15 Janoben, 229 A.G.S.

A torrential rain doused the Southern Valley. Lightning shattered the predawn darkness, creating wicked shadows amongst the forest of pines, firs, and oaks outside Fallheim. Gusts of wind made the rain fall at awkward angles. Five riders made their way through a narrow alley to the un-walled outskirts of town. The weather was perfect, though it soaked them to their skin. Scarcely a dog barked as they picked their way through the twisting streets. Miraculously, in the midst of the lightning and thunder, they had kept their horses calm. Not a whicker betrayed them. The downpour masked the splashing of the horses' hooves in the puddles of the unpaved streets. Rain never cleansed Fallheim of its waste. It simply stirred it up and turned the streets and alleys into filthy, stinking sewers.

The riders' leader halted at the end of the alley, which was the edge of town. Less than a hundred yards away, the forest stood across a space of cleared land. He looked left and right, watching for signs of unwanted eyes. There was a trail through the trees across the open space, which led to the main road running north to the Borvik Pass.

Individually, the riders crossed the clearing, driving their mounts at a brisk trot, trying to time their crossing between lightning flashes. Once inside the trees, they joined back together before moving on. Their leader located the narrow trail and the rest of them followed. They wound their way through the blackness of the woods. The closeness of the trees lining the trail kept them from losing each other. Intermittent lightning tore the shroud of darkness enveloping the woods, blinding the riders and taking away their night vision. After a half-hour, they came to the road and followed it north. The rain lightened to a steady shower and the wind abated. The lightning slowly died out.

Not counting the leader, two of the riders were men and two were women. Each of them wore a plain peasant's robe of brown, rough-spun wool. Hoods concealed their faces. Two of the Chelts were small in stature and rode with bows hooked to their saddles. The other two were large, with one slightly larger than the other, who had a greatsword angling across his back, while the slightly smaller one had an ugly, double-headed axe hanging from a ring on her saddle.

The leader wore a rough-spun cloak, too, which had tripled in weight from the rain. The plain cloak covered him to his knees, where it contrasted with his expensive, knee-length riding boots. He wore a gentleman's sword - a rapier - that stuck out from below the cloak's edge.

Pendros cursed Jurdana for plopping the weighty bag of gold in his lap. He still could not believe she had located him before dawn of the previous day. He also could not remember the last time he had been a victim of such rudeness. It amazed him that the High Priestess had set foot inside a brothel at all.

When the knock at the door awakened him, he had been fast asleep, wrapped in the arms of a wild Vhanti temptress. He had flung open the door and, out of habit and precaution, greeted the knocker with the tip of his sword. A cloaked figure stood in the hall. The figure drew back the hood of her black cloak a little to reveal her face. Pendros had nearly dropped his sword when he saw that it was Jurdana. He was naked from the waist down, and his manhood pointed at her from beneath the tails of his shirt. Jurdana's face had been solemn and dark patches lined her eyes. She glanced at his waist and quickly returned her eyes to his.

"We need to talk," she had told him as she pulled the hood over her head and entered the room. "Get dressed."

Pendros, looking dumbfounded, stepped aside. The whore still lay on the bed, propped up on her elbows. Her uncovered nipples pointed at Pendros like accusing fingers.

"Is this your wife?" the whore asked.

"Get out," Pendros ordered. He then helped her from the room by shoving her, naked, into the hallway. He threw her dress to her as he slammed the door shut.

Pendros sat on the room's only chair, without offering it to Jurdana. He dropped his sword on top of the small table beside the chair. He rubbed his eyes and yawned. When he felt more awake, he tried to sound as if nothing were out of the ordinary. "So, what can I do for you?"

Jurdana pulled back her hood. "I need you to go north and meet with Orius Candell. The Holy Tower has ordered his arrest and time is running out for us. I know you love your country." She then tossed the bag of gold at him, striking him in the groin.

Pendros had jumped when the bag landed on him, but he ignored the pain and ran his fingers through the coins. They made a lovely tinkling noise, but he was a little insulted by her shameless appeal to his greed. "There *is* more to me than a lust for gold, but if a person throws enough gold at you, it is difficult to control oneself. And I will not have another chance at making money before the spring thaw, so I accept the job," he said. "But this gold is not for me. I will use it to finance the journey. Normally, I would charge a personal fee."

"What you hold is only an advance," Jurdana told him.

The rain pattered on Pendros's head and shoulders. *Yes. Too bad it's too late to organize another caravan. I could've done this job and quadrupled my money by hauling back more iron.* But the autumn rains would have turned the road into a spongy morass before the snow could even have a chance to stop him. The mules could not pull iron over roads like that.

At least Jurdana's money had allowed him to pay his four best guards again that year. It would ensure they would be around when the snows melted and the ground firmed up next year. Success in business equaled surviving the competition, and surviving the competition meant Pendros had to hire strong guards for his caravans. *Always have to find the best in everything. Always.*

He only recruited guards from the warrior stock of the Northern Tribes. Burly, rugged, and well paid, they discouraged rivals from raiding his caravans. Even brigands roaming the mountains and the pass thought twice about attacking Pendros's wagon trains. He also kept a few of them with him year round, when he wintered in Fallheim. With his guards, he had foiled not a few attempts on his life in Fallheim's dark alleys.

Pendros glanced over his shoulder to check on his escorts. They rode behind him, scanning the trees for unseen foes, as he knew they would be. That is why he employed them, but in his experience, it was always wise to check on things for oneself. He returned his attention to the road ahead. He did not expect any serious trouble along the way. Maybe a gang of robbers would try to waylay them, but he felt he could stay ahead of the real danger - Father Laigren's party, which would be heading in the same direction the next day.

Jurdana had assured him that Father Laigren would delay his departure for a day, giving him a head start. It had factored heavily into Pendros accepting the job. But the rainstorm would eat away at his lead on Father Laigren and the knights. The muddy roads would slow his journey. He knew once the knights were given their orders, they moved swiftly. He would need every minute he could get to ensure he arrived in the North before the knights, because he wasn't sure about where to find Orius Candell.

But Pendros was sure he had kept his preparations secret. After Jurdana left him, he had made his way to one of his warehouses, while the streets were still empty and the people of Fallheim slept. He had sent a runner to locate and summon four of his hired blades to join him there for a meeting. By the noon hour, they had gathered to hear what their master had to say.

"I have agreed to run an errand for a reputable person," Pendros had told them. "It involves traveling to the Northern Valley to arrange a meeting and then to return to Fallheim. You will be paid half the money prior to leaving." He tossed Jurdana's fat bag of gold coins onto the warehouse's dirt floor for emphasis.

Gritta Kalbat, a huge woman with cropped blond hair and shoulders wider than most men, knelt down and emptied the pouch. She peered up at Pendros. "Who would pay this much money for such a simple task?"

"I cannot reveal the employer's identity," Pendros said.

Breedon Ulath, a Chelt with a massive chest and arms and a thick, ruddy beard, said, "Who're we suppose to see in the Northern Valley?"

Pendros nervously shuffled his feet. "A business associate of the employer, whose identity I shall reveal to you later."

Una Merwyd, a petite, muscular Chelt, who wore her dirty blond hair in thick braid that hung down to her left breast, asked, "Why do you need to hire only four bodyguards?"

"I need your answers today," Pendros said, ignoring her. "I intend to leave before daylight tomorrow."

Kelwyn Camerod, a Chelt with a slender body and an angular face, said, "Count me in. I always need more gold."

The others then reluctantly joined in, as well.

Pendros then gave them his practiced smile. "There will be adventure for all and – more gold."

*Gold. Is that why I'm out here on this wretched night? I'm already rich, and I have enough gold to last me into old age. Jurdana's errand was an act of treason.*

It had taken him a year to come to grips with his feelings about the independence of Southern Cheltabria. He remembered the time, two years prior, when Father Laigren visited his home late one evening. The priest wanted to quietly purchase the finest quality metal that Pendros would be bringing back from that summer's expedition. Father Laigren had promised him a good price for the ore. So, when he returned from the North, Pendros had set aside the metal for Father Laigren. Metal that was usually snatched up by buyers from Fringia, to be sold to smiths to be hammered into weapons.

Pendros had not asked where the metal went, or what it had been for. He had been satisfied with the payment and had kept silent about the arrangement. To him, it just seemed like another scheme by someone in the Holy Tower, or he figured it could be for the contingent of the Black Hand guarding Fallheim's temple. The Fringian merchants had not been especially happy with picking over the remnants of Pendros's metal stocks, and they had asked Pendros for the reason why the metal's quality was poorer than the previous years. Pendros had simply explained that another buyer had contacted him earlier.

He had nearly forgotten about it until last year, when Father Laigren again came to him in the night and arranged to purchase more metal. Again, the priest had insisted on secrecy. But the secrecy had made Pendros suspicious and concerned. So, he had refused to sell the metal to Father Laigren, unless he gave Pendros some answers. The Fringian merchants would have more questions for him, and they would be interested in knowing who was buying up all of the weapons-quality metal. Merchants like to know their competition. "Do you love Cheltabria?" Father Laigren had asked him, and that is how Pendros came into the folds of conspiracy.

Pendros knew the plotters whom Father Laigren was involved with stood little chance of succeeding. They were a small group, biding their time until an opportunity presented itself to break away from Fringian hegemony. In the spring of 229, the opportunity seemed to emerge. Orius Candell was thought to be that opportunity. If he could unite the tribes of the northern valley, perhaps he could be persuaded to send his army south and unite the rest of Cheltabria. *But first he must know of the plans to arrest him. Get him to trust us. Then Orius will owe a debt to Jurdana.*

The rain continued and chilled the air. Pendros's breath flowed in white clouds from beneath his hood. He risked much, as Jurdana did, in communicating with Orius, but he was disgusted with the vassalage of his home to the throne of Arshapel. Duke Malcomb's reign was a sham. Pendros thought him the poorest excuse for a Chelt he had ever met. *Spineless snake.* It angered him further to know that more than half of the taxes levied by Malcomb were shipped south to line the coffers of Arshapel. Fringia was the great leech of Iningia. It sucked the lifeblood out of Cheltabria, and Malcomb did nothing to stop it.

Pendros thought of the coming winter. The long line of grain carts from Fringia would soon leave after the harvest. Much produce would be hauled south to feed Fringia's huge population. He thought of the Cheltan families who would struggle to find food when the temperature plunged and the wind and snow whipped in from the North.

The gaunt faces of hungry children from his dreams appeared to him amongst the forest's trees. They stared at him with large hollow eyes. They had rags wrapped around their feet. They held out their hands to him, pleading for his charity - the charity of a powerful, wealthy man. *For once in my life, I'll do something to benefit others.*

The rain ceased. For three hours, Pendros and his guards moved along at a brisk trot. Mud splattered the horses' flanks and speckled the riders' cloaks. The air was cool and damp and heavy with the scent of wet earth and foliage. Sunlight had broken through the clouds.

"Pendros," Gritta called out in her husky voice. "You move us along as if this were some kind of race."

Pendros reined to a halt and spun around to face his companions. "This is a good spot to rest the horses. And, yes, we must reach the North quickly."

"Tell us more about this," Breedon said as he dismounted his brown shire.

Pendros dismounted and removed his cloak. "There are competitors we are trying to beat," he said, as he shook mud from his cloak.

"Competitors?" Una asked.

"That is correct."

"I want to know where you're taking us," Breedon demanded.

Pendros put his cloak back on and flashed a smile. "Of course you do. But to be honest with you, I do not know exactly where to find the man we seek, but I know where to start looking."

Breedon, Gritta, and Una groaned. Kelwyn kept a stoic face and quietly scanned the forest and the road behind them.

Una spoke first. "In case you've forgotten, it's not safe to travel the Borvik Pass. With the Oruks in the Drenga valley, we all risked our necks bringing back that last load of iron."

"For all we know," said Gritta. "They may have already reached the pass, and we may not be able to get through."

Pendros replaced his smile with a serious look. "I agree with both of you."

Breedon crossed his thick, rippling arms. "My fee just doubled."

Pendros ignored the weakness in his knees and smiled again. "The Oruks *are* a threat, and I did say there were risks involved. And, Breedon, you need to discuss your fee with the employer."

Breedon snorted and walked over to the trees to relieve himself.

"Where do we begin looking?" asked Una sounding annoyed.

"Drenga," Pendros answered.

Una's jaw dropped; so did Gritta's. Kelwyn ceased looking into the forest, but only for an instant. Breedon's water stopped flowing, like someone had closed the spigot on a cask of wine.

"Of all the lowdown..." roared Gritta.

"You should've told us!" Una shouted.

"Scoundrel!" Breedon yelled and rushed at Pendros.

In a smooth motion, Pendros stepped backwards and drew his sword. He pressed the rapier's tip against Breedon's throat. Breedon's eyes bulged with anger. His breathing was heavy.

"I think I need to remind you of the bargain," Pendros said. "I told you that once we were on the road, I would reveal the details."

Breedon took a step back, but Pendros kept the blade against his neck. "You may turn back if the risks are too great for you," Pendros told him. "But I insist you hand over your share of the advancement to the others, if you leave."

Sweat rolled down Breedon's forehead. The corners of his mouth twitched. "I'll stay."

Pendros smiled and withdrew the blade. "You really need to control that temper of yours."

Breedon snorted again, tucked in his manhood, and tied up his breeches.

Pendros slid the rapier into its scabbard. "The last word I was given was that the person we are supposed to meet was going to Drenga. That is why we are all being paid a lot of money to do the work."

"Pendros," Kelwyn called out. "Someone's coming up from behind."

Through the trees, sunlight glinted off metal. Flashes of white were visible. The staccato thudding of hooves on the ground resonated through the forest.

"Who are they?" Gritta wondered.

Fear gripped Pendros's chest. "The competition." He slapped Breedon on the arm. "Mount up!"

"It's the Black Hand," said Kelwyn.

"What're you getting us into?" Una asked.

"You are already in it," Pendros said. "Now ride!"

The five of them spurred their horses to a gallop, placing distance between them and the Black Hands. Pendros hoped the trees hid their flight. His knuckles were white as he clenched the reins and struggled not to pull on them. The appearance of the knights was humiliating, and he felt like a fool. The plan had collapsed. All of his advantages vanished the instant Kelwyn spotted the knights. A hundred questions flooded his mind, but he set them aside and focused on getting away. A race had begun.

The horses plodded through the road's thick mud. Pendros did not believe their tired mounts could be driven very far at that pace. He needed to know if the Black Hands had seen them flee. If they had, it must have looked suspicious. *They shouldn't be looking for us, though.* Only he and his hired blades were privy to his preparations. And he had been purposely vague in his explanations to Gritta, Breedon, Una, and Kelwyn, and none of them had been out his sight since they had gathered in the warehouse the previous day. *What happened to Father Laigren?*

The thick Cheltan forest hugged the edges of the road, forming a tunnel through which it wound its way north. In a green blur, trees and foliage streaked past Pendros, Gritta, Breedon, Una, and Kelwyn. They then came to a stretch of the road where the forest became sparser.

A little way further, the forest opened into a small clearing. It was the place where his caravans camped when they were a day out of Fallheim. Pendros's horse soon burst from the woods and into the clearing, bathed in sunlight. The road cut a muddy brown swath across the green grass. A tree-covered knoll stood on the clearing's opposite side, and Pendros led the way to it. The road wound around the base of the knoll. As they disappeared into the trees, Pendros charged his horse up the reverse slope to a sagging log hut on the knoll's crest. His guards followed and the party dismounted behind the hut. Lathery sweat dropped from the flanks of their horses.

"We will rest the horses here for a few minutes," Pendros said, though a few minutes would not do much for them. "I have to know how fast they are coming." He gestured toward the south. "We can see a good distance back up the road from here."

Pendros slid along the hut's wall and knelt on the damp ground beside its southwest corner. The air was still and muggy. The hut's walls were covered with moss and were crumbling from rot. Cool moisture soaked through the knee of his breeches. Kelwyn and Una joined him; Gritta and Breedon stood by the horses, keeping them concealed behind the hut.

"Do you think they saw us?" Una asked.

"Maybe," Kelwyn said. "If they did, hopefully we looked like a gang of bandits, scared away by the sight of the Hand."

"Oh, if it ever were that easy," said Pendros. "I doubt we were betrayed, though. *Very* few people know of this." His admission seemed out of place, and it brought a concerned look from Una; Kelwyn seemed to ignore it.

The three of them knelt and scanned the road leading south. There was no sign of the Black Hand. After ten minutes, they scampered back along the wall to where the horses were.

"They aren't pursuing," Una said. "We would've seen them by now."

"Mount up," Pendros commanded. "We will ride until we reach the inn at Okernau."

# Chapter 24

## Strike, Counterstrike
## 14-15 Janoben, 229 A.G.S.

The mounted scouts raced back to the main column, nearly trampling the warriors at the front.

"The woods are filled with Oruks and they're heading this way!" they shouted. One of them dropped from his horse, with an arrow in his back.

Orius and Culley rode forward. "Send word down the road to prepare for a fight," Orius ordered. He dismounted to lay hands on the wounded Chelt, but the man was already dead.

Within minutes, the underbrush came alive with movement. Rabbits and deer scurried through and around the Chelts. Then, scores of Oruks crashed through the foliage. Ringing metal and screams shattered the forest's peacefulness. The Oruks wrapped around the sides of the road. In seconds, the situation became confused. The Oruks' charge split the Chelts into small groups. They became little islands in the center of a swirling sea. Swords and axes flashed. Clubs and maces smashed bones and battered shields. Limbs and bodies fell to the forest floor – though more Oruk than Cheltan.

The struggle engulfed Orius and Culley. Orius held Worgoth's axe in his hands. He and Culley stood in the center of a circle of warriors at the head of the column. The Chelts used gaps in the pine trees to funnel the Oruks into killing lanes, which evened the odds.

Then a horn keened from somewhere, and the Oruks withdrew. The noise of battle subsided as quickly as it had begun. The Chelts did not pursue the Oruks far, except to dispatch the wounded ones, crawling away from the road.

Orius moved back along the line, tending to the severely wounded. He laid hands until he exhausted himself and could no longer stand. He was strong with the Gift, but there were many wounded. He ordered a halt, and the Chelts rested for several hours before moving on. The attack had killed no warriors, but several of the wounded needed to be sent back to the valley to recuperate with the Chelts wounded in the last battle. The rest of the warriors then marched on, until they camped when the light failed.

Orius rode his horse after the ambush and was rested by the time his army halted for the night. He spent the evening checking the wounded. He laid hands on wounds that had reopened, and on wounds he had not been able to heal earlier. Again, he worked to exhaustion. Moreena accompanied him and helped him afterwards to where he would sleep for the evening. Culley and Chief Condin took care of posting guards and organizing the watches. No fires were lit.

Orius felt his Healing skills lessening as his fatigue increased. "I doubt we can keep up this pace," he said to Moreena. "The shortage of food weakens us. It is weakening me. But advancing quickly after being attacked keeps the Oruks off balance."

"Hard choices," said Moreena. "But we can't allow them time to set up another ambush. And we don't have the time to travel off the trail."

"We must stick to this road," said Orius with disgust, "or retreat. And that is not an option."

The exhausted Chelts bedded down with empty stomachs. Those with any food consumed the mouthful or two they had left in their packs and pouches. They then slept with their hands wrapped around their weapons.

Distant rumbles and stark lightning preceded the storm. A strong, cool breeze rustled through the boughs of the forest's canopy. The skies opened up an hour before dawn. The Chelts awoke to find they lay in pools of muddy water. Sore muscles tightened up in the chilly wind and rain. They gave up trying to sleep.

The rain ceased and droplets pattered down from the branches overhead. Thin shafts of light penetrated the forest's canopy. Moisture saturated the air. Clouds of insects floated amongst the trees and undergrowth. The rain had transformed the road into a sloppy paste. The stink of blood and the Chelt's unwashed bodies smothered the forest's piney scent.

Orius sent five mounted warriors, led by Kathair, to scout the road. They returned less than an hour later with word that the Oruks had camped no more than half a mile from them. "They left a dozen dead and there are many footprints leading west," Kathair said. "I can't tell how many there were. I don't have Fayne's tracking ability."

Orius sighed at the mention of Fayne. "Ride out again. The rest of us will follow. The Oruks have to be found or they could set up another ambush."

The road ran along the base of the mountain at the eastern end of the Drenga Valley. It wound back and forth, following the contours of the mountain's draws and spurs. To the left, the land ascended through the trees and foliage to the mountain's peak. On the right, it sloped away to the stream, which ran back east. Pines and boulders clung to the edges of the road, which narrowed in many places to the width of a cart. Orius's column was strung out in single file. The road continued higher up the mountain's side. The foliage there was not as dense, and the pines did not grow as close together at the higher elevations. The upper part of the mountain was encrusted with rough outcroppings. Above the road, a row of boulders became visible through the trees. Up ahead, a large spur ran downhill and the road went over it, bending sharply to the left and out of sight. Kathair and the scouts sat their horses near the bend. Orius halted the tired Chelts along the road and steered his mount next to Kathair's.

"What news do you have?" he asked.

Kathair pointed to the bend in the road. "That bend's a good spot for an ambush. I decided to wait for you to close up. I have two warriors up there, checking those rocks."

Orius shaded his eyes with his hand and watched the warriors crawl up the slope. "Drenga should not be much farther. I want to be in a position to observe the town while the light remains."

"I wonder what can be seen from those rocks." Kathair pointed at the ridgeline of the mountain's spur, where large boulders jutted from the ground.

"Chief Condin," Orius called behind him. "Join us."

The Chief, wearing his yellowing white wolf's hide, trotted his horse up beside Orius and Kathair. "Father Orius, what need do you have?"

"Take a handful of your Wolf Riders up to those rocks along the spine of the slope. Look westward to see if there is a view of Drenga. I wish to look if there is one."

Chief Condin bowed his head. When he did, the wolf's eyes glared menacingly at Orius. "As you wish, Father Candell." He twisted in his saddle. "Alroy, Calum, Bevyn, Arturo - follow me."

He squeezed his horse past Orius and Kathair's and trotted up the road. The four Wolf Riders followed him. They rounded the bend and were lost to sight.

Orius shielded his eyes and again gazed at the Chelts scouting the mountain's side. Boulders near them stuck out of the ground like a row of teeth. Dozens of shadowed spaces existed between the rocks. Orius thought he saw movement in the midst of a shadow. The darkness there seemed deeper. An unsettling feeling twinged in his gut.

The two warriors approached the rocks. "Check the shadows!" Orius cried. But they were out of earshot.

Then, the warriors stopped climbing. Something streaked from the shadows. A black object crossed the distance between the rocks and Orius. An arrow struck his horse in the neck. The animal reared in pain, and Orius struggled to keep his grip on the reins. A second later an arrow flashed in front of his face. The fletching scraped his forehead, leaving a cut. Another arrow drove through boot leather into his calf. Up the mountain, the Chelts searching the rocks tumbled down the slope - their bodies riddled with arrows.

Orius cried out at the sharp, stabbing pain.

"Follow me!" Kathair roared at his remaining scouts. "We have to warn Condin of the danger!"

The other Chelts scrambled to find cover behind rocks and trees as arrows landed among them. Cries and shouts filled the air. Arrows imbedded into tree trunks and clattered off rocks. Some found marks and the wounded dragged themselves off the road.

Borgar, from Ragnaar, braved the missile storm and pulled Orius from the saddle. Orius grimaced and clutched at the arrow protruding from his leg. More arrows pelted the rocks and trees.

Further down the line, Culley lay behind the trunk of a pine. "Argus!" Culley called out to the big Chelt. "Argus!"

Argus stood off to the left behind another tree, glaring at the rocks concealing the Oruks and screaming curses at them. He looked around and saw Culley waving at him.

Culley made a hooking motion with his left arm and yelled. "Gather some warriors and clear out those rocks!" He repeated the hand signal, until Argus nodded in understanding.

Argus scrambled to the left, tapping warriors on the shoulder as he did so, motioning them to follow. Moreena joined him and they disappeared into the trees.

At the front of the line, Orius groaned and clenched his teeth. Blood ran from his forehead and down his face. "Push the arrow...the rest of the way through my leg. Then...snap off the tip."

Borgar's face was grim, his voice reluctant. "As...as you wish, Father Candell." He looked at the Chelts nearby, huddled behind the trees and rocks. He pulled a knife from his belt. "Hold him down. I have to cut off his boot."

Oruks appeared and disappeared among the rocks, exposing themselves long enough to loose arrows downhill. Soon, the arrow barrage halted, and the Chelts peered around the rocks and trees. Up the slope, several boulders shifted and shuddered. Slowly, they tilted as the Oruks wrenched them loose. The boulders turned over and over, gaining momentum, raising clouds of dust and dragging smaller rocks and boulders with them into a growing rockslide. The mountain came to life.

Standing firm against a wave of Oruks was something Chelts prepared for from a young age, but tons of rock yielded to no one. They broke and ran downhill through the trees. Borgar and another Chelt grabbed Orius and dragged him as they fled. Orius screamed in agony as the arrow in his leg was knocked about. He passed out from the pain.

The wave of rocks rumbled across the road and crashed through the trees, knocking over some large pines. Their heavy trunks ricocheted off the neighboring trees, knocking several others over before crashing to the ground. The cracks of splitting wood filled the air, along with the crash of stone against stone. Falling trees crushed several Chelts and their branches buried many more. Their cries replaced the chaos of the rockslide and clashed with the cheers of the Oruks.

The Black Rider stood behind his soldiers. "Line up. We are leaving. The ambush is sprung."

Fifty Oruk archers and infantry scampered along the mountain's face. The narrow path they had climbed to their perch lay beyond the bend in the road. The Oruks began to disappear over the ridge of the spur. The Black Rider mounted his horse and trotted alongside them. He was near the middle of the group when the Oruks in the lead suddenly stopped, causing the ones behind to pile into each other.

Wolf howls rode on the wind from the west. Panicked cries came from the Oruks. Sunlight glinted off weapons, and a pack of wolfskin-clad Chelts came over the rise. The leader, wearing a white pelt, buried his axe into an Oruk's shoulder. A few Oruks formed a line and offered resistance, but the warriors in the wolfskins rode them down.

The Black Rider drew his sword. "Form a line and advance! Archers, loose!" *Scum! There are only five Chelts, and they panic. I have fifty to throw against them.*

The Oruks gathered and moved toward the Chelts. Arrows zinged over their heads from their supporting archers. An arrow struck a Chelt in the leg and he spun his horse around and fled over the rise. The other Chelts followed him. The Oruks unleashed a cheer as their opponents fled. Freedom and safety lay to the west.

*I will not to die on a barren slope in Cheltabria.* "Move forward! Advance!" The Black Rider struck the Oruk nearest him with the flat of his blade.

As he hit a second Oruk, an arrow struck that one between the shoulder blades. He spun his hooded head around and saw a dozen winded Chelts coming at him from behind. A snarl came to his bloodless face. His thin, pallid lips curled back from rotten, blackened teeth.

"Turn about!" he barked in the harsh Sytish tongue.

Some of the Oruks nearby turned to face the new threat, but most broke and scrambled up the mountain. The Black Rider swung his horse around.

"Follow me!" he called to his soldiers, and he charged the Chelts in his rear.

The black stallion moved nimbly across the rock-strewn ground. A Chelt notched an arrow and drew back the string. The Black Rider reared up his horse and it stomped him with its hooves. Another moved in to attack, but the Black Rider swung the horse around, slammed the animal's rump into the Chelt, and knocked him away.

A handful of Oruks joined their leader and a tangled melee broke out. The tired, hungry Chelts did not fight with their typical energy, but neither did the surprised, frightened Oruks. Slow, clumsy blows were exchanged. The combatants stumbled amid the rocks. The battle turned into an ugly brawl - fists flailing, arms grappling, rocks flying.

The Black Rider steered his horse through the fight. The animal kicked and bit at the Chelts, without guidance from its master. The Black Rider swung his sword and took the arm of a Cheltan warrior. Ahead of him, a huge Chelt swung an axe and nearly hew an Oruk in two. *He is the leader. The Chelts are so predictable. They always follow the biggest and the strongest.*

The Black Rider pointed the stallion at the giant Chelt and dug his spurs into the animal's ribs. He raised his sword and prepared a heavy blow. But as he closed in, a wild female warrior screamed at him in the garbled Cheltan tongue. She appeared out of nowhere. She was tall, beautiful, and muscular, with long, brown hair. She wielded a two-hander.

The Black Rider was seldom surprised, even during the most chaotic engagements. He had survived dozens of battles, great and small, but the woman moved with dexterity. He hardly noticed it when her blade struck him. Sword and hand spun away together. The pain took a moment to register. Deep, unnaturally dark blood poured from his open stump. He unleashed a bone-chilling howl.

The Black Rider spurred his horse and it bumped the female Chelt away, before it galloped out of the melee. The Black Rider slumped forward and cradled his arm as the horse raced up the mountain and over the crest of the spur.

The fighting ended with the Black Rider's flight. The Oruks scattered and fled to the west. The tired Chelts did not pursue them, but the Wolf Riders cut into them for a short while.

Down the mountain, the road had been wiped out. Debris covered it completely. Arms and legs of the dead hung limply across branches and rocks. Dusty, injured Chelts pushed aside the debris. Slowly, they got to their feet and helped get others out of the tangled mess.

Orius lay on his back. His face was twisted in pain and streaked with mud, blood, and sweat. He breathed heavily. "Get on with it. Cut the boot. There are...many wounded to care for."

Borgar nodded wearily, crawled across the rocks, and began cutting away at Orius's boot. He had to stop cutting a couple of times to sharpen his knife on a rock.

Culley picked his way through the rubble. "Orius," he called out. Close by, a group of Chelts knelt in a circle. Someone lying on the ground groaned loudly. One of the crouching Chelts threw aside a tall, black leather boot. The same Chelt then reached down and the person on the ground cried out.

One of the kneeling Chelts raised his head, "Over here. He's here."

Culley's grizzled face was firm, but his eyes betrayed the worry underneath. Orius lay on a small patch of ground cleared of rocks. A bloody arrow shaft protruded from the muscles of his lower leg. Borgar broke off the arrow's tip.

"Sit me up!" Orius screamed. The Chelts lifted him by the armpits. His palms glowed with the amber Light of Ghyo. "Pull it...out!"

Borgar wrapped his blood-encrusted fingers around the shaft, took a deep breath, and yanked the arrow from the leg.

Orius's eyes bulged and his body convulsed with pain. He covered each of the bloody holes with his glowing palms. Veins bulged from his forehead as he directed the Gift to flow into the wound. The amber light seeped in, like a warm, soothing salve. The warmth soon reached every inch of his body – hypnotic and comforting. The bleeding stopped as the wounds closed. The sensation of pain subsided, and the Gift knitted the torn flesh. Orius' eyes grew heavy with the need to sleep. He released his hold on his leg and fell back on the ground.

"It appears you'll live, boy." Culley sounded relieved.

Orius looked up with heavy eyes at his mentor. "How many...did we lose?"

"It's too soon to know, but it doesn't look good. Their leader is a cunning bastard." Culley pointed uphill. "I saw him up there."

Orius did not have the strength to hold up his head. "They tried to kill me outright. I...was lucky. Bring the injured to me. I must help them...do what I can." Though he felt little pain, Orius' body still sensed a serious wound. His calf muscles twitched violently.

"Father Candell," Borgar said. "We need you to be healthy. Rest now. We'll do what we can for the wounded until you are stronger."

Orius moaned. "I could have waited...to heal myself. The arrow was holding back the blood. Warriors will die now...because I did not help them first."

Culley knelt and spoke quietly. "You can't blame yourself. All warriors die. Everyone knows that. It's just a matter of when."

Orius shook his head. "They deserve to grow old...raise crops and children. There has been enough death."

Culley dismissed the Chelts around Orius. "Tend to the others. Father Candell will soon be on his feet. Spread word of that. Tell it to the wounded."

Borgar and the others left.

"You're the leader, my boy," Culley said when the others were out of hearing. "People live to serve you. You make the choices that guide their lives."

Orius waved away the comment. "I still do not have to like it."

"Don't lose sight of your goal. Take back what is rightfully yours. Until the end, I'm with you - one way or the other." Culley then chuckled. "Besides me giving you the best years of *my* life, I owe it to your mother. She's a great woman who must redeem her reputation and claim what's hers, too."

"But days like this..." Orius began.

"Are to be expected," said Culley.

"That is not...what I was going to say," Orius muttered as sleep pulled at him.

"I know." Culley patted him on the shoulder. "I know. Rest now. We'll need you tomorrow."

# Chapter 25

## Summoning the Spears
### 15 Janoban, 229 A.G.S.

A scribe sat in a shadowed corner of the council chamber, scratching a message on a piece of parchment. A brass lantern hung above his head from a hook screwed into one of the rough ceiling beams. His quill wiggled back and forth. He dabbed sweat from his forehead and the tip of his nose. An errant drop would make the ink run.

Despite the heat, Rodrigo had ordered the windows to be closed and the curtains drawn. He sat in his high-backed chair at the heavy trestle table with the map of the nation on it. He quietly studied the positions of the wooden blocks, identifying the locations of the marquis's soldiers, the Semotecs, and Todu's troops. The marquis's militias had delayed the invader's advance and bought time for the Royal troops to reach Spandel March. The March's fate now depended on Todu's army.

"Sire," the scribe said wearily. "I have finished the letter to Don Yulazar."

"You do good work, Edero," Beltram answered. He sat in the shadows, in a high-backed padded chair. His silver staff shone in the darkness of his cornered recess. "Don Yulazar should receive this within a day or so. I will send it by bird. He will gather many lances for the Crown." Then his voice quavered. "And we will need every one of them."

"The next message will be to Ernesto Characo. Let me know when your quill is primed," said Rodrigo, seeming not to hear Beltram. There was a hint of impatience in his voice.

It had been a long morning of drafting messages. They had been working since daybreak, and the midday hour was fast approaching. Edero wiped his face and hands with a cloth. He lifted the lid on his portable wooden desk and retrieved another sheet of parchment. He flexed his fingers and massaged his hands. He picked up the quill and dipped it into the inkpot, which rested in a carved opening along the top of the desk. "I am deeply sorry, Your Majesty. I am at your disposal."

The back of Rodrigo's chair faced the scribe. Rodrigo sat with his elbows propped up on the armrests, his fingers steepled in front of his nose. "To His Lordship Ernesto Characo, Duke of Vorencia. Old friend, I call upon your services in this time of great need. Our country is threatened with invasion by forces of His Holiness, Arch Priest Ignater. As this message is being drafted, columns of knights of the Black Hand are marching toward our borders."

He waited until the scratching of the quill stopped. "They intend to march through our land as they head for Spandel March. They have no obligations to fight under our banner, or to follow the orders of our commanders in the field."

He paused, pondering his next words. "There has been a breakdown in relations between the Eagle and the Sunburst. The Church does not recognize national borders, nor any authority but its own. It is clear His Eminence no longer recognizes the sovereignty of this nation."

Rodrigo cleared his throat and continued. "A ship will depart Harluer bound for Vorenica. The vessel carries a contingent of the Black Hand charged with protecting a cargo of one hundred thousand gold pieces. The money is to be used for the licensing of Azari vessels to wage war upon the lands of Semotec. The Church again, under the guise of necessity, has chosen to settle its temporal matters with temporal methods. I find it distasteful when His Eminence sanctions the use of force."

Rodrigo sipped wine from a gilded goblet and continued. "Times are different, old friend. The political makeup of Iningia is shifting. The Church is asserting itself at the expense of Soriazar. I hereby issue this Warrant of Reprisal to His Lordship, Ernesto Characo, Duke of Vorencia. I task you with the seizing of all vessels flying the Sunburst of Ghyo, whether that banner be in the superior or inferior position, by the forces His Lordship deems necessary to the completion of this warrant."

Rodrigo took another sip as Edero scratched furiously to catch up. "All prizes won by His Lordship shall be his to dispose of, excepting the Royal Fifth."

Edero finished writing, laid down the quill, and set his desk on the floor. He carried the stiff parchment to the trestle table and set it down. Rodrigo leaned forward and read the document. He showed no sign of approval or disapproval as he reached for his quill lying next to a gilded inkpot. He dipped it in the ink and signed his name with a flourish.

Beltram slowly stood. Soft creaking from his bones accompanied his movements as he walked to the broad table. A stick of dark green sealing wax sat across the tabletop from Rodrigo. Beltram placed the item within his reach. Edero carefully folded the letter, while Beltram pulled down one of the lanterns hanging from the ceiling beams. Rodrigo flipped open the lantern's door and stuck the tip of the wax into the flame. He then dripped a blob of it onto the letter and sealed it with his signet ring.

Beltram spoke softly. "Your Majesty, there is time to consider another path. This aggression will not go unnoticed by other nations, especially Fringia. The vessel with the money will most certainly be Fringian."

Edero quietly returned to his seat. Rodrigo gave Beltram a hard look. "Fortune grants victory to the bold, old friend. Over three decades, we have worked to make our nation strong and stable. It is time to settle old scores. The Khelduni hate us. The Fringians fear us. The Iduin envy us. Prosperity for Soriazar lies to the west, but its security depends on matters to the east. A hundred and twenty-five years ago, this kingdom dominated trade along the western coast of civilized Iningia. And like all prosperous nations throughout history, jealous rivals plotted to steal a share of the wealth. Seventy-five years ago, Kheldune seized the port of Balbo from my grandfather after he ascended at the age of fifteen. They would not have succeeded without Church assistance, and the youth of my grandfather. Fifty years ago, Idu sacked Morzon and carved Galorica out of the heart of our country. Though I was very young at the time, I can still see the great black cloud rising from the city and smell the air, saturated with the odor of death." Rodrigo thumped his hand on the table, knocking over a couple of the painted blocks. "No one expects us to lash out. That is our advantage. We will have a year, I figure, to exert our influence upon those who seek to do us harm. By then, we will have a sizeable stockpile of firearms. It will then be very difficult for our enemies to attack us. They will wear themselves out and sue for peace."

Beltram shook his head with sorrow. "Your Majesty, war is uncertain. There is too much unpredictability, too much fog. We move too rashly."

"Edero, leave us," Rodrigo ordered. The scribe retrieved his desk and hurried from the room. "We have a new army with powerful weapons. By ourselves, we have the ability to drive the Semotecs off our land, but the Church insists on being involved in the fighting. They have declared our struggle to be a holy war, worthy of their intervention. They are spending huge sums on this venture." Rodrigo placed a finger on the map and traced the course of the Gudor River. "If we do not make a stand against them, foreign soldiers will march through our land and inflict untold havoc upon us. It is bad enough having our own troops marching through the land."

"But, Your Majesty," Beltram said. "You...we have not pushed negotiations with the Church very far. Perhaps..."

Rodrigo stared hard into Beltram's eyes. "The Holy Council is applying pressure on us to force us to go along with their plans. Before we agreed to their assistance, they dispatched their money and knights. Their arrogance knows no limit. The heart of the problem is simple. The Church does not recognize national boundaries. In their eyes, there is no sovereignty but Ghyo's. All kings need be suspicious of the Church."

"May I speak my mind, sire?" Rodrigo wearily flicked his hand, giving his approval. "The issue is even simpler than Your Majesty admits. Personal vanity is at the heart of the matter."

Rodrigo snorted. "The king and the nation are one. The lowborn exist to support the Crown; thenceforth, they are supporting the nation. You know that, old friend. I think this terribly hot summer has been hard on you. I know it has sapped some of my energy, and I am ten years younger than you."

Beltram sighed. "Your Majesty, we are overmatched. We are faced with a serious invasion of our land by the Semotecs. It is not prudent to launch attacks in opposite directions."

"One direction," Rodrigo corrected. "We attack to the south, but we will hold to the east and north. Our enemies will ruin their strength attacking our defenses in the mountains and around the walls of Vorencia. The lessons learned fighting Kheldune would serve us as well as they did thirty years ago."

"You are asking too much from Todu's untried troops," Beltram said. "Our militia is equally green. Thirty years of peace have produced no battle-hardened fighters for Soriazar. Three quarters of the Order of Olantaro have seen no fighting outside the tournament field."

For a long moment, Rodrigo considered Beltram's counsel. *Nothing's certain in war, but the prestige of Soriazar won't recover from subjecting itself to the Church's authority.* "Beltram, you puzzle me. You agree with your king that the Church is moving to increase its influence at our expense. Yet you see no other choice but to bend a knee to it."

Beltram slowly sat down in Javior's chair, third from Rodrigo's right. "Rodrigo, I cannot help the way I feel. You must understand. I speak for the future of the country. You will not be the last king. We must make policy that perpetuates the monarchy. I do not see this war with the Church as a means to that end."

"My legacy is at stake, old friend. My grandfather is remembered as the king who lost Balbo and Morzon. My father is remembered for his unending border wars with Idu and Kheldune, which accomplished nothing but to drain the Royal coffers. I hadn't a *doblay* when I ascended to the throne."

"Please accept my apology, sire." Beltram sounded ashamed. "My office exists to counsel His Majesty, but I have overstepped myself. You have always been most gracious in allowing me to voice my opinions. I trust you understand that if I do not voice my views; I do not properly serve the nation."

"Of course you have served me faithfully, but we must be of one mind when our plans go into motion. We owe the nation nothing less."

Rodrigo placed his hands on the table and stood. He went to the table by the wall and picked up the silver decanter containing wine. He returned to his table, filled his goblet, and took his seat again. "Borrowing gold from the Church thirty years ago was the beginning of our problems, but we could not avoid doing it. Khelduni troops were breaking through the passes of the Yunars. The Gudor Valley was at their mercy. We had militia to put into the field, but the knights of Olantaro were more interested in settling personal scores and competing in tourneys for fat purses. The knights had no faith in my abilities and most had yet to swear fealty to me." He sipped his wine. Beltram nodded slowly. "So, I broke with tradition and married the High Priestess of Golandar - out of love, yes, but for the good of the country, too. I bound us to the Holy Tower, and Damiana violated Church canon by marrying a noble, a king no less. But the Holy Tower sent us the gold anyway. They had their own score to settle with Kheldune. I used their gold to buy Olantaro's assistance – I had to *buy* Azari knights. I then gathered the militias of the Gudor Valley and led my army against the Kheldunii. Fate smiled on me, and I drove my enemies back into the mountains."

"That victory was your finest hour," Beltram said.

Rodrigo sipped his wine again. "Later, the Khelduni traitor, Menkus, rode into my camp with news that the enemy had gathered a massive army. At the time, my few royal troops were battered and the militias wanted to return home to harvest crops. Thankfully, the snows in the mountains arrived early that year. They blocked the passes, delaying the Khelduni invasion until the spring thaw. Fate *gave* me one winter to save Soriazar."

Rodrigo stared into his goblet. "During winter, the Duke of Ariandor answered my request for soldiers and money. He recognized the disaster facing the country and his personal interests, but his assistance came with a price. His wished for his grandchildren to be the heirs to the throne of Soriazar." An ache formed within his chest. "For the nation, I made the greatest mistake of my life. I left the woman I loved, for the cunning and clever Khalia, whom I have never loved. A piece of me died that winter, old friend. It tore a hole in my heart that has never healed."

"Being king is a terrible burden for anyone to carry," Beltram said. "The opulence and riches of monarchy blind many a claimant to the thrones of Iningia. It takes a great person to rule."

"Khalia is a jealous woman," said Rodrigo. "The presence of my former wife and lover in Golandar humiliated her. The annulment of my marriage to Damiana offended the Church more than the marriage had itself, but they nonetheless offered more money to finance the spring campaign against Kheldune. And we desperately needed the gold - but placing Serophia, Damiana's main rival, on the High Priestess's chair in Golandar was its price. And she has made me pay for that mistake ever since."

There was a low rapping at the door. "Enter," Rodrigo said.

A page entered and announced, "Rufina Manda, Mistress of Trackers, sire."

Rodrigo's mood switched from gloomy to attentive. "Send her in."

Rufina entered the council room, striding confidently. Her leather doublet, gauntlets, and boots, all dyed green, creaked softly with each step. Her red hair was pulled back into a long, tight braid, showing off her emerald eyes. A pair of short swords bounced rhythmically from her hips.

Rufina placed a hand to her chest in salute. "Your Majesty, what service may I render you?"

Rodrigo smiled and rose from his chair. "The services I require are of the highest importance." He extended his arm toward the decanter of wine. "Would you share a cup with your sovereign?"

Rufina bowed. "It is always a pleasure to drink from your cup, sire."

Rodrigo poured a goblet of wine and handed it to her. "Please, take your seat." He glanced at Beltram. "You, too, Master Steward. Page, you are dismissed. Tell Edero to remain outside." Rodrigo returned to his seat, and Beltram sat in his corner. Rufina took the third chair on Rodrigo's left and slapped her leather gauntlets along the edge of the map. She studied the positions of the painted blocks.

"The green blocks will remain in the mountains," Rodrigo told her. "My travel plans have changed. I will not be journeying south to join the army."

Rufina pulled her eyes from the map and furled her eyebrows.

"The political situation has changed," Rodrigo said. "It will not be safe for me to venture outside the Alcazar, let alone the city."

Rufina asked, "Your Majesty, is there a plot against your person?"

"Against my person and the nation. But the threat is from without."

"Who has raised their hand against the nation?"

Rodrigo smiled a tight, content smile. *Ah, my tigress's teeth are always sharp.* "Tell me, Mistress. What is your opinion of the Church?"

"I...I am not sure I understand where His Majesty is going with this question," Rufina said.

Rodrigo sat up and folded his hands together. "Do you agree with Church doctrines and teachings?"

Rufina sipped her wine. "With due respect to Your Majesty, my family has never subscribed to the teachings and doctrines of the Church of Arshapel. The earth and the Creator are one being. Ghyo does not exist among the stars as they wish us to believe. He is of the earth."

"But the Church of Arshapel is Ghyo's vehicle for reaching the people, both high and lowborn," Rodrigo told her.

"If I have offended Your Majesty. It was not my intention. I simply wished to answer His Majesty's question."

"No, Mistress, no." Rodrigo chuckled heartily. "It is I who offend with my peculiar questions. Your honesty is one of the qualities that makes you a great leader."

"I am flattered Your Majesty thinks so highly of my abilities. But I cannot accept those accolades without acknowledging my father's doing."

"Quite right!" Rodrigo rapped his knuckles on the table. "The blood of my old friend runs thick within your veins. Do you agree, Master Beltram?"

"I do, sire. We are favored at having Mistress Manda among the defenders of our realm."

A slight blush came to Rufina's cheeks. "I do not believe His Majesty summoned me here to review my portfolio."

Rodrigo composed himself. "Yes, Soriazar requires your services. The Church of Ghyo has seen fit to exert its interests upon us. They wish to subordinate our sovereign power to theirs. The Holy Council has declared our struggle with the Semotecs to be a holy war – a crusade. Therefore, they believe they should play a major role in its resolution."

"Your Majesty, I have heard nothing of this until now. Secrecy has been well maintained. Though, I do admit noticing the comings and goings of the High Priestess."

"The negotiations with the Church have advanced quickly. Too quickly for third parties to become involved," said Rodrigo. "At least, we hope so." He gazed at the map, absently setting up the wooden pieces he had knocked over. "Knights of the Black Hand are marching toward our borders. At this moment, a column of three hundred, plus their usual entourage, moves through Kheldune. I wish I could tell you which pass they intend to use. They wish to march south through our land to wage war on the Semotecs. This is unacceptable. Mistress Manda, your Trackers must bar their way through the Yunars. Destroy them, if possible. You shall command all militia and Royal troops operating within the provinces of the Yunar Mountains."

Beltram shifted in his seat. "Master Beltram, do you have some insight to offer?" Rodrigo asked.

"No, sire," he said. "His Majesty's course has been set."

Rufina pulled her eyes away from Rodrigo and studied the area of the map around the Yunar Mountains. Her eyes darted back and forth. "There will be nine hundred to a thousand marching with the knight's column, counting squires and servants. I have five hundred guarding the entire frontier with Kheldune. If I strip the outposts to bare bones, I can muster two hundred Trackers at the crossing point. Depending on where that will be, but it could take up to three days to have forces in position to slow their advance."

"I have ordered the militias of the Yunar provinces to serve at your command," Rodrigo said. "That will give you around fifty mounted troops and three hundred infantry."

"The mounted soldiers will serve us some good, but the dismounted will be useless. Too slow for what I have in mind," Rufina told him.

"Then I will leave them to defend the keeps of the local lords. The Black Hand cannot leave hostile garrisons behind them. That should buy you time to mass at the crossing point. I have every confidence in your abilities, Mistress Manda."

"King Mendio, you have bestowed a great honor upon me. I am Mistress of Trackers, not one of your generals."

"The mountains are your ancestral home. There is none other more suited to their defense."

"Majesty, will you grant me this simple request?" she asked. "I require the services of His Highness, Prince Masuf."

"I cannot grant you that request," Rodrigo apologized. "His Highness is serving as the eyes and ears of the Royal Army. You alone, my mighty warrior, are up to the task."

Rufina furled her brows and took a long sip of wine. She set the goblet down and wiped her mouth with the back of her hand. "The Black Hand will receive a sharp welcome."

Rodrigo stared at his beautiful commander. *A sword has beauty, and so do you.* He turned to Beltram. "Master Zepio, I wish to speak with Mistress Manda in private. You are dismissed, but do not go far."

Beltram's knees popped as he rose to his feet. "As you wish, sire." He grasped his staff.

The doors clicked as Beltram shut them behind him. Rodrigo waved for Rufina to move closer to him. He laid his hand on the first chair to his left. Rufina took the seat next to her king. "I have another task for you," he said quietly.

Rufina glanced toward the doors. *She's intrigued by the fact I've dismissed my most trusted advisor.*

"Master Zepio is not to be privy to this?" she asked.

Rodrigo ignored her question. "You swore fealty to me, when you inherited the command of the Trackers from your deceased father."

"Yes, of course, sire."

"Ghyo's temple in Golandar poses a real danger to the success of your ability to defend the border. Within the temple, there is a device that allows the High Priestess to communicate with the Holy Tower. The device is very ancient. I need you to storm the temple, seize the device, along with the High Priestess and the Princess Drucilla, and return with them to the Alcazar."

Rufina exhaled and slumped forward. "I now know His Majesty's interest in my religious views."

Rodrigo remained silent for a few minutes, allowing time for Rufina to sort through her thoughts. *Her loyalty is essential to the execution of my will.* "The Trackers that have been gathered to serve as my escort south are the swords I offer you to complete this task."

"When does His Majesty wish the raid to be done?" said Rufina.

"The day after tomorrow. Time is short. The Holy Tower has dispatched its forces some two weeks ago. They are that far ahead of us. We must slow down the pace of their designs. We need time." Rodrigo pulled a silk kerchief from his tunic sleeve and wiped sweat from his forehead.

Rufina was direct. "Majesty, how will the people of Soriazar feel about us raiding a temple?"

"It will be easier to deal with them if the High Priestess and the Princess are taken unharmed."

"A day is not much time for me to plan this, but I understand the nature of our plight. I thank Your Majesty for the opportunity to serve in this way." Her voice rang with conviction, and she raised her goblet. "Will the king honor me with a toast to our success?"

Rodrigo raised his goblet and touched it to Rufina's. "No, it is I who should offer a toast to your loyalty."

# Chapter 26

## No Respite
### 15 Janoben, 229 A.G.S.

Pendros and his hired blades walked the last mile into Okernau. Dry mud clung to their cloaks. Fatigue lined their eyes. Their horses' heads hung low. They passed a caravan of twenty wagons, laden with iron ore, camped in the field on the western side of the road. A number of armed guards circled the wagons, and drovers sat in small circles, rolling dice and smoking pipes. Pendros recognized the caravan as the one that had arrived in Ragnaar as his was leaving for the south. He pulled his hood a little further over his head. Attention was the last thing he needed - attention led to questions.

Thatched roofed log huts defined Okernau, squeezed in among a forest of pines and oaks. The village marked the edge of the civilized north. The mountains of Northern Cheltabria rose up a dozen miles to the north, denoting the extent of the Law. Farmers worked fields along the sides of the road as Pendros's cloaked band passed by. They warily watched the mud-splattered strangers limp along, whose rough-spun capes contrasted with the quality of their weapons.

The road bisected Okernau. The brewer's long log building sat on the left, beside a small trail cut through the trees. A row of empty oak barrels stood along its wall, stacked two high and leaning in different directions. The ripe odor of fermenting grain wafted from the building, tainting the scent of the pine trees. Further up the road, the Golden Acorn became visible through the trees on the right. Pendros and his comrades kept their heads bowed as they passed the people moving about the village.

The heart of Okernau was the Golden Acorn Inn, a two-story, half-timber structure. The entire village worked to support it. They grew its food and brewed its beer, ale, and mead. They ran the blacksmith, cooper, and miller shops that served the merchants who stayed at the inn.

Pendros led the way down the short path to the front door of the Golden Acorn. A young groom sat on a bench in front of the inn, waiting for customers. He stood as Pendros's group approached.

Pendros spoke in a low tone, keeping his head to the ground. "Tell the innkeeper I wish to bargain for goods."

"As you wish, sir," the groom replied with a drilled formality. "May I ask who's calling?"

"A business opportunity," said Pendros.

The groom did not hide his surprise at Pendros's answer. He raised his eyebrows, shrugged, and disappeared into the Golden Acorn.

Pendros turned to his companions. "Keep quiet and let me do the talking." Breedon, Gritta, Una, and Kelwyn nodded their heads.

The door to the Golden Acorn's great room stood open. A wall of noise passed through it. Drunken caravan guards and drovers filled the inn. The Golden Acorn was the last place to get a drink before moving into the Borvik Pass, and the first place to get one on the way back.

The groom returned with the innkeeper, Clust Kampynn, an aging Chelt with thin arms and a round belly. Clust regarded the caped figures with suspicion. Pendros handed the reins of his horse to Gritta and motioned Clust to follow him. Pendros stopped a few paces away beside an oak tree, keeping his back to the inn.

"This is...unusual," Clust said. "What can I do for you?"

Pendros reached up and pulled back the edge of his hood. Clust's face instantly brightened with recognition. Pendros made a shushing sound. "I need to trade horses."

"Master..." he began.

Pendros cut him off. "There will be extra in the deal for you, for your discretion. I plan to leave this evening, but my horses are exhausted. I need to trade for fresh mounts."

"I...I am afraid...I have no horses to trade with you," Clust told him. "The stables are filled with the horses of others. I would have to find the owners and bring them to negotiate with you one trade at a time. I can't see how I can keep the transactions discrete."

Pendros grit his teeth. "Then we will not be trading." The last thing he wanted was to stay the evening in Okernau and risk allowing the Black Hand to get ahead of him on the road - or worse yet, should the Black Hand stay the night with his party still in town. "Please care for our horses, Clust. We leave in a few hours. We also need food and drink and supplies for the road." He gently pulled the innkeeper closer. "Above all, we need privacy."

"Of course, Master Pendros," Clust said quietly. "May I ask why?"

"I am taking advantage of a business opportunity." He reached into his pockets, produced four gold coins, and pressed the money into Clust's hand. "Here is an advance to hold your tongue. I will give you more when I leave."

"Master..." Clust stopped himself. "Sir, you are more than generous. He scratched the stubble on his chin and sucked at his lower lip. "I can quarter you in one of the servants' huts behind the Acorn. Good and private, but not exactly what you're used to, or deserve."

Pendros rolled his eyes at Clust's flattery. "That will do. Peace, quiet, and *privacy*."

Clust called out to the groom, "Lead our guests to the stables. I'll meet you down there."

Clust returned to the inn, and Pendros and his hired blades led their tired mounts down the path to the stables. The Golden Acorn maintained two stables for its guests. The stables were half-timber structures like the inn. The groom called to someone in the stables, and two boys appeared from one of the buildings and sank pitchforks into a large pile of straw. Pendros and his guards turned the horses over to the grooms, who reeked of manure.

Pendros lowered his head, keeping his face shadowed while he spoke. "Give them your finest fodder. Rub them down, as well."

Clust Kampynn quickly walked down the trail toward the stables. He stopped a short distance away and waved for Pendros to follow. His voice mirrored his anxiousness. "I'm ready for you. The cooks are preparing your suppers. Come along."

Pendros sensed something odd and walked over to Clust. "What has you so agitated?" he asked as they started back toward the inn together.

"A troop of the Black Hand has arrived," Clust told him. "Their captain is rather demanding. I must hurry and get you settled in, so I can attend to them."

Fear clutched Pendros's chest. Beating the Black Hands to Oker-nau had been a close thing. His mind raced. *Do I risk telling Clust anything else?* "Why are they here?" he asked, trying to not sound too curious.

"I don't know. They just arrived and marched into the great room, demanding to see me," Clust said. "I was in the kitchen and slipped out the rear. I must be getting back." He pointed to a hut near the kitchen's entrance. "I opened the servants' quarters for you. Opida will bring your food."

Clust left Pendros and entered through a back door leading to the kitchen.

"Get inside," Pendros told his companions.

The door to the hut had hardly closed when Breedon complained, "Why are we holing up in here? I want to spend some of my advance on the whores." He made a pumping gesture with his hips.

Una wrinkled her nose. "Those sluts give womanhood a bad name. It's hard enough being a female fighter in this world."

"You're a fighter, Una," Breedon agreed. "A fighter no *man* can conquer." He glanced at Gritta and chuckled at his own joke.

Una slipped a dagger from her sleeve. It appeared so quickly that Breedon seemed to not know what had happened.

Pendros grabbed Una's wrist. "No." To Breedon, he said, "You need to keep your mouth shut." He jabbed a thumb toward the inn. "If you want to attract attention, why not go inside and talk to the Black Hand."

Breedon swallowed hard.

Gritta stepped over to the small window next to the door. She peeked out. "Do you trust Master Kampynn?"

Pendros released Una's wrist. He tried sounding confident. "I am paying him extra. He makes a lot of money off us when we come through town. He will not jeopardize our good business relationship."

Kelwyn pulled a stool close to the window, where he could watch the back of the inn and the path leading around to the front.

"Pendros, you have a lot of faith in gold," Una said. "The Church has gold to throw around too, if the Black Hands know about us."

"More money than I have," Pendros admitted. "I do not plan to stay long. We are slipping out of town after nightfall, but we have to figure a way to get provisions for crossing the pass, without attracting attention."

Kelwyn said, "That will not be easy. The townspeople will recognize us. I recognized four of the caravan guards. Two of them I've worked with."

A gloomy silence hung over the hut. *This is worsening by the minute*, Pendros thought. *Worse, yet, Clust said nothing of Father Laigren being with the knights.*

Gritta leaned with her wide back against the door, still peering out the window. "Pendros, no one should know why we're here. You practically held us hostage yesterday. Now's a good time to tell us the details."

Breedon folded his arms and cocked his head to one side. Una returned the dagger to her sleeve and folded her arms too. Kelwyn kept his eyes on the window.

*I hate it when the hired muscle gangs up on me.* Pendros had grown close to his guards over the past few years, except for Breedon, who had trouble getting along with anyone. They had survived ambushes and had saved each other, once or twice. *I'll tell them, but not everything.* "Our employer sends us north to arrange a meeting with the heretic priest, Orius Candell, before the Black Hand arrests him."

Pendros's words landed like a hammer. Gritta, Una, and Breedon stood slack-jawed. Kelwyn took his eyes away from the window, but just for a moment.

"Since when did politics interest you?" asked Una. "Or the Church?"

"Who's the employer?" Breedon's loud voice seemed to shake the dust from the roof.

"What could he want with a heretic who hides out from the law?" Gritta added.

Pendros cleared his throat and looked at the floor. He slid his boot across the dirt, making a semicircle. He did not give an immediate answer. *What would they think if they knew the truth?*

"He has an army for hire." Kelwyn surprised everyone. He was a man of few words, but they usually hit hard.

Pendros nodded. "He *does* have an army."

"You would risk your life, our lives, to deliver a message for someone wanting to buy the services of a mercenary?" Una asked.

"No," Gritta said. "He never does anything save for profit."

"What do you gain from this, *Pendros*?" Breedon said spitting out the last word. "What's this trouble you put us in?"

Pendros moved his eyes from person to person. "You do not wish to know the truth. It could cost you your lives. Being ignorant is sometimes better."

Breedon grabbed the edge of a small table. With one hand, he flung it against the hut's logged wall. "I'm tired of your puzzles!"

Pendros backed off a little, giving himself room to draw his rapier. Breedon's northern temper usually got the best of him. Una and Gritta gave Pendros hard stares. Only Kelwyn seemed uninterested as to what was happening, but Pendros knew he listened to everything that was said. He flashed his practiced smile. "Fine, then. Anyone who wants to leave can go and keep your share of the advance." He sat on the bottom bunk of a bunk bed. "But I will not reveal the employer's identity." His nervousness surprised him. He licked his lips and wiped his sweaty palms on his breeches. Only a year earlier, he had come to grips with his own opinion of the situation in Southern Cheltabria. *I'm still not sure if I'm comfortable with my feelings about it.* "You may know there are Chelts who consider Duke Malcomb to be the most un-Cheltlike Chelt in the Southern Valley. Those same people feel Cheltabria should be ruled by Cheltabria, and the duke does not fit into that scheme of things." He looked into the faces of his companions, who seemed unimpressed. "These same people agree that what is happening in the Northern Valley needs to happen in the Southern Valley, as well."

Muffled sounds of revelry coming from the inn were the only noises heard inside the little hut. Pendros sat on the bunk, expecting his companions to tongue lash him. Breedon shook his head slowly. Gritta stared at the floor, frowning in contemplation. Una's eyes were wide; the color had drained from her face. Kelwyn kept looking out the window.

"Count me in," Kelwyn said. "I don't think our secret's out. I want the gold."

Pendros smiled. "That is one. The rest of you can go. No shame. Your pay is secure for the winter. Though, I will need you again in the springtime."

"Our pay's secure," Breedon grumbled. "Only if you aren't dead."

"Yes." Pendros's face became serious. "Treason is hazardous."

Gritta's husky voice was critical. "We know what we get from this. You still haven't said what you get if the duke is overthrown."

"I have no idea what is in it for me," Pendros said soberly. *No tax burden, maybe?* "We have only been sent to arrange a meeting. I know nothing past that."

"Who's being positioned to replace the duke?" asked Una.

"I do not know," Pendros said. "I want the change. I know that. That is why I am here. Every winter the Chelts of the Southern Valley suffer for want of food, while the Fringians break bread every day." He would not tell them about the images of the starving children that disturbed him. *These hardened souls will see it as a weakness.*

"Pendros, when have you given anything to the poor, or cared about them?" Una asked.

His eyes dropped to the floor. He heard Jurdana's voice, appealing to his conscience and his love of his country. He remembered running through the filthy streets of Fallheim when he was young. For an instant, the hunger pangs of childhood returned. "Let me say, I have remembered my roots."

Breedon scoffed at him. "I've heard you twist your words time and again. Believing you is difficult." He shook his head in disgust. "I'm out."

"I believe you're telling the truth," said Gritta, sounding surprised to hear herself say that. "If the North is rising, I must stand by Tydorhagen."

Una's nostrils flared and she pouted. "Well, I guess I can't go against Lunevik. I'm already up to my throat in this treason."

"Three in, one out," Pendros said. "Can we trust you to keep silent about this?"

Breedon huffed and ignored him.

"What'll you do in Fallheim if Pendros dies?" Gritta asked Breedon, like a friend would. "This scoundrel pays us double what he pays his other guards. No one else in Fallheim will pay you those wages. Keeping Pendros alive is in your best interests."

Breedon shook his head in frustration. He pounded his fist on his thigh. "Gold and women. One can't get by without either." He spat on the dirt floor.

"Opida's coming with the food," Kelwyn announced.

In the great room of the Golden Acorn, four long trestle tables and benches stood in parallel lines. A half-dozen square tables sat along the walls. Twenty guards and drovers ate, drank, and listened to a minstrel playing a mandolin. Coins, playing cards, and dice were mixed in among bread bowls and wooden trenchers with scraps of food on them. Oil lanterns hung from hooks in the rough-cut rafters, lighting the inn's interior. A wispy cloud of pipe smoke swirled around the lanterns.

Argamone Bilayr, Knight Captain of the Holy Order of Ilyas, stood next to the door, waiting for Clust Kampynn. Splatters of mud dotted his white surcoat, with Ghyo's sunburst centered on it. He held his polished barbuta in the crook of his arm. The helm's gold-plated spikes and the gold stitching on the backs of his white gauntlets identified his rank. He was tall, wiry, and clean-shaven. His angular face was devoid of emotion.

Clust walked through the door leading from the kitchen, kneading his hands as he crossed the great room. "Accept my apology, sir. I came as quickly as I was told of your arrival," he said in Tradespeak.

Captain Bilayr's Fringian accent was unmistakable. "Spare me your flattery, innkeeper. You assumed correctly that I do not speak your barbarous Cheltan tongue. My men and I require three rooms with two beds apiece. Make the arrangements. I do not care if it requires throwing half the scum in here out into the street. I pay in gold."

"Y...yes, sir," Clust said. "Th...there is plenty of room for you and your knights."

"We will take our mounts to your stables. My men are hungry and thirsty. Clear off one these tables for us and get rid of the whores. We will return shortly."

Clust smiled. "My other patrons are paying customers, too. There's room enough for everyone."

Argamone Bilayr looked at Clust Kampynn as though he were looking at a tool on a workbench he needed to use. "Stabling our horses will not take long." He turned and left the inn.

Clust dabbed at the sweat on his forehead. He faced the room and waved his hands. "Pardon me, everybody..."

The ten knights led their horses down the path around the inn. They gathered at the opening to the stables. "Sergeant Dennger," Captain Bilayr said in Tradespeak. "Find the grooms. Put them to work, and assign two knights to stand first watch here. The rest will follow me to the inn."

"As you command, sir," the sergeant acknowledged the orders in his guttural Imbrian accent. "Kidekos, Heymar - you two pull first watch."

The two knights remained with Sergeant Dennger and the horses, while Captain Bilayr and the others marched back up the path toward the inn.

Dennger entered the stables. Three grooms were inside, rubbing down and feeding a group of exhausted horses. "Boys, do you know Tradespeak?"

The shortest of three came forward. He held a feeder bag in his hand. "I do, sir," he said meekly.

Sergeant Dennger eyed the sweaty horses. His voice showed concern. "These are fine animals. Who did not spare the horseflesh?" He walked over to the shire and patted its forehead. "This looks like one of the horses I saw earlier. Are the riders here?"

The groom hesitated. "Yes...they're here."

"Did you see them? Do you know them?"

"I...I saw them, sir," the groom said. "I can't tell you...who they are."

Sergeant Dennger hardened his voice – just a little. He placed his gauntleted hands on his hips. "Why not?"

The corners of the groom's mouth sagged and his lips quivered. "Th...they wore cloaks. I couldn't see their faces."

"Did they say anything to you when they left their horses?"

"No," the groom answered. Then his face lit up, like he remembered something important. "Only one of them spoke. The one with the shiny boots."

Sergeant Dennger nodded. "Stop tending to those horses. Those of the Order of Ilyas need tending first." He spun around and marched off down the path toward the inn. "Do not allow the owners of those horses to leave." The two knights bowed their helmeted heads.

Kelwyn had watched the knights lead their horses around the Golden Acorn and disappear from sight, moving in the direction of the stables. He, Pendros, and the others hastily ate the beef and vegetable stew, served in bread bowls, and drank the beer that Opida Kampynn had brought for them.

"How much longer do we stay here?" Gritta asked.

"Not as long as I had figured on," said Pendros.

"By my count, two of the Hand did not return from the stables," Kelwyn said. "The sergeant just went by, though. His steps seemed hasty."

Una took a drink from a wooden tankard. "They left two by the stable. Are they guarding against something, or making sure their horses are being tended?"

"No one should know why we're on the road, or what is our task," Breedon said. He glared at Pendros. "Or is that not true?"

"I do not know," Pendros told them. "The Black Hand showing up so soon is a surprise."

"You *knew* the Black Hand would be following us north?" Una exclaimed.

"Yes, but they were not supposed to ride out of Fallheim until tomorrow morning." Pendros set his bread bowl on the bed next to him and pulled a soggy chunk from it. "That is what went wrong." He tore off a piece of bread with his teeth. "Before we make a move, I have to find out if someone is traveling with the Hand."

"Tell me who to look for," Breedon said. "I'm restless sitting here."

Pendros shook his head. "I have to go." He drank some of his beer. "If the situation goes sour, get to the horses - Black Hands in the way, or not."

Kelwyn set his bread bowl on the dirt floor. He stood and strung his bow.

"We have to get the horses saddled before you go look," Gritta said. "Should trouble come up everyone ride to the east."

"Gritta and Breedon saddle the horses. Una and Kelwyn find a spot in the woods and cover them," Pendros said. "I will wait in here and give you time to get started. I will enter the Acorn through the kitchen."

"Keep your faces covered," Breedon told them.

The Chelts pulled their hoods over their heads. Kelwyn cracked open the door, looked left and right, and slipped out. Una followed him. They disappeared into the trees and undergrowth behind the Golden Acorn. Gritta and Breedon walked from the hut and strolled down the path to the stables.

Pendros stayed inside, watching the kitchen door and the trail running beside the inn, but his excitement compelled him not to wait as long as he had said. He had to know. *Is Father Laigren inside?* Every second he waited seemed like a missed opportunity. He moved quickly toward the kitchen door.

Breedon and Gritta approached the stable, great sword and battle-axe resting over their respective shoulders. Seven of the Black Hands' horses stood in front of the entrance. The grooms were visible through the open doors, unsaddling three horses. Two knights of the Black Hand talked to each other among the horses in front of the stables.

The knight named Kidekos turned his head toward the inn, let go of the reins he held, and walked toward Gritta and Breedon. His gauntlet-covered hand grasped the hilt of his long sword.

"Stop where you are," Kidekos commanded in Tradespeak. Breedon and Gritta kept walking. He spoke again with his Khelduni accent. "In the name of the Holy Tower and Canonical Law, I cannot allow you to go further."

The arrow struck the golden sunburst on his chest as his sword was halfway out of its scabbard. At such a short range, the arrow punched through his mail hauberk and the padding beneath. Breedon hopped forward and swung his sword in a broad arc, hewing one of his legs. Kidekos landed hard on his back, and the fall knocked his helmet cockeyed. His high-pitched shriek filled the air. Like a giant cat, Gritta pounced on the wounded knight. Her axe blow caved in his chest; blood rapidly darkened his white surcoat.

Heymar sprinted through the stable's open doors. He was through them before Gritta and Breedon could slip past the horses. Kelwyn crashed noisily through the bushes beside the stables. Una burst out of the undergrowth, reaching behind her ear for another arrow. Heymar knocked over one of the grooms and squeezed by the horse he worked on.

"Boys, find the Sergeant!" he screamed in Imbrian-laden Tradespeak. "Find him if I die!"

Heymar emerged from the opposite end of the stables and stopped his flight. His head whipped around frantically. Two huts stood to the right and he started in that direction, but he only took a few steps before an arrow struck him low in the back. He cried out and spun around. His long sword flashed from its scabbard. In the midst of the undergrowth, Kelwyn stood up, notching another arrow. Una, Breedon, and Gritta came thundering out of the stables.

Heymar stood on-guard. "Those who strike at the Order of Ilyas will find no refuge."

His Tradespeak fell on uncomprehending ears. An arrow plunged into his chest, then a second. His lifeless body collapsed to the ground. Breedon handed his sword to Gritta and walked over to Heymar. He bent down, grasped him under the armpits, and dragged him into the stables.

Kelwyn moved out of the woods. "Get the other one out of sight. I'll cover the trail." Breedon laid down the knight and went to get the body of the other one.

Una yelled at the grooms. "Saddle our horses!"

Onion and garlic smells greeted Pendros as he stuck his head through the kitchen door. Potatoes hung in nets from hooks in the ceiling, alongside air-cured pork legs. Opida Kampynn stood beside a heavy table. She wore a scowl as she rapidly chopped carrots with a long knife. Opposite Opida, a stout older woman, with her graying hair tied into a bun, sprinkled flour on her side of the table and sunk her thick fingers into a mass of wet dough. A young female bent over a stone fireplace, spooning stew into a bread bowl.

None of them noticed Pendros until he stepped inside. Opida Kampynn set down the knife and placed her hands on her hips. "If you want more food, talk to Clust. I don't like patrons in my kitchen. Use the front door if you want to come in." Opida's helpers stopped working and stared at the cloaked figure in the doorway.

Pendros shook his cowled head. "May I please use this entrance? I am looking for someone. I just want to peek into the great room."

Opida became irate. "You can *peek* through the front door. I have no time for this."

Pendros did not press the matter. Unwanted attention had to be avoided. He made his way around the back of the inn to the side where the path to the stables ran alongside it. He found an open window.

A terrible scream tore through the air. The sound chilled his blood. The closeness of the trees around the Golden Acorn concealed the direction of the noise, but he knew something had gone wrong near the stables. He wondered if the occupants of the great room had heard the scream. Cautiously, he peered through the window. The sounds of laughter and talking spilled out of the Golden Acorn. Pendros could not see much. The knights of the Black Hand sat at one of the trestle tables. Father Laigren was not with them, but Pendros could not be certain, unless he stuck his head through the window.

"There is one of them," a voice called out in Tradespeak.

Pendros jumped up and his hood slid back. Sergeant Dennger and Captain Bilayr stood at the corner of the inn. The distinguishable barbutas of the Black Hand covered their faces, but the whites of their eyes were visible through the T-shaped slots.

Captain Bilayr pointed at Pendros. "You! I know you. Explain this behavior."

As the captain and sergeant drew their swords, Pendros dashed off down the trail, cape flapping behind him.

"Stop! Only the guilty flee the Knights of Ilyas!" Sergeant Dennger yelled.

Pendros emerged from the trees near the stables. He saw the horses of the Black Hand, standing in a loose cluster. A large, dark stain lay in the middle of the trail. A black boot lay at the edge of the stain. Breedon ran out of the stables. Pendros sprinted toward him. The look of concern on Breedon's face told Pendros the plan had failed.

"Gather the others. We are out of time." Pendros slid to a stop next to Breedon and looked down. The boot contained a severed leg. "Why has this...happened?" He panted heavily.

"He challenged us. Said something in Tradespeak and drew his sword," Breedon said with a grin. "It ended quickly."

"Take that smile off your face. You have killed one of the Hand." *This is totally out of control.* "I was seen. I think the captain recognized me."

A voice sounded from up trail. "Halt! Go no further."

Captain Bilayr came into view, striding arrogantly toward Pendros and Breedon. "In the name of Arch Priest Ignator and his Exalted Office, surrender to me," he called out. "I have summoned the knights who travel with me. You will not escape."

Captain Bilayr doubled over in mid-stride. Kelwyn's arrow burrowed through mail and padding. The Knight Captain curled up on the ground, wailing in agony, clutching at the shaft of wood protruding from his belly.

Kelwyn stepped from the trees. "We've killed three of the Hand," he said, correcting Pendros's count.

Pendros stared at him in disbelief.

"Our horses are inside," Breedon told Pendros.

Pendros pulled his eyes away from Kelwyn and turned his attention to the horses of the Black Hand, waiting to be unsaddled. "There is no time. Everybody take one of these and lead your own. Scatter the rest."

Kelwyn, Pendros, and Breedon quickly judged which of the knight's horses seemed fresher than the others. They slapped the six they passed up on the rump and sent them scurrying into the trees. They led the chosen horses into the stables. Inside, their horses were not ready. Only the bridles had been fastened to the animals' heads.

"Leave the saddles," Pendros ordered. "We will transfer the Hand's saddles onto ours when we are clear of Okernau."

A commotion came from the direction of the Golden Acorn. Men shouted and flashes of white were visible through the trees.

"Mount up!" Kelwyn cried, surprising his comrades with a rare outburst of emotion.

Everyone moved with urgency except Breedon. "I can't leave the shire." He raced around the giant horse and threw the overly large, specially crafted saddle on his horse's back. He hastily buckled the cinch just tight enough so that the saddle would not fall off.

"Hurry up, you fool!" Gritta roared. "They'll torture us if they take us alive."

The Black Hands were in sight, but they stopped and gathered around Captain Bilayr. Sergeant Dennger bent a knee beside his leader, while the other knights watched their horses being ridden out of the opposite end of the stables by Pendros's party.

# Chapter 27

## An Abrupt Goodbye
### 15-16 Janoban, 229 A.G.S.

The Alcazar was visible through the window. Dusk's waning light bathed its smooth walls in a deep reddish hue. Stark shadows were etched upon the steep, rough slopes of its granite cliffs. Drucilla sat before an elongated mirror, slowly stroking her long hair with a gilded brush. She gazed at her reflection, pondering her taking sides against her family and her people. Her thoughts were a mixture of sadness and guilt, but a firm foundation of resolve supported them. *The Creator has given me the Gift. His blessing's a source of power and influence.* It had ultimately bolstered her decision to stand by the Faith.

But turning her back on her family was more agonizing than she cared to admit. She was twenty-two and had spent half of her life in the care of the Church, but the other half had been spent in the palace with her family. She now had two families, who were at odds with each other. Her siblings had followed royal tradition and served Rodrigo and Soriazar. Sandovar was heir to the throne. Her sister Caermela had married Borto Camidor. Masuf was First Captain of Trackers, and her baby brother, Javior, served in the Royal Army. Drucilla was supposed to have married at her father's discretion, but when she became a priestess, the circumstances had changed. A new pathway had opened to her.

Tears ran down her face as she stared at her reflection. *A person has to serve some master. No one can go through life without pledging fealty to someone. No one, not even kings, can deny the Creator his due worship.* Drucilla now cried openly. *Father! Mother! I weep for your sacrilege. Change your hearts. You're the leaders of a great people. Do not divorce them from their Church.*

A warm breeze entered her bedchamber, carrying with it Golandar's sharp smells. Drucilla stood and turned her bloodshot eyes out the window to the street below. Her new room was in the High Priestess's tower. A cobblestone street ran along the tower's base. The temple had no protective wall. The city had always been a safe, stable place, compared to the rest of the continent. War had not touched the walls of Golandar for nearly two centuries. Drucilla watched as the Golandarii walked past the temple. Their voices drifted up to her

◆215◆

ears. She imagined about what would be their entertainment for the evening.

For a change, she had no functions to go to. Usually there was a dinner party to attend or some religious duty to complete. She was glad for the respite; she needed time to sort out her feelings - and time to cry.

Torchlight flared atop the Alcazar's western tower. One by one, other fires appeared along the road carved into the cliff sides. *Who's attending dinner at the palace tonight?* She sighed as she wondered if she would ever attend dinner there again. The temple lay less than half a mile from the Alcazar, but it may as well have been on Eo's moon. To Drucilla, the rift between her and her family seemed that wide.

That afternoon, the acolytes had moved her into her room. The move had elevated her status. Serophia was rewarding her for her loyalty, but Drucilla did not need such gifts to secure her loyalty. Her decision to stand by the Church came from her heart and her faith. *I made a moral choice. In time, the justification will come to me, or I'll find it.*

A group of men and women strolled down the street, laughing and singing. Their apparent oblivion to the events concerning the Se-motecs baffled Drucilla. *Danger lies not two weeks south of here, and the Golandarii are as cheerful as ever. Are they too preoccupied with the pursuit of their appetites? Or are they simply keeping their spirits high? The city's walls insulate them too much from the world's prob-lems.* Drucilla moved away from the window and blew out the lantern on the small table beside the mirror. She pulled back the covers of her bed and climbed in.

Birds welcomed the dawn. Drucilla awoke at the sound of their twittering. Her bedclothes clung to her sticky skin. Summer nights in Golandar rarely brought relief from the heat. The air outside was still and thick with the odors of manure and garbage and oven smoke. The city was still shrouded in shadows. The sun glowed faintly over the peaks of the Yunar Mountains. The calls of bread vendors echoed through the streets as they pushed their carts from door to door. A drunken voice sang out from somewhere.

A light rapping at the door startled her. An acolyte's voice called out. "Mother Drucilla, are you awake?"

"Yes, thank you." She stretched, walked to the window, and waited for the sun to appear. She loved the dawn. Each day brought new opportunities to serve the followers of the Faith.

A ray of sunlight appeared over the tops of the mountains. The shadows of the Gudor valley and the streets of Golandar melted away. From somewhere below her window, a rhythmic grunting caught Drucilla's ears. She peered through the darkness, squinting. The grunting changed to moaning, mixed with gleeful squeals. She stared into the gloominess of the street as the sky continued to lighten. Her eyes caught sight of a jerking movement against the whitewashed wall on the opposite side of the street. The silhouettes of two embracing figures became clearer. Drucilla watched a pair of pale legs and buttocks thrusting rapidly into the other figure. Her eyes widened and she muffled a startled gasp. Yet, the sight provoked a yearning inside her. She gently slid her hand up her leg to where her bedclothes were matted to her sex. She held her hand there only briefly and smiled sheepishly. She had never known a man; she had never taken time to enjoy that diversion.

*I'll explore lovemaking when the time's right,* she promised herself as she watched the man climax.

Drucilla turned from the window and peeled off her sweat-soaked clothing. She powdered the dampness on her body before she pulled a white dress from her wardrobe.

She descended the tower's stairs and exited through the door at the bottom, which led to the temple's sanctuary. She walked behind the colonnade, running the length of the sanctuary. Smoky braziers provided minimal lighting. Their fuel was burning out. She joined the priests, priestesses, and acolytes worshipping before the altar, performing their Sunrise Devotions.

The altar sat atop a marble dais along the temple's eastern wall, so that the members of the priesthood faced the dawn. Above the altar an immense, round stained glass window allowed the light of the new day to illuminate the sanctuary. An identical window adorned the western wall, which allowed the last light of day to shine upon the altar.

Drucilla knelt and placed her palms together. She bowed her head and raised both hands skyward. Silently, she mouthed a prayer to the Creator. She separated her hands and lowered them until they were held parallel to the floor, palms up. She then took a seat on the first row of benches.

It was not long before the contingent of the Order of Ilyas arrived together, twenty-five in all, dressed in mail hauberks and crisp white surcoats and gauntlets. They knelt before the altar in two lines. En mass, they drew their swords and held their blades in front of them, upon their palms, and offered their lives and steel to the Creator. They rose together, sheathed their swords, and silently took their places on the benches behind the priests and acolytes.

An acolyte struck a small gong. The consistory rose to their feet. Serophia strolled down the burgundy carpet, running between the rows of benches and ending at the foot of the altar. Her face was solemn. The delicate material of her gown flowed behind her. The sun now shined through the green, red, and blue glass of the window above the altar. She quietly ascended the dais's steps. She halted before the engraved sun of beaten gold, which seemed to hang in the air, but was fixed to the temple's wall by metal bars.

Serophia completed her devotions and faced her temple's consistory. She raised her right hand and the palm glowed with the Light of Ghyo. She conducted the Celebration of the Light:

> *Blessed be Ghyo's glory, and His creation, the World.*
> *Blessed be His Light that He sends to Earth, which manifests*
>     *through His Gift.*
> *Blessed be the Cycle unbroken.*
> *Life perpetual.*

Serophia dismissed the consistory to break their fast, except for Drucilla.

Drucilla followed Serophia up the winding steps of the High Prietess's tower. They passed the door leading to her room and continued upward. Serophia's chambers occupied the tower's third and fourth levels.

Serophia pulled a key from the pouch at her waist and unlocked the stout oak door. She turned and half-faced Drucilla. "We can speak privately in here."

Her chamber took up the entire floor of the round tower. Six high-backed chairs surrounded a trestle table with two silver candelabrums upon it. Tall shelves, bursting with scrolls and books, lined the walls in the spaces between the room's three windows. A thick Muori rug covered the floor, displaying the repetitive patterns of that culture.

Serophia motioned Drucilla to be seated at the end of the table opposite her. "Are you satisfied with your new accommodations?"

"They are most excellent, Holiness. Far above my status within His Church."

Serophia smiled. "You have received what you have earned, sister. You have demonstrated that your loyalty to the Faith is unbounded."

Drucilla's ears turned hot. "My loyalty is a small price to pay for the Gift of Ghyo."

A knock at the door interrupted them. "Enter," Serophia commanded.

A hooded acolyte opened the door; followed by a second, carrying a silver tray of fruit, cheese, and bread, and a third, bringing a decanter of wine. They divided the food between the two women and poured wine for them. The scent of the bread made Drucilla's mouth water. One of the acolytes opened the windows. When they were done, they lined up near the door, bowed their heads, and left the room.

"I can hardly remember my time as an acolyte," Serophia said. "But, I detested having my face hidden by a cowl."

Her frankness surprised Drucilla. The cowl taught priests humility. Drucilla's memories of her time with the acolytes were still clear. It had only been six years since she spent her year wearing the cape and cowl. It was not meant to be enjoyable. "The duty *is* onerous," Drucilla agreed.

"Break your fast, sister," Serophia said. She popped a piece of cheese in her mouth and drank some wine.

Drucilla tore off a small piece of the hot bread. She quickly placed it in her mouth and blew on her fingertips. "The bread here is always delicious. They rival the cooks of the Alcazar."

Serophia swallowed her cheese. "Thank Duke Camidor. He released one of his cooks and gave her to me."

Drucilla sipped her wine. "Holiness, how may I serve you and His Church?"

Serophia cut up a pear with a dirk. "I have need of your abilities. Actually, the Church has need of you. The Holy Council requires your presence in Arshapel. Your familiar background is more useful to the Church if you were serving there."

Drucilla was stunned. "I am to leave Soriazar?"

"The Legate Plenipotentiary needs your unique insight into the affairs of Soriazar. Relations between your father and the Holy Tower are always strained at best. Brother Gaetan believes you can help shape a workable relationship with King Mendio." Serophia snapped off a piece of pear with her teeth and chewed it rapidly.

*How does Brother Gaetan know that the negotiations with father have broken down? It's only been a little over a day. It's impossible to contact him so soon. Maintain your composure. Control your emotions.* "Events are moving quickly," said Drucilla, aware of the slight quaver in her voice.

"They always do when the Holy Tower demands action," Serophia told her. "Brother Gaetan does not know of the king's refusal of the Church's offer. He cannot," she added quickly. She sipped some wine and eyed Drucilla over the top of the cup. "Regardless, he wants you there."

Brother Variki cared for the temple's rookery and he was supposed to let Drucilla know of the arrival of messages. As part of her training, she joined Serophia when messages were read and deciphered. "I was not aware of the arrival of a message from the Holy Tower." Drucilla studied Serophia to glean her reaction.

Serophia remained impassive. "Not *all* of my correspondences with the council are made known to you. That should not surprise you."

*Knowing what is unseen is power.* Drucilla silently recited a maxim of diplomacy. "I apologize, Holiness. My assumptions have overstepped my position."

"Do not apologize, sister. You are highborn. Ambition is in your blood. Ambition, double-edged as it is, can carry you a long way in the Church. Humility is not becoming of you. Stop hiding your ambitious spirit behind your piety." Serophia had never spoken to Drucilla like that before.

She continued. "You belong to the Holy Legation, as do I. More than the other offices, we are involved in the temporal affairs of the Church. We are immersed in the intrigues and double-dealings of kings and lords. That is the irony of what we do. Our work keeps the Church from becoming a tool of the monarchs."

*That's the cold truth.* It was not a new concept to her, but it was something she did not dwell on when she helped the poor and comforted the sick and injured. "Arshapel is a great distance from Golandar. With the respect due High Priest Gaetan, what better good could I serve there, versus here?"

Serophia selected another piece of cheese and chewed it slowly. She raised her cup, drank, and wiped her mouth with a cloth napkin. She did not look at Drucilla as she spoke. "I do not presume to know the mind of the Legate. He wants you to go to the Holy Tower." Her eyes then met Drucilla's. "Being assigned to Arshapel is a great honor for a priestess." She then looked out the window. "In time, I am sure you can return here, unless..." Her eyes glided from the window and landed on Drucilla. "You are promoted to some higher position elsewhere."

Drucilla's mind was suddenly filled with thoughts of being a high priestess. She stared at the little bunch of grapes before her, but she stopped her mind from wandering. *Give them something they need, but something that will do you little or no harm.* It was another maxim of diplomacy. Drucilla plucked a grape and ate it. She mulled over Serophia's words. *Her Holiness knows the reason why I'm to be sent to the Holy Tower. The signs are subtle, but I can read them.* "How does Your Holiness feel about the Legate's wishes?" she asked.

Serophia cleared her throat. "I will miss you. There is still much I wish to teach you." Her impassiveness faltered. She closed her eyes and ran her tongue across her lower lip. "Like you, I have masters whom I serve. I expect my subordinates to follow my wishes. In turn, I owe the same to the Arch Priest and the Holy Council."

*That seemed genuine. She seems to care about me.* "May I ask when I leave?"

"Tomorrow. You shall draw sufficient coin. Secure passage on a ship from Vorencia to Harluer. A knight will serve as your escort to the Holy Tower."

Surprise squeezed Drucilla's heart and her limbs suddenly trembled. "D...Do I get to say goodbye to my family?"

"I am afraid that will not be possible. The Alcazar must not know you are leaving. Your father may try and prevent it." Serophia pushed her chair from the table and walked over to the bookshelves. She selected a thick book, opened it, and reached inside it. A hollow space hid a letter within. A thick blob of wax sealed the folded parchment. "This letter must be handed to Brother Gaetan upon your arrival. Another reason for you to leave so soon."

*Things* are *moving fast. She could be right about father trying to hold me hostage. He nearly begged me to remain with him inside the fortress. It may not be wise to tempt fortune by going to the Alcazar.* "I understand, Holiness. I do not have many things of value in the temple, but I will need a few hours to gather what I do have."

Serophia handed her the letter. "Pack this with your things. You again demonstrate your loyalty by facilitating an early departure. You will be sorely missed here, but you are serving a higher purpose by leaving."

Drucilla sensed the finality in Serophia's voice. The meeting had finished. *Is that a tear in the corner of her eye?* She hid her amazement, stood, and bowed her head to her mistress.

Serophia raised her hand and Ghyo's Light radiated from it. "May the Light of Ghyo guide you through the darkness." She closed her palm and extinguished the Light.

# Chapter 28

## A Bitter Defeat, A Blessed Retreat
### 16 Janoban, 229 A.G.S.

*M*y *crown.* The inlaid emeralds and diamonds sparkled from a light, which shone on it from nowhere and everywhere. *Always, you've been there, far from my reach.* The crown hung from a weather vane, high atop a castle tower, which itself was atop a rock outcropping. Like he had done time and again, Orius scaled the outcropping and climbed the tower's narrow, winding, unending stairwell. But never had he come close to reaching the top, until his dream had changed in the spring of that year. It had changed when he, his mother, and Culley came down from Malagorn's tower and entered the village of Torveg.

Orius reached the top of the tower. His legs ached from the hundreds of steps he had climbed. But uncertainty was always the prevailing mood of his dream. He emerged from the stairwell onto the tower's roof, and there he found the metal weathervane to be smeared with a slick, black, foul-smelling oil. He tried to grasp it tight enough to climb it and retrieve his crown, but the oil stopped him, again and again. *I'm closer to having you than ever before, but the end is the most difficult part of my journey.*

A dust cloud then obscured the crown, and the light dimmed around him. Orius watched as the silhouettes of rocks silently rolled through the dust before him. A sickening feeling twisted his stomach as a familiar shape took form behind the rolling rocks. He stared into the roiling dust clouds, catching only glimpses of the figure. *The Black Rider is there. I can feel his corruption.* He sniffed at his oily hands. *I can smell his corruption.*

Orius reached for his sword, but it did not hang at his waist. He knelt to place a hand upon the ground to summon fire, but he felt nothing. He looked down and saw only swirling dust clouds beneath his feet. He stared ahead again. The rocks no longer rolled by, and the Black Rider had gone. A hand reached through the dust toward him, startling him. Orius tried to flee, but the hand wrapped around his shoulder and grasped him tightly...

"Orius," a gravelly voice called his name. The dust faded, and Culley's rough face and gray beard appeared before him. "Wake up, boy."

Orius woke suddenly, breathing heavily. "Wh...what is wrong?"

"Dawn's breaking. It's time to move out, and there's nothing left to break your fast."

Orius sat up and grimaced at the wound in his leg. It was swollen and tender. The Gift had sealed the holes, but it would take a day or two to complete the healing and drive out any infection. "I suppose the others have no food, either?"

Culley nodded grimly. "Aye. It will be a slow, hungry walk home."

Orius held up a hand to Culley. "Help me to my feet." The old Chelt took Orius's hand and pulled him up. He put some weight on his leg to test it, and a wave of pain and weakness in the leg greeted him. He switched his weight to his other leg; he would limp for a few days.

Orius had slept with the rest of the wounded in a small space that had been cleared of rocks and debris. He had exhausted himself the day before, healing as many warriors as he had the strength for. The thirty-six Chelts who lay around him suffered mostly from broken or smashed bones. More than half wore crude splints made of tree branches bound with strips of cloth, or slings fashioned from torn shirts and blankets.

Two-thirds of Orius's army was dead or wounded. Eighteen warriors had fled when the rocks came crashing down the mountain and had never returned. Most of the horses had scattered. He could now only field thirty warriors.

"Are Condin and his Wolf Riders ready?" Orius asked Culley.

"They're saddling their horses," he answered. "But only Chief Condin and four others have horses, and those are weak."

Orius frowned. Blood and dirt soiled his white surcoat. "Drenga is a half day's ride or less from this place, but we must retreat. With one stroke, the Oruk's leader has shifted the momentum in his favor. He is a cold, bloody commander. He knows we cannot survive the attrition. He is drawing us into a trap, or he may advance today and finish us off. Unless, he has died of his wound - but I have a peculiar feeling that is not the case."

"Aye, we shouldn't fight him in the trees," Culley said. "They can cut us off too easily. If we can get the army back to the valley, there's a chance we can escape, and maybe even bloody his nose if he sticks it out in the open."

The sun peaked over the mountaintops. Orius looked at the chaotic scene of his army. Tons of rock, mingled with the broken trunks of pines littering the road and the mountain's slope. The legs and arms of dead Chelts still protruded from the rubble, mixed with the legs and heads of dead horses. The dead had begun to stink; the air was tainted with their sickly-sweet odor. But there was no time to light funeral pyres, nor did any have the strength to move the heavy debris.

One of his mother's lessons returned to him as Orius swept his eyes across the aftermath of his first defeat. *The commoners exist to serve the nobility. But the nobility cannot survive without them. But the commoners bleed, laugh, and love like we do.* "I want you to accompany me to Drenga, Culley. Moreena and Argus will help Kathair retreat the army."

Culley's face was stolid. "I would like to see Drenga for myself, but I fear you're not up to the journey. You can hardly stand."

Orius hobbled around and faced him. "True, but I cannot let this stop me. I must see Drenga. I must stop him."

Culley's face reflected his concern. "You mean to kill their leader."

Orius's desire for revenge shamed him. "The body dies when the head is severed. I owe it to the warriors who died here."

"I have some hard news to give you," Culley said. "Every warrior from Tydorhagen has died."

Orius exhaled and slouched his shoulders. "It will be a hard winter for the Chelts of Tydorhagen. The village is tiny. The ten warriors who rode south with me made up three-fourths of the Chelts of fighting age living there. When I return north, I must ensure that the neighboring villages do not take advantage of Tydorhagen's misfortune." *If I live that long.* "I fear the Chelts of the Northern Valley will return to their customary squabbles after the harvest."

Kathair walked over to Orius and Culley. "Father Orius, my horse is saddled and ready for you. Your horse bled to death from the arrow in its throat."

"Thank you, Kathair. You are most loyal. I place you in command of leading the army back to the valley we fought in. Culley, Chief Condin, and I will lead a small patrol toward Drenga. If we encounter the Oruks heading this way, we will delay them as best we can. Move the warriors along as best you can."

"I'll see to it," Kathair said. "It'll be difficult to move them at any good speed. There are as many wounded as not. The lack of food will slow us, as well."

"No hunting parties," Orius ordered. "Not until you reach the valley. Get the army there in one piece and gather up those we left behind." *I know you're as hungry as the rest of them.*

"As you wish," Kathair said, not liking his orders.

"Orius," Culley said quietly. "What do you wish done with those who've deserted?"

The subject put a knot in Orius's stomach. *I have to spill blood to deal with deserters.* The thought disgusted him. He tried to sound sure of himself, but he was certain his fatigue made him sound less so. "Any warrior who is missing and returns will be pardoned. Any warrior who returns to us after, or if, we return to Ragnaar will be dealt with then. We are not defeated." *Not defeated. That sounds hollow.* "Do not let the tribes squabble between each other, Kathair."

Kathair glanced around at the wreckage of the road. "I'll do my best, but the desire to return and defend their homes and crops is stronger now than it was before you killed Egon. Another Challenge is to be expected."

That fact struck Orius like a heavy blow. Each Challenge threatened to tear apart the fragile peace between the villages, because he was the glue that bound them together. "I am the Chief. I must defend my place."

Kathair's eyebrows rose. His voice echoed his worry. "Please. Stop this. Crown yourself and end the Challenges."

"Kings are not crowned after a beating," Orius said. "Kirkvold won his war, and then he crowned himself."

Culley interrupted. "Kathair, just keep this bunch together. We'll join you again. Then, we'll see where our paths lead us."

Kathair held out his hand to Orius. "You're the Light of Ghyo. You push back the darkness in the North." Orius shook Kathair's hand, and Kathair left to organize the retreat to the east.

Orius limped to where the horse waited. It was slow going, hobbling around rocks and branches. Culley walked behind him. Orius grasped the horse's bridle and coaxed the animal to kneel. He grit his teeth and swung his right leg over the horse. He gasped as his injured leg briefly supported his weight. He clicked his tongue and the horse rose to its feet. He guided it around and faced Chief Condin and four of his Wolf Riders. "We should get moving."

Condin's intense eyes stared back at Orius from beneath the snout and fangs of his white wolf's hide. "I sent Arturo and Bevyn out before first light. The road is clear for at least a mile."

"Good, with warriors like you how can we not prevail," Orius said. His spirits picked up.

Culley grunted as he climbed into the saddle. "Hopefully, the road's clear for a bit further than that, Chief. We need time."

"The road continues around the mountain before it descends into the Drenga Valley," Condin said. "My scouts could not see the village, but they saw several plumes of smoke rising from behind the forest on the valley's floor."

"Campfires?" Culley asked.

"The smoke was too thick for campfires."

*Are they putting Drenga to the torch?* "Move out," Orius commanded. "I must see this for myself." *If they're leaving, I'll miss my chance. I feel stronger now. I can do this work.*

Orius had awoken stiff, sore, and tired. He had considered using the Gift to take away his fatigue, but he would need his strength. Using the Gift in that way would make him feel rested, but it only masked the energy he drained away from himself in healing himself. He would feel stronger than he actually was. The Gift healed wounds and mended broken bones, but real rest was always required to complete the healing.

Orius's small band rode in single file. The seven men guided their tired horses westward. They disappeared up and around the bend in the road. Up the slope to the left, the pine trees thinned out after a short ways, and above that point, scrubby bushes and boulders covered the ground. Condin's scouts, Arturo and Bevyn, led the way.

Orius rode with his hand resting on Worgoth's shining axe. It was his tangible prize for killing the powerful chief, a symbol of power. The Black Rider's sword hung from the saddle next to Orius's twohander. Orius wondered if the sword was a symbol of power over those the Black Rider commanded. Moreena had brought the sword to him late the previous night. The Rider's severed hand, still in its glove, had clutched the hilt. Moreena had described to him the melee among the rocks. She told Orius how she had taken the Black Rider's hand, how he had bled unnatural, black blood. She then pried the stiffened fingers from the hilt and shook the pallid hand from the black leather glove. A gold ring on one of the fingers had sparkled in the torchlight, shining with unusual brilliance. Orius put on his gauntlets before he pulled the ring from the dead finger. Holding his enemy's hand had given him a queer feeling. He had expected to sense the Rider's presence, as he had on the battlefield, but the severed hand was dead flesh, human, yet inhuman, with thick, yellowish nails. He placed the ring in his belt pouch. He was not certain if it was an object of power, or not, so he would not put it on. He would save it for Malagorn to scrutinize, when, or if, they returned to the Northern Valley.

The Rider's long sword gleamed like polished silver and showed the ripples of countless folds. The sword's forger was a master. Unlike the ring, the sword was engraved with a script unrecognizable to Orius. Moreena had foregone her claim to her victim's weapon and given it to Orius to honor his victories over the Oruks. Orius had smiled at her tenacity and generosity and had thought, *Did you survive the same ambush I did?*

The full light of day blazed over the tops of the mountains as they followed the road down its winding descent into the gloomy woods of the valley floor. Condin's scouts halted and waited for the others.

"The land's opening a bit," Bevyn said. The snout of his gray wolf's skin mimicked his movements. "Arturo and I'll ride ahead and see if the trees below are occupied."

Chief Condin nodded. "Bows," he said to the two Wolf Riders in the rear of the line.

The warriors dismounted and notched arrows. Culley held the reins of their horses. Bevyn and Arturo headed for the thick forest that the road led into. The valley was quiet. The sound of horseshoes scraping on stone seemed to carry for miles. There was no wind to stir up the piney air. No birds chirped. The warriors left the road before reaching the trees and veered left. They disappeared into the blackness beneath the pine trees.

Minutes passed without a sign from Arturo or Bevyn. Orius strained his eyes to penetrate the murky shadows between the pines. If there were no Oruks watching the road and the mountain, the scouts should have returned. "The silence of the morning is unnatural," Orius said. *Forest dwellers grow quiet when danger's close.* He turned in his saddle to speak to Culley, but the old Chelt's eyes were riveted on the forest. *He senses it, too.*

A scream rent the air. The heads of the Chelts and their horses jerked upward. The warriors with the bows shifted their feet and drew back their bowstrings. Then...

Silence fell over the valley floor. Drawn-out seconds passed. Orius's heart thumped; his chest tightened from holding his breath. *Something moved.* He swore he saw movement in the shadows beneath the trees. He strained his eyes again, wishing they could cut the through the shadows. *There it is again.* Something crashed through the bushes and broke into the open. A stocky black figure raced across the ground on stubby legs. His arms flapped at the air, like a bird trying to take flight for the first time. *An Oruk!*

Arrows crossed the distance between the Chelts and the fleeing Oruk. The black figure curled up, rolled across the ground, and moved no more. Two horsemen appeared from beneath the trees to the right of the road and trotted slowly toward Orius and the others. Their lighter wolf skins contrasted against dark background of the forest. Arturo and Bevyn halted and waved to their comrades.

"You two mount up," Orius commanded as he followed Chief Condin down the road.

"What happened?" Condin called to his scouts.

"There were four of them," Arturo answered. "They were camped where they could watch the road. Three were asleep. That one walked up on us as we were killing the others."

"He must've been relieving himself," added Bevyn.

"Are you sure there are no others?" Orius said.

"Only the four, Father Candell," said Bevyn. "I think they were scouts. Their ponies were saddled, and they slept on the ground."

"A pony's whicker gave them away," Arturo added. "They hadn't even built a fire last night."

"There could be another ambush further along," Chief Condin said.

"Aye," Culley said. "He's a fox, that one. But he lost a hand yesterday. If he lives, he has to be weak."

"From where they slept," Arturo said, "they could've fled up the road without us seeing them and spread word of our advance. I think that was their plan. That's what I would do."

"If more are waiting for us, they could easily overwhelm our tiny number," Condin pointed out.

"We will move on," said Orius. "There is no way to be sure of the Oruk's situation unless we see it for ourselves. Kathair and the wounded can move only so fast. We must know if the Oruks are coming back for us." *I must see my enemy one more time.*

A tense silence followed Orius's words. "The seven of us are the eyes and ears of a retreating army, an army in danger of being destroyed if our foe catches up with us," Culley said.

"All warriors die," said Condin. "If this is our day, then we shall meet it with courage and weapons drawn."

Orius and the others followed Chief Condin, Arturo, and Bevyn into the woods. The sun rose higher above the mountains, but the road and the forest remained shrouded in deep-green shadows. The air was cool and damp. No breeze stirred the branches of the pines. They rode through clouds of insects. Deeper inside the forest, the tree trunks grew stouter, and broad ferns and saplings choked the ground. The birds returned to their chirping. Small game darted about the underbrush.

Orius and the Chelts moved down the road at a steady trot, all of them warily watching the trees. The road was a set of parallel wagon tracks. It wound back and forth around the forest's great pines. Toward mid-morning shafts of sunlight broke through the canopy, illuminating the forest in a greenish-yellow hue. Signs along the road told Orius a welcome tale - an Oruk corpse, bits of armor, and blood-stained clothing lay beside the road. They passed the remains of a campsite where a couple more bodies had been left behind, stripped of their clothing and weapons.

A heavily wooded hill rose out of the valley floor before them. The road broke off to the right and wound around the base of the rise. Chief Condin held up his hand and halted near the bend in the road. He spun his horse around.

"Father Orius, I mean to ride to the top of this hill. It may give us a view of the ground ahead."

"Your lead," Orius responded.

The seven of them steered their horses up the slope. The hill was actually a spur running off the mountain to the south. When they reached the crest, the valley opened up before them. Drenga lay a mile's distance in the center of a circular piece of ground, cleared of trees. Beyond the village, a stark, rocky mountain closed off the valley's western end.

Drenga was a large village. Dozens of log huts with steep thatched roofs stood on top of a carpet of green. Low stone walls radiated from the edges of the village, marking the boundaries of crop fields and the cow pens of the villagers. But the crops had been trampled flat, and the pens were empty. A large wooden watchtower stood on the village's eastern edge. Earthworks had been thrown up around the village proper. Columns of smoke rose from a few of the huts. Black specks circled them, throwing flickering balls of orange light through the air onto the roofs.

Orius tore open a saddlebag and dug out his spyglass. Culley had his out already. Through the glass, he watched a long line of dark figures winding back and forth up the side of the stony mountain and disappearing through a notch in the mountain's crest.

"May the Light of Ghyo be praised," Orius said. "Our enemy flees before us."

"Aye," said Culley. "Never before in all my years have I seen so few turn back so many."

"No," Chief Condin interrupted. "You are wrong, old man."

Culley gave him a disgruntled look.

Condin dismounted his horse, faced Orius, and touched a knee to the ground. "The Chelts have been struggling against such numbers for generations. Never before has *one* turned back so many. The Creator has sent you to lead us from the darkness, Father Candell. Today, I have seen it for myself. You, who wield the Light of Ghyo, have been sent to unite the Northern Tribes, to mend the wounds we Chelts inflict upon ourselves. This day, I pledge to you my life and my support. Never again shall you answer a Challenge, for I will Champion you, King Orius."

Orius was stunned. *Fate leads me in a strange direction and grants me a victory.* Tension made his mouth dry. "Chief Condin, I accept your pledge. And I ask your support of my claim to the Throne of Cheltabria, for I mean to don the crown of King Kirkvold, and then I shall face my father."

Condin's intense eyes met those of Orius. "You shall have it, and you shall have the loyalty of my Wolf Riders. Let us serve as your personal guard. The King's Guard."

"You shall have that honor, but we must finish the business at hand," Orius said. "I mean to kill this Black Rider. He is the head of the snake." Orius spurred his horse and led the way downhill. *Saying that felt good, but vengeful feelings are part of the corruption that power brings. Remember the feelings, and don't let them overwhelm you.*

Chief Condin jumped onto his horse. Culley gave him a curt nod of approval, and together they followed Orius through the trees.

Orius trembled with exhilaration. The goal of his army's campaign lay but a short distance ahead. The long road neared its end. He rode quickly, but not recklessly. There could still be Oruks waiting in the trees to bar their way. It would be a disaster to be killed so close to the end.

He arrived at the edge of the forest and stopped. Across the fields surrounding Drenga, he saw the extent of the Oruks' occupation. The earthworks bristled with an abatis. Dozens of short, thick training posts stood in rows in the fields south of the village. Ten quintains were in a field on the north side of Drenga.

Culley and the rest of the Chelts formed a line to either side of Orius. "This camp would be suitable for a southern army," Culley said.

"A most unnatural sight," said Chief Condin. "First, we see Oruks fighting in formations. And now we see this."

"There are forces moving within the Wastes of Sytor that threaten all humankind in Iningia," Orius said. "When I first saw the Black Rider with my own eyes, I felt the evil of it before we fought in the valley."

"You can feel evil?" Bevyn asked. His natural Cheltan suspicion of foreigners surfaced. "What other abilities do you hide from us?"

Orius did not face the Wolf Rider. "The Gift works differently for every priest, but in all ways, it must be used for Goodness."

He fetched his spyglass again and scanned the village. He watched the Oruks go about their work, putting Drenga to the torch.

*AARRoooooo!!!! AARRoooooo!!!!*

"There's a guard in the watchtower," Culley said. "We're spotted."

"Keep a sharp eye!" Condin called to his Wolf Riders.

"It does not matter," Orius said. He dismounted, removed his gauntlets, and tucked them into his belt. "Watch for the Black Rider." He raised his spyglass to his eye again.

The alarm raised by the watchtower created a panic. Oruk soldiers dropped their torches and disappeared into the village. The

Oruk in the tower scrambled down a rough, makeshift ladder. Once on the ground, he threw down his spear and scampered away. Orius stared intently at the village, but his prey was nowhere to be seen.

# Chapter 29

## Adrift in the Sea of Duty
### 16 Janoban, 229 A.G.S.

The myth was shattered. Magnificent Roda was a thing of legend. Only the size of the city, sliced into thirds by the dirty, sluggish Roda and Kelebas Rivers, lived up to its reputation. A quarter of a million people were crowded into conglomerates of tenement houses and opulent manses. The summer heat putrefied the smells of the mass of humanity hemmed in by the city walls. Tarik had spent much time in smaller cities like Spandel, Vorencia, and Golandar. All of them were held together by a system of walls, as well, but the similarities ended there. Roda was filthy. The smells of the other cities could not compare.

The legends also did not speak of the obscene contrasts between the impoverished and the wealthy Rodii, the true Roda. The western part of the city consisted of rough, brick apartments and shops. Beggars and homeless children choked its narrow, crime-ridden streets, alongside the carts and shops of merchants. The middle of the city was wedged in between the forks of the rivers, which boasted the famous white marble edifices of the Senate, on the Capitol Hill, and the Temple of Ghyo, on the Hill of the Light. But dull-brown brick shops and homes butted haphazardly against the feet of those seats of power, resembling the jumbled aftermath of a rockslide. The manses of the wealthy and the ruling class crowned Roda's eastern hills, overlooking the houses of the merchant class below them. There, the city guard heavily patrolled the streets, strictly enforcing the laws.

Tarik stood upon the balcony of the manse that served as his jail, looking northeastward toward the city's southeast gate. It stood only a half-mile away, a quick dash through the winding streets and alleys to freedom. He placed his hands on the peristyle's unpolished marble railing and peered over the edge. The slope of the hill fell away sharply from the foundation of the house. He figured he had a fair chance of scrambling the fifty feet to the street below, but only in daylight, but the Iduin soldier standing guard nearby would not let that happen.

Tarik studied the view to the east and south. He pondered which direction to take should he escape. The balcony's height allowed him to see just over the walls. To the southeast lay one of the ridges, rising out of an undulating plain that shaped the valley of the Roda River. Orderly olive groves and rows of grapevines covered its slopes. He wondered if there were merchant pavilions, like the ones on the western side of the Roda, close to the eastern walls. *If so, are any of them breaking camp soon and heading off to Terghu?* He had to get home. The day before, he had watched a legion approach from the east, march south of the city, and head westward.

It was a hot afternoon. A cool breeze blew in from the north, stirring the hot, muggy air. A line of dark clouds had formed along the northern horizon. The wind carried a hint of coming rain. Tarik breathed it in deeply. The breeze brought a little respite from the still, stagnant air from earlier, but it still smelled of sewage. *Even the lofty homes of Roda's rich can't rise above the stench of the city's shit.* He watched a caravan of twenty wagons, laden with barrels and wooden crates, rumble through the southeast gate. Mounted guards flanked the columns of wagons, moving back and forth. *Caravans are always in need of an extra sword.* Tarik tucked that piece of information into the back of his mind. *Now I need to find a rope.*

He turned away from the balcony and walked to a table with a bowl of fruit on top of it. He picked out a pear and bit into it. He rolled the pear's sweetness across his tongue and studied the Iduin soldier guarding him. The soldier stared straight ahead, but Tarik knew he kept track of his movements. The guard wore a simple, but well-made mail shirt. He was armed with a short stabbing sword, a javelin, and an oval, body-length shield. His helmet was plain, rounded on top, and fastened beneath his chin by thin leather strings attached to the classic Iduin cheek plates. He admired the uniformity of Idu's soldiers. Their equipment was practical, simple, deadly, and able to be produced in great quantities. An Azari fighter's panoply reflected the wealth of the soldier or knight. The militias and knights of Soriazar went into battle with every conceivable combination of weapon and armor, and Tarik believed the Azari militias to be not as skilled at arms as Idu's professionals. *But I could take him if I had my sword.*

A young bonded female entered the peristyle. She wore a loose gray shift of rough-spun wool. Her long black hair was pulled back from her smooth face and braided down her back. She smiled as she approached Tarik, displaying innocence and shyness.

She looks at me like that each time she comes to me, Tarik mused. But her eyes betray her and show her hunger for men. He guessed she was not yet fifteen, but he figured she was experienced in the ways of pleasure. The master of the house probably saw to that.

The girl was called Otilia, and she spoke neither Azari nor Tradespeak. She took Tarik's hand and led him to the atrium on the opposite side of the manse. The Iduin soldier followed them discreetly. Murius waited in the atrium beside a white marble impluvium, streaked with wavy black veins. He wore his officer's panoply. He removed his red-crested helmet with both hands. "You are being well treated here?" he asked in Tradespeak, leaning his head toward Otilia. "Just like in those inns we stayed at."

"This place is better than jail," Tarik said. "But I have not been in the mood for that."

Murius smiled mischievously. "By the look of her, this thrall would let you have at it as a gratuity."

Tarik allowed himself to chuckle. It felt good to hear some humor. It lessoned the frustration about his treatment by the Iduin Senate, but only a little. "Why have you come, Murius? The last time you came to my jail you took me away. Is that going to happen now?"

Murius's smiled faded. He spoke harshly to Otilia in Iduin, and she bowed and left them. "No, it is not that. But I wish to speak with you in private."

Tarik glanced at the guard. "I do not think he will allow that."

Murius spoke to the soldier in Iduin. The soldier looked concerned and said something back to him. Murius's voice sounded sharper the second time he spoke. The soldier snapped to attention and stepped aside. Murius turned to Tarik. "He will not bother us. Where can we speak?"

Tarik gestured toward the peristyle. "Over by the railing."

Together, they walked through the house, and Murius's accoutrements quietly clicked with each step. Tarik wore a dark blue cotton tunic, which hung halfway to his knees, in the Iduin fashion. When they were beside the railing, Tarik said bitterly, "Well, we have privacy."

"I understand you are upset," Murius said. "I came here to give you some company and some news, too." He glanced in the direction of the guard. "Mostly, I came for the news."

"Are you here to tell me of my appointment with the courts?" asked Tarik. "My crimes *must* be terrible."

"I am glad you brought that up. I have something to say about that, as well."

Tarik's pulse quickened. No one had told him anything. All he knew was that Murius had used his family's connections with certain senators to get him moved from the jail to a senator's house. "What is to be my fate?"

Murius shrugged. "I have no idea. But I have been sitting in on the debates. Your situation is better than it was."

The back of Tarik's neck turned hot. He clenched his fists. "That tells me nothing. I am still a prisoner. How is my situation any better?"

"There are senators - not many, but some - who show you a little sympathy," Murius said. "Though their party, the Blues, has the minority in the Senate."

Tarik was taken back. He shook his head in disgust. "What can these Blues do for me? They can be outvoted. Your Republic leaves much to chance. A king moves more decisively."

"Not necessarily," said Murius. "Getting business done in the Senate takes skill. Negotiating and compromising requires shrewdness. Even kings have to work with councilors to be successful." He changed the subject. "There is another party, the Golds, whose numbers can give the Blues a majority."

"Golds?"

"Yes," Murius smiled. "A most fitting name. They grow rich off bribes from the Greens and Blues to vote one way or the other. The Greens do not have a majority either, but they are the largest party. The Golds are made up of successful merchants who buy enough votes to win senate seats. They promise their people much, but give little in return. They have smooth tongues."

"Which party does Bulbius belong to?"

"He is a Green. The Greens represent the wealthiest class."

"Which party does your family belong to?" Tarik was leery of the answer. Though Murius had helped him, and they shared many private secrets on their journey from Novium, Murius was still an officer in a foreign army whose country was not friendly to Soriazar.

"My father is a Green, of course," Murius answered. "The leading party appoints the army and garrison commanders. It keeps their base of power secure. Some things are the same everywhere." Murius's family politics made Tarik uncomfortable. He could tell that Murius sensed it. "Be calm. I prefer the Golds. I rather like the way they kick up the dirt – but please do not tell my father. Anyway, I must tell you of the debates. That letter you bore is causing much trouble."

Tarik perked up. "What kind of trouble? What did the letter say?"

Murius was surprised. "You really do not know what your king's message contained?"

"He simply handed it to me and gave me his instructions."

"King Mendio offered to assist Idu in driving out the Semotecs from Apumium, but the price of his help is the concession of the land between the Azari border and the River Boro," Murius told him. "But, if Idu declines his assistance, your king said he will pursue the Semotecs as far south as the River Boro, and if Soriazar has to go it on its own, King Mendio will declare the northern part of Apumium be part of Soriazar proper, without the approval of the Senate. Soriazar will reclaim what it calls the 'Lost Province' of Galorica. Since, in King Rodrigo's words, Idu has abandoned it to the Semotecs." Murius's voice turned icy. "Your king wants war."

Tarik was stunned. *What's Rodrigo's game?* He recalled the sights he had seen around Orpresa - the distant fires of burning farms and villages on the horizon, the narrow streets choked with exhausted, hungry Azaris. *How can the king expect to launch a campaign when his own land isn't free of the Semotecs?* He looked at Murius, who stared back at him. "His Majesty's designs escape me. I cannot and do not presume to know his mind."

"You have a brain. You can guess what his motives are."

*Why'd he ask me that?* Tarik became defensive. "It is not my place to comment on such things. I was never privy to any planning." His training told him to be alert and listen carefully.

"Tarik, I suggest you think of something. You have recently come from the seat of your nation's power. You have seen things that will be important for the Senate to know about. They will be coming to ask you about such things." Murius was serious - *deadly* serious.

*Oh, Murius.* Tarik said to himself. *You risk much to tell me this.* "It is dangerous for you to be here talking to me."

"Tarik," Murius said quietly. "I know you are loyal to your Sovereign and to Soriazar, but, like me, there are things about our homelands we do not like."

*He owes me nothing, yet he's here.* "When are they coming to ask me *things*?" Tarik asked. "Did a senator send you to me?"

"I came here of my own wishes. Senator Bulbius is heavy handed. Emissaries should not be treated in such a manner. You were only doing your duty."

"Too bad you are not in the Senate. You could help me, but your influence is only a little greater than mine. Go on, tell me more."

"You have more influence than you know," Murius said. "I believe that is why they have not sent anyone to question you yet. The Senate is rigorously debating the proper course to take. King Mendio's letter is causing much distress. The Blues want to accept an alliance with Soriazar, though they are naturally concerned about the language of your king's demands. The Greens consider the message to be belligerent and, for them, the price of cooperation with Soriazar is out of the question."

"The Iduin army took a beating," Tarik said. "So say the people flooding across our border. The size of the Semotec host was monstrous, they say."

"Yes," Murius admitted. "Part of that army was defeated. But the remainder withdrew and now hold the mountain passes."

*Why'd he reveal that to me? Because the Senate believes it has the strength to fight both Soriazar and the Semotecs.* "The combined strength of Idu and Soriazar could defeat them," Tarik went on. "Idu has suffered worse than Soriazar. Surely the Greens know this."

"Are not your father's lands overrun as we speak?" Murius asked him. "Spandel is nearly as large as Apumium. I think the amount of suffering is mutual. King Mendio sees our defeats as a sign of weakness."

"When I left Spandel, my father's troops were resisting and holding their ground." Tarik's instincts told him to say no more. *My brothers are probably where the action is.*

"Holed up inside their walls, and unable to venture out. The story is the same in Apumium. The Senate, the Greens mostly, believe King Mendio's message boasts of Azari strength that does not exist. Our army will strike back by itself long before the Azaris can muster enough soldiers to do the work. Our army is a professional one, yours is mainly militia and a few Royal troops."

He's fishing for feedback. Even if no one sent him, I must watch what I say. But Rodrigo would want to hear about the speed at which Idu is mobilizing. Tarik tried to sound as though he were growing weary of the political talk. "You know more than I do, Murius. I have been on the road nearly three weeks. Events may have already changed. You said my situation is not as bad as it was."

"Correct. The Blues wish to send you home with the Senate's response, with no further action taken against you. But the Greens agree with Senator Bulbius and believe in his indictment of you as a criminal. The Golds are trying to decide which way to go and how much profit their votes can bring them."

"I am no criminal!" Tarik blurted out. "The messages and the words of the king are above the law. King Mendio is the law, like the Senate of Idu."

"Not in Idu. Here, no one man makes the laws, and no one is above them."

"I am an emissary. Customs dictate I be treated in a certain way." Tarik covered his face with his hands and cursed under his breath. "Do you have any guess at which way the Senate will vote on the matter?"

Murius shook his head slowly. "I know the Greens are spending much money buying off the Golds. It was a Green general who commanded the legions in Apumium. Losing the province was embarrassing to the Greens. Senator Bulbius is keen on regaining lost prestige. Peace is not an option with Pavilius Bulbius." He paused. "The Greens have more money than the Blues."

Tarik rubbed his eyes then lowered his hands. "I have to escape. It is right that I do so," he whispered. "Help me." *Why have I asked him this? I ask him to commit treason.*

Murius gave a sideways glance toward the manse's interior. "Helping you would be treason. I am an army officer. I have sworn oaths." His voice became quiet, and he leaned close to Tarik and offered his hand. "But should an opportunity come up." He patted the railing a couple of times. "I suggest you take it." They then shook hands like old friends saying goodbye.

Tarik blinked several times. A hundred thoughts and questions ran through his mind. Murius turned and walked across the peristyle's shining marble floor. Tarik hurried after him. "Where are you off to, Murius?"

Murius stopped. "Legions are moving westward. I am returning to Novium to join the army gathering there. My Charge ended when I delivered you to the Senate." A hint of gloominess tinged his eyes. "I stayed longer than I should have, because of you. I admire your dedication. I did not wish to abandon you. You have a rare quality, Tarik. Sometimes the law is not served with justice." He smiled and touched Tarik on the shoulder. "You faced the Senate with poise, even when they were stripping you of your sword. I almost feel an obligation to help you. I know that sounds strange. We met only a week ago, but soldiers honor dedication."

Tarik smiled wanly. "We could have been great friends, I think. But now we serve opposing masters."

"Fortune always twists the road of life in strange directions," said Murius. He grasped Tarik's hand with both of his. "Goodbye! And good luck."

# Chapter 30

## The Enemy is Within
### 17 Janoban, 229 A.G.S.

A stiff southerly breeze blew across the plains of Spandel March to the village of Turela. It whipped up the dirt loosened by the picks and spades of the Royal Army, adding to the men's misery. The soldiers wiped the gritty soil from their necks and eyes as they dug entrenchments. The sky was devoid of clouds, and the sun beat upon the rows of tents outside Turela.

As with all armies, rumors abounded throughout the camp. The soldiers knew their foe was within a day or two's march of Turela. They overheard their officers talking about it and spread what they heard to others, who in turn spread what they heard to still more soldiers. Eventually the stories got back to the originators, who thought they heard a completely different tale and passed it along in kind. But despite the numbers of rumors, all of them had a common, ominous theme - there were tens of thousands of Semotec warriors, *everywhere.*

The rumors had reached Todu Mazrio, but he had the luxury of knowing which ones were true and which ones were not. Masuf's Trackers had done a splendid job of scouting and providing him with an accurate picture of what was happening throughout Spandel March.

The leather flaps of Todu's tent slapped against the sides of the entrance. Inside, several men stood around a small, square table. Sunlight flooded through the tent's entrance. An unlit lantern hung from a hook screwed into the center pole. Todu sat beside the table on a leather folding-chair. To his left stood the tall Nestor Solanto, Captain of the First Tercio; to his right stood the grizzled and sun-burned Marco Xerezo, Captain of the Second Tercio. Prince Sandovar stood opposite Todu, between the potbellied Basilio Gapacho, Captain of the knights from the Gudor Valley, and the graying Roldan Torrero, Captain of the knights from Vorencia. Prince Javior stood alone beside the tent's center pole. The quatrefoil medallion of the Order of Olantaro hung from the necks of all the men except Todu, Nestor, and Marco.

An unrolled map covered the table. It depicted Spandel March. Wooden blocks, painted black, were set around a red block on the

spot marked as Orpresa. Another cluster of black blocks were near
Spandel City, with more scattered between Orpresa and Spandel. Two
red blocks, noting the location of the marquis's troops, sat between
Spandel and the black ones near it. The four red blocks around
Turela represented the battalions of Todu's men.

"Your Highness," Todu said, while looking up at Sandovar and
forcing himself to remain patient. "The knights must be positioned
upon the flanks of the army." He rapped his knuckles on the table for
emphasis. "Lining up the heavy cavalry in front of the infantry and
charging forward is an antiquated mode of fighting. My army is not
trained to fight in that manner. It will not work."

Sandovar, Basilio, and Roldan grumbled.

"So, the glory of breaking the enemy now goes to the commoner,"
Sandovar said. "The knight is no longer valued as the 'King of the
Battlefield.'"

"Well put," said Basilio.

"Agreed, Your Highness," Roldan added.

"General Mazrio's infantry, with their uncivilized firearms, are to
claim the day, while the heavy horse sits around until called upon to
mop up," Sandovar said.

Roldan and Basilio gave him supportive nods. "Most uncivilized,"
Basilio said. "Honor is gained by personal combat. The notion of a
small metal ball punching through my armor is - disturbing." His
face reflected his concern. "Yes, quite uncivilized."

Todu ignored Sandovar and Basilio. "Senyor Roldan, your attitude
surprises me." He pointed an accusing finger at the aging knight.
"You fought alongside me and the king against Kheldune. Are you so
old, your memory fails you?"

Roldan showed astonishment at being chastised.

"If that is not the case," Todu continued. "Please tell these gentlemen how the Knights of Olantaro were employed in *that* conflict."

Roldan looked down at Todu and gave him an icy stare. "The
knights were used in an undignified manner. I remember fighting
mostly on foot and riding around a lot, in circles."

"Senyor Gapacho, you simplify things. That is why I am High-
General of Soriazar and in command of this expedition." Todu looked
into the faces of the three men opposite him. "Flexibility, cooperation,
and obedience, senyors. That is what we need here." He found himself staring into the eyes of Sandovar when he made the last comment.

"Senyor, you forget I am above a gentlemen," Sandovar said. "You
may be in command, but you *will* address me as Your Highness."

"Prince Sandovar, I love your father dearly, and he tasked me with teaching you, his heir, how to conduct a war. I can teach you my ways, but I cannot make you listen, or learn."

Sandovar's face reddened. "Now you mock me. When I am king, if you are still breathing, it will be me you must swear fealty to."

Todu glowered at the *still breathing* comment. "Prince Sandovar, the future is of no interest to us at this time. We must first survive this campaign." He swept his hand over the map, motioning to the blocks representing the locations of over sixty thousand Semotec warriors.

Todu's sarcasm brought smirks to the faces on his side of the table, including Javior, who quickly suppressed his. Sandovar slapped his fist into the palm of his hand and stormed toward the tent's entrance. Everyone was silent.

Todu's voice broke the awkward stillness. "Your Highness." Sandovar paused, but he kept his back toward Todu. "Please return when you are ready. You are the Second of this army. Masuf should be returning early this evening. We shall dine together."

"I will be dining elsewhere," Sandovar told him.

Todu was unprepared for that reply. His eyes widened and he sat up straight. "Prince Sandovar, I insist you join the rest of us tonight. It will be a working dinner. There are orders to be issued."

Sandovar slowly shook his head and said nothing.

The back of Todu's neck turned hot. "Your Highness, my command tent will not be pitched in Lady Petra's bedchambers," he said referring to the place where Sandovar had spent the previous evening. In fact, many of the knights had visited the homes of the men of Turela who had been called away to defend Orpresa or Spandel. It had been the same all along the march through the Gudor Valley. The knights disappeared into the villages at sunset and returned at dawn. Todu found their lack of personal discipline repugnant, but heavy cavalry was expensive, and the knights provided their own equipment and mounts.

Sandovar clenched his hands and left the tent.

Todu leaned back in his chair and folded his hands in his lap. His face was gloomy. He wondered which was the greater threat to the army – the Semotecs, or Sandovar and the nobility. *The nobles mustn't put the best interests of the country before their personal pride or status.* It had always been that way, even while growing up in the dusty port of Jucar. Todu's family had land and money, but it was not inherited wealth.

"You are all dismissed," he ordered. "Dinner will begin at sunset. Ensure your commands are ready to march before daylight."

As he emerged from the tent, Sandovar headed for his quarters a
hundred yards south of Todu's tent. Todu's slight dominated his
thoughts. He crossed the parade ground in the center of the camp,
which shimmered in the heat.

   The camp's center was a busy place. Sergeants drilled squads of
pikemen, barking orders that resonated across the field. As Sandovar
passed the blacksmith's tents, clamorous metallic ringing replaced
the sounds of the bellowing sergeants. Four blacksmiths hammered
at their anvils, repairing bits of armor and weapons. Sweat trickled
from their foreheads and droplets flew with each swing of their burly
arms. Their work was unending, but they watched Sandovar as he
passed by. The pace of their hammering did not slacken, but their
eyes were on him and not on their work.

   Sandovar looked away for a split second, blinked, and gazed back
at them. *Why are they staring so?* But the blacksmiths no longer gave
him any notice. They went about their work, chatting amongst themselves as if they had not seen him in the first place.

   Sandovar then looked to his right at a collection of tents fifty
yards away, belonging to the officers of the First Battalion of the First
Tercio. Runners came and went, delivering reports and leaving with
messages. Several officers stood around a table with rocks holding
down the papers on top of it. They too had their eyes fixed on
Sandovar, but strangely, they continued talking to each other and
pointing to different places on the table. Sandovar rubbed his eyes,
and from between his fingers, he saw that the officers no longer paid
attention to him. They were engrossed in their work.

   *How could they know of our argument? Does word spread that
rapidly? They think I've dishonored their general. They believe I'm
unworthy to lead.* His thoughts raced along, but Todu's insult about
Lady Petra remained foremost in his mind. *No, the argument just occurred. It's impossible. We weren't talking loudly. News of it couldn't
have spread that quickly. Todu must mock me when I'm not around.*
He nodded unconsciously. *That's why all of the officers hate me. And
then the common soldiers find out by eavesdropping on their officers.*

   Sandovar continued walking, furtively glancing into the eyes of
the soldiers he passed. He swore he saw the same accusing expressions from them, too, all of which lasted barely a second. His insides
trembled and he fidgeted his fingers. He clasped his hands behind his
back. *I can't let them know their hatred of me affects me so. One day
I'll be their king, and I'll remember all of this.*

Sandovar approached his tent with the forest green banner of the Crown Prince in front of it, fluttering in the warm breeze. His son Tyrel was there, whacking away with a wooden sword at his servant, Devio, who parried with a wooden staff. Devio stopped fighting and greeted Sandovar, but Tyrel gave a gleeful squeal and struck him squarely on the shin. Devio howled in pain and landed on his back, cradling a fast growing lump on his leg.

When Sandovar saw this, his mood flip-flopped and he shook with laughter. "A well placed blow, son." Then, he grew angry. "Devio, you are entrusted with protecting the prince, but you took your eyes off your opponent. In battle there are many distractions, and mistakes are lethal."

Devio gave Sandovar a quizzical look and rose to his feet, favoring his sore leg. "We were playing, Your Highness."

Sandovar's voice remained harsh. "You are not paid to play with the prince. I picked you because you are a faithful servant. Not to mention your horseback skills are exceptional..." Sandovar interrupted himself with the wave of a hand. His face twitched. "Never mind. Fetch me some wine." Devio limped off and disappeared into the tent.

Tyrell approached his father. "Please do not be angry with Devio. I was bored and had no one to play with."

Sandovar placed his hand on Tyrell's shoulder and smiled weakly. But he did not hide his ire well. "I understand, but no more playing for today." Tyrell bit his lip and looked away. Sandovar breathed deeply and softened his voice. "I mean...it is too hot to play so wildly. There will be time later." He patted his son's shoulder and entered his tent.

Sandovar sat at the small table near the entrance. His leather tent was larger than Todu's. In fact, it was the largest in camp. Twelve soldiers and their accoutrements could be sheltered inside. His tent's center pole was twice the height of an average man.

Devio set a tray on the table, holding a flagon of port wine and a glass. Sandovar mechanically held up the glass. Devio filled it, and then he left. Sandovar sipped the wine and the tawny liquid bit into the tip of his tongue. The sweet wine cleared the stickiness from the back of his throat. He placed the glass on the table and brooded. From somewhere behind the tent, he heard Tyrell's shrill voice as he chatted with Devio.

Through the open tent flaps, Sandovar could see the officers' tents opposite his. He stared at the tents, unconsciously tapping his foot on the canvas covering the ground. He watched soldiers and officers appear and disappear at the tent entrances. He listened to the conversations of people walking past, straining to hear anything said about him or Todu Mazrio. Todu's insult about Lady Petra still echoed in his mind. His emotions flowed back and forth, between hatred and humiliation. His mind was a tempest.

A shadow blocked the light entering the tent. Sandovar snapped out of his daze and saw a man duck down to enter. It took a moment for his eyes to adjust, but he recognized his brother Javior. "Devio, a glass and a chair for Prince Javior!" he bellowed.

"I came to see if I could change your mind about dinner," Javior said.

Sandovar shook his head and his eyes narrowed. "If Mazrio issues orders tonight, he can send a runner to my tent. I will not dine with that lowborn son-of-a-bitch. Can you believe the audacity of the man, telling *us*, the nobles, who we can and cannot sleep with. If he were a knight, he would understand."

Devio entered through the backside of the tent and the two of them ceased talking. Like a good servant, Devio went about his business, pretending to ignore his master. He set up a chair for Javior and opened a small cabinet. He retrieved another glass, filled it with wine, and left as quietly as he had come.

Javior sat down and sipped his wine. "The army needs discipline. I say your opinion of the general is in the minority. He is Father's oldest friend and a master of war. He is willing to try new ideas. Usually men his age are unyielding to change, but Todu Mazrio is different. He is one of a kind."

Sandovar stared at the canvas floor, brooding. "Even my family is against me. Javior, listen to yourself. You worship the man like he was your god, or your king." He glared at his younger brother. "He is a prude. It is our right to seduce any woman we admire, or drill any common slut who asks for it. Todu is of low birth and takes joy in his elevated status. He uses it to force his morals on those of higher birth." He gulped down the rest of his wine. His thoughts raced by faster than he could make sense of them. His eyes darted about.

"I do not worship him," said Javior, calmly. "It is respect, and my respect is based on how he handles the troops. I have learned much from him. He is an excellent teacher. That is why father wishes for you to learn from him, too."

"He hates me," Sandovar hissed. "He hates me, because I am heir to the throne and have yet to see a battle. He hates the knights, because the Azari people adore us. They love the mysticism of knighthood and our affirmation of manhood in single combat. He probably hated Father too, until Father bloodied his sword in battle."

"You need rest Sandovar. The heat disturbs you."

Sandovar smirked. He pointed at Javior's chest. "The War Masters of Olantaro know their business, too. You wear the medallion of a knight, yet you disavow the practices of knighthood. General Mazrio's ideas are a threat to the existence of our ancient brotherhood. These new weapons are impersonal. Any idiot can be taught to use them in less than a month." Sandovar's eyes then became gloomy. "Personal honor will no longer have a place in battle. It is good for a king to prove his valor in battle."

"There will always be conflicts between old and new ideas," Javior said. "I have found a place in this army, and I have discovered that the duty and the honor of knighthood are useful traits to the army. I do admit his ideas clash with those of Olantaro, but I see my service to Soriazar as something larger than the service I owe my brotherhood."

Javior's comments stunned Sandovar. His blood boiled, but he tempered himself, so that his words could come out clearly. "You swore an oath. Olantaro is the nation. The king is the Master of the Order. When you serve Olantaro, you serve both. Mazrio's army may defend the nation, but it really serves to promote his interests. Do not let Todu Mazrio fool you, he is cunning and ruthless." He poured himself another glass of wine. "Thirty years ago Father let him taste power, and Todu discovered he liked the flavor of it."

"Good day, Brother. I must be leaving," Javior said. He ducked through the entrance and departed.

Sandovar muttered something unintelligible, raised his glass, and swallowed the contents.

# Chapter 31

The Tiger is Unleashed
17 Janoban 229, A.G.S.

Rodrigo sat on his mahogany throne in the audience chamber. He wore a yellow damask tunic with buttons fashioned from emeralds. His tight hose were dyed forest green, and his knee-high black boots had a high sheen. Beltram stood on the bottom step of the marble dais, to Rodrigo's right. He wore the black robe of his office and held his silver staff in his right hand. A small table with tall thin legs stood beside Beltram. Two small sand clocks rested on top of it. Half of the Illustrious Council sat in the six high-backed chairs arranged in a semicircle before the dais. Three of the chairs sat to the left of the green carpet and three to the right. The doors were locked and a pair of Eagle Guards was posted outside.

Beltram thumped his staff three times on the dais's step. "The Illustrious Council of His Majesty, King Rodrigo Mendio, First of His Name, shall convene. His Majesty wishes to open the session by allowing the members an opportunity to speak." The scratching of pens on parchment followed Beltram's announcement, from the three scribes to the right of the dais.

Borto Camidor rose to his feet from the first seat on the right. He was the only council member seated on that side. Todu Mazrio's empty chair stood to the right of his along with Grand Admiral Amadora's, who was in Spandel directing sea-borne raids against the Semotec coastal villages. Borto wore a light blue tunic tailored to fit his girth.

"I wish to address this council." Beltram turned over one of the sand clocks. Borto smiled. "Your Majesty, the City Guard is working diligently at enforcing your wishes. The jails are filled to bursting with merchants arrested for ignoring your decree on the prices of goods. The magistrates can scarcely keep up with their caseloads." He stroked his neatly trimmed goatee and then his smile faded. "There have been problems here and there, but nothing the City Guard cannot handle. However, the shop windows are becoming increasingly...bare. The merchants are holding back and creating shortages, and many Golandarii no longer have work."

"Are you saying more problems are to be expected?" Rodrigo asked.

"As time passes, people will grow hungry. But I do have better news, Your Majesty. In the last week, my offices have turned over one thousand gold pieces in fines to His Lordship, the Royal Exchequer." Borto returned to his seat.

Lord Igulio Berexo sat opposite Duke Borto to the left of the green carpet. His gold Chain of Office, made of square links with a gold coin dangling from each link, jingled as he rose to his feet. He tugged at the bottom of his ash-gray tunic, smoothing the material over his paunchy stomach. He was sixty years of age and it showed in the creases beside his hazel eyes and his lips. His gray hair was pulled back into a ponytail running halfway down his back. His thick beard masked his double chin and jowls. "Master Steward, I require a turn at speaking to counter the claims of Duke Camidor. His boasting cannot erase certain facts."

Beltram nodded solemnly. "You shall have the time."

The edge of Igulio's lip curled up as he gave Borto an indignant sideways glance. "Your Majesty, for every thousand Duke Borto gives my office, he keeps three for *his* coffers. I pose this question to you, sire. How I am to fund the Royal Army and other endeavors when your other servants do not hand over the Exchequer's rightful share?"

Borto brushed the accusation aside with a wave of his hand. Rodrigo remained impassive, on the outside. *Greed, Borto. Your greed causes me much trouble.* "Duke Borto, I order your bookkeepers to inspect their records. If there are errors, your office shall pay arrears to the Exchequer. This matter is closed."

Borto rose and bowed. "It shall be done."

*It had better be*, Rodrigo thought. Borto took his seat. The scratching of the scribes' pens faded away.

"Lord Berexo," said Rodrigo, "the harvest is approaching. How are the numbers?"

"The fields of the Juahana Valley are bursting, sire. My assessors figure half a million gold pieces is a fair estimate. The produce of the Gudor Valley is likely to be one million. The Turio region will fetch the same..."

Rodrigo cut him off. "And what of the losses from Spandel?"

Igulio hesitated. "I have no reports. Historically, the region gives the Crown a million in taxes. It is reasonable to figure we lost all of it this year. And for many future years, if this war is not soon ended." Igulio took his seat.

Rodrigo placed his elbows on the armrests of his throne and steepled his fingers. *The Juahana Valley must be saved. Spandel March borders the valley. Most of the food in Spandel has been destroyed or carried off by the Semotecs. And the Semotecs will need more food, or they'll have to leave. They mustn't advance farther than Spandel City. The Semotecs may be primitive, but they're not stupid. They'll learn of the Juahana Valley if they don't know of it already.*

"Lady Rosalyna," Rodrigo called out to the woman sitting to the left of Igulio Berexo. She rose and held her hands together against her midriff. Sandovar's empty chair sat beside her's. She wore a full-length blue velvet dress. A string of pearls circled her neck, and a caul of silver bound up her curly red hair. *She's the vision of Khalia, minus fifteen years.* "I call on you to communicate with your brother the Duke of Ariandor, to inform him of my call for two thousand militia for service in Spandel. The levies are to be taken from municipalities, whose *fueros* obligate them for no less than nine months military service."

"It shall be done, Your Majesty," Rosalyna replied. "But Your Majesty needs only draft the order and my brother will carry it out. What more can I do?"

"Sometimes, the intended meanings of letters are not communicated accurately. You can hasten him. Soldiers are needed to complete the work. Right now, we are only capable of holding our positions in Spandel. Make him aware of my desire to drive out the invaders before spring. How long has it been since you have seen your home?"

"Two years, sire."

"Then, I deem it time for you to make that journey and see your family, but return to me as quickly as possible. I will have need of the Council in the near future," said Rodrigo.

Rosalyna curtsied, smoothed out the cloth of her dress, and sat. Rodrigo nodded to Beltram, signaling it was time to move on to new business.

Rodrigo's voice was serious. "I invite the Council to remain in the Alcazar to dine with me at midday. I wish to extend my gratitude for your support of our struggle against the hordes of Semotec."

Duke Borto raised his hand, requesting permission to speak. "It is always a pleasure to break bread with Your Majesty. However, I humbly beseech you to excuse me from the gathering."

"I deny you, Borto."

"B...but."

Rodrigo gave Borto a hard glare, and Borto bit his lip and took his seat.

"You are a most trusted and honored servant, Borto," Rodrigo complimented him. "That is why the Eagle Guard have brought my grandchildren and your wife to dine with us, as well."

Borto fidgeted in his chair. Igulio gave the king a puzzled look, and Rosalyna seemed intrigued.

"I will not accept a request for excusal from you two, either," Rodrigo told them.

Rosalyna's eyes widened at Rodrigo's bluntness and she glanced at Igulio.

Igulio raised his hand to speak, and Beltram granted him permission. "Your Majesty, this dining arrangement concerns me. Why are we being held in the Alcazar? Are we prisoners?"

"No," Rodrigo said, flatly. "But it may not be safe for *any* of us to leave the fortress."

Rosalyna stood up, ignoring protocol. "When will we be able to leave?"

Rodrigo sniffed. "Later this afternoon, possibly, and after a proper escort can be arranged for you to leave safely." *They're not satisfied with that answer.* "I will reveal my reasons to you all after we have filled our bellies, but before then, I shall retire to the gardens for a bit of archery and shooting."

Stunned and insulted faces met Rodrigo. *They're irate. So be it.* "The Council is closed. Master Beltram, make sure the Council's personal guards are fed. No one leaves the fortress. The gates are already closed. You are all dismissed, except for Duke Camidor."

Beltram left the dais and crossed the audience chamber. He rapped on the doors with his staff and the guards outside opened them. Lady Rosalyna stepped onto the green carpet, lowered herself to one knee, and walked the carpet's length to the hallway outside. Lord Berexo touched his knee also and followed her.

"Master Zepio, I wish to be alone with Duke Borto," Rodrigo said. Beltram's face had a sour look, but he bowed and left. When the doors clicked shut, Rodrigo gestured to the queen's seat beside him. "Borto, come here."

Borto nearly ran up the dais. "Sire, you have never invited me to sit on the throne with you. You honor me too much."

"You sit upon the queen's throne. My seat is the symbol of power in the land," Rodrigo said. "I have beckoned you up here, because I want you to remember this meeting."

"Yes, sire." Borto said. "Your examples are always most - vivid."

"Borto, there is a plot against my majesty," Rodrigo told him. "This morning I shall deal with this plot."

Borto sounded worried. "S-sire, have I knowledge of who these plotters are or their motives? Is it the merchants? Have my spies failed?"

"I doubt it," said Rodrigo.

"King Mendio, who are these *wretches*? Tell me what I must do. I will have them arrested."

"You will do nothing to the plotters. I have made the arrange-ments," Rodrigo said. "What I need is for your spies and the City Guard to serve me at a moment's notice."

"It will be done, sire. Permit me a question?" Rodrigo dipped his head. "I gather the plotters are in the city. I beg your pardon, but why was I not told? Have I lost your confidence?"

"No, Borto," Rodrigo replied. "This plot is an international one, outside the circle of your responsibility. But be satisfied with what I am revealing now. You will know the rest at midday."

Borto sounded letdown. "I understand, Your Majesty. What do the powers of my office need to prepare for?"

Rodrigo's face was grim. "It may be necessary to close the city's gates and putdown riots."

Borto's face went blank, and he blinked his eyes a few times.

Rodrigo marched down the corridor that divided the royal family's private apartments. As he walked, he glanced sideways at the sculp-tures and the paintings of the Mendio Kings of Soriazar. Two footmen followed close behind. Farther up the corridor, Sandovar's youngest son Broen waited by the door to Rodrigo's bedchamber. A smile split the three year-old boy's face. Broen unleashed a shrill squeal and charged as Rodrigo approached him. Rodrigo smiled warmly, squat-ted down, and held his arms out to his grandson. Broen jumped into his embrace and wrapped his arms around Rodrigo's neck.

"How is my little prince?" asked Rodrigo. I hold the future of my kingdom in my arms.

"Bam-pa," Broen said, giggling.

"Where is your mother?" Rodrigo asked in a soothing tone. Broen absently pointed a little finger in a random direction. "Ah, I see. Are you coming with the king to the gardens?"

"Gaaden! Gaaden!" Broen said, giddily.

Rodrigo stood and handed his grandson to a footman. In a flash, his tone changed and he was the king again. "Take him to his mother and have them gather with me in the gardens."

The footman carried Broen away, who waved goodbye to Rodrigo over the servant's shoulder. The other footman held the door open, and Rodrigo entered the Royal Bedchamber.

"I will be shooting this morning," Rodrigo told him.

His footman moved to the tall, wooden wardrobe and shifted around Rodrigo's clothing. Rodrigo stood beside his bed and studied the tapestry hanging from the bed's canopy. It depicted his triumph over the Kheldunii. *Those were great moments in our national story, but most of those brave fighters are gone now.* Rodrigo's eyes moved across the tapestry. He had not done that for some time. He silently recited the names of the men in armor, whose likenesses had been hand-stitched into the fabric. *I need your strength now, old friends. I need it from all of you.* A nostalgic smile came to Rodrigo's lips and his eyes brightened with recognition. He ran his fingers over the tightly woven texture of a figure on foot wearing a breastplate, a morion, and carrying a double-headed axe. "Culley Magolin," whispered Rodrigo.

Rodrigo let his hand fall. He pulled his eyes from the tapestry, walked to a window, and pulled it open. A light breeze blew in. Rodrigo glanced over his shoulder and saw that his footman was shining a pair of boots, so he turned back toward the gardens outside. The sounds of trees brushing against each other filled the air. Rufina Manda sat a black horse beneath the trees. Rodrigo ran his eyes up her green hose, which hugged her thigh and rump. He moved his eyes further up her athletic body, until they met her piercing green eyes. Rufina's face was stoic. The horse whickered and shook its head, but she sat there unmoving. Rodrigo swallowed hard and breathed deeply. *My tigress. Do your duty.* His insides quivered as he raised his right hand and touched his forehead. He then lowered it to the windowsill and slid it across the lacquered wood. Rufina smoothly raised her right hand and lowered it.

Rodrigo turned from the window and his nervousness melted away. The order had been given; the deed would be done. He unbuttoned his yellow tunic and walked over to where the footman laid out his clothes. Rodrigo dressed himself in a brown leather tunic and breeches. He sat in a chair and the footman set his boots before him. Rodrigo grunted as he leaned forward. Old age had not been too unkind to him, but his stomach had grown a little over the years. He pulled the boots on and folded down the tops of them.

Queen Khalia and her sister Rosalyna sat on chairs beside the patch of grass used for archery and shooting. Khalia sipped wine from a golden goblet inlaid with sapphires. Four handmaidens stood nearby, holding bows and quivers. Khalia wore a delicate, lemon colored dress, with a silver belt, resembling three parallel ropes. A manservant held a silver tray out to Rosalyna, offering her a golden goblet of wine. She looked at Rodrigo as she spoke to her sister.

Conrado Juarez, Captain of the Eagle Guard, stood a short distance away, puffing on a cigar. Four Eagle Guards accompanied him, their burnished breastplates shown like mirrors. Captain Juarez wore his panoply, including his morion, heavily engraved with images of vines, leaves, and acorns, a matching breastplate, and forest green tunic and hose. He cradled an arquebus in the crook of his arm. A manservant stood beside him, holding another arquebus and a leather bandolier. The manservant with the tray offered a goblet to Rodrigo as he approached Khalia. Rodrigo sipped at the dry, yellow Manzanilla wine.

"His Majesty is looking rugged today," said Khalia. "I must say Masuf has better taste in clothing."

Rodrigo chortled. "Masuf gave this to me as a gift before he went south with the army. Leather will not smolder like cloth if touched by powder sparks."

"You should stick to archery," said Khalia. "Guns are beneath your status."

"My great queen forgets these guns are the future of warfare," Rodrigo said. "Nations will emulate us when word of the gun's might spreads."

Khalia raised an eyebrow and sipped her wine. "My sister tells me you have sealed off the Alcazar. Are we all prisoners?"

Rodrigo wet his tongue with wine. The morning was warm, aside from Khalia's heated words. "The king will make his reasons known in due time. Until then, shall we relax and enjoy the morning's activities?"

"The Eagle Guard is manning the walls," said Khalia. "There is not a Tracker in sight, nor that ruffian Rufina Manda. What can my son see in her?"

Rodrigo defended the prince. "He sees what I see - strength and loyalty." *And great, great beauty.*

"You need to end that disgraceful relationship," Khalia told him. "It does not serve the nation, and our prince, though he does not act as one, needs marry a noble to secure an alliance."

Rodrigo was tiring of the talk. "The relationship binds the Trackers more tightly to me."

"Rufina Manda is bound to you for life by oath," Khalia reminded him. "Anything else is overkill."

Lady Rosalyna remained silent and sipped her wine. Rodrigo turned from Khalia when a child's laughter found his ears.

Livia Mendio, Sandovar's wife of seven years, glided across the grass. She was the daughter of Maxo Trubedo, Duke of Aliantro. Her face was pretty, though not beautiful, and her hips, widened from bearing Sandovar's two sons, contrasted with her petite torso. She wore a bodice of red damask with white enameled buttons. A ring of wildflowers circled her curly red hair, and a black velvet choker supported a golden Sunburst of Ghyo. A maidservant walked a few steps behind her, holding Broen by the hand.

"Good day, Your Majesty," Livia said as she curtsied. Her voice was plaintive.

"Princess Livia, you look exquisite this morning," Rodrigo said. He did that often when he met her. She had the sweetest smile of the royal family, but her melancholy concerned him. No love existed between Sandovar and Livia, which affected Rodrigo, because he yearned for love too. "Can you draw a bow in that outfit?" he asked her.

"Sire, I shall be a spectator this morning. I am not feeling up to it."

"As you wish." Rodrigo dipped his head to her, eyeing her neck. "I have never known you to wear religious items."

Livia took a chair beside Khalia and her maidservant stood beside her, still holding Broen's hand. "Times are different, Majesty. Perhaps we can all do with more of Ilyas's teachings. I got the idea from the people, sire. The Semotec invasion has made the Sunburst fashionable."

Rodrigo was unimpressed. "I believe my Eagle upon your bosom would be more appropriate." He sipped his wine and set his cup on the servant's tray. "Captain, we will commence."

Captain Juarez gave Rodrigo a crooked smile as he clenched the cigar between his teeth. He touched a cotton cord to the cigar's glowing tip, until it too began to glow and smoke. Khalia and Rosalyna handed their cups to the servants and took up places near Captain Juarez. Their servants strung their bows for them, while Khalia packed cotton into her ears.

Across the field, two round canvas targets stood, stuffed with straw. Red circles marked the targets' centers. Two other targets dangled on chains from wooden frames to the right of them. A mail shirt had been draped over a straw-filled burlap sack and a plate armor cuirass over another sack hung beside it.

Captain Juarez handed the lighted match to Rodrigo and lit another one with his cigar. Rodrigo motioned the servant holding the arquebus to approach. He took the bandolier from him and draped it over his shoulder, so the leather pouch containing paper cartridges hung at his right hip. The servant handed Rodrigo a small powder horn. Rodrigo then took the arquebus and cradled it in his left elbow.

Holding the smoldering match in his left hand, Rodrigo pushed aside the small lever of the flash pan cover. He filled the pan with powder from the small horn and swung the cover back into place. He placed the butt of the arquebus on the ground and fetched a cartridge from the leather pouch. He bit off the end of it and poured the powder down the barrel. He then stuffed the remaining paper into the muzzle and dropped in a lead ball. He pulled the ramrod from beneath the barrel and rammed down the powder, ball, and paper. He lifted the gun and took the match into his right hand. He blew on the end of it, making it glow, and placed it into the serpentine shaped lock. He put the arquebus to his shoulder, flipped open the flash pan, squeezed the lever beneath the stock, and the burning match touched the powder in the pan...

*Phuff-PHOOM!*

Thick gray smoke spewed from the gun. Rodrigo's body jerked back from the recoil. The ball struck low on the mail target, spraying pieces of the metal rings into the air. The flattened ball imbedded itself within the burlap sack. Rodrigo roared with laughter.

"Excellent shot, sire!" Captain Juarez exclaimed as he discharged his arquebus at the plate armor target. The ball clipped off a piece at the top of the armor. "Ach! That one drifted."

Khalia harrumphed and drew her bowstring. Her arrow struck dead center. "Really Rodrigo, I agree with the nobles. Guns are uncivilized. Let alone inaccurate."

Rodrigo laughed some more and slapped his thigh. "Reload!" Rodrigo plucked the match from the lock, flipped open the flash pan, and blew out the remaining powder.

Broen squealed with delight and clapped his hands together. The maidservant stood behind him, with her hands over his ears. Khalia loosed a third arrow by the time Rodrigo prepared to discharge a second time. "Those guns are clumsy, dangerous, and fire much too slowly," she said.

"Maybe so," replied Rodrigo. "But a bow requires months of training for the arm to build strength for sustained fighting. Guns require only a couple weeks training and no great strength is needed."

Rodrigo's second ball struck the plate armor at a bad angle and ricocheted into the ground, throwing up a plume of grass and dirt. The chains holding up the target jingled as it bucked wildly. Broen howled with delight and jumped about.

"These little balls hit harder than war hammers," said Rodrigo. "Even if they do not punch through the armor, they still stun the victim." He undid the match and blew into the flash pan again.

Captain Juarez's second ball struck true and punctured the plate cuirass dead center. "A killing shot," he said, unlocking his match and blowing out his pan.

Rosalyna spoke up. "Guns are cruel weapons, Majesty. They leave ugly, dirty wounds, which breed infection."

"That they do," Rodrigo answered her, as he pulled a paper cartridge from his bandolier. He rammed the ball into the barrel, while Khalia and Rosalyna loosed two more arrows. Broen continued to squirm about, and Livia gave the maidservant a scornful look. The servant lost her grip on Broen and he darted off toward Rodrigo.

He was a fast little boy. The maidservant had to raise her skirt to chase after him. Rodrigo shifted the match to his right hand and blew on it. Broen ran up to Rodrigo, his face wild with excitement. He grabbed the pouch at Rodrigo's waist, stuck his hands into it, and pulled out some of the cartridges. Rodrigo was startled and bent down, grabbing at Broen's hand. Angry words formed on his lips as the glowing match touched off the powder residue on the cartridges in Broen's hands.

In an instant, Rodrigo's world turned ashen gray, streaked with red fire. A shrill scream pierced in his right ear, before his hearing became muffled. His knees buckled and the right side of his face was rent by a searing pain. The smell of burnt meat found his nostrils.

A woman's voice screamed, "Blessed Ilyas! No!"

Rodrigo collapsed.

# Chapter 32

## Sanctuary Defiled
### 17 Janoban, 229 A.G.S.

Drucilla took one last look at the city where she had spent her entire life. She would miss the whitewashed facades. There were no white cities in the north, and the food was not spiced the same way. Everything would be different.

After her things had been secured to a packhorse, Drucilla had retreated to her private quarters to look at the city. She gazed upon the fortress walls of the Alcazar. The Mendios had occupied its precipitous cliffs for centuries. They looked down upon and ruled Soriazar from their towering perch. An eagle was a fitting symbol of her family's power.

The fat brown Gudor River was visible to the left of the Alcazar. Trees lined each bank, and a merchant's barge moved against the current, heading for the city docks. In an hour, Drucilla would travel the high road that followed the Gudor River to Vorencia.

She placed her hands on the window ledge and leaned forward. She watched the Golandarii go about their business. Two well-dressed men huddled near a recessed door, covering their mouths as they spoke. By their style of dress, Drucilla assumed they were merchants. Women wearing plain dresses and aprons carried baskets with items purchased in the city's innumerable stores. Children ran back and forth, chasing cats and dogs and each other. A cart filled with barrels of salted fish passed beneath her window. The driver was a white-haired man with a pipe clenched between his teeth. A thin trail of smoke rose from the pipe's bowl. The mules pulling the cart brayed loudly.

The tromping of boots then rose above the street noises. People moved off to the sides of the street, clearing a corridor down the middle. Ten Trackers ran down the street beneath her window. Each carried a crossbow with the bow cocked. Drucilla watched as the Trackers stopped and gathered along the base of the wall beneath the windows of the temple's kitchens. She knew her father used them from time to time to maintain order within the city, especially when a plot against him was discovered. Drucilla watched with curiosity. It saddened her to know one of her last memories of home would be watching her father flex his muscles. The cook, given to Serophia by Borto

Camidor, appeared around the corner of the temple. The Trackers pulled bolts from the quivers at their waists and charged their cross-bows. The last Tracker in line turned and looked over his shoulder. He raised his gloved hand above his head and lowered it quickly. The line of Trackers then disappeared around the corner of the temple, opposite the Oaken Cask.

Drucilla shut the window and walked to the door. She took a last glimpse at her room. She did not want to leave, but the Church was greater than one temple and one city. She turned the latch and pulled open the heavy wooden door.

A scream disturbed the tranquility of Ghyo's temple. A brief silence followed, and then the sounds of steel clashing with steel shattered the quiet like breaking glass. Drucilla gasped and cold sweat broke out across her stomach.

"Father, no!" she screamed. Her heart pounded, tears filled her eyes and spilled over her cheeks. "Father, you wretch!"

Drucilla gathered her dress and rapidly descended the winding stairs of the High Priestess's tower. She came to the last turn and crashed into a terrified male acolyte trying to run upstairs. Drucilla careened into the unyielding stone blocks of the tower wall. She cried out from the sharp pain that stiffened her elbow and hip.

The acolyte ended up on top of Drucilla. He picked himself up and pulled back his white hood. "Treachery, Mother!" he cried. A curving line of blood spattered the front of his robe. "The Trackers are killing everybody!" He raced past her up the stairs, trampling the loose folds of her dress and leaving dark smudges on the cloth.

Drucilla got to her feet and limped to the doorway. The acolyte had left it ajar. She leaned against the wall for support. The coolness of the stones passed through the silk of her dress and chilled her as much as the horrible screaming coming from beyond the door. Drucilla stayed there and listened carefully. A woman's voice caught her attention.

"In the name of His Majesty, lay down your arms," the voice called out.

"Never," a male responded. "Your treachery will not succeed. By Oath, our lives and our steel are married to this temple."

That was Captain Ercanbold, Drucilla told herself.

"Then your Oath will be your epitaph," the woman declared.

Shouts rang out and the cacophony resumed, followed by screams of pain. Drucilla pushed the door further open and limped through the opening. She made her way to one of the wide columns running the length of the temple. She slid around it, pressing her body to the smooth sandstone. A wild melee raged in the sanctuary's center among the wooden benches. Seven knights and ten Trackers

weaved around and stumbled over them. Eight Knights of the Order
of Ilyas lay sprawled on the floor, with bolts sticking out of their white
surcoats. She recognized Captain Ercanbold among the dead. Drucilla watched in horror as her father's Trackers traded blows with the
knights. White mixed with green in a swirling kaleidoscope. Swords
flashed, sparks ignited, and blood splashed onto the combatants and
the floor. Drucilla felt bile rise to her throat as see saw a Knight of
Ilyas take away the top of a Tracker's head with his sword.

In the middle of the fray, Drucilla saw a beautiful woman in green
leather, thrusting and slashing with two short swords. The Tracker
fought with feline grace and her long red braid swung through the
air, following her movements. *Rufina Manda!* Rufina's lips were
curled up into a vicious snarl. Drucilla could see her teeth and her
eyes. Drucilla saw joy in those green eyes. *Battle lust.*

Rufina squared off against a knight armed with a helmet, sword,
and shield. The knight kept his shield between him and his foe.
Rufina did not hesitate. Drucilla watched her move toward the
knight. In a flash, she jabbed the point of her left hand sword into the
inside part of the knight's elbow. The knight's sword dropped from
his grasp. Rufina withdrew the sword, hooked the top of the knight's
shield with the quillon, and pulled it down. Drucilla blinked her eye
and nearly missed Rufina opening the knight's throat with her other
sword. The knight fell to his knees and his helmet slumped forward.
Crimson blood washed over his white surcoat.

There was a commotion down the arcade on Drucilla's side of the
temple. Trackers poured out of the kitchen doors. They loosed their
crossbows into the backs of the knights struggling against the Trackers in the sanctuary's center. The melee ended. Sobbing replaced the
sounds of fighting.

Across the sanctuary, a dozen Eagle Guards held the temple's
priests, acolytes, and servants against the wall with the pikes of their
halberds.

Rufina's voice echoed throughout the sanctuary. "Find the High
Priestess and Princess Drucilla. Bring them to me alive."

*Where is Serophia?* Thoughts rushed into Drucilla's mind. *This is
insane.*

"Princess Drucilla," said a voice from behind.

The sound shocked her senses and weakened her knees. Drucilla
held the column with both hands as she slid to the floor and curled
into a ball. "The princess is here, Mistress." A hand gently wrapped
around Drucilla's arm and lifted her to her feet.

Drucilla could not speak. She kept her head down and stared at
the floor. A gloved hand touched her beneath the chin. The glove's
brown leather was sticky with blood, and the coppery smell filled her

nose. The hand raised Drucilla's head, until she was face to face with the Mistress of Trackers. Rufina's fair skin was speckled with blood; her red hair was matted with it. A wry smile came to her lips. "Your Highness, I have come to take you home."

Drucilla jerked her head out of Rufina's grasp. She wiped at the blood Rufina had left on her chin. "I will not go willingly. The Alcazar is no longer my home. If I am to go there, I go as a prisoner. This aggression against the Church is nothing short of war."

"See it as you wish," Rufina said. "You *will* sleep in your old bed this evening." She turned to the three Trackers standing by. "Keep her safe. We still need to find Serophia." Rufina turned her piercing emerald eyes back to Drucilla.

*Here it comes.* Drucilla thought.

"Where is Her Holiness?"

"I do not know," Drucilla answered truthfully. "I have not seen her since Morning Rituals." Drucilla somehow found the courage to smile. "Maybe she has slipped through your fingers."

Rufina smirked. "I doubt that." She walked away from Drucilla and stood in the pooling blood among the bodies in the middle of the sanctuary. "Tear the temple apart! Find the High Priestess! Anyone caught looting will be punished by pain of death!"

Drucilla had no idea where Serophia was. The thought of her escaping raised her spirits. She looked at the trio of Trackers guarding her. One had an ugly scar on his face, beginning at the corner of his mouth and ending where his left eye should have been. She did not recognize him.

"Are you proud of yourselves?" Drucilla asked, not taking her eyes off the old Tracker's scarred face. "You have betrayed your Faith and slaughtered innocent people."

The three Trackers glanced at each other. Finally, the one with the scar said, "Your Highness, we are sworn to obey your father. It is his bidding we do."

Drucilla laughed. It surprised her she that was able to do it. "And that washes away your guilt?" She laughed some more. *Where am I getting this courage?* "My father is a criminal. You follow the wishes of a criminal."

"You are wrong," the scarred Tracker said. "Rodrigo and I fought side by side against the Kheldunii. I am Casimo, and the king is a good man. The country is in danger. He will save us again." He pointed a gnarled finger at his face. "Thirty years ago, I gave an eye in his service. I will give the other, too - or more, if need be."

"Mistress," a male voice called out. "There is a locked door behind the altar."

Drucilla watched Rufina Manda stroll across the sanctuary and stop before the people guarded by the Eagle Guards. "Who can unlock that door? Where is the key?"

Her questions were met by silence. Rufina placed her hands on her hips. "Trackers, pick up a bench and batter it down."

Four Trackers carried one of the heavy benches to the doorway. The noise of the battering resounded throughout the temple. Clouds of dust flew from the cracks along the edges of the thick door. The Trackers grunted as they rammed. The metal bands holding the top and bottom of the door together began to loosen. The wood groaned with each hit and began to crack. The iron of the lock mechanism bent increasingly. The Trackers breathed heavily. Sweat lined their brows.

*Is Serophia in her private chamber?* Drucilla wondered. Serophia had never spoken to her much about the depths of the temple. On only one occasion, she had hinted about her private collection of valuable books.

The door gave way as the lock shattered. Pieces of metal clanged as they hit the floor.

"Bring a torch!" a Tracker by the door called out.

It took time before a Tracker appeared with a lit torch. Rufina waited beside the broken door. The Tracker with the torch led the way down the steps, and Rufina followed close behind, with both swords drawn. Two other Trackers followed her down the stairs.

A loud scraping noise soon resonated from within the stairwell. The sound intensified until it abruptly ended in a fulminating roar. A thick cloud of dust rolled out of the doorway. Shouting echoed from the stairwell. Two dusty Trackers crawled out on all fours and fell on their faces, gagging on dust.

The pair of Trackers waiting outside stormed into the dust cloud. Drucilla heard them calling out for Rufina. Minutes later they reappeared carrying Rufina Manda between them. She was caked in a thick layer of beige dust. Slimy mucous darkened the dust around her mouth. Rufina wheezed and hacked, but the noises grew weaker. Blood gushed from a wicked gash on her forehead.

"Princess!" one of the Trackers shouted across the sanctuary. "Mistress Manda is dying. Your skills are needed."

The Trackers with Drucilla grabbed her by the arms and dragged her to where Rufina lay on her back. Drucilla's feet hardly touched the floor as they moved her across the bumpy stones. She stared at the woman sent by Rodrigo to storm Ghyo's temple. She had watched her Trackers slaughter the knights, who had died protecting her and the other priests. Blood had soiled Ghyo's sanctuary, and now the Trackers expected Drucilla to heal the architect of that blasphemy.

"We couldn't see," a dusty Tracker said. He coughed harshly. "I stepped right on top of her. That's how we found her, covered with dust."

"Princess Drucilla, lay hands upon her," another Tracker demanded.

Rufina's emerald eyes bulged as she struggled to breathe. Drucilla's feelings hardened. *This wicked person doesn't deserve the blessings of the Gift. She brought this ruin upon herself.* She felt no pity for Rufina, but the Tenets of the Faith were deeply rooted within her. *Let not the affairs of temporal matters keep you from healing the sick and injured, which you can render aid to.* Tears filled her eyes. *No! I will not cry like some scared child in front of these barbarians.* An amber light grew out of her palms. Drucilla knelt down. Rufina clutched desperately at the hem of Drucilla's white dress. Drucilla placed her hands upon Rufina's chest and the Gift sank into her lungs. Rufina coughed up globs of black mucous, until she breathed normally again. Drucilla then placed a glowing hand on the gash in her forehead.

The Light of Ghyo faded from Drucilla's palms. "I can do nothing more for her," she said quietly. "But she will recover."

"Where is the High Priestess?" Casimo asked one of the Trackers who had followed Rufina down the stairwell. "Was she down there?"

The Tracker answered, "She was down there when the ceiling fell on top of Ernio. I fear she was crushed."

Casimo assumed a commanding tone as if it were his place to lead in case of Rufina's death. "We must leave. Two of you carry our Mistress to the carriage. Eagle Guard! Move your prisoners out of the temple and prepare to return to the Alcazar." His one-eyed gaze turned toward Drucilla. "You will accompany us to the palace." There was no room for negotiation in his voice.

# Chapter 33

The Darkness Abates
17 Janoban, 229 A.G.S.

Orius's party was in no mood for mercy. They had passed by several wooden racks with rotting corpses suspended from them with ropes – Cheltan corpses. An Oruk shrieked as Chief Condin buried his axe between his shoulder blades. Blood speckled the Chief's horse and stained the white wolf's pelt he wore. Another Oruk threw up his hands, but Culley's sword sent one of the outstretched arms spinning to the ground. He followed up with a smooth slash that opened his foe from breastbone to waist. The Oruk wailed as he fell to the ground, clutching his spilling entrails. Culley flashed his eyes around. To his right, a wild-eyed Oruk pressed his back against the wall of a steeped roofed hut. He spurred his horse in that direction, but a Wolf Rider beat him there and pinned the Oruk to the wall with an arrow.

Orius and his patrol pursued the fleeing Oruks around the huts and through Drenga's narrow, twisting dirt streets. The keening of the horn in the watchtower had announced the Chelts' approach and sent the Oruks into a panic.

Orius and the Chelts pursued their foes no further than Drenga's western edge. They stopped there and watched a score of Oruks flee across the fields and disappear into the forest at the foot of the western mountain. Orius sat his horse and watched the tail of the Oruk army slowly disappear over the mountain's summit.

"They shall have a long, hungry walk home," he said. "The Sytish frontier is three or four days ride to the west, for a lightly encumbered party with proper mounts."

"Aye, they number at least a thousand," Culley added. "From the looks of Drenga, there cannot be much food left back that way, either. A host that size is difficult to feed in these mountains, even when the countryside hasn't been plundered."

"It is difficult to feed an army of two hundred in these mountains," said Chief Condin. "Many of them will not make it back to Sytor." A sideways smile came to his face. "Hopefully, they will remember this defeat before they think of another invasion."

"For we may not be able to resist another," Culley growled. "We have lost many of the North's finest warriors, but I doubt the Oruks know that."

"This is just the beginning. There are wicked powers at work within the Wastelands." Orius's words landed hard.

"Father Candell," said Chief Condin. "You have my curiosity."

"Chief, I will withhold my opinion until I have spoken with Malagorn and my mother."

Bevyn broke in. "Father Orius, your words are a mystery. The cold will soon blow in from the north, and the weather will keep the Oruks off our land. This is the end of our troubles."

Orius pursed his lips and sighed. "It is unwise to assume the Black Rider is the only one of his kind. When the weather warms next spring, the Oruks will again sally forth through the mountain passes. They may not return to the Northern Valley, but they may strike the Southern Valley, or move into Fringia. One does not train an army as hard the Oruks have been training, not to use it."

"Fringian fields can support huge armies," said Culley. "And the Southern Valley is large enough to feed ten thousand mouths for months."

"We must also consider the speed at which the Oruks breed. The Wastelands conceal their true numbers. The South needs to be warned," Orius said.

"The southerners must fend for themselves," said Arturo. "Never have they cared about the happenings of the North."

Condin scowled at his Wolf Rider. "Father Candell is Chief of the Northern Valley. He will soon be crowned King of Cheltabria. You will do his bidding."

Arturo glared at Condin.

"Arturo," Orius said. "The Northern Chelts have a right to distrust foreigners. I know this first hand. But the Chelts of the Southern Valley are of your heritage, too. If I am to be King of the Chelts, it must be of *all* the Chelts. Your brothers in the south must be made aware of what has happened here." *We may need their numbers.* Arturo spoke no more of it.

The Chelts followed Orius back into the village. The air was thick with the acrid smell of burning wood and thatch. Plumes of smoke rose into the sky. Three of the steep roofed huts were fully engulfed and several more would be. The hungry flames sucked in the neighboring air, creating an artificial breeze. Bits of broken pottery, furniture, and weapons littered the streets. The Oruks had left behind fifty two-wheeled carts, most of which were smashed up. The carcasses of butchered mules, dangling by their back hooves from wooden poles, cluttered the village center, which was no more than a patch of dirt. The air there was ripe with the smell of entrails and spoiling meat. Embers smoldered beneath a half-cooked slab of a mule on a wooden spit.

A blacksmith's hut sat on the edge of the village square. The wide double-doors hung open, revealing the shop's interior. A reddish glow emanated from the smithy's forge. A hammer lay on top of the anvil in the hut's center. Unlike the rest of Drenga, the smithy was not in disarray. Tools hung in neat rows from hooks screwed into the rafters. Workbenches and stools were unbroken. Only a purplish head, mounted above the entrance, was out of the ordinary. There was no mistaking the locks of golden hair hanging from the head. It was Cheltan. The dead man's jaw hung open, frozen in a mute scream.

"All of the Cheltan bodies left here are men and boys," Orius said. "No women or girls."

"It is always like that," said Chief Condin. "The Oruks carry them home to fuck them. They can pump them until they drop from exhaustion, because no living child will ever be gotten from their efforts. They will produce no extra mouths to feed."

Culley's face reflected his disgust. "Drenga had many people. If any of the women survive the journey through the mountains..." His voice trailed off.

"Drenga must be rebuilt," Orius broke in. "The Drenga Valley is the best way for the Oruks to move a large army into Northern Cheltabria. We have the entire autumn and winter to gather settlers to do the work. In the spring, fields here will need to be sown, and a stockade must be erected around the village."

"Only a king can do such things," Chief Condin pointed out.

"Only if a king can stop the tribes from fighting one another," Orius told him. "The tribes banded together with me to drive the invaders back into the Wastelands, but I fear they will soon return to their old squabbles."

"Orius Candell, King of the Chelts," Culley quipped. "Fate is a fickle mistress."

"My throne is not in Cheltabria," said Orius. "But the Oruk rising changed things. I may have no other choice but to first ascend to the Cheltan throne."

"True, but Fate has placed a capable person in a position to take advantage of the times," Culley said. "You have the tools to do the work. Having a nation behind you strengthens your legitimate claim."

*But Kirkvold's crown is not ringed with emeralds and diamonds.* "I have only you, my mother, and Malagorn to thank for my training and schooling," said Orius.

"You are too modest, boy. It takes skill to use tools properly."

Orius turned toward the Wolf Riders. "Search the huts. Look for survivors. Then we will leave this sad place."

The Wolf Riders split into pairs and rode off through the village. Orius, Culley, and Condin stayed together and searched the huts around the village center. The scene inside the dwellings was the same as in the streets. All was wreckage and chaos. Shelves, tables, and pottery lay in pieces. The Oruks had broken up the furnishings to light fires. Only beds remained intact. The Oruks had lived well in Drenga, though the bedding and the air inside the huts stank of sweat and urine.

Outside, ravens and lammergeyers picked at the hundreds of discolored, putrefying bodies. The stench of death tainted the air, making breathing an uncomfortable thing. Orius stood before a log frame with twenty bodies hanging from it. "It sickens me to know such vile creatures exist. These men deserve a proper funeral, but that is impossible. We are too few."

Culley gestured at the bodies. "This was meant to be a message for us."

Chief Condin said, "These Chelts have been hanging here for a few weeks. The Drengans must have resisted fiercely to be punished like this." He pointed to a couple large mounds of charred bones lying outside the village. "Oruk funeral pyres."

"Why did they not have walls around their village?" Orius asked no one in particular.

"Memories always fade," Condin said. "The Oruks have not caused such troubles in generations. Drenga's earthworks, like those around my village, Skorva, were sufficient to drive off small bands of Oruk raiders, but no one would have dreamed of such numbers coming out of Sytor." He clenched his jaws. "That is why Skorva exists no more."

"Come spring, the North will be ready," Orius promised.

"We should head back. There's nothing more for us here," Culley said.

"Call back the scouts," Orius ordered. *I want to scour every inch of the village for anything identifying the Black Rider, but there's no time.* The Cheltan army had to return home. The warriors were restless; the harvest was near. *Many crops will remain in the fields this autumn. The labor of the dead will be missed.* Winter would be long and hungry for many families of the Northern Valley. Orius wondered how long Kathair could maintain order among the warriors he led.

Orius believed Malagorn could provide answers to his questions about the Black Rider. He had the Rider's sword, a shining ring, and a gruesome piece of evidence, in the form of the Rider's severed hand. Malagorn had crammed his keep with old books, dusty scrolls, and thousands of other oddities. The old conjurer possessed a thirst for knowledge equal only to the scholars of the Holy Tower. Malagorn was the last of a vanishing breed, forced to live in seclusion to avoid persecution by the Church of Ghyo. He guarded ancient knowledge that had been passed down from conjurer to apprentice for millennia.

Before heading east, Orius and the Chelts rested a while and let their horses graze. They had no food and they dared not fetch water from the village well. The Oruks had thrown two of their dead into it and the water stank. After an hour, they mounted up and left Drenga.

# Chapter 34

## The Tide Crests
### 17 Janoban, 229 A.G.S.

Todu stood between two cannons atop an earthen mound at the southwest corner of the camp. He watched the soldiers of the First Tercio's Second Battalion labor beneath the hot sun. The square camp was taking shape. The soldiers had worked throughout the morning. The ditch was nearly complete, and Torigo Azano, the Royal Army's engineer, had passed out the mauls to drive the wooden stakes into the dirt, transforming the ditch into an abatis.

Todu shielded his eyes from the sun and gazed down the road leading to Spandel. The city lay fifty miles away, beyond the rolling foothills south of the Blancuro Mountains. Masuf's Trackers reported over thirty thousand Semotecs were near the city. Only the marquis's militia and the city's walls stood between the invaders and Spandel's vital port and dockyards. He turned his head south and watched lines of haggard old men, women, and children approach Turela. He had issued orders to not allow the refugees into the army's camp. He ordered his officers to urge the people to head north, through the Rojera Pass. Extra mouths would eat up the food around Turela and leave little for the army. Todu lowered his hand and opened the letter that had just arrived via messenger.

*To Todu Mazrio, High General of Soriazar, Spandel City, 15 Janoban, 229*

*Great Warrior, I beseech you to hasten your march and come to the aid of this city. The Semotecs oppose me with tens of thousands of warriors. Our militia numbers less than ten thousand. I have yet to order the withdrawal of my forces into the confines of Spandel's walls, but I will issue this order within a day or two. We are burning everything of benefit ahead of the enemy. My intention is to offer the Semotecs a siege, unless you can arrive in time with the Royal troops.*

*I can feed the city by sea, but the countryside is another matter. I cannot provide for the security of the Juahana Valley, including the merchant traffic traveling along the river. I must inform you that the Turela-Spandel road has been cut near Buraluz. Prudence tells me to not attempt to clear that line of communication. The operation would require me to split my forces in the face of my foe.*

*Gregoro Torenyo, Marquis of Spandel*

Todu placed the letter into the supple black leather of his tunic. His face reflected his deep contemplation of the military situation. He considered the information he had received from Masuf's Trackers. *Five to six thousand Semotecs surround Buraluz, so too in Tuaste, east of there. But how many Semotecs actually block the road? And do they come from the numbers around Buraluz or not?* He tucked the questions into the back of his mind. He would send scouts to have a look, but there was a more immediate and closer problem - Orpresa.

Twenty thousand Semotecs rampaged around Orpresa, twenty miles to the east and about five thousand were sacking the village of Burbagona, not fifteen miles to the southeast. Five thousand more were seventeen miles directly south, completing their sack of the village of Turzaga. Plus, five to six thousand warriors were twenty-two miles to the southwest, near the village of Tramoce.

*This isn't a safe place for the army to be, but it's the place to be to launch an attack.* Images swirled around his mind like tealeaves in a Terghui fortuneteller's cup. A plan was forming. He visualized the army's next move. They would act when the soldiers finished their camp and when Masuf returned from scouting Turzaga.

"General," a voice called out. Todu spun around and looked down upon Captain Solanto. "May I join you there?"

"You may approach."

Nestor Solanto walked up to his general and bowed. His blue eyes beamed with pride. "Despite the heat, the men have worked well. My Second Battalion is made up of good troops. Better than the First."

"I am sure you are correct, Captain," Todu said. "But we will not know how good any of them are until the ground runs red." *Thirty years of peace has been good for Soriazar, but not for its army or knights.*

"The sergeants have done us a valuable service. Those old veterans have trained the men hard. The movements of drill have become second nature to the troops," Nestor said.

*Captain Solanto, you're an excellent officer, but we will soon find out if you are an excellent commander.* "The initial clash of arms renders most plans unworkable, but good training lessens the confusion," Todu said.

"'Discipline and the training come into play when the situation is most chaotic,'" Nestor quoted Todu Mazrio. "I have taken it to heart."

"Very well, Captain." Todu ended the small talk. "I wish to commence the inspection."

"Yes, General."

Todu descended the cannons' mound, kicking up little clouds of dust with each step. Nestor accompanied him. He walked along the southern rampart until he came to the main path, running north to south through the camp. Soldiers stopped what they were doing and stood at attention as Todu passed. He paused briefly, now and then, and spoke to a particular sergeant or a junior officer. He shouted words of encouragement to the common soldiers, and they returned to moving earth with their picks and shovels.

He turned left and headed up the path leading to the parade ground in the camp's center. The Knights of Olantaro had their tents and horse pickets set up along the path. Their part of the camp bustled with activity, but the greetings toward Todu halted. As he passed by them, none of the knights, or their squires, stopped what they doing or paid him any respect or attention.

They do not look me in the eye, but I can feel their cold stares on the back of my neck when I'm past them. I must gain their confidence.

Beyond the knights' tents stood the officers' tents of the second battalions of both tercios. Visible respect for Todu Mazrio returned as suddenly as it ended when he had approached the knights. Soldiers came to attention and there were cheers for their leader.

Sandovar's immense tent sat along the parade ground's southern edge. The Crown Prince's banner flapped lazily in the warm summer breeze. Devio sat on a stool beside the tent's entrance, polishing a pair of elaborate greaves. Todu's shadow fell across Devio's feet. The manservant looked up, squinted into the sunlight, and his eyes widened with recognition. He set the greaves aside, stood, and bowed.

"Senyor, what service can I render you?" Devio asked. He did not look Todu in the eyes.

"I require the presence of your master." Todu's dislike of Sandovar made him conscious of the words he used in public. "Please inform His Highness."

Devio's mouth worked about nervously. "H-His Highness is not within."

Todu's neck muscles tightened. *Steady.* "Where can the prince be found?" His tone was flat.

Devio hesitated in answering. He nervously opened and closed his hands.

"Answer the question," Todu said.

"General, please do not tell the prince it was I who told you this. My work is all I have."

*This is ridiculous.* "I need not promise you anything. Where is he?"

"His Highness had business to attend to in Turela," Devio said.

Todu clenched his teeth and his hands. "Send word to His Highness to return immediately."

Todu walked away. He found it strange when he suddenly realized he was angrier with Rodrigo than he was with Sandovar. *Rodrigo, you gave your wretched son to me and tasked me with teaching him of war. I warned you of the difficulties that the arrangement would create.* His pace quickened as his anger grew. He marched across the parade ground toward the lines of swordsmen awaiting his inspection. Nestor Solanto hurried along to keep up with him.

Sunlight glittered off the breastplates and morions of the soldiers gathered on the parade ground. The swordsmen of the First Battalion of Nestor Solanto's Tercio were the most undisciplined formation in Todu's army. Four hundred twenty of the original five hundred had completed the march from Golandar to Turela. Sweat rolled down their faces. Many had thick beards. Their officers had formed them up on the parade ground a half-hour before Todu arrived. The swordsmen had labored throughout the morning, digging out their portion of the ditch before their officers lined them up.

Todu spent an hour and a half walking up and down the ranks, randomly picking out men to inspect. "Rust spots on the helmet." "Improperly oiled vambrace." "Dull sword edge." Afterwards, he harangued the officers and sergeants for not enforcing discipline and said, "Captain Solanto, punish the worst offenders with hard labor on the entrenchments."

Todu ended the inspection by scolding everyone present. "Bloodthirsty savages, who carry off our people to have their hearts torn out upon sacrificial altars, have overrun the country. A dull blade and rusty armor do Soriazar no good!"

He returned to his tent to rest and eat the meal he had passed on earlier. He sat in his chair next to the map table, placed his elbows on the table, and rubbed his eyes with his fingers. During the inspection, his anger with Rodrigo and the thought of Sandovar bouncing up and down on Lady Petra never left his mind. *Sandovar is something I've never had to deal with before during a campaign. Have thirty years of peace taken the edge off my wits?*

Vigo, his servant, came through the open tent flaps with a plate of food. The slices of roasted meat on the plate were no longer warm and the fat and grease had congealed. A lump of hard bread sat beside the meat. "General, please allow me heat up your meal."

Todu shook his head. "I am too hungry to wait. Bring some wine."

Vigo left the tent and returned a minute later with a flagon and a cup. "Is there anything else I can bring?"

Todu waved him away and said nothing more. He tore off a hunk of bread, dipped it in the wine, and put it into his mouth. The wine's strong, sweet flavor squished out of the bread as he chewed it. *Planning battles troubles me less than dealing with that pathetic prince. The nobles hate self-made men.* Todu picked a slice of meat from the plate. He put aside his preoccupation with Sandovar as he chewed the meat and focused on the wooden blocks on the map. A line of black blocks ran from east to west, and each one stood beside an Azari village. Orpresa, Burbagona, Turzaga, Tramoce, Tuaste, Buraluz, and lastly, Spandel. But they were spread out over seventy miles, and the Semotecs used few horses. *Coordination will be difficult for them. Communications will be slow.* His eyes rested upon Orpresa, surrounded by four black blocks. *Orpresa must be relieved. The road allows us to quickly move cannons and wagons there. I can't march to Spandel with twenty thousand Semotecs in our rear around Orpresa. They could sweep down the road and destroy Turela, making it impossible for reinforcements and gunpowder from Golandar to reach me. It's late summer, and I must end this threat. Autumn and the harvest are not far off. Many Azaris will starve this winter, while the Semotecs grow fat off our produce.* "I must strike them now," he said aloud.

Sounds of cheering rolled through the open tent flaps, followed by the sound of horse hooves. Todu licked his fingers and took a sip of wine. A shadow darkened the light shining through the tent's entrance. He turned in his chair, and his mood was lightened by what he saw.

A dusty Masuf Mendio ducked as he entered the tent. "General," he said as he pulled off his brown leather gauntlets. "Blasted hot day. I much prefer the cooler air in the mountains."

Todu gestured to one of the chairs at the map table. Masuf removed his mottled green and brown cloak and draped it over the back of the chair before he sat.

"Vigo!" Todu called out. "Wine and food for Prince Masuf!" The servant briefly peered into the tent and acknowledged his master's orders.

"Thank you, General," Masuf said. "I haven't eaten since before daybreak."

Todu drank the last of his wine. "Well, Your Highness, what did you see?" He liked being direct in matters of war.

Masuf reached inside his tunic and pulled out a blue peacock feather and a green one. "I plucked these from the headdresses of dead Semotec warriors. My scouts and I ambushed a small group meeting in a field near Turzaga. The blue one is from the Semotecs around Burbagona, and the green feather is worn by warriors around Turzaga and Tramoce."

Todu frowned. "Semotecs from different cities and kingdoms are fighting together?"

"It does go against their nature." Masuf leaned forward and pointed to the black block near the village of Buraluz. "These warriors wear the skins of jungle cats." He slid his finger across the map to a nearby village. "Tuaste is being attack by warriors wearing eagle feathers."

Todu nodded slowly as he swept his eyes across the map. "They are quite organized. It appears different cities have been given certain pieces of land to pillage." He looked into Masuf's eyes. "Who is directing them?"

He shook his head. "I would love to put a few of them to the torture, but we have no one who speaks Semotec."

Todu leaned back in his seat and stared at the tent's ceiling. He absently patted his right hand upon the armrest. *Yes, I have it.* "There *has* to be a sailor inside Spandel city who has traded with the Semotecs."

"Do you wish for me to send someone?"

"Yes, send one of your best Trackers. Send him out today, and make sure Your Highness passes along to the Tracker that the Spandel road has been cut by the Semotecs, near Buraluz."

"As you wish, General."

"Now, if Your Highness would please update the map."

A pang of anxiety stabbed Todu in the center of his chest, and he held his breath. Masuf slid the black block from the village of Tramoce to a position halfway between that village and the town of Turela. He released a little of his breath as Masuf picked up the black block near Turzaga and set it down next to the block he had moved closer to Turela.

"Linked up?" Todu asked. His plan for marching on Orpresa suddenly crumbled to dust.

"Yes, General." Masuf looked up from the map and added. "They've gathered."

"Ten miles. They are only ten miles from here." His eyes moved erratically around the map. "Do they know we are here?" he asked himself more than he asked Masuf. *I'd concentrate if I knew my enemy was this close.*

Masuf shrugged. "It's possible. There are scattered bands of Semotecs running about the countryside. One of those could have come within eyesight of our camp."

Todu pushed his chair back from the map table, rose to his feet, and clasped his hands behind his back. "What news of Tramoce?"

"Tramoce's burning. But the Semotecs aren't looting the villages. My scouts say they seem interested only in food and moving prisoners south. A Tracker named Basuz crept into Turzaga last night - a very brave woman. She reported the Semotecs are taking nothing of value."

"Azaris are valuable to them," Todu said.

"True," Masuf said quietly.

Todu walked around the table, keeping his eyes on the map, viewing the situation from different angles. "It is possible, though unlikely, that the Semotecs do not know of our presence. Turela is the next logical place to raid, and it is the largest town in the area. How would you judge the speed of their march?"

Masuf raised his eyes to the tent's ceiling as if the words he searched for were written up there. After a moment, he looked down and said, "With no urgency, General."

A smile came to Todu's lips. He silently swept aside the dust of his broken plans for Orpresa. He studied the map. *There are no other villages between Turela, Tramoce, and Turzaga. Turela is the next natural objective.* A surge of excitement filled every inch of his body. "We shall have a battle on our hands on the morrow, Your Highness. There will be a fight, whether we force one or they do."

Masuf stood rigidly. "What are your orders, General?"

"You and your veteran fighters will remain here with the army. We march tomorrow and you will have the lead." *I'll need your leadership. Your brother will be nearly useless to me.* "Your Trackers have done us an invaluable service in gathering this information. We could have met disaster if you had not discovered these movements. Tomorrow your Trackers will wet their blades for Soriazar."

"A just reward for our labors." Masuf smiled wickedly.

# Chapter 35

## Royal Penance
### 17 Janoban, 229 A.G.S.

The throbbing was oppressive. *It will not let me sleep.* The side of Rodrigo's face felt as though someone held a hot iron against his flesh. A sickening, wet smell filled his nostrils, accompanied by the scent of singed hair. A dull ringing filled his right ear. One of his hands hurt too; the right one. A burning sensation covered it. He tried to flex his fingers, but they responded clumsily. His mind then clouded over and sleep pulled him into its grasp...

He suddenly cried out in agony, as an excruciating pain shot through his right eye. *Stop! What are you doing to my eye?* Rodrigo tried to speak, but his thoughts were translated into moaning. He opened his left eye; his right one was useless. His vision was blurred, but he could make out the shape of a face hovering above him. He blinked several times and his vision cleared somewhat.

"Sire," a male voice said quietly. "Please, sire. Lay still. I beg you, lay still."

"Rodrigo." *Khalia?* "Be strong, Great King. We have sent for the doctors and a priest." Khalia sat beside him on the edge of the bed.

*Priest.* The word sparked something within the cloudiness of his head. *Priest. Oh, no!* He suddenly remembered ordering the Trackers to seize Serophia. A hazy image of a woman, standing before him, appeared in his mind. She spoke to Rodrigo with Drucilla's voice, but her form was ambiguous.

"You have sinned against His Church," the woman said. She walked away and disappeared into the haze.

Another shock of pain produced a rush of cold sweat across his body. He heard a man moan, and then he realized it was his own voice. He passed out, but woke again. *I'm grievously injured. This was to be a great day in my reign, but it looks to be my last.*

"Am...I...dying?" Rodrigo whispered. Someone wept outside of his range of vision.

Another wave of pain washed over him. Another vision appeared to him. *Broen!* His grandson's face appeared like an apparition. *Oh...* The voice inside his head cracked with grief. *I remember.*

"Broen," he muttered. The sound of the weeping increased.

"Rodrigo." Khalia's voice was quiet, but somehow it broke through the weeping. "Broen is gone, my king."

Her soft voice touched off a pang of sorrow in the center of his chest. He knew what she said was true.

A shadow fell across Rodrigo's face. "Your Majesty." *Captain Juarez.* "Save your strength."

There was a knock at the door.

"Enter," Khalia ordered.

"The Trackers are approaching with a priest," a male voice announced. "It is the Princess Drucilla."

"Bring the princess here immediately," Khalia said. "Why do the Trackers escort her here?"

"Coincidence, Your Highness," Captain Juarez answered.

"I have never believed in coincidences," Khalia said. "There is a reason behind everything." Captain Juarez fell silent.

A male servant delicately dabbed at the blood welling up on Rodrigo's torn cheek. Rodrigo cringed at each touch. The raw, exposed tissues magnified each dab of the cloth a thousand fold.

"Steady, Your Majesty," the servant said. "I must absorb some of the drainage from your eye." The manservant lightly dabbed Rodrigo's injury.

A bolt of pain shot through Rodrigo's head. He writhed in agony. His back arched as his legs squirmed. "No more!" he wailed.

"Out of here, you fool!" Khalia shouted.

The side of Rodrigo's face twitched. The skin was charred black and red; it was cracked and oozing. He lay back on the bed inside the servant's quarters he had been brought to after the pouch of powder charges had exploded in his face. He panted while waiting for the next wave of pain.

"The leather spared him further injury." It was Captain Juarez speaking again, changing the subject.

"I...would look...on my grandson's body...if you will move me to him," Rodrigo said. His throat was parched.

From his right, Khalia's face appeared above him. Worry etched deep creases along the sides of her mouth. "It would do the king no good. The king must await his treatment."

Rodrigo gazed into her green eyes. *Khalia, I've never loved you like I should have. It wasn't possible.* His lips moved lazily as he tried to speak, but nothing coherent came out. He drifted off again.

A woman's beautiful face came to him. The woman smiled at him. Her face was serene, familiar. Tears rolled down her cheeks. *Damiana.* Rodrigo sensed tears forming in his own eyes. *Stop looking at me like that. Please. I'm vulnerable now. I don't have my wits about me...Oh, how I hurt you. I'm sorry, my love. I'm so sorry.* Pain crept into his dream, causing him to return to the servant's quarters.

As he awoke, he was relieved to see Damiana's face fading, but as she faded, he felt the anguish of losing her again. His inner voice cried out, and the words bled over into the conscious world. "Damiana, come to me." Rodrigo's uninjured eye flickered open, and the scorn on Khalia's face greeted him. Her nostrils flared.

"The king is delirious," she said, looking around the room. "He drifts in and out consciousness." Her eyes returned to Rodrigo. "Rest, Rodrigo. You are not making sense."

A tear flowed from Rodrigo's good eye. It rolled across his temple and vanished into his peppered hair. "Khalia...you are...a great queen." He licked his dry lips. "I wish...I loved you...more." He paused to catch his breath. "But...you broke...my heart."

Khalia's face became a cold stare, but she softened her expression with practiced ease. "Leave us, everyone," she commanded.

Rodrigo saw shadows walk past him, but the sounds of footsteps only registered in his left ear. The other ear felt like it was stuffed with cotton.

Khalia smiled crookedly. "The others have no need to witness your ramblings. But I must admit, I feel an affinity for you. It was not there in the beginning, thirty years ago, but it grew. I find Your Majesty attractive. You have become a magnificent king and brought great wealth to me."

She turned toward the door of the servant's quarters. As she did, her thick red braid slid across her shoulder, and its tip brushed the burn on Rodrigo's face. He gritted his teeth. Her hairs felt like a hundred tiny needles digging into his ruined flesh. She looked back down at Rodrigo, green eyes darting about his face.

"I am ashamed to admit I am jealous for you. Her Holiness, Damiana, was a threat to me, both personally and politically. I would not share my place in your bed with someone so influential and beautiful."

Rodrigo grimaced as another wave of pain throbbed across his face. Khalia's words hurt too. *I know what you did to her.* "Our...marriage...was payment...for troops," he said, trying to wound her back.

Khalia's nostrils flared again. "I was sold off like a piece of property. Our union aggrandized the wealth and position of my father, solidified the country, and won a war for you. But no one ever considered *my* position. That is the curse of being born noble." She snapped her head, whipping the braid behind her shoulder. "So, I came to my own aid. I determined to give you an heir as soon as possible. Remember how I coaxed you each night, again and again. I gave myself to you, *freely.*" She smiled mischievously. "Pleasuring each other was something we always did well." The smiled faded and her seriousness returned. "My influence grew as Sandovar grew within my womb, and I used that influence to my benefit. It was difficult to arrange Damiana's reassignment. It cost me a fortune. Her death would have been the best solution, but the backlash would have been unconscionable."

"I sacrificed my love...of her...for my country," Rodrigo whispered. *I was too late in knowing of the child.* Rodrigo closed his eye and drifted away again.

"Father!" Drucilla's voice cut through his pain-laced shroud of sleep. Her astonished gasp followed her shout.

"Come forward, my dear." Khalia said. "Your father, your king, needs you."

Rodrigo watched his daughter scrutinize his injuries. Her chin was smudged with dirt and blood. "Are...you hurt?" Rodrigo asked.

Drucilla was taken back. "Yes, Father, but I find your concern to be misplaced. Your reckless raid on the temple has wounded me deeply. I have scars which will not heal anytime soon." She swallowed hard. "The blood. I have never seen so much blood. Do you understand what I have seen?"

"You sent the Trackers to attack the Church?" Khalia asked.

"It was...in our interest...to do so," answered Rodrigo.

"You cold bastard!" Drucilla's outburst was unbecoming of her priestly status. "You murder what is good and beneficent in this world, and hide it behind the guise of nationalism." She made a fist as though she meant to strike him.

Rodrigo saw Captain Juarez appear behind Drucilla and place his hands upon her shoulders. "Princess, please. The king has need of your skills," he said.

Drucilla unclenched her hand and let it drop to her side. She jerked her shoulder and broke away from Juarez's grasp. "Take your hands off of me. Your Eagle Guardsmen have the stain of this crime upon them, too. I promise you, Arch Priest Ignater will call *you* to account as well."

"Only if the other nations do not have their way with us first," Khalia broke in. "Rodrigo, have we not enough trouble with the Semotecs?"

"The Church offered Father assistance in driving back the heathens," said Drucilla. "But he declined the offer. His pride would not let him accept."

"That...is Serophia talking," Rodrigo said.

"Yes. Her Holiness has opened my eyes to the workings of the world."

Rodrigo groaned and his head lolled to the left. His breathing was rapid and shallow.

"Drucilla, we have brought you here to heal your father," Khalia said. "Soriazar needs its king."

Rodrigo turned his head. "Can you...save my eye?" His head swam through waves of pain. It made his voice sound distant and unreal to him.

Drucilla bit her bottom lip. "No, Father. Some injuries are irreversible."

Khalia sighed heavily. "Very well, then. Do what you can for him."

Drucilla shook her head slowly. "No, Mother. I will not heal an enemy of the Faith."

"Treason!" Captain Juarez shouted.

"How *dare* you turn your back on your father!" Khalia exclaimed. "You are an Azari, and he is your king."

"No, Mother," Drucilla said, almost mechanically. "My priestly loyalties supercede temporal loyalties. Iningian custom recognizes this."

Khalia chuckled. The sound of her voice mocked the seriousness the scene. "Custom means nothing when compared to Law." Her voice hardened. "You will heal your father. Use the Gift to ease his suffering. You cannot refuse the requests of the sick and injured. I command you to do it. The Faith commands you to do it."

"Child..." Rodrigo's soft voice caught Khalia and Drucilla off guard. "Help me."

Anxiety overwhelmed Drucilla's face. Tears glistened in her eyes. "His pain is his penance for raising his hand against the Church," she said.

"You are not the Creator. You cannot judge him. Captain Juarez, take the princess to her room!" Khalia screeched. "She is a prisoner. Post guards on her."

"Come with me, Your Highness," said Juarez.

"Of course I will come with you, Captain," Drucilla said. "I have witnessed what happens to those who resist the Eagle."

Rodrigo watched Drucilla give Khalia a menacing stare.

"This madness clouds your judgment too, *Mother*," Drucilla said.

"The surgeon!" Khalia cried. "Bring in the surgeon!"

Rodrigo watched his daughter depart. The last glimpse he had of her was the fluttering of her delicate dress as she disappeared from sight. His good eye wandered from the door to the ceiling of the servants' quarters. The pain in his right eye felt as though it ran completely through his head. It felt like an iron rod had been lodged in his eye. *A surgeon can do little but reduce my pain. Today, I have lost my family, my reign, and my life?*

Rodrigo closed his eye and let sleep overtake him.

# Chapter 36

## Turela - The Tide Breaks
### 18 Janoban, 229 A.G.S.

odu Mazrio sat his white-faced, chestnut mare at the peak of a hill five miles south of Turela, along with Sandovar, Masuf, Javior, and Todu's captains. Down the slope and a mile further south, a host from Semotec was drawn up for battle in two massive blocks of men standing ten rows deep. A large cotton farm occupied the land between the armies. A whitewashed manor house and three smaller buildings stood on the left, surrounded by persimmons and a low stone wall. Six brown, stone buildings stood in rows of three on the far right, in the midst of thousands of tiny white puffs of cotton covering the fields. A steady, southwesterly breeze blew in from the ocean fifty miles away. The slender persimmons rippled rhythmically in the wind.

Todu admired the splashes of color displayed on the shields and wooden headdresses of the Semotecs. He held a spyglass to his eye, scanning his foe. The Semotecs' line extended beyond the edge of the white manor house, disappeared out of sight, appeared again in the space in the middle, vanished behind the servants' quarters, and re-appeared beyond the right.

Masuf's estimates were correct. *Ten thousand Semotecs are approaching Turela, and I can field barely five thousand untried troops against them.* He clenched his jaw to hide his concern about the difference in numbers and his fatigue from not sleeping much the previous night.

The army had marched out of camp an hour before dawn. One battalion of Marco Xerezo's Tercio remained behind to guard the camp. Preparations had been completed during the night, and the soldiers had only slept three hours. Masuf's sixty Trackers had led the way through the darkness. By mid-morning the army had reached the hill that rose above the surrounding farmland. The hill sloped to the left from its highest point on the right.

Todu had decided to fight the battle from atop the hill. He wasted no time in issuing orders. He had charged Captain Solanto with positioning the pike squares, cannons, and swordsmen. Todu had scattered five hundred arquebusiers and an equal number of swordsmen among the buildings and the cotton field. He placed the knights from

Vorencia on the far right, and the knights from Golandar and the Gudor Valley were sent to the far left. Masuf's Trackers remained close to Todu, in reserve.

Six pike squares and their accompanying arquebusiers were staggered along the hill's crest, resembling a checkerboard. Pairs of cannons were placed between the three pike squares of the front line. Smaller pike squares, numbering around a hundred men, stood behind the cannons. Captain Solanto had positioned the other three pike squares on the reverse slope of the hill, hidden from sight to the approaching Semotecs. Three blocks of swordsmen waited in reserve behind the second line of pike squares.

Not long after the preparations were complete, word had arrived from the Trackers observing the Semotecs in the area of Tramoce. The enemy was marching to the northeast, toward Turela. Their path would place nearly five thousand warriors behind the right flank of Todu's army.

Dust clouds had preceded the arrival of the Semotecs approaching from the south. Two long columns had appeared over the tops of the rolling hills of the plains of Spandel. It was now two hours past midday.

"I wish we had more time to prepare," Todu said. "But circumstances have not cooperated with us."

"This ground is miserable for the horses," Sandovar complained. "The hill is strewn with boulders and the fields are hemmed in by stone walls. General Mazrio, we crossed open ground back towards Turela. We should have deployed back there."

"Your opinion is out of place," Todu responded. "The proper place for it was last night, but you were not present for the planning."

Sandovar's face reddened. "Do not mock me. I am heir to my father's throne. I am second in command here. Though, you have yet to truly define my responsibilities."

"Your Highness, you will command the entire army in the event of my death." Todu saw that Sandovar's response lay just beyond the contemptible look he gave him. *My death would please you. Indeed, it would.*

"You were sent here to learn about war from the general," Masuf butted in. "But your mouth's a dangerous handicap." Shocked expressions followed his words from the knights and officers gathered nearby.

Sandovar shifted his focus to his brother. "Masuf, I will call you out when this is over. I will not suffer the outrage of your insults. By the Laws of Knighthood, before my brothers-in-arms, I swear to avenge this injury to my honor by challenging you to single combat."

Masuf sneered and drew his short sword halfway from its scabbard. "Why wait."

Sandovar's eyes widened with fear. His mouth worked about nervously.

"Stop this!" Javior rammed his horse between his older brothers'. "This is a disgrace. I am ashamed to call myself a Mendio." Senyors Gapacho and Torrero sat upon horses in silence, looking over their shoulders at the closest soldiers.

Todu's voice got everyone's attention. "I do not think the Semotecs will give us time to settle family arguments. Prince Sandovar, please take your place next to me and await my instructions. Standby for orders." Sandovar glared at Todu and purposely moved his horse a short distance away. "Captain Xerezo, keep a sharp eye on the right flank. I must have good warning of the Semotec's approach from that direction." Marco bowed and rode off to his post. "Captain Solanto, have the cannons commence firing on the enemy's center, between the buildings. We need to draw them into a fight." Nestor saluted and called for messengers.

Masuf moved his horse closer to Todu. "My brother is a power-mad fool, General. I'll not allow him to spread the stain of his arrogance to you. Our nation owes you its existence."

"Prince Masuf, you have inherited your father's sense of honor," Todu said. "I know not what Sandovar inherited, besides the power of sitting on a finely carved chair."

Masuf smiled a little. "Let's hope my father lives another thirty years."

Todu nodded. "Let us pray we survive this day." He raised his spyglass to his eye. "Prince Javior, stay close to me when the fighting begins. The army needs to know the location of the Commander's Banner."

"As you wish, General," Javior said, adjusting his position in his saddle.

"Prince Masuf, I wish for you to remain close to me, as well," he said. "I may have to call upon you and your Trackers in a moment of crisis."

"Our swords are sworn to you and to the king," Masuf assured him.

*POOM!*

A cannon in the center opened the battle. A fifteen-pound iron ball formed a black arc in the air. A plume of dust shot up from the ground in the distance, then another and another, as the ball skipped across the ground. Through his spyglass, Todu saw a perceptible ripple in the Semotecs lines, as the cannonball bowled over several of them.

"The Royal Army's first shot in anger," Todu announced.

*BOOM!*

The second gun in the center belched forth a cloud of smoke and sent its message of death across the field. Todu pulled his eye away from the spyglass, waited for the ball to kick up the dirt, and then he trained the spyglass on the area where the ball landed. The second ball skipped twice before burrowing into the Semotec's wall of hide and wooden shields.

*PHOOM! BOOM! KOOM! POOM!*

The cannons on the flanks commenced firing on the center of the Semotec's line. The wind caught the clouds of powder smoke and blew them back over the Azaris. In the lulls between cannon blasts, the fearful cries of the knights' horses, not conditioned to the reports of gunpowder, could be heard. For a quarter of an hour, Todu's gunners worked their cannons. Visibility worsened as each cannonball kicked up dust amongst the Semotecs. Todu peered through his spyglass, checking the damage being inflicted on his enemy. Occasionally, he caught a glimpse of the Semotecs through the dust. Their line was ragged and the warriors moved about with agitation, as they tried to dodge the incoming balls.

*How much longer will their commander allow his men to take this punishment and not answer to it?* Todu knew the stress of those heavy balls, pounding their friends into pieces, had to be wearing on them. *It's offensive to their honor as warriors to be struck down at such long range.*

He spun his horse and signaled two riders to approach. The young men eagerly answered his summons. Sunlight glinted off their breastplates and morions. Todu pointed at one of them. "Ride to Captain Solanto. Gun crews cease firing. Restock powder and shot. Cool the guns. Then you return to me." He repeated the order to the second rider, but directed him to find Captain Xerezo. Todu turned his horse and turned his spyglass westward. He studied the horizon for the telltale dust clouds that would signal the approach of the Semotecs from Tramoce. *Every minute that passes brings them closer.*

Javior Mendio sat his horse nearby. He wore a full suit of plate armor. The army's banner, attached to the pole he held, fluttered above his head. "The guns are performing smartly, General."

Todu maneuvered his horse beside Javior's. "We have inflicted some damage. We will shortly commence firing again." *I have to reach a decision here before the numbers against us become overwhelming.* "We do not have sufficient powder to blast away all day."

The pair of guns on the right fired for a few minutes longer. *Marco, you need to react faster than that. Solanto has twice the numbers under his command.* The wind carried the dust thrown up by the cannon barrage toward the Azari lines, and for a while, it obscured the Semotecs.

Todu handed the spyglass to Javior. "Your Highness, can you make out what is happening over there?"

Javior studied the haze. "It is clearing up a bit...wait." The keening of many horns filled the air in chaotic dissonant waves. "I see...they are coming!"

Javior returned the spyglass to Todu, who watched figures appear from the haze. The Semotecs walked steadily across the fields. Their thousands of high-pitched and undulating screams washed over the Royal Army. The enemy had a half a mile of ground to cross before they reached the manor house and the servants' quarters; it would take them many minutes to do that. Todu whipped his horse around and called for more riders. He instructed them to have the cannons open fire when the Semotecs reached the buildings.

*CLACK-clack! CLACK-clack! CLACK-clack!*

The rhythmic pounding of weapons on shields replaced the shouts of the Semotecs.

"They are using that sound to keep a cadence, are they not?" Javior asked Todu.

Todu smiled. "You have learned much. They do it to frighten us, too."

Movement in and around the buildings of the farmstead caught Todu's attention. The skirmishing troops readied themselves for action. Minutes passed slowly. The Semotecs kept coming. Todu scanned the western horizon three times, but no dust cloud was yet in sight. He looked again across the battlefield. The colorful Semotec army drew nearer to the buildings. *They have to be close enough by now.* He was surprised to discover that his palms were sweaty, and he wiped them on his breeches. *The cannons did their work well. They coaxed the enemy into advancing.* He was anxious to see if his ideas about the use of the arquebus would survive their baptism of fire. *How much closer?*

Dozens of puffs of smoke appeared from inside and around the manor house and the brown buildings on the right. The popping sound of the arquebus shots reached the hill a second later. Through his spyglass, Todu watched the Semotecs. Their lines wavered a bit and gaps appeared in their ranks, but they kept coming.

A pause seemed to take forever before the next arquebusiers stepped to the front of the line to fire. The white puffs appeared again. Fewer Semotecs fell this time. *They're firing at the maximum distance.* Sporadic puffs of smoke continued to blossom as more arquebusiers moved to the front of their lines and fired into the Semotecs.

The Azari cannons again belched forth smoke and flame. Black streaks of cannonballs arced through the air and skipped across the ground into the gap between the buildings. In some places, the Semotecs halted and milled about in confusion; in other places, they continued. The further they advanced, the more often their comrades fell, but they kept coming. Sunlight glinted off swords and shields as the Azari swordsmen moved about the manor and the servants' buildings. They would have to check the Semotecs advance, so that the slow-firing arquebusiers could safely fall back.

Todu steered his horse alongside Javior's again. His voice reflected his excitement. "We are witnessing the first land battle in Iningian history where massed firearms have been employed!"

"It is a great day for Soriazar. May Fortune grant us victory," Javior said.

*Yes. But if Fortune abandons us, we'll have our hearts cut out.* Todu raised his spyglass and looked westward again, but shouts of the Semotecs pulled his attention back to the battle in front. He watched them rush forward. The firing of the arquebusiers slackened as the swordsmen began their work. Violent melees broke out along the wall beneath the trees surrounding the manor house and among the buildings on the right side of the battle.

On the left, the arquebusiers streamed through the holes they had earlier knocked into the wall and formed into lines, five deep. Todu watched them frantically load their guns. Soon after, the line of swordsmen around the manor house came into view, hacking and slashing with their swords and bashing with their shields. The arquebusiers opened fire on the Semotecs, who were trying to surround the swordsmen. After shooting, the arquebusiers pivoted left and made their way to the backs of their lines to reload. The second shooters then fired and executed the countermarch. Bit by bit, the skirmishing swordsmen and arquebusiers gave ground.

But the fighting on the right developed differently. No wall surrounded the servants' buildings to slow the enemy's charge. The officer in command there had been slow in ordering a withdrawal, so the Semotecs flowed around their flanks like water and swamped the swordsmen and arquebusiers. Azari order and discipline dissolved in a flash. Pockets of swordsmen and arquebusiers fought for their lives. Empty guns were quickly turned into clubs. Survivors streamed back toward friendly lines. Some turned to fire another shot or stab at a Semotec, but most just ran.

Todu pounded his fist on his thigh and called for another messenger. He sent him downhill, into the cotton field. Within minutes, arquebusiers and swordsmen rose up from where they knelt among the cotton and moved off toward the right. The Azari cannons continued firing, pausing only to adjust for range. A horn blast on the left ordered the skirmishers to fall back to the rear. On the right, Todu's reinforcements slowed the Semotec advance, but they fell back as they fought, dragging wounded Azaris with them.

Todu ordered the cannon to cease firing as the Semotecs halted and formed lines for an assault. He gazed westward again and surprise grabbed at his chest. A cloud of dust had appeared in the distance. He figured it could not be more than five or six miles away.

"Rider!" he called out. "To Captain Xerezo - the enemy approaches from the right. Have you seen this? Are you prepared?"

"As you command, General." The rider raised his hand to his brow and whipped his horse into a gallop.

Prince Sandovar appeared next to Todu. "I see the dust in the west. We must withdraw or be destroyed."

Todu lowered his eyebrows. "They are two hours away. The main force is here and will attack us long before they arrive. We have time to confront both threats." He turned his horse from Sandovar and continued to observe the battle.

"You dare turn your back on me!" Sandovar exclaimed. He spurred his horse alongside Todu's. "You will take counsel of me. I am the Crown Prince."

Masuf Mendio wedged his horse between Todu and Sandovar. "Back down, Brother. You're an infant when it comes to matters of war."

"He is reckless," Sandovar said. "He gambles with the safety of this army. We have been placed between two foes."

"War *is* a gamble, you fool," Masuf spat back. "It's always a balance of cost and gain."

"Prince Sandovar," Todu said calmly. "Get a grasp on your wits. We are all scared, but our discipline helps to contain it."

Sandovar's eyes bulged. "Are you calling me a coward? It is not my fault. Father never sent me to fight. He sends my brothers, but never me."

"I believe the prince needs to retire," Todu declared.

"No!" Sandovar shouted. "I will not be shuffled aside like some half-wit." He jerked his horse's reins and galloped away downhill.

Todu turned to Masuf to ask him to chase down his brother, but Javior broke in before he could speak. "Merciful Creator, I have never seen such a terrible sight."

The Semotec horns keened again, and the entire host stepped off in unison. They held their round shields close together, resembling an immense string of colorful beads coming to wrap around and strangle the Azari army. Low grunts were interspersed between the rhythmic poundings of weapons on shields. The noise increased as they closed the distance. Todu dispatched riders with orders for the cannons to again commence their work. It took precious minutes for the firing to begin; the Semotecs were a little over a quarter-mile away.

*BOOM! PHOOM! KOOM! BOOM! BOOM! POOM!*

Gaps opened up in the Semotecs' lines. The enemy was now close enough for the Azaris on the hill to see debris and body parts spinning through the air. Todu watched one cannonball bounce off the ground at a sharp angle and bowl over twenty warriors, but most knocked them down in threes and fours. The rhythmic pounding on their shields ceased as the cannonballs tore into the Semotecs' ranks. Cries of anger and screams of agony replaced the pounding. The Semotec line became ragged and confused, but still they came.

"They're quite disciplined," Masuf said.

"Another reason never to underestimate your opponent," Todu told him.

The cannon crews ceased firing to reload with grapeshot and lower their barrels to point-blank range. Then they waited. The Semotecs were two hundred paces away. An oppressive, ominous quiet fell over the battlefield. Only the sounds of the wind and the trampling of the cotton plants could be heard, until...

A few brave Semotecs began the charge. Their aggression became contagious and spread like lightning. The stress of prolonging the engagement gave way to a maddened rush. The distance between the armies decreased rapidly. Sheets of smoke and flame spewed forth from the ranks of arquebusiers arrayed in front of the pike squares. The gunmen countermarched and kept up a steady rate of fire. Here and there, Semotecs fell in mid-stride and rolled across the ground. Todu's cannons fired for a final time, spraying the enemy with hundreds of bits of iron, which whistled eerily as they tore through the air. The cannons ripped wide holes in the horde of charging Semotecs, mowing down a dozen with each burst of grapeshot. Todu saw many warriors fall into the cotton in two or three pieces.

The Semotecs inundated the lower portion of the hill. The arquebusiers fired into them at fifty paces. Todu saw puffs of dust appear, as the lead balls struck the enemy's cotton armor. Splinters of wood flew as bullets penetrated shields. He saw blood spurt from wounds and he heard the smacks of lead against flesh. The small pike squares behind the cannons moved forward and enclosed them within their ranks. The soldiers leveled their long pikes at the enemy, forming a steel-tipped wall. The larger pike squares leveled theirs likewise as the arquebusiers fell back amidst the first couple of rows of pikemen and knelt. The sounds of pike shafts clattering against each other filled the air. At thirty paces, the Semotecs unleashed a

hailstorm of arrows and sling stones. The projectiles banged and
clanged off of Azari breastplates and helmets, though some struck
flesh and caused a few gaps to open in their tightly packed formations.

The Semotecs crashed against the pike squares like an angry
wave on massive rocks. Where they could not break in, they flowed
around, like the currents of a great river. Many Semotecs met death
on the end of an Azari pike as those behind them pushed against
them. The Semotecs fought past their impaled, dying comrades and
used their shields to knock away the tips of the thrusting pikes. The
arquebusiers fired or clubbed at the Semotecs with empty guns. The
Semotecs showed skill in handling their obsidian-spiked wooden
clubs and opened wicked wounds on their victims. Many of them, in
the midst of the forest of pikes, killed or wounded an Azari before being impaled by a pike or being blown backward by a gunshot.

In the center of the line, a tempest raged around the cannons.
The small pike square was swamped and lost cohesion. Their flight
gave heart to the Semotecs, who hacked at the fleeing Azaris with
their obsidian clubs. The screams of men fighting and dying filled the
air. The acrid smell of burnt gunpowder, overlaying the sanguineous,
coppery odor of blood, saturated it as well.

Todu, Masuf, and Javior took refuge in the center of the great
pike square on the highest part of the hill. From there, they watched
the melee rage around them. The common soldiers now controlled the
battle. The arquebusiers of the squares on the reverse slope opened
fire as the Semotecs flooded around the squares of the front line. The
first volley nearly stopped the onrush in its tracks. Scores fell or panicked at being fired on from two, or three sides. Dozens of Semotecs
continued to fall as the arquebusiers discharged volley after volley
into them. The blocks of swordsmen held in reserve were then ordered up the hill and into the battle.

As the impetus of the charge in the center was spent, the Semotecs in the rear flowed toward the ends of the Azari line, but the
Knights of Olantaro gave them a bloody welcome. Senyors Gapacho
and Torrero rode at the very tips of the wedges of heavily armored
knights. They crashed into the enemy like two ships plowing through
heavy seas. Dead Semotecs weighted down many lances, and the enemy crumbled before the Order of Olantaro. The knights then drew
their swords and continued their work. The flight of the Semotecs on
the flanks was infectious and spread throughout the entire host.
Within a minute, the Semotecs fled across the trampled cotton fields.
The knights pursued them for a few hundred paces before returning
and re-equipping with fresh lances. On the hill, vengeful Azaris drew

their daggers and dispatched scores of wounded Semotecs. Blood flowed in rivulets down the slopes of the hill.

The muscles between Todu's shoulder blades ached from tension. "We did well, but they will come again," he said. He looked to the west. The dust cloud loomed closer.

"General, they're rallying near the farm," said Masuf.

"I would attack them and finish them, but the threat to the west precludes that," Todu said.

Todu, Masuf, and Javior left the square. Soldiers made way for them and cheered their general. Their horses stepped gingerly around the dead. The priests of Ghyo had begun healing the wounded, but to conserve their strength, they did not fully heal the seriously wounded. They did just enough to keep death at bay.

"I never imagined it would be this horrible," Javior said to his brother.

"Fighting is never pleasant, but remember, they forced it upon us," said Masuf. "You don't have to get used to it, but you must deal with it."

"Stand to your positions men! This day is not done!" Todu cried out to the soldiers who had broken ranks to finish off the wounded Semotecs. "Riders! Riders to me!" But none were around to respond. The fighting had scattered them. "Prince Masuf, I need messengers." Masuf nodded and rode off to find his Trackers. To Javior, Todu said, "Your Highness, wave your banner high. Summon the commanders to me." Javior waved his banner in circles above his head. "Such confusion, and we are winning."

Marco Xerezo arrived first. A bloodstained bandage circled his head beneath the brim of his morion. "General," he said smoothly, as though it were an ordinary day.

"Captain Xerezo, are you well?"

"Well enough, senyor. A sling stone ricocheted off of someone's helmet."

Todu dropped any semblance of formality. "Marco, have you seen the approach of our enemy to the west?"

"I have," he answered.

"I fear your battalion will be assailed from two directions. You cannot withdrawal. You must be stubborn." *You're tough, Marco. But I wish Solanto were on the right.*

"As you command, General."

"I give you command of the Knights of Olantaro on the right. Use them as you see fit."

"I will, senyor," Marco said.

"I will inform Senyor Roldan of your command. Now, return to your men and make ready. Have your cannons bombard the Se-

motecs to our front. They are regrouping." Todu's tone dismissed him
without saying so. As Marco rode away, he passed Roldan Torrero.

Streaks of drying blood dulled the luster of Roldan's armor. "General, Olantaro made a good account of itself today."

"You did as well as the infantry," Todu responded. *Arrogant bastard.* "I am placing your knights under the command of Captain
Xerezo. You will obey him."

Roldan Torrero was stupefied. "G-general, that is a slap of dishonor to the Order."

"Take it up with king the next time you see him," Todu said. "We
will be flanked in an hour. You will cooperate with Captain Xerezo or
we are all dead, and the Semotecs will cross the Rojera Pass and dine
at your table."

Roldan spat in disgust. "As you wish, *General*," he snarled and
rode away.

Nestor Solanto and Basilio Gapacho arrived last. "Nestor, we will
stand and fight. Move the skirmishers back into the fields and harass
the enemy's next advance. Have your cannons pound on them as
they regroup." Todu turned to Basilio. "Keep up the good work, and
do not give up our left."

The Azari cannons bombarded the mustering Semotecs, but the
guns in the center remained quiet. Their crews lay among the dead
there.

The Semotecs aimed their second charge at the center of the hill.
Their numbers swirled about the field as they advanced. They
crowded toward the center until their masses resembled an immense
spear point. The Azari skirmishers fired five or six shots into them
and then retired to cool the barrels of their guns.

The middle pike square bore the brunt of the onslaught. The Semotecs crashed into it and flowed around it. Hundreds of them penetrated the Azari line and reached the wagons in the rear, where a melee broke out amongst the baggage train. The Azari skirmishers had
fallen back there to rest and rearm, but they suddenly found themselves fighting for their lives. Swords flashed, guns fired, clubs
bashed. Semotec and Azari blood darkened the ground. Barrages of
arrows from the Trackers and a counterattack from the nearest block
of swordsmen won the fight amongst the wagons. The knights again
charged the flanks, and the main Semotec host fell back in confusion.

Ghyo's priests had exhausted themselves; many of the wounded
now went unattended. Their cries and pleas filled the air. The center
pike squares had suffered heavily and were severely weakened. The
storm of sling stones and arrows preceding the last clash had caused
much confusion, and the center square had nearly given way under

the strain. A quarter of their strength of four hundred lay dead or wounded.

"We nearly broke," Javior said.

"But they have broken twice," Todu countered. "Remember, Your Highness, the enemy knows fear as well as we do." *But if we break once, it's over.*

The Azaris had reaped a greater slaughter on the second assault than on the first one. Todu summoned his commanders again. The enemy warriors approaching from the west were now visible. Blasts from their horns announced their arrival to their embattled comrades. A triumphant cheer arose from the retreating Semotecs in the front, and they rallied around the farm buildings.

Todu turned to his commanders. "We know the numbers arrayed against us, but we are all that stand between the invaders and our homes. We cannot leave this spot. No matter the cost."

"No matter the cost!" Sandovar screamed from behind the gathered officers. Tears flooded his cheeks. He walked towards Todu Mazrio, carrying his son Tyrel in his armored arms.

"Merciful Ghyo!" Masuf exclaimed.

"Oh, Brother. My dear Brother," Javior lamented.

Todu was speechless.

Sandovar's eyes had a crazed look. He knelt and placed Tyrel upon the ground. "He and Devio took refuge among the wagons." He rose to his feet and broke into uncontrollable sobbing. "They murdered my boy! I will wet my blade with Semotec blood! I will bathe in it!" He slapped a gauntlet to his breastplate. He then headed downhill. Prince Javior rode after him, but Sandovar refused to speak with him, so he returned to Todu.

Todu stared at the dead prince. "Time is robbing us again. There is no time to properly deal with this. Prince Masuf, assign a Tracker to take the prince's body back to camp."

"It shall be done," Masuf said.

The Semotecs arrayed before the Azaris blew their horns in answer to their countrymen to the west. The newly arrived Semotecs mustered into lines less than a mile west of the hill. Horn blasts preceded the third assault upon the Royal Army of Soriazar, as the two groups of Semotecs attempted to work in concert with each other. The weary Azaris stood by in their formations, growing hungrier and thirstier by the minute. The afternoon had reached its hottest point.

*We're cooking in our armor. Why don't you attack?* The tension also wore on Todu. His battered army had given better than it had received, but the Semotecs to the west were unbloodied, and the obsidian of their clubs was unchipped.

An immense roar announced the beginning of the attack. The colorful masses of the enemy beat out their cadences. The Azari skirmishers and cannons opened fire again, wearing down the enemy as best they could. On the far right, the skirmishers of Marco Xerezo's battalion gave the Semotecs a warm welcome. The land there contained scattered stands of trees and was strewn with large rocks and boulders. The skirmishers used the ground to their advantage.

A rider approached from the right. "General Mazrio, I beg to report." He sounded anxious.

"Get on with it, man," Todu snapped. *Fatigue's getting to me, too.*

"Captain Xerezo says Prince Sandovar has disobeyed his orders. The Knights of Olantaro are charging the enemy to the west. Prince Sandovar convinced Senyor Torrero to defy you."

A sense of dread overwhelmed Todu. A thousand thoughts flooded his mind, but only one broke through the chaos. *They'll blow their horses. The enemy's too far away.*

Sandovar's banner, fluttering from the tip of his lance, was visible through Todu's spyglass. He rode at the tip of the wedge of armored knights. The charge moved sluggishly. The knights rumbled passed the line of skirmishers, and the rough ground broke up their wedge. The skirmishers waved for the knights to turn back.

The Order of the Olantaro collided with the Semotecs. The warriors fled before their deadly lances, but the horses' momentum failed. The sixty knights from Vorencia found themselves surrounded by hundreds of Semotec warriors who began pulling them from their saddles. The knights drew their swords and hacked at the grasping arms. One by one, however, they disappeared among a swirling storm of sling stones and spiked clubs.

Todu watched the spectacle in horror. A dozen knights hacked their way out of the arms of death and fled northward. Through his spyglass, he recognized the knight leading the rout by the style of his armor. *Have you had your fill of blood, Sandovar?*

"Your Highness," Todu called to Masuf. "Your Trackers must fill the gap left by our reckless companions." Masuf gathered his Trackers and moved west with alacrity.

Todu and Javior moved to the highest spot on the hill to observe. The battle again raged at the foot of the hill. Todu drew his sword as the Semotecs inched their way up the blood-soaked slope. Arquebus balls tore into their ranks; the pikes leveled again and the melee recommenced. Todu and Javior moved and took refuge inside the center pike square behind the center of the hill. The hordes of Semotecs again swamped the Royal Army. The air was filled with the sounds of screaming, the clattering of pikes knocking together, and smoke from powder discharges. Then the sounds of the fighting changed. Panicked cries rang out, as the battered pike square in the center broke. Fleeing Azaris appeared over the crest of the hill, pursued by the Semotecs. A smaller square of reserve pikemen moved up to the crest to plug the wide hole.

Todu's heart sank. *The center is folding.* "Hold men!" he shouted to the soldiers surrounding him. "For the sake of your wives and mothers, hol..."

A sling stone struck him across the bridge of his nose. His world became a mass of stinging pain, and he felt like he was floating.

Todu opened his eyes and saw the blue sky.

"General." A frightened soldier was talking to him. "General!"

The noise of the fighting rushed back into Todu's ears. The soldier helped him to his feet. He had no idea how long he had been on the ground. Blood filled his mouth and throat. He spat it on the ground.

"General, you're alive!" the soldier exclaimed. His eyes were wild with fear. "We need you, General."

"My...horse," Todu managed to say. He felt sick to his stomach from the blood he had swallowed.

"Here, General," a voice called from behind him.

Todu groggily turned around. A soldier held his horse for him. "Help me up," Todu ordered. The center of his face was a mass of sharp pain. Blood ran down both sides of his nose and saturated his goatee.

Three soldiers lifted Todu into the saddle as cheers rang out among the Azaris around him. Todu looked to his left and saw Prince Javior on foot, leading a formation of swordsmen into the melee swirling around the small pike square, which had plugged the hole left by the routed pikemen. In his left hand, Javior held the Eagle Banner; in his right was his sword.

Javior was in the thick of the fighting. With a stroke of his sword, he took off a Semotec's leg beneath the knee. Another warrior banged his spiked club against the side of Javior's helmet. He took a clumsy step back; the Eagle Banner fell from his grasp. He raised his helmet visor, recovered from the blow, and moved with surprising grace in his plate armor. The Semotec's club arm dropped to the ground.

Javior and the swordsmen broke the Semotecs in the center and pursued them over the hill's crest. Pikemen and arquebusiers from the other formations broke ranks and joined Javior's charge. A slaughter ensued. The battle in the center ended. The Semotecs on the wings lost their will to continue and routed with the warriors in the center.

The commanders gathered around Todu who lay on the ground, holding a cloth to his face. Masuf rode up and dismounted. Someone had opened a bottle of wine, and the men passed it around.

Todu was dizzy. His nose was swollen and black. "Give me...a drink," he said. A lieutenant handed him the bottle. "This...is still an army. All officers...form your men...in the event...the Semotecs return." He filled his mouth with wine.

Masuf knelt beside him and took a drink for himself. "I'll see to your wishes, Todu Mazrio, High-General of Soriazar."

"A rider approaches!" someone cried.

A Royal Messenger galloped up the hill and halted next to Masuf, who had waved him over. "Prince Masuf, where is your brother, Prince Sandovar?" the messenger said.

"I know not where he is," Masuf lied. "There's still much confusion."

"Your Highness, it is urgent that he be found. Master Zepio sent me to summon the Crown Prince to return to the Alcazar. There has been an accident. The king is dying."

A gasp rose from the officers gathered around Todu Mazrio. Their revelry ceased.

Todu had not the strength to respond. *Why? On the day of one of our greatest victories, why?* Tears welled in his eyes as he lay on his back. *Our cause is just. Why?*

# Chapter 37

## No Time for Laurels
### 18 Janoban 229, A.G.S.

The remnants of the Cheltan army camped along the road near the piles of blackened bones marking the spot where they had routed the Oruks. Though they had driven their enemy before them, they were a defeated army. Hunger weakened them and their surviving horses. Exhaustion is hunger's cousin. They still had a four or five day march ahead of them, if the wounded did not slow them too much.

Kathair had been faithful to Orius's wishes. The army did not stop to gather food until the survivors camped in the valley. It was not a popular decision, but being in command requires making unpopular choices. Earlier that morning, Kathair had sent six of the strongest remaining warriors to scour the valley's woods for game. With luck, the army would not have to spend another day with empty bellies.

Half the Chelts suffered from fractured arms, legs, and other broken bones. Orius had done everything in his power to patch them together before he headed into the Drenga Valley. The Gift accelerated the body's healing processes. But healing times could only be shortened and never avoided. The warriors lay in the grass where they had halted the previous evening. For the first time since leaving Ragnaar, they would spend an entire day resting. They had marched and fought for ten days with little respite.

The further the Chelts moved from their enemy, the more they grumbled and bickered amongst themselves. They grew increasingly restless and looked forward to taking up their usual vendettas. Traditional rivalries flared, but luckily, none came to blows. The warriors lacked the energy for it, but it was only a matter of time before their strength returned.

The sun approached its midday zenith and the day became warmer. The overnight temperature had been cool, though. The wind carried the unmistakable scent of autumn to the valley. The chill had been hard on the wounded. It stiffened their battered bodies and caused much discomfort.

Kathair stood by the edge of the road, scanning the forest to the west. Moreena sat cross-legged on the ground at his feet, drawing a stone along the blade of her two-hander. Argus sat nearby on a large rock, picking and scratching at himself. The rest of the Chelts clustered around the smoking embers of their campfires, separated into their particular villages. They watched each other with sideways glances, muttering quietly to their fellow tribesmen.

"There's movement along the road," Kathair said.

Dark shapes could be seen moving in the shadows at the forest's floor. Moments later, Orius, Culley, Chief Condin and four Wolf Riders marched out of the forest, leading their horses by the reins. Their horses plodded along, with heads hanging low, but the men walked with their heads high.

Orius saw his companions and waved to them. It felt good to be together again. They had shared many hardships since the spring. The sight of his companions nearly erased the horrors he had seen at Drenga, but he knew that he must recount what he had witnessed. *They need to be told of the victory they've bled for, and of the fate of the people of Drenga.*

Kathair walked up to Orius and grasped his hand, smiling broadly. "Father Orius."

"I see we still have an army," Orius said. "You have done well."

"Six did not return to us," said Kathair. "We know their names."

"Thank you, but that is best left for another day." Orius looked around at the Chelts gathered in the field. "Our warriors need to be told of their victory."

"Victory?" Kathair was amazed.

"Aye," Culley's gravelly voice broke in. "Like a snake, the Oruks've slithered back into their hole. Gone home, they have."

"It is a miracle," added Chief Condin. "A real tale of legend. I would not have believed it myself, but I saw it with my own eyes. The Light of Ghyo has turned back the Darkness."

"Kathair, gather the warriors," Orius commanded. "We are heading home!" *To their home, mine is still far away.*

The Chelts took the news with elation. There would not be another battle. They had saved their homes from destruction, and they had survived. Their spirits were high. The harvest and the New Year were fast approaching; they would be home with their families for the celebrations. They immediately forgot their hostile overtones. Chelts from different villages congratulated and hugged each other.

The hunters returned after midday, carrying a pair of deer dangling from tree branches propped on their shoulders. The famished

Chelts wasted no time in slaughtering their meal. Within an hour, they had lit cooking fires and the scent of roasting meat filled the air. The eighty survivors stretched out the venison so that everyone got something to eat. They even spitted and roasted the kidneys, hearts, and tongues. Another hunting party was sent out in the afternoon. Meanwhile, Orius checked the injuries he had treated and healed wounds he had lacked the strength to deal with after the rockslide.

At last, sleep covered Orius like a heavy blanket. It was the deep sleep of physical exhaustion. He lay on the ground with his head propped on a saddle. Puffy clouds glided by, occasionally blocking out the sun's rays. The day grew warmer. A fresh breeze blew through the valley, which maintained a pleasant temperature. Orius found the pleasure of relaxation to be what he needed. The sunlight felt good on his face. Its warmth permeated his clothing and sank into his tired body, like a deep massage. He was content to lie there forever and let his mind drift, like a ship on calm seas...

A rough pat on the shoulder startled him. "Wake up, boy," Culley said. "Riders are approaching."

Orius struggled to sit up. Sleep kept his limbs from doing what he wanted them to do. His head was groggy; he could make no sense of what his eyes saw. He looked westward, expecting to see the hordes of Sytor rolling out of the woods like an angry tempest. "Wha?"

"No," Culley pointed east. "That way."

Orius blinked his eyes and rubbed them. He turned and saw five riders approaching at a gallop. "Chelts?" he asked.

"Aye," Culley grumbled, muttering a curse beneath his breath. "Two of them are huge."

"I suppose Alana sent them," Orius said.

The riders slowed to a trot as they rode up to Culley, who held a hand up for them to see. "You're a bit late. The fighting's over."

The newcomers' leader pulled back the hood of his robe. "I did not come to fight. I came to talk." He looked beyond Culley, at Orius. "I come to talk with the priest, Orius Candell."

Culley placed his hands on his hips and twisted around to look at Orius. "The man's blunt isn't he?"

The newcomer snorted. "My, my. You are quite the crusty old buzzard are you not, old man?" Culley gave him a scornful glare. To Orius, the newcomer said, "Priest, does this man speak for you? Do you have a voice, or does Ghyo's voice descend from the sky when you are around?"

"You speak to the Chief of the Northern Tribes," Kathair said. "Show him his due respect."

"I speak to those who present me with their names," Orius told the newcomer. "Do I get that courtesy from you?"

The newcomer scanned the groups of Chelts camped around them. "I never knew there was such a position as Chief of the Northern Valley. I know that Duke Malcomb rules the Southern Valley in the name of Abella of Fringia. I also know that Kirkvold ruled the whole of Cheltabria as king, but knowledge of *your* title escapes me. I do, however, see that one rumor is true. There is a priest, or someone who claims to be one, at the head of an army of Chelts - albeit a small one."

"Who sent you?" Culley asked.

"My employer is to remain nameless. I am being paid well to keep that secret. I am Pendros Lilellin, the Iron Merchant." He bowed and smiled his practiced smile.

"Come down off of your horse, Master Pendros, and join me," Orius said.

Pendros dismounted. He removed his ragged cloak with flair and draped it over the back of his horse. Beneath his rough covering, he wore a fine silk tunic and hose. A rapier and a dagger dangled from his belt.

Kathair quickly stepped forward. "Remove your weapons."

Pendros frowned and hesitated, he then reached for his sword and handed it over, along with the dagger. He smiled once more. "I am not an assassin."

"You handle a gentleman's weapon," Orius said.

"The streets of Fallheim can be dangerous for a man of my stature," Pendros replied smoothly. "And I am a gentleman. At least, the ladies say so."

"You have my attention," said Orius. "Say what you have come to say."

"Is it too much to ask to speak with you away from the others?"

"You need not worry about them. They are my confidants." Orius could tell by Pendros's reaction that he was used to getting his way.

"Master Orius..."

"*Father* Orius," Orius corrected.

Pendros smirked. "Father Orius, you are a stubborn man, but my employer insists I speak to you alone." He lowered his voice. "My employer has much to lose."

Orius's patience began to fail. "Master Pendros, these Chelts have been fighting and dying here. Each warrior has risked everything to stop the Oruks. I have born wounds. Do not play with us."

Pendros smiled warmly. "I meant no offense to you and your brave warriors. These piles of burnt bones tell your tale to me, but I must act in the best interests of my employer. You can understand that, can you not?"

Orius clenched his teeth. *What fool would send such an irritating man to do their business?* "Master Pendros, I will grant a moment of my time. For your sake, it had best be worthwhile." He turned and walked a dozen paces.

Pendros quickly caught up. "I can tell you are a man of purpose, used to being in command."

Orius faced him. "Drop the niceties. Your mannerisms sicken me."

Pendros nodded. "I can tell you are a warrior, as well, and not a man of business. I am used to negotiating arrangements which benefit all the parties involved."

Orius's patience was ending. "Who has sent you to me?"

Pendros cocked his head to one side. "I cannot reveal that to you." Orius's face went taut, and Pendros quickly added, "But I can tell you what my employer offers you."

"Master Pendros, return to Fallheim. Tell your employer I do not entreat with buffoons. Tell him it is not flattering to his reputation." Orius walked past Pendros and left him standing alone.

"Who said my employer is a man?"

Orius stopped abruptly. "I will tolerate no more of your vagueness. Speak plainly, or I promise we will be done with this."

"My employer has been collecting arms to be used in a revolt," Pendros said. "She has money. There is support in the Southern Valley for a revolt, but there is no leader."

"I am not a mercenary," said Orius. "I do not fight for pay."

"My employer does not offer you money. She offers you a crown and a bride's dowry."

"A *bride's* dowry?"

"Yes. My employer wishes to unite the Northern and Southern Valleys. She wishes to overthrow Duke Malcomb and give you the throne of the Southern Valley. I was sent here to prove the rumors that you are a priest and chief of the Northern Tribes." There was tension in Pendros's eyes.

*Something's wrong here,* said a voice in the back of Orius's head. "Tell me of these rumors."

In a blink, Pendros drew a knife from a small pocket sewn into the interior of his sleeve. Orius took a step back. Kathair and Culley ran in his direction, but Pendros made no lunge toward Orius. His face twitched as he slid the blade across the palm of his hand. Blood ran in a steady stream from the deep cut. Pendros's face turned pale; he let the knife fall to the ground. "Heal me, priest."

Orius held up a hand to his companions. "Stop!" he said as Culley and Kathair grabbed Pendros's arms. Pendros's bodyguards reacted, too, and spurred their horses to where Orius and Pendros stood.

"Everyone stop!" Orius said loudly. Culley and Kathair gave him puzzled looks. The bodyguards reared in their horses; they had already drawn their weapons.

"Let him go," Orius commanded. Culley and Kathair released their hold on Pendros. Orius stepped towards him and his palms began to glow. "Here is your proof," he said calmly, as he covered Pendros's wound with his hands.

The strain on Pendros's face subsided as the Gift closed the cut. He breathed a sigh of relief, and smiled his practiced smile. "Luck is usually on my side."

Orius was not amused. "Enough of this ridiculousness. Tell me who employs you."

Pendros leaned forward and whispered to Orius, whose eyes widened with amazement. He jerked his head away from Pendros. "When does she wish to see me?"

"Before the snows block the Borvik Pass, but there are complications. I was to wait for you and escort you to her, but that is no longer possible."

*Are there not always problems?* Orius thought. "Master Pendros, you strike me as man who makes a lot of trouble for yourself. What has happened to change things?"

"The Holy Tower has ordered your arrest for the crime of heresy. The Black Hand was sent to arrest you. They were supposed to leave the day after we left Fallheim, but something went wrong. We ran into them in Okernau. My bodyguards killed three of them." Pendros's eyes fixed on Orius's white gauntlets with the black palms. "I never knew priests to wear the gauntlets of the Black Hand."

"The priests of Arshapel do not, but I do not belong to their Order." Pendros gave Orius a quizzical look. Orius continued, "Does the Hand still ride northward?" *They killed members of the Black Hand.* Orius was surprised. He tried to sort through the challenges the deaths of the knights would present.

Pendros shook his head slowly. "I do not believe so. We stole most of their horses from the stables of the Golden Acorn in Okernau and scattered them throughout the forest. It will take them a couple of days to round them up, but there were only ten knights coming for you. They lost three of their number, so I do not think they will risk continuing on without reinforcements."

*That sounds logical.* "Is the identity of your employer known to the Black Hands?" Orius asked, fearing that possibility. *If they do, Pendros's trip was for nothing.*

"I do not believe so, but..."

Orius rolled his eyes. There's always a "but" with this man.

"Their captain recognized me," he said. "I must assume the Black Hands know I was there. That is why I cannot wait for you. I must return to protect my interests in Fallheim. Assaulting the Hand is a serious crime."

Orius was surprised to discover he had developed a speck of admiration for Pendros. "You are a wealthy man, are you not?"

Pendros smiled and puffed out his chest. "I am the wealthiest man in the Southern Valley. And the most popular with the ladies."

*And you're completely enraptured with yourself.* "You and your guards may rest here with us, though we have little food to offer. I will arrange the meeting with your employer. Tell her it will not be before the snows. That is impossible." Orius paused for a moment before deciding to ask another question. "May I ask why you choose to risk everything for a cause that does not actually exist?"

"No, you may not," Pendros answered.

"I understand and respect your wishes," Orius said. "I believe there comes a time in each person's life when that someone must give of themselves freely to a cause which is greater than themselves, their family, or their nation. It is oftentimes a decision which is personal in nature and not easily explained to others."

Pendros smiled. "You are a man of great insight, Orius Candell, and I wish you luck. There is a great opportunity for us on the horizon. Foreigners rule the Southern Valley and they must go. I will tell my employer I believe you may be the one to guide us to our destination. Do not make her wait long for your response. It is dangerous for her."

*Yes, but there's enough danger for everyone.* "Fate is a fickle mistress, Master Pendros. The future is never certain." He raised his right hand and an amber glow radiated from the palm. "May the Light of Ghyo guide us *all* through the Darkness."

The End

# The Star Calendar of Merchants and Sailors

The calendar is used by nearly every nation as a means of regulating trade. Also, the calendar dates legitimize contracts and treaties.

Each month is named after the star that appears in a particular spot in the sky on the first of each month. There are 18 months of 20 days, each month containing 4 weeks of 5 days.

The current year is 229 AGS. (After the Great Schism)

1. Ixlor (iks LOHR) 1 Ixlor (new year's day)
2. Pylec (pee LEK)
3. Tranifar (trahn NEE fahr)
4. Meryloc (mayr EE lohk) 10 Meryloc (beginning of winter)
5. Cranius (krah NEE us)
6. Cronius (kroh NEE us)
7. Calispo (kah LEE spoh)
8. Kaltar (KAHL tahr)
9. Ferilax (fayr EE lahks) 1 Ferilax (beginning of spring)
10. Rema (RAY mah)
11. Tusla(TOOS lah)
12. Alfar(AHL fahr)
13. Keptis (KAYP tis) 10 Keptis (beginning of summer)
14. Grigor (GREE gore)
15. Xenoban (zenn OH bahn)
16. Kaltus (KAHL tus)
17. Janoban (JAH noh bahn)
18. Gastus (GAHS toos) 1 Gastus (beginning of autumn)

# Thank You

Thank you for purchasing this premier title from Runestone Hill, Ltd. Co. We hope you have enjoyed this first installment of Timothy Brommer's exciting tale. Our mission to seek out new talents and bring them to you, the science-fiction- and fantasy-loving reader, is off to a great start. While mainstream authors are enjoyable to read, the serious fan of the genre is often left wanting more... something different... something fresh to seek their teeth into. To help us continue this effort, we'd appreciate your support. If you liked the book, encourage your friends to buy and read it as well. Each book sold helps keep the world of small press and the dream of every would-be writer alive.

If you've got questions or comments for Mr. Brommer, he would love to hear from you and so would we. For the latest news and address information, visit our website. Also, be sure to join our mailing list to stay up to date on new title releases and interesting news. All this and more at...

## www.runestonehill.com

Printed in the United States
17827LVS00004B/1-24

9 780972 634403